WELCOME TO THE CORNISH COUNTRY HOSPITAL

JO BARTLETT

Boldwood

First published in 2023 in Great Britain by Boldwood Books Ltd.

Copyright © Jo Bartlett, 2023

Cover Design by Alexandra Allden

Cover Illustration: Shutterstock

A CIP catalogue record for this book is available from the British Library.

Paperback ISBN 978-1-80483-921-8

Large Print ISBN 978-1-80483-920-1

Hardback ISBN 978-1-80483-922-5

Ebook ISBN 978-1-80483-918-8

Kindle ISBN 978-1-80483-919-5

Audio CD ISBN 978-1-80483-927-0

MP3 CD ISBN 978-1-80483-925-6

Digital audio download ISBN 978-1-80483-926-3

Boldwood Books Ltd
23 Bowerdean Street
London SW6 3TN
www.boldwoodbooks.com

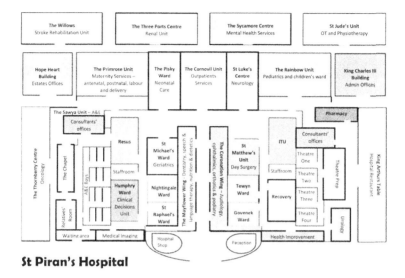

The Willows
Stroke Rehabilitation Unit

The Three Ports Centre
Renal Unit

The Sycamore Centre
Mental Health Services

St Jude's Unit
OT and Physiotherapy

Hope Heart Building
Estates Offices

The Primrose Unit
Maternity Services – antenatal, postnatal, labour and delivery

The Pisky Ward
Neonatal Care

The Cornovii Unit
Outpatients Services

St Luke's Centre
Neurology

The Rainbow Unit
Pediatrics and children's ward

King Charles III Building
Admin Offices

The Sawya Unit – A&E

Consultants' offices

The Thornberry Centre
Oncology

The Chapel

A&E Bays

Resus

Staffroom

Humphry Ward
Clinical Decisions Unit

Relatives' Room

St Michael's Ward
Geriatrics

Nightingale Ward

St Raphael's Ward

The Mayflower Wing – Dentistry, speech & language therapy, nutrition & dietetics

The Coronation Wing – Audiology, ophthalmics, orthotics & podiatry

St Matthew's Unit
Day Surgery

Tewyn Ward

Govenek Ward

ITU

Staffroom

Recovery

Consultants' offices

Theatre One

Theatre Two

Theatre Three

Theatre Four

Theatre Prep

Urology

Pharmacy

King Arthurs Table
Hospital Restaurant

Waiting area

Medical Imaging

Hospital Shop

Reception

Health Improvement

St Piran's Hospital

1

If Danni could have stopped it from happening, she would have. If she'd had any say at all, she would rather have hated her best friend's fiancé on sight than spent the last seven years falling more and more in love with him. But life didn't play fair like that and, by the end of the year, the only man she'd ever loved would be walking down the aisle with the woman Danni thought of as her sister.

'This was supposed to be a fresh start.' Danni muttered the words as she headed up the coastal path on the cliffs above Port Kara. Brenda didn't answer, but then basset hounds weren't exactly famed for their ability to give relationship advice. The only thing Brenda was famous for was leaving trails of slobber that no cleaning agent in existence could remove.

'I've taken a job I didn't even want and spent every penny I had buying a house on the opposite side of the country, and what do they do?' Danni kicked a patch of loose gravel on the path ahead of her. 'They both take jobs at St Piran's Hospital and buy a house half a mile away. Half a bloody mile!'

Brenda looked up, the sudden movement sending some of her

trademark slobber through the air as her jowls swung from side to side. She'd heard all this from Danni a hundred times before, but she still gave her owner the same look of sympathy she'd given her every other time, those soulful eyes seeming like they wanted to say so much. It was just as well Brenda couldn't speak; she'd probably have told Danni to pull herself together and get a grip. God knows Danni had looked in the mirror and told herself that often enough.

She didn't want to be this person, someone who'd wasted 2,500 days praying for a miracle that involved Esther falling for someone who made her far happier than Lucas ever had. That revelation would be followed by a short interval, the bare minimum that decency dictated, before Lucas finally realised it had been Danni he loved all along. Then they'd all get on with the rest of their brilliant lives, their old friendships completely intact and with none of the complications that having an ex hanging around so often brought. It was like Danni was trapped in a romcom, except somehow, *she*'d ended up as a supporting character in her own life story.

Taking the job in A&E at St Piran's Hospital had felt like a huge step backwards in her career. The seven years she'd spent secretly loving Lucas had been the same seven years the two of them had spent undertaking specialist training at a teaching hospital in London. When they'd both been offered jobs in their chosen fields at the same hospital, Lucas as an associate specialist trauma surgeon and Danni as a consultant in A&E, it had felt like a dream come true. They'd be working in parallel some of the time, with part of Lucas's role involving assessing trauma patients in A&E.

Danni had tried not to admit, even to herself, how relieved she'd been that they wouldn't be working in different hospitals, and going out for a drink to celebrate the news had seemed the most natural thing in the world. It was the second bottle of champagne that had changed everything; she'd suddenly looked across at Lucas and realised that if she didn't tell him now, she never would.

Halfway through that second bottle of champagne, she'd opened her mouth to say the words, but nothing came out. She sat there, not moving, with every fibre of her being screaming at her to *just say it*, to tell him she loved him before she lost him for good. But even in a haze of Veuve Clicquot, she couldn't do it to Esther. Not to the woman who'd sent a congratulations bouquet to Danni that was so big she could hardly see over it. Or who'd taken her call just days before, when there'd been a young patient Danni's team couldn't save and she'd woken herself up sobbing at 3 a.m. Esther had let Danni cry on her shoulder so many times in the ten years they'd known one another and it was Esther who'd got Danni through when the training had felt like it was going to overwhelm her, or when her day had seemed tougher than she was.

Esther was the person Danni confided all her fears to, and all her secrets. All except one. Loving Lucas was something she hadn't admitted to a soul. And, in that moment, staring across the table at him, in the corner of a noisy pub, she'd realised that she never would, because as much as she loved him, she loved Esther more. It was why she had to get away, because if she stayed she'd never be able to get over him. Any doubts she might have had disappeared when Esther had texted her later that night.

Oh my God, he's finally asked me! Not like I'd imagined, but I don't care. Apparently it was drinks with you that got him thinking and 'the ring' was something he made in the taxi on the way home, out of the wire from one of the bottles of champagne you two so rudely drank without me 😌 He's promised there will be an upgrade, but I don't care about that either. Let me know when you can do lunch and I'll fill you in on all the rest. I promise not to be a bridezilla and you can wear whatever dress you want! Love you xx

Danni had wanted to get in her car and leave the moment she'd read the text, to just keep going until she could outrun her feelings. Instead, she'd sat there staring into the darkness of her empty flat. It was like being torn in two, wanting to feel happy for the kindest, most generous person she'd ever met, but finding it impossible when her heart felt like it had been ripped out of her chest.

When she'd told Esther she was turning down the job in London to go back to the same stretch of Cornish coast where she'd grown up, it had been her best friend's turn to be heartbroken. She couldn't understand what on earth would make her want to leave, or to reject a job in one of the most prestigious hospitals in the country to go and work in a tiny Cornish hospital, an eight-hour drive away from the people who loved her most. Especially as Esther knew it didn't even feel like home to Danni, not any more.

Danni had been ten years old when she'd decided to become a doctor. The same age she'd been when her father, Trevor, had died from a massive heart attack at work. There'd been no one around to save him and Danni had vowed, then and there, that she'd learn how to bring someone back from the brink of death, to stop other families going through what hers had been forced to endure. Her mother, Nicola, had never been the same after that. She'd coped by trying to find solutions to her problems at the bottom of a bottle of gin, and by sending Danni and her brother to boarding school so she didn't have to try to be there for them. School had been Danni's solace and losing herself in books had been a refuge from the real world. It didn't matter if it was the textbooks she clung to during the day, or the novels she read under the covers at night – those books, as well as the snatched days she got to spend with her brother, Joe, when their mother reluctantly had them back for the holidays, had been the only things that had felt like home since losing her father. Until she met Esther.

Esther had been just two weeks into her first full-time nursing job the day that Danni had started a two-year foundation programme at the same hospital, straight after finishing medical school. They'd clicked straight away and within three months they'd been sharing a flat. By that time, Joe had settled in Australia, where he'd gone for his post-university gap year. Her mother was living on a houseboat in Bristol, with her boyfriend, Paul, who she'd met on an art therapy course, eight years after her husband's death. These days, Danni's mother seemed content to scratch a living as a part-time artist, selling the paintings she and Paul did from the back of their boat. Danni was glad her mother had found some level of happiness, but Nicola still couldn't cope with anyone's problems but her own, so their relationship consisted of superficial conversations and meet-ups over lunch every couple of months or so.

Meeting Esther really had felt like coming home for the first time in years, and through her she'd found a whole new family too. Esther's parents and paternal grandparents had treated Danni as if she really was one of the family. Esther's mother, Caroline, often told Danni she thought of her as another daughter. They were the family Danni had always wanted and, even if she didn't love her best friend as much as she did, she'd rather have died than hurt any of them. Which was why she had to leave, and why she could never reveal the real reason for going.

'Please stay. Nothing here is going to be the same without you. I know I've moved in with Lucas now, but he's just a boy. I still need my girl around too.' Esther had taken hold of both her hands. 'I can't for the life of me understand why you'd want to leave London and go down there. I know it's beautiful, but there's so much more scope for your career here. And, more importantly, you've got all of us.'

Everything Esther had said had made perfect sense, but she had no idea that seeing Lucas almost every day felt as if it was slowly killing Danni. She'd tried to tell herself at first that her feelings for him would pass and that the initial spark of attraction would die out. Then she'd got to know him and any hope she'd had that her feelings would just fizzle out had been lost. Danni and Lucas understood each other in a way no one else seemed to. They'd bonded during late-night shifts, sharing bleary-eyed conversations over hospital canteen coffee, cramming for assessments and talking about all the things they wanted to do with their careers. But most of all they'd bonded over both having lost parents at a young age, which no one else quite understood.

Sometimes, when the three of them were together, Danni wondered if Esther ever felt left out. If she did, she never showed it. She still invited Danni along to everything – meals out, movie nights, even on holiday, and the three of them laughed together over shared jokes no one outside their inner circle would have found funny. Despite the torture of watching Esther and Lucas's relationship from the sidelines, Danni had accepted every invitation. Hoping that one day he'd show a side of himself that would make her fall out of love with him. But she was still waiting…

'Cornwall is where all of my memories of Dad are.' Danni's eyes had filled with tears, but only partly because it had been true. 'I need to be there for a while and work through some stuff that seems to be coming to the surface just lately. I buried it all when Dad died and just threw myself into schoolwork, then medicine. I need to do this, Essie, but I'm going to miss you all more than you'll ever know.'

It had been one of the hardest conversations Danni had ever had and her throat had been raw with the effort of trying not to cry. The tears had come when she'd started packing up her stuff, photo frames where all her memories seemed to feature Esther and Lucas. She'd had a wobble the day before she'd been due to exchange contracts on the purchase of the cottage in Port Kara.

When the former holiday cottage where they'd spent their last family break together, before her father had died, had come up for sale, Danni had been sure it was a sign. The cottage was in such an idyllic spot it couldn't have felt more magical. It had also been the last place she remembered feeling happy, before her whole world had come crashing down.

But on the night before she was due to sign the final paperwork, and hand over almost every penny of the inheritance her father had left her, she'd felt nausea grip her stomach at the mere thought of leaving London. Danni didn't want to go; she was suddenly as certain of that as she'd previously been about needing to leave. And then came the knock at the door.

'Lucas.' His name had caught in her throat, as he stood in the exact same spot he'd been standing on the first day they'd met, when he'd come to collect Esther for their date. She'd been terrified of her feelings for him even back then, but the impact of those feelings had turned out to be far worse than she'd ever have thought.

'Don't go, please. I've come to beg you not to.' He'd moved past her, catching hold of her arms and spinning her around to look at him. Those dark eyes of his that were so often smiling, more serious than she'd ever seen them.

'Did Esther send you?' Danni had struggled to keep breathing and her whole body had felt as though it was pulsing with longing.

'She doesn't even know I'm here.'

In that moment, when he'd looked at Danni, she'd known for certain that she hadn't been imagining it. The feelings she had for him didn't go just one way and, if she'd moved even a fraction, he'd have kissed her. God knows what would have happened after that, because she'd have been powerless to stop it. So, instead, she'd stayed rooted to the spot; the only movement she made at all was to shake her head.

'I've got to go, Lucas, you know I do.' Even then, part of her had been desperate for him to touch her, seven years of pent-up emotion pounding in her chest, but somehow she'd taken a step back. 'You need to leave.'

'If things had been different, we could have been—'

'Don't!' She'd pushed him then, out of the door, slamming it behind him and leaning against it for good measure. It was only when she'd finally heard his footsteps as he walked away that she'd allowed herself to sink to the floor and the tears had come.

It had been the hardest thing she'd ever had to do, but it had driven her on, overriding any doubt she might have had about leaving. The next day she'd signed the paperwork and finished packing up her flat. She'd refused the offers of help from Esther and her family with the move down to Port Kara. And she'd started her new job, burying herself in work when she was on shift and escaping between the pages of a book at night. But, at first, even that hadn't worked the way it used to and she'd rung Joe, just like she'd done when they were at separate boarding schools, hundreds of miles apart, and the longing for their beloved dad had got too much.

'I've made a mistake moving to Cornwall.' Her voice had been small, almost as if she was afraid to admit the magnitude of her error out loud.

'No you haven't.' Joe hadn't even asked why she thought that, and his tone had been so certain, somehow she immediately felt a bit better. 'You're just lonely that's all, and you miss having someone to take care of.'

'What do you mean? I've got just as many patients who need me here and—'

'I'm not talking about your patients.' Joe's voice had taken on an edge, the way it always did when a certain person's name cropped up.

'I know what you're going to say, but I don't *look after* Lucas. We're colleagues and friends, and we're on an equal level.' She'd hesitated for a moment, concern about taking a step down in her career stabbing her all over again. 'Or at least we were.'

'No, you weren't. You were his loyal cheerleader, always there to massage his ego. I bet he can't stand the fact his number one fan is no longer around.'

'You just don't like him.' Danni had sighed. Joe's first meeting with Lucas, on one of his annual trips home from Australia, hadn't gone well. Somehow, a couple of bottles of wine into the evening, the conversation had got on to the subject of their schooling. Esther was the only one who'd been to state school and Lucas had made some throwaway comment about that being obvious, given the jobs the three of them had ended up doing. Joe was a psychiatrist, with a practice in Melbourne, and a string of academic publications to his name.

'There are three doctors at this table, so you can see the value of a proper education.' Lucas had nudged Esther, and they'd both laughed, but Joe had felt the need to jump to her defence, telling Lucas he was condescending and a snob. Lucas had laughed again, explaining to Joe that he'd got it all wrong; what he'd been implying was, if Esther had been given a similar private education, she'd have been more than capable of being a doctor too. That had just seemed to inflame Joe even more and he'd argued that the best doctors he'd met in his career were those who'd had to work the hardest to get where they were, not the ones who'd been given every advantage. Lucas had said that they'd just have to agree to disagree about the value of a private education, because there was nothing that would dissuade him from making that the top priority for his own children when they came along.

'I'd have traded my education to have the sort of family life Esther clearly did. That's something money can't buy.' Joe had shot

Danni a look at that point, and she allowed herself just the smallest nod. She hadn't wanted to say out loud that she'd agreed with Joe, because she'd known Lucas hadn't meant anything derogatory by what he'd said. The two men had just got off on the wrong foot, that was all, and she'd been convinced it was a blip they could quickly overcome. But, if anything, Joe's view of Lucas just seemed to harden every time they met. So, it shouldn't have come as a surprise that her brother's opinion of Lucas was still unfavourable.

'You're right, I don't like him, but that's beside the point.' Joe's voice had softened again. 'I understand why you feel like you've made a mistake. It took me more than two years to stop feeling that way about living out here. Having Lucas and Esther to prop you up wouldn't have lasted forever anyway. Once they get married and have a family, things are going to change. I think it's brilliant that you were the one to walk away first and take the step to start making a life for yourself. It might not feel great now, but it will be worth it. Trust me. Just hold on for a bit, and fake it until you make it, like I did. Then, one day, you won't have to pretend any more.'

So she'd followed Joe's advice, surviving and getting through life a day at a time. Then things had started to change, just like he'd said they would. Adopting Brenda from a rehoming service had been a huge part of finally making it feel like she was starting a new life, rather than just escaping from the old one. She'd formed some friendships at the hospital and was particularly close to one of the nurses, Aidan, who made her miss Esther just a tiny bit less. Things were going well, and her boss had suggested it wouldn't be long before a consultant's post came up, and had told her he'd support her in going for it. Everything Joe had promised was happening and eventually her feelings for Lucas would fade too. Not seeing him every day would make that so much easier. She'd been so certain of it... until she'd got the voicemail.

'*Hey, anyone would think you were screening my calls!*' The sound of Esther's voice had immediately made Danni feel homesick. '*You're not going to believe this, but we're moving to Cornwall! Mum, Dad, Nan and Pops have been talking for ages about all getting a place together and they found the perfect house down there a few weeks ago. I didn't want to say anything, but it got me and Lucas thinking. There's no way we want to be hundreds of miles away from everyone we love, so we contacted St Piran's Hospital to see what jobs might be coming up and it was like everything falling into place. We've found somewhere to rent in Port Kara and we'll be moving down as soon as we've worked our notice. Now ring me, Haggage, and tell me just how excited you are that we're coming down! Love you.*'

Esther's laugh had still been ringing in Danni's ears when the voicemail came to an end. They'd always shown their affection by calling each other silly names. Danni's nickname had come from the day she'd gone out in the drizzle and had come back with hair like Hagrid, which no amount of anti-frizz serum had been able to tame. In turn, she called Esther Nugget, after her friend had been on a date – before she'd met Lucas – with a guy whose idea of a romantic night out was ordering a sharing box of chicken nuggets from the McDonald's drive-through. Esther had been too nice to tell him she didn't even like nuggets and, after managing to eat one or two, had hidden the rest of her share in the pockets of her coat. The nuggets had then fallen out all over the floor of their flat, when she'd chucked her coat over the arm of the sofa after she'd got back from her disastrous date.

Danni has missed all of that familiarity, the sound of Esther's laugh, and most of all her friendship, even more than she'd thought she would, but the voicemail had still filled Danni with dread. She'd called Esther straight back and tried every argument she could think of to persuade her that moving to Cornwall was the worst idea in the world, including that Danni might well be moving again herself soon, but none of it had made any difference.

Esther had made her mind up and nothing Danni said was going to stop her.

She'd thought about phoning Lucas and telling him to do something, but she hadn't spoken to him since the night he'd turned up at her flat. And now Esther and Lucas were moving into their new house and, in twenty-four hours' time, they'd be starting their first shifts at St Piran's Hospital too.

'You'd think he'd have put a stop to it, wouldn't you?' Danni looked at Brenda again, who was sniffing a damp patch of unknown origin, when a text suddenly flashed up on her phone.

Major incident reported on the A3689 Port Tremellien to Port Kara Road. Multiple casualties. All available critical care staff to contact the major incident team leader.

'Come on, Bren. I'm really sorry, girl, but we've got to go.' Clipping the lead onto the dog's collar, Danni pulled the reluctant basset hound back down the track as fast as she could, scrolling through the contacts on her phone to find the team leader's number at the same time. There were people out there who needed her help and for once, as the call connected, Lucas was the last thing on her mind.

2

Connie craned her neck to try and see over the high bank, which was topped with hedgerow, in the hope of catching a glimpse of the sea. But this was Cornwall, and the tall hedgerows were as much a characteristic of the landscape as the coastline itself. It was all coming back to her now. Whenever she'd thought of Port Kara, as she had so many times in the thirty-eight years since her last visit, all she'd pictured was the seemingly endless stretch of sand. Back then, if she'd gone there at the right time of day, the only trace of human life existing would have been two sets of footprints. Hers and Richard's.

'This driver wants to slow down a bit. If a tractor comes round the corner with him going at this pace, one of us is going to get run off the road.' The woman sitting next to Connie jabbed her in the side with her elbow as though they were old friends, rather than total strangers who just happened to be crammed in next to each other on the only bus heading to Port Kara from the station at St Ives. It was a single decker that had already been three-quarters full when they'd left the station, but by the time they were twenty minutes into the journey, it was standing room only.

Port Kara had become a lot more popular in the last ten years. Connie had seen it in her Sunday supplement, only the week before, in an article about the most popular locations for celebrity staycations and second homes. It was clearly drawing in the celebrity-spotters too and she'd heard two young women in the seat behind talking about Harry Styles being spotted there filming for a new movie. Apparently, it was why they'd simply had to get down to Port Kara before everyone else found out. Connie was just impressed with herself for knowing who he was. She had to google most of the celebrities her history students spoke about these days, but then they'd probably never heard of Led Zeppelin either. Years ago, Connie and her sister, Janice, had spent every bit of money they could scrape together trying to get to one of their gigs, and she'd been convinced she was going to marry Jimmy Page. Or Harrison Ford if she decided to go the movie star route. No one had come close to either of them – all through her uni years, or for a whole decade afterwards. But then she'd met Richard.

'He's driving like a lunatic; I'm going to tell him to slow down before he kills us all!' The woman sitting next to Connie moved to get up, just as the bus lurched violently to the right, sending her crashing back down into her seat.

At the same time, a man at the front of the bus started shouting, 'He's collapsed. The driver's collapsed!'

Suddenly everyone around Connie seemed to be screaming and all she could do was watch as a couple of the passengers at the front of the bus tried to get into the cab. Everything was happening so fast, but at the same time it almost felt as though the world was moving in slow motion. Connie looked down at her hands; she was gripping the bar of the seat in front of her so hard that her knuckles had gone white. But she still couldn't scream.

For a few seconds the noise of metal scraping against a stone wall, as one side of the bus peeled open like someone had taken a can opener to it, was so loud it drowned out the sounds of panic. But then the bus left the ground, flipping in the air as if it were made from paper, and Connie finally let out an ear-piercing scream. By the time the bus landed, everything in her world had turned black.

3

The new hospital had developed its own definition of what constituted a major incident and protocols for dealing with such a situation, should one arise. Danni had been asked if she was willing to be part of the on-call pre-hospital critical care team, which allowed A&E doctors to be sent out to provide emergency care to patients, alongside paramedics, at the scene of an incident. It hadn't even taken a moment for her to decide, even though the likelihood of anything major happening in Port Kara had seemed pretty remote. Now she was heading for Port Tremellien, with no idea how bad things were going to be when she got there, but it didn't take long to find out.

'Oh God.' There was a sea of blue lights ahead of where Danni pulled into the layby. Poor Brenda had been shoved unceremoniously through the door of the cottage five minutes after the major incident alert, and Danni had changed into her uniform in a time that Wonder Woman would have been proud of. She had the on-call kit provided to every doctor in the pre-hospital critical care team. Anything else she needed would be provided by the paramedics.

For a moment it felt like she was back in London, where working with ambulance crews delivering pre-hospital care was something she'd done as part of her specialist training. She'd even had a stint working with the HEMS crew on the air ambulance for three months. But, in London, there was always the reassurance that specialist hospitals in every discipline were within relatively easy reach. Providing emergency care in rural Cornwall, and stabilising patients for long enough to get the specialist care they might need, was a whole different ball game.

There were two ambulances, an advanced paramedic vehicle and a fire engine already on scene. And, when Danni got out of the ambulance, she could hear the wail of more sirens approaching. As soon as she got closer, she could see it – beyond the fire engine – a single-decker bus with its side ripped open like an ugly scar. It looked so alien it was barely recognisable as the same sort of bus that stopped outside the hospital every day. The angry gaping hole exposing the inside of the bus looked almost aggressive, like a big 'keep out' sign.

The sounds of people shouting for help, and wailing in agony, carried on the still autumn air, the cloudless, almost turquoise sky making the scene below it seem all the more out of place. It was a beautiful September day, the Indian summer Port Kara had been having showing no sign of abating. As soon as Danni arrived, she checked in with the incident coordinator and was handed another pack containing some of the medication she might need. The coordinator told her the situation was changing so quickly the best thing Danni could do was get into the thick of things and find out who needed her most, which was exactly what she did.

However bad the accident might be, Danni was thankful it hadn't happened two weeks before, when the bus would have been crammed with children and young families making the most of the final days of the school holidays. And she was silently praying, as she hurried towards the bus, that none of the passengers were children and that by some miracle every single person on board would somehow have escaped without serious injury. But as soon as Danni walked around the ambulance furthest from the scene, it was obvious her prayers weren't going to be answered.

'I'm Danni Carter, one of the A&E doctors; what can I do to help?' she called out to a fire officer who'd just sent some other emergency personnel towards the bus.

'Those two have been working on the driver since they arrived on scene.' The fire officer gestured towards two paramedics leaning over a man lying on the tarmac; there was blood on his face, and so much broken glass in his hair that it was sparkling in the sunlight. 'I'm sure they'll be grateful of any support you can give.'

'Thanks,' Danni breathed out as she hurried towards them. These situations were always a weird mixture of adrenaline and fear, but she'd never wanted to do any other sort of medicine.

'I'm Danni; can I give you a hand? They said this was the driver?'

'Yes and he bull's-eyed the windscreen, but it looks like the accident was caused by him going into cardiac arrest.' The female paramedic looked up and shook her head. 'Two passengers who were in a car that witnessed the crash managed to drag him free and they were still attempting CPR when we got here. He's been asystole since our arrival, despite adrenaline and mechanical CPR. Without any electrical activity in the heart we can't defibrillate, so I think we're going to have to call it.'

Danni tried not to look too closely at the man lying on the ground, knowing that if there was even the tiniest likeness between him and her father, it had the capacity to send her spiralling back to the moment when her mother had told her she was never going to see him again. Her eyes seemed to slide towards him anyway and, from his colour alone, she could tell he was gone. His jacket and shirt had been undone and there was an open wallet lying close to Danni's feet, with some of its contents spilt out on the ground. There was a debit card, a family photo depicting at least three generations, and a money clip with the words: *Here's to the next 40 years! Love Karen xxx* engraved on it. The thought of how many people his death was going to hurt felt like a weight pressing against her neck.

'He was probably dead before he even hit the windscreen.' The male paramedic sighed and Danni curled her fists into a ball, her fingernails digging into the palms of her hands. There were those echoes again, words so similar to those her mother had been told, which she'd repeated to two children who'd never needed to hear them: *They said your father was probably dead before he even hit the floor.*

'You're right to call it.' Danni blinked twice, trying to focus more on the driver all of a sudden, so that she really saw him and not her father's face. There was nothing she could do for him and she turned as one of the fire officers came hurtling towards them, his eyes wide.

'Can we get some more help in the bus? There's a woman trapped, with serious blood loss; it looks bad.' Even as he spoke, the fire officer was already turning away again.

'I'll go.' Breaking into a run to catch up with the man, Danni didn't stop to look back at the other paramedics or the driver. She had to keep moving forward, just like she'd been doing for the best part of twenty years.

She passed a row of passengers sitting at the base of a bank, looking at first sight like they were waiting for another bus to turn up. It was only when Danni got closer that she could see the anguish on their faces, and the cuts and bruises they'd been lucky to escape with. One of the men had a makeshift bandage tied around his head, fashioned from a cream-coloured scarf that was now soaked with blood, and someone else was supporting their arm in a sling made from a leather belt. Members of the public, who must have pulled up in the cars abandoned further down the road, were taking blankets, bottles of water, or whatever else they might have to offer to try and give the accident victims some comfort. Even those passengers who looked completely unscathed would be suffering from shock and they'd all need medical attention eventually. But for now there were more urgent priorities for the emergency team.

Going inside the bus was like stepping into a warzone. The other paramedics and some of the fire crew were tending to patients in need of the most critical care, while the rest of the fire officers were fighting to free some of the most critically injured patients. The team leader had assured Danni that any equipment she might need to treat the patients would be made available on site, but first she needed to assess the patient and hope there was something she could do to help.

'She's over here; her name's Connie. She's got a lump of metal embedded in her leg. I can't... I just couldn't...' The fire officer shook his head. 'She was lucky to be on the side of the bus that didn't hit the wall, but we need to move the seat in front of her to get her out; it's bent backwards. There are other patients trapped too and we're having to prioritise until more crews arrive. They're en route and the air ambulance has been dispatched too. I really wanted to stay with Connie to make sure she's okay, but I can't do that and do what I need to.'

'It's okay – you do your job and I'll do mine.' Danni touched the man's arm briefly and he seemed to sag with relief.

'Thank you. We'll get to Connie as soon as we can, but let us know if you think she needs to be prioritised. We've brought in some oxygen.' He gestured over to some cannisters lying on an abandoned seat. 'Just take one, if you need it.'

'Okay.' She didn't look at him again as she moved towards the patient, who appeared to be in her sixties. The neatness of her ash-blonde bob looked so at odds with the fact that she was partially pinned by the crushed seat in front of her.

'Hi, Connie, I'm Danni, one of the doctors from St Piran's Hospital. I can see you've got an injury to your leg and I'm going to stabilise that until the fire crew can get you out and into the ambulance. But I need to know if you've got any other injuries you're aware of?'

'I feel like someone has hit my left hip with a sledgehammer and there's a tingling feeling in my pelvic area that's travelling down to my thighs.' Connie grimaced, pain etched on her face, as she struggled to keep her eyes open. 'It's numb and painful all at the same time. Although that's nothing compared to my hip; I've never felt pain like it. Never.' The fawn-coloured trousers Connie was wearing were stained bright red by the blood seeping from the wound in her thigh and the shard of metal the fire officer had described looked like a bolt of lightning piercing her skin.

'Okay, Connie, I'm going to give you some pain relief before I do anything else.'

'Are you going to take it out?' Connie's eyes flew open with panic and Danni shook her head.

'They'll need to do that in surgery so that they can control any bleeding. But I'm going to secure it with some dressings to try and stop anything moving on the way to the hospital. Once I've given you the pain relief, I'm going to give you some saline and oxygen too, to help make up for the blood you've lost, as well as some antibiotics to help prevent any infection. I promise all of that will really help.' Danni kept her voice steady, not waiting for Connie to answer before she swung into action. She could tell the older woman was struggling; her breathing was quick and shallow, and when Danni touched Connie's skin it felt cold and clammy. Grabbing one of the oxygen cannisters, Danni placed the mask over Connie's nose and mouth. Watching her breathing start to steady, Danni finally felt like she could breathe again too.

But as she turned away from Connie to look for some support, Danni's heart sank. There were multiple casualties, and the medical teams were spread far too thin. The young female paramedic she'd seen earlier was already holding the head of another patient, as some of the fire crew tried to cut away the twisted metal around them. The fact that so many of the patients were trapped as well as seriously injured was making a difficult situation even worse. There was no sign of the other paramedic who'd been with the bus driver, but even the fatalities had to be taken care of. He'd probably be liaising with the police by now, before they transported the driver to the mortuary. The poor man's cause of death would undoubtedly be the subject of an autopsy and all Danni could do was pray that he ended up being the only fatality.

Turning back towards Connie, she shivered. The amount of blood pooling by her patient's feet was much bigger than Danni was comfortable with, and there was a good chance she had some internal bleeding too. The pain she'd described could be down to a broken hip or pelvis, both of which could cause significant damage to blood vessels close to the bones.

'How are you doing, Connie?' The pain relief should be kicking in by now, but Danni didn't like the way the colour had continued to drain from her patient's face; it looked almost waxy now.

'I feel like all the energy is being sucked out of me; I'm so tired.' Connie closed her eyes. 'I just want to go to sleep.'

'I need you to try and stay awake for me, okay?' Danni bit her lip as she took Connie's pulse; it was weak and rapid and neither was a good sign. Setting up the IV saline fluids to help replace what Connie's body had lost, she would have given almost anything for a second pair of hands or another opinion, but it was a luxury she wasn't going to get. Checking Connie's blood pressure did nothing to alleviate her fears; it was much lower than it should have been and all the signs were adding up to hypovolemic shock, which could prove fatal if she didn't get the treatment she needed. They had to get Connie to hospital as soon as possible, but she wasn't the only person in need of urgent help and the fire crew were still working on freeing a younger passenger further up the bus. Despite all that, it was time for Danni to bump Connie up the list.

Keeping her voice at the same even tone she'd fought to use all the way through, Danni gently touched her patient's arm. 'I need to go and speak to one of the fire officers, but I'll be right back.'

'Don't leave me!' The older woman suddenly made a grab for Danni's hand and when she couldn't find it, ripped the oxygen mask off her face.

'You need to keep the mask on, but I'll be right back. I promise.' Danni put the mask back over Connie's face and squeezed her hand briefly. 'I need to make sure we can get you out quickly, so we can get you to the hospital.'

'Am I going to die?' Connie widened her eyes, her chest rising and falling as she breathed in the oxygen so deeply that the skin on her neck seemed to pucker.

'Not if I can help it.' Danni had promised herself during her training that she'd never knowingly lie to a patient who asked her a direct question, but over time she'd realised that the truth wasn't the only option in situations like this. She had no way of knowing if Connie was going to make it, but it was clear she was in a bad way.

'I need you to take the letter, please. I can't go without telling Richard.' Connie was grabbing at her own clothing this time, trying desperately to get something out of her jacket. 'It's in my pocket, please.'

'You can give it to Richard yourself.' Another thing Danni had learnt over the years was how important it was for patients to have hope. If she let Connie believe for one minute that she wasn't going to make it, then the chances of her dying would probably treble.

'He needs to know I love him, that I never stopped.' Connie's voice was muffled by the mask, but nothing could disguise the pleading in her eyes. 'I should have told him thirty-eight years ago, please. I can't stand the thought of dying without Richard knowing the truth. I don't care about anything else. Just promise me, please.'

Danni had no idea why Connie had held on to her secret for so long, and the older woman could never have guessed how easy it was for Danni to identify with what she was saying, but she could feel Connie's desperation as if it was her own. The thought that anything could happen, and that she could die, without Lucas ever knowing the truth, hit her hard.

'I promise.' Her hand was shaking as she reached out to pull the crumpled letter from Connie's jacket pocket. Four words were written on the front in loopy handwriting.

Richard Bruce, Trengothern Hall

'He needs to know... please.' Connie repeated her plea as a single tear rolled down her cheek and Danni stuffed the letter inside her uniform. She might have made a vow never to tell Lucas how she really felt, but she'd keep her promise to Connie if she had to. She just hoped with all her heart it wouldn't come to that.

4

If there was anyone still querying whether the Three Ports area needed its own hospital, the scene in A&E when the emergency teams began bringing in the casualties from the bus crash would surely have been enough to convince even the most diehard of doubters. The most seriously injured passengers had begun to arrive first, after being stabilised on scene. There was a 'golden hour' to start treatment at the hospital to give them the best chance of survival, with the larger group of less seriously injured patients being transported as soon as other crews became available. It was like something out of a TV drama.

Connie was the last of the critical patients to be transferred and, by the time she and Danni arrived at A&E, some of the others had already been taken to other specialist centres. Connie's condition was amongst the most serious being treated at St Piran's and Danni felt as if the letter was burning a hole in her pocket. Connie had been in and out of consciousness since handing her the letter, and she'd only stopped fighting the oxygen mask being put over her face when she was certain that Danni had agreed to deliver it. Whatever the contents, it clearly meant the world to Connie and Danni would do everything she could to make sure her patient got to pass on the message herself.

'This is Connie. She needs a CT scan, she's in hypovolemic shock as a result of blood loss from a puncture wound and I suspect there's an injury to the pelvis or hip causing internal bleeding.' Danni's voice as she filled in the team in A&E sounded matter of fact, even to her own ears, all those years of training enabling her to flick an invisible switch that allowed her to stay professional, regardless of the emotions racing through her head. Despite being a new hospital, in the middle of a very challenging incident, the team seemed to be rising to the occasion and there was a flurry of activity as they took over Connie's care, while Danni continued to fill them in on the checks and treatments she'd had so far. Even as more pain medication and fluids were administered, Danni still couldn't walk away. She needed to know Connie was going to be okay.

'We'll get her down next.' Aidan put a hand on Danni's shoulder ten minutes after she'd brought Connie in. 'Are you okay? You look shattered. The paramedics said it was awful on scene.'

'The bus was packed, and with that many people on it, it could have been even worse than it was, but it was pretty bad.' The sound of a teenage boy screaming as the bus seat in front of him was cut away and the extent of his injuries was revealed was one Danni didn't think she'd ever forget. His foot had been completely degloved by the impact of the crash and from the updates the paramedics had got on the way in, it sounded like he was already undergoing the surgery that was the only chance of saving his foot. All non-emergency surgery had been cancelled as soon as the major incident had been announced, but Danni still didn't know if Connie might need to be transferred elsewhere. There were only four operating theatres at the hospital and a small surgical team, who had suddenly seen an influx of patients that even much bigger hospitals would struggle to cope with.

'If you need a break, take one. You'll be no good to man nor beast if you run yourself off your feet.' Aidan had a beautiful lilting Irish accent and just listening to his voice was usually enough to ease some of the tension on a long shift, but not today.

'I'm fine, but thank you.' Danni gave him the briefest of smiles, before leaning closer to Connie. 'You'll be going down to have a CT scan soon, so they can take a look and see what's causing your pain and decide the best way of removing the metal from your leg. Then we can get you all sorted and back on your feet.'

'Will you be here when I get back?' Connie's voice was hoarse and she was still deathly pale, but there was a fire in her eyes when she looked at Danni.

'I'm not leaving until I know what's happening with your treatment. Are you sure there's no one we can call for you?' She'd already asked the question twice and Connie had been insistent there was no one. She had a niece, Darcy, but she was due to have her first baby soon and Connie didn't want her worrying. The rest of her family – her mother and only sister – were long gone. The only phone call Connie had agreed to anyone making, when Danni had first asked, was if the worst came to the worst.

'You can call Darcy if I don't make it. Her number's in my phone and tell her there's a letter for her too, inside the treasure chest. It explains everything.' Connie had closed her eyes after that, until they'd reached the hospital, as if she was trying to cut off any further questions. But this time, Connie was looking straight at Danni.

'Darcy doesn't need to know anything unless I die. She won't be on her own now she's got Jimmy, but she might have more questions once their baby arrives and I'm the only one who can answer them. Tell her it's all in the letter and that I'm sorry I lied for so long. I'm sorry I lied at all. The only people who ever knew the truth were me, my sister and her husband, and we all thought it was better that way. They're gone now and I thought the secret should die with me, but keeping it means I'm still lying to Darcy.' Connie let out a long shuddering sigh. 'That's the problem with lies: they multiply until you can hardly even remember what the truth is any more. If I die, I need Darcy and Richard to know what really happened and you're the only person I can trust.'

Part of Danni wanted to ask why Connie was so convinced she could trust a total stranger with what sounded like a decades-old secret, but maybe when you were keeping a deep, dark secret of your own, it gave you the power to see it when someone else was doing it too. Either way, she didn't want Connie to worry about anything other than getting better. 'You can trust me, but I need you to believe me when I tell you that you can get through whatever injuries you've got and tell Richard and Darcy for yourself.'

'But if I don't, you'll—'

Danni cut her off. 'If you can't tell them yourself, I'll make sure they know about the letters.'

'Thank you.' Connie reached out for her hand and Danni squeezed it.

'Let's get you down for this scan, then.' Aidan smiled at Connie, before turning towards Danni, raising his eyebrows and mouthing a silent question. *'What was all that about?'*

But she just shrugged and shook her head. Even if she discovered Connie's secret, she wouldn't share it with anyone other than Richard and Darcy. She was good at keeping things hidden, and she knew only too well the potential for damage if a secret found its way into the wrong hands.

* * *

The last people Danni had expected to see walk into the A&E department were Esther and Lucas. They should have been in the midst of unpacking their new home. She'd even pictured them there, laughing at shared memories as they took photo frames out of boxes and exchanging kisses as they arranged their furniture in the place where they'd be starting their married life. Danni had needed to focus really hard on other things to try and get that last image out of her head the night before. Not even Brenda's snoring, from her basket near the end of Danni's bed, had been able to drown out the internal voice reminding her what a loser she was for still being fixated on Lucas after all these years. So seeing him walk into the hospital, with his hand in Esther's, made her gasp. For the last few months this had been her safe place. Somewhere she didn't need to worry about being confronted on a daily basis with everything she didn't have. And yet here they were again, right in front of her.

'What on earth are you doing here? Shouldn't you be up to your necks in boxes?' Danni was trying and failing to keep her tone light. She wasn't ready for this. She'd counted on every one of those remaining twenty-four hours before she needed to adjust to seeing Lucas again.

'We heard about the accident and thought we might be able to do something to help. Are you okay? You look really pale.' Esther's eyes were round with concern and this was just like her, worrying about everyone else even in the midst of the stress of moving house. She deserved a much better best friend than the one she'd got.

'I'm fine. It's just been…' She looked at Esther, who knew her well enough to understand what she was about to say. 'They think the bus driver had a cardiac arrest and when he was lying there, I just—'

'Oh, Dan.' Esther flung her arms around Danni. They'd always been the odd couple in many ways and for a moment she couldn't help smiling. She could probably have lifted Esther over her head, like Patrick Swayze in *Dirty Dancing* if she wanted to. Danni was five feet ten, with long, dark, wavy hair, and Esther was a good nine inches shorter, with a blonde pixie cut, earning her the nickname of Tinkerbell from the other staff back in their old hospital. They couldn't have been more different, their backgrounds included, and yet they'd somehow been soulmates from the first day they'd met. Every time Danni had discovered she'd be on shift with Esther, it had lifted her spirits and, when they'd got a flat together, they'd become each other's confidantes. She might not have the shared experience of losing a parent that Lucas did, but Esther knew how hard it had hit Danni when she'd lost her father and the feelings that seeing the bus driver would have raked up for her. 'Do you think you should go home? You don't look well.'

'I need to be here.' She looked at Esther again, as her best friend finally let go of her, knowing she'd understand that too. But it was Lucas who responded.

'Seeing the driver must have been so tough. Those situations always are. We had a whole family involved in an RTC on my last day in London. The two kids were in the back and got out completely unscathed. But it was too late for the surgical team to help their father. Thank God I managed to save their mother.' He exchanged a look with Danni that made it feel for a moment as if no one else existed. Esther might understand her pain, but Lucas could *feel* it, just like Danni could feel his pain, when something triggered a memory for him of losing his parents, the way this conversation was clearly doing. It took everything she had not to reach out and comfort him.

'I'm fine.' She deliberately glanced away, breaking the intensity of the look he'd given her. 'And I'd better get back to it.'

'There must be something we can do to help?' Lucas ran a hand through his hair as he spoke and Danni cursed the fact that he always managed to look so good. He had thick-rimmed black glasses, ever-so-slightly messy dark brown hair, hazel eyes and a hint of stubble, making him look like a poster boy for the thinking-woman's fantasy. She just wished to God she could stop thinking it.

'Can you do anything when you don't officially start until tomorrow?'

'I don't care even if it's making tea, or taking down details for the walking wounded in reception. Anything is better than just sitting around, worrying about how much you and the rest of the team are having to cope with.' Esther looked from Lucas to Danni. 'Is Dr Moorhouse on duty?'

'Yes, he's in resus. Do you want me to go and speak to him?' Danni was already walking in that direction, before her best friend could answer. She'd seen Lucas's hand curl around Esther's again and she was done being the third wheel. Coming to Cornwall had been the start of a new life, even if they'd made that more complicated by following her, and she was determined not to slip straight back into how things had been.

Less than three minutes later she was back, with instructions from Dr Moorhouse, the consultant in charge of A&E. It sometimes confused patients that their consultant was a doctor, rather than a Mr, but it was only surgeons who got to change their title when they were promoted. Dr Moorhouse had said that because their DBS and reference checks were in, Lucas and Esther could help out with anything non-clinical, like the other volunteers at the hospital. St Piran's had an unseen army of volunteers, who'd already become its backbone, from the team who ran the hospital radio to the staff who ran the shop, as well as mealtime volunteers, patient transport and befrienders. Until they were contracted, Esther and Lucas couldn't provide any medical support, but right now their help could still be invaluable in other ways.

'Where do you think we should start?' As an A&E nurse, Esther was well used to doing anything asked of her and she was clearly ready to get stuck into whatever would help. What was perhaps more surprising was that Lucas was too. In Danni's experience, not all surgeons were as willing to roll up their sleeves to do more routine jobs. But he wasn't like everyone else. That was the trouble. Lucas needed to be needed, exactly like Danni. It was the one thing Joe had been right about.

'There are quite a few people in the relatives' room, waiting to get updates on how their family members are doing. So maybe you could start there? See if they need drinks or if you can make any calls for them? After that, there might be patients who are okay to have a drink or a sandwich. The porters would probably appreciate the offer of some help too, if you can speak to one of them.'

'It's good to have the old team back together.' Lucas smiled and reached out to touch her arm, sending a jolt of electricity up her spine. Her stupid, treacherous body just wouldn't listen when she told it to stop reacting to Lucas.

'I've got to go and see a patient, but I'll catch up with you guys later.' Danni forced a smile and turned towards the cubicle where she'd be checking on a patient whose dislocated shoulder had just been put back in place, to see if he might be able to be discharged. Work had always been the best medicine for whatever ailed her, and she just had to hope that having Lucas and Esther around wouldn't change that too.

* * *

Connie didn't return to A&E after her CT scan and, when Danni went to get an update, she found herself holding her breath, wondering if she was going to need to deliver on her promise after all and tell Richard and Darcy about the letters.

'She's been taken straight up to surgery.' Aidan's gentle lilt made the prospect of undergoing an operation seem almost appealing. 'They're going to remove the metal shard, but she's got an unstable fracture in her pelvis too. The surgeon said she'll perform an external fixation of Connie's pelvic fracture during the op, until the team can decide on any plan for further surgery. At the moment she isn't well enough to tolerate a longer surgical procedure, but she'll almost certainly need one further down the line. It looks like she's in for a long stay. I meant to come and tell you, but it's still like herding cats in here.'

'Oh, that's good news, then.' Danni breathed out, relief at knowing that Connie would almost certainly be okay, allowing her shoulders to relax at last. Richard and Darcy would be able to speak to Connie themselves and she just hoped that the second chance would bring her patient everything she was hoping for. The weird thing was she hadn't once been tempted to open the envelope and find out what the big secret was. Maybe it would have been different if she wasn't carrying a secret of her own, one she felt would kill her if another living soul ever found out. So, she'd keep the letter safe until she had a chance to go up and see Connie on the ward.

'Why won't anyone tell me what's going on!' The voice of a woman, who was clearly distressed, carried through from reception. 'I just want to know he's okay, please.'

Danni didn't hear the response, but a moment later the double doors separating A&E from reception flew open and a woman came running in. 'Someone needs to tell me where the hell my husband is. I just want to see him!'

'It's okay, let me see what I can find out.' Danni put herself in the woman's path, waving away one of the reception staff who'd followed her.

'It's my husband.' The woman didn't seem able to lower her

voice, despite the fact she was standing less than a foot away from Danni. 'I heard about the accident on the car radio, when I was on my way back from meeting my friends for lunch and I can't call him to check he's okay because I'm waiting for a new mobile phone. The old one doesn't charge properly any more.' The woman was gabbling now, but some of the adrenaline finally seemed to go out of her as she looked up at Danni.

'How do you know your husband was on the bus?'

'Because he was driving it.'

It felt as if iced water was dripping down Danni's spine as she faced the woman. Maybe she was wrong, maybe her husband had swapped routes with another driver, but even as the thoughts ran through Danni's head, she somehow knew there was no mistake. There was one way to check for certain, though.

'What's your name?'

'Karen. Karen Bradshaw and my husband's name is Dave.'

There was no doubting it now. The money clip Danni had seen had been a gift from Karen, and their surname matched the one found on the debit card. There couldn't be that many coincidences.

'Shall we go somewhere else where we can talk?' Danni kept her tone as soft as she could, but there was no fooling Karen. She knew something was wrong and wild horses probably couldn't have moved her from where she was standing.

'Just tell me now.'

'I really think it's better if we—'

'Tell me, for Christ's sake, just tell me!'

'I'm so sorry.' It was as far as Danni got before the woman started to wail and every pair of eyes in the unit seemed to be on them.

'No, no, no, no, no, no, nooooooooooooooo!' As Danni reached out to try and comfort Karen, the other woman's legs seemed to give way and she collapsed into her arms. Barely able to hold her up, Danni called out for help.

'I need a wheelchair.'

Lucas got to her first, helping to lift Karen as she continued to wail. Danni didn't even try to give her more information. She just wanted to get Karen out of view of everyone witnessing her agony. It felt horribly intrusive that her raw grief was on display to a group of strangers.

'All the bays are full, so I'm going to take Karen to Dr Moorhouse's room.' Danni looked at Lucas and he nodded. She was desperate to ask him to come with them, but it turned out that a look between them could still say so much.

'Let's go.' He followed her as she pushed Karen through the department to the consultant's office and, not even bothering to knock on the door, they went in. Danni knew Dr Moorhouse wouldn't be there with everything going on.

'I'm so sorry you had to find out this way, Karen.' Danni crouched down by her feet, trying to remember if anything anyone said to her after her father's sudden death had been in the remotest bit helpful. But she'd been so young, and her over-riding feeling had been terror that the one person she could always rely on was gone. 'The police will have been trying to get in touch with you and they should be able to explain a lot more about what happened.'

'Are you sure it was him?' Karen's words were still punctuated with sobs and there was such hope in her eyes when she turned her face towards Danni. It would have been so easy to play along and pretend there was still a chance this might all be some kind of horrible mistake.

'I was at the scene.' Danni swallowed hard, not sure if she could go on, but then she felt Lucas's hand on her shoulder. 'Did Dave have a silver money clip in his wallet?'

'It was platinum and it was for our... for our—' Karen gave a shuddering sigh. 'Our fortieth wedding anniversary. You saw it, didn't you?'

Danni nodded, taking hold of one of Karen's hands. 'Is there anyone we can contact to come and be with you?'

'Our daughters, but I don't know their numbers, not without my phone. Dave was sorting it out for me. He takes care of all of that kind of thing.' The tears were still rolling down Karen's cheeks, but silently now.

'I'll go and sort it out, don't worry.' Lucas sounded so certain that even though Danni had no idea how he was going to find Karen's daughters, she believed he could.

'Will I be able to see him?' Karen asked as Lucas left the room.

'Of course you will.' Danni didn't want to mention that someone would probably need to formally identify Dave's body; Karen had more than enough to cope with for now.

'How did it happen? Did he suffer?' Now that Karen had started to ask questions, she didn't seem able to stop, but Danni hoped what she said next might help a tiny bit.

'It all happened really quickly and the paramedics did everything they could to help, but I don't think Dave would have been aware of anything, not even the crash. We don't know for sure yet, but they think he had a cardiac arrest.'

'I keep telling him and telling him to cut out the ciggies, but he just won't listen.' Karen wasn't ready to talk about Dave in the past tense and, over the next ten minutes, it was almost as if speaking about him would somehow keep him alive. Danni understood that and it seemed to be helping Karen cope. By the time Lucas got back, Karen had shared highlights of the forty-two years she'd been married to Dave, and the lives of their two daughters and five grandchildren. The ripple effects of his death would be felt by so many people.

'The police had already managed to get hold of one of your

daughters, Kelsey, from Dave's records at the bus company.' Lucas spoke as he came back into the room. 'They were on the way to take her over to your place, but they're going to come straight here instead.'

'Oh my poor baby, she had to hear about her dad all on her own.' Karen was suddenly gulping for air again and clawing at her throat. 'I can't do this. I can't!'

'I know this is awful, and that you feel as if you want to start running and keep going, but Kelsey is going to need you and so are Jessica and your grandchildren.' Danni almost felt as though she knew them already. 'So, for now, I just need you to concentrate on your breathing, slow and steady.'

'Do you want me to see if there's a bay free?' Lucas exchanged another look with Danni and she knew what he was asking. If they got her into a bay, they could give her some medication to help with her anxiety, but Karen was shaking her head.

'I don't want you to take me anywhere or give me anything.' Her breath was still catching in her throat, but she sounded determined. 'My mother went on something after her mum died and she was never the same again. Dave wouldn't want me taking that, I know he wouldn't.'

'No one is going to make you take anything you don't want to.' Danni took hold of her hand again. 'Let's just concentrate on our breathing together.'

They stayed liked that, the three of them doing nothing but breathing until the police arrived with Karen's daughter. Danni held the older woman's hand the whole time, and a wave of complete exhaustion swept over her when she finally left the police to talk Karen and Kelsey through the details of what had happened.

'You were amazing.' Lucas stopped, turning her to face him in the corridor outside.

'I should have found a way of getting her out of the department before I said anything.' Danni shivered, all the emotion suddenly hitting her hard.

'You couldn't have done things any differently and I wouldn't have been able to do a better job – no one would. Karen will never forget your kindness.'

'You were the one who sorted everything out, getting hold of the police and making sure her daughter got here.' She was close enough to hear Lucas's breathing, the scent of his familiar after-shave clinging to his skin.

'Speaking to her daughter was tough, but it was nothing I couldn't handle. Why can't you ever see how amazing you are, how amazing we've always been together?' Lucas put a hand under her chin and she felt it again. That almost irresistible pull towards him, as her body ached for just the slightest touch.

'Esther will be wondering where on earth you are.' Stepping away was like a physical wrench, but she had to do it. 'Come on. You must have a million things to do at home and I've got other patients to check up on.'

'Danni, wait. Danni—' She had no idea what he wanted to say, but one thing she knew for certain was that she couldn't afford to let herself hear it. She sped up, breaking into a run, because that was all she could do: keep running and running in the hope that, one day, she might finally be able to outrun her feelings for Lucas.

5

Danni could hear Brenda snoring as she hurried down the pathway to her home. She still had to pinch herself to believe she lived in Castaway Cottage. If someone had painted it and put it on the front of a tin of biscuits, people would say it was too perfect and that nowhere that quaint could exist in real life, let alone perched on a ridge overlooking the bay in Port Kara. That came with its own risk, of course, and she could still hear the surveyor's sharp intake of breath when he'd come to take a look at the property.

'You'll never get a mortgage on this. Too much risk of it crumbling into the sea before you've even had the chance to pay it off, never mind that it's timber-framed.'

'Just as well I don't need a mortgage, then.' It had probably been foolhardy of her to be quite so blasé, when the risk of coastal erosion was very real, and her father would probably have been horrified that her inheritance had been spent on something that wasn't guaranteed to last. But then Trevor Carter had been cautious his whole life and where had that got him? Dead on his office floor the week after he'd turned forty-two.

It hadn't mattered to Danni that Castaway Cottage might not be a sound financial investment; it had filled her heart with joy back when she'd been a kid and that hadn't changed when the estate agent had walked her around the place again. Since joy had been in short supply for a long time, it was enough to convince Danni the cottage was a good investment in other ways. Brenda loved it too. Her favourite spot was at the end of the mercifully long garden, which separated the back door from the edge of the cliffs, howling at the boats coming in and out of the harbour. Ever since the day Danni had brought her home, Brenda had claimed that spot as her own. When she was indoors, she mostly slept – recovering from the exertion of all that howling – and her snoring was loud enough to wake the dead. On more than one occasion, Danni's Apple watch had warned her she was in a loud noise area which could put her in danger of permanent hearing damage if she exposed herself to it for too long. It turned out that Brenda's snoring matched the decibel levels of a snow-blowing machine, and sometimes even the dog would wake herself up with a start.

'Hey, girl, sorry I've been so long.' Danni reached down to pat Brenda as she went into the kitchen. She had her bed by the Aga, whatever the weather, and on the one occasion when Danni had attempted to move it, the dog had taken the corner of the bed in her mouth and dragged it back to her favourite position. Danni had never made the same mistake again.

'Do you want to go outside?' It was already dark and Brenda's usual enthusiasm for barking at boats had waned as a result. She opened one eye, looked at Danni and promptly shut it again, dropping her head down onto the bed. 'Come on, girl, you need to go and do a wee, at least, and then I'll make us both some dinner.'

Danni had considered grabbing a takeaway on the way home, but she'd been so exhausted after the day she'd had that even the thought of stopping somewhere had made her bones ache. Danni hadn't seen Lucas or Esther again, which had been a relief. It had been another two hours before she'd felt able to leave work, when the A&E department had finally started to look less like a post-apocalyptic scene, and the next shift of staff had arrived to take over. Danni had thought about going up to see Connie, but she'd still be recovering from her op. So she'd taken Connie's letter home with her.

Pushing the still resistant Brenda out into the garden, she shut the back door and opened the fridge. To say the contents were uninspiring was an understatement. There was some tenderstem broccoli with a serious case of droop, some fresh Parmesan and three yoghurts, a week after their best-before date. This was not how she'd envisaged life when she finally bought her own place. She'd wanted one of those big American fridges, filled to bursting with ingredients she could whip up into delicious meals in minutes, like every other advert she saw on TV. But cooking for one had turned out not to have nearly the appeal she'd thought it would and trying to think of something to make every night seemed beyond her. Esther had always been the cook when they'd shared a place and Danni had learnt to be self-sufficient years before, because there'd been no family members she could call to bleed a radiator or put up some wallpaper. They'd made a good team back then and she still missed Esther's cooking.

'When I leave, you'll have to get yourself another 1950s house-wife.' Esther had made the joke on the night before she'd moved in with Lucas, when she'd cooked a lavish farewell dinner for herself and Danni. 'But God knows what I'm going to do without you. Lucas struggles to change a lightbulb. You'd think being a surgeon would have given him some transferable skills!'

'I'm sure he's got other talents.' Danni hadn't meant for it to come out the way it did and the last thing she'd wanted was to hear about Esther and Lucas's sex life. Before Esther had started dating him, those were exactly the sort of details they'd shared with one another – the good, bad and the downright ugly of their dating lives. She still couldn't hear a cockerel crowing without starting to laugh, not since Esther had described the sound her boyfriend before Lucas had made when she'd stayed over at his place for the first and only time. But it had been different with Lucas. Maybe Esther had sensed it wasn't something Danni wanted to hear, or maybe it was because from the very first date, Esther was clearly more serious about Lucas than she had been about any other boyfriend she'd had.

'My nan always used to say when you know, you know, and I thought it was rubbish. Until now.' Esther's face had taken on a wistful look whenever she'd spoken about Lucas in the early days of them dating. Even now, seven years on, and after almost two years of living together, it didn't seem to have changed. Maybe Esther's nan had been right all along. It was just a shame that Danni's 'one' already had a 'one' of his own.

'Come on then, girl, it's dinner time.' She waited as Brenda came through the door. The basset hound was surprisingly quick for a dog of indeterminate age and unwieldly proportions. Having such a long body and little legs could be a challenge. She insisted on being lifted into the car, because she couldn't possibly jump up by herself. But when Danni had left a pizza cooling on the table, while she went to get a drink, Brenda had somehow managed to heave herself onto a chair, just high enough to be able to snake her body along the length of the table and take a big, slobbery, uneven slice out of the pizza. It was certainly the best diet Danni had ever tried, because she went right off the idea of deep pan pepperoni after that.

'Here you go then, sweetheart.' As Danni put the bowl of dog food down, her stomach gave a loud grumble. It came to something when a bowl of Tender Chunks almost looked appealing. One of the downsides of living in Port Kara was that the takeaway delivery service was limited at best and all she could think about now was how much she wanted a bag of crispy, golden chips from Penrose Plaice, the fish and chip shop in neighbouring Port Agnes, which did the best chips she'd ever tasted.

'Do I want them enough to get back in the car and drive over there, Bren? That's the question.'

Brenda might not have been able to answer, but Danni's stomach could, giving another loud rumble in response to her question.

'Do you want to come with me for a ride out? I don't want to leave you all on your own again.' It was another rhetorical question, and the truth was Danni was the one who could use the company. 'You finish your dinner and then we'll go and get mine. We might even have time for a walk around the harbour in Port Agnes, seeing as you've been stuck in all day.'

Danni had just got to the hallway to grab Brenda's lead, when someone rapped loudly on the front door, making her jump. It was a long way from the neighbouring property and not the sort of place you could chance upon accidentally, so getting an unexpected visitor was definitely out of the norm. Freezing to the spot, she tried to decide whether to pretend no one was home, or to call out and ask who it was. But then the average axe murderer probably wasn't going to announce that he was standing outside ready to strike. Instead, she stood perfectly still, so much so that the only sound she could hear was her own breathing. But then the mystery caller knocked again and, having finished her dinner, Brenda decided to leap into action. She hurtled along the hallway as fast as her stubby little legs would carry her, howling a greeting to whoever had knocked on the door, then looking back at Danni and howling some more.

'Shush, Brenda, shh.' Danni's attempts to quieten her down came to nothing. The dog clearly couldn't understand why her owner could obviously hear someone at the door, but was doing absolutely nothing about it. 'Oh, for God's sake! Well, if we both end up in a tin of Tender Chunks after the axe murderer has done away with us, you've only got yourself to blame.'

'Dan, it's me. Let me in!' As the voice outside finally rose above the noise of Brenda barking, Danni's shoulders slumped with relief. It was Esther and unless she'd somehow discovered that Danni had been harbouring secret feelings about her fiancé for the last seven years, the chances of becoming the victim of an axe murderer had fallen sharply.

'Sorry, I was in the kitchen, and I couldn't even hear you knocking over the sound of Brenda howling.' Danni didn't want to admit that her imagination had been in overdrive. She was even more relieved to discover that Esther was on her own. The prospect of seeing Lucas again so soon was only marginally more appealing than facing an axe-wielding maniac. 'What on earth are you doing here?'

'Mum made about six lasagnes for moving-in day and, even with all the family coming over to help out, there was still masses left over. And I know you – the chances are you'll have come in from an epic shift like you've had today, with nothing more than a packet of Super Noodles in the cupboard.'

'I wish I had some Super Noodles! You know me too well, thank you.' Danni stepped to one side to let her best friend come in; Brenda was already drooling as the smell of lasagne drifted down the hallway. 'Shouldn't you be busy unpacking? You must be way behind schedule after helping at the hospital.'

'You'd think so, wouldn't you?' Esther rolled her eyes. 'Except that by the time we got back, Mum, Dad, Nan and Pops had unpacked almost everything. I'm never going to know where to find my cheese grater, or the blender, but I nearly passed out when I saw Nan putting the underwear Lucas got me for his birthday into the drawer, although apparently not even she's got the skills to fold a basque!'

'It could have been worse; it could have been Pops!' Danni laughed, deliberately picturing the look that would have been on Esther's grandmother's face at the impracticality of un-foldable underwear, rather than imagining the look that had been on Lucas's face when he'd given it to Esther.

'Oh my God, don't say that!' Esther laughed too, and they headed down the hallway into the kitchen.

'I was just about to go out for some chips, but this is much better.' Danni took the dish of still warm lasagne from her friend, the rumbling in her stomach even louder than it had been before as she set it down on the kitchen counter. 'Can I get you a drink?'

'I can't stay, even though I'd love to. I've got to get back to everyone, especially after they all worked so hard for us today. I just wanted to make sure you had something proper to eat and to check you're okay.' Esther tilted her head slightly, giving Danni the appraising look she always did when she was worried she might not be looking after herself properly. 'It must have been tough today, especially seeing the bus driver the way you did and then having to wait with his wife until her daughter arrived.'

'Lucas told you?' Danni shouldn't have been surprised. He and Esther probably told each other everything.

'Yes, and he told me how well you handled things too.'

'I don't think I did.' Danni could still picture Karen's face as the news that her husband had died hit her.

'You never do, Dan, but it's part of what makes you, you, and it's why we love you.' Esther reached out and squeezed her hand. 'Maybe one day you'll see yourself as you really are and then...'

'Then what?' They knew each other so well, but for once Danni couldn't read the expression on her friend's face, and then Esther shook her head.

'Oh nothing, just maybe then you'll realise that you deserve to be happy.'

'I am happy.' Danni's voice had gone an octave higher and she knew she sounded like she was protesting too much. But she'd been getting there. A new lightness had come without the daily reminder of her feelings for Lucas, or why her love for Esther meant she had to fight so hard against them. But now it was like all the progress she'd made had disappeared, and she was completely torn. Having her best friend standing in her kitchen should have made her happier than she'd been in months. But, even when he wasn't there, it was like a Lucas-shaped shadow was looming over them. Danni shook herself, painting on a smile. 'It suits me fine, always the bridesmaid. Some of us don't want to be the bride, that's all.'

'Well, I'm glad you have no objections to being my bridesmaid.' A slow smile crept across Esther's face. 'Because Mum and Dad made an enquiry with Noah, the vicar at St Jude's in Port Agnes, and he's said we can move the wedding down here, as long as we're happy to do it on a weekday.'

'What about all the deposits you paid in London?' Danni leant against the kitchen counter. It was one thing playing the part of maid of honour miles from home and never again having to pass the venue where Lucas and Esther had promised themselves to one another for the rest of their lives. It was quite another to have it in a church that Danni had no chance of permanently avoiding.

'Even with losing the deposits we're going to save money doing it here, and this already feels like home.' Esther squeezed her hand again. 'Because you're here.'

'If you're happy, that's the best news I've heard for a long time.' Danni's head was starting to ache from keeping her smile in place. One day soon, if there was any justice in the world, the only thing she'd feel about Lucas and Esther's wedding was happy for them. God knows she was trying.

'I'm so glad you're glad. I didn't know if you were looking forward to going back up to London, especially as you never managed to find the time once you moved down here.' There was no bitterness in Esther's voice, but the appraising stare was back, and Danni couldn't bear the thought of her friend seeing the truth.

'I really am glad and, as soon as you get back to that wonderful family of yours, I'll be diving into this lasagne and opening a nice bottle of something to celebrate.'

'All right, I can take a hint.' Esther laughed again.

'Say thanks to your mum for dinner, won't you?' Danni hugged her when they reached the door. 'And thank you too, you really are the best friend a girl could ask for.'

'Don't you ever forget it!' Esther was still laughing as she waggled a finger in Danni's direction, but for a split second she thought she saw something else in her friend's eyes and then it was gone. 'I'll see you at work tomorrow.'

'Looking forward to it.' Danni kept waving until Esther had gone. Closing the door, she stood with her back against it, wondering whether that momentary look in Esther's eyes really had meant something, or whether she was just tired. She was probably overthinking things, the way she always did. She needed something else to think about, that was all. Reaching inside her pocket, she pulled out the crumpled envelope containing the letter Connie had given her for safekeeping.

Richard Bruce, Trengothern Hall

Taking her phone out of her other pocket, she keyed the name into Google. It was time to focus on someone else's problems for a change.

6

Connie hadn't expected to wake up. She'd been certain that something would go wrong during one of the operations. When it became clear the external fixation wasn't working and her pain levels remained unbearably high, a second operation had followed, just twenty-four hours after the first and her pelvis was now held together with a series of screws and metal plates.

The surgeon had warned her it was a more complex operation and having two anaesthetics so close together came with some level of risk, so it was only natural that she expected the worst. Well, only natural for her perhaps. The damage she'd sustained had been severe and there'd also been some injury to her bladder, intestines and one of her kidneys. A lovely nurse had reassured her it was all fixable, but with the likelihood of further operations, monitoring of the damage to her internal organs and the need for physiotherapy, she was going to be in hospital for quite some time.

Connie had never liked hospitals and, until now, she'd only ever had to stay in once and that had been enough to make her hate them even more. Then, after her sister and brother-in-law had both died within eighteen months of each other, she'd decided she'd seen more than enough of hospitals to last her a lifetime. To Connie, they always symbolised the end, so waking up to hear the operation had been a success had been unexpected.

For the first few hours after she opened her eyes, all she'd felt was relief. And then suddenly, when she was back on the ward, she remembered the letter.

'I need to get up.' Connie was struggling to move and the nurse who'd appeared at the side of her bed looked absolutely horrified.

'Oh no, not yet. You can't get out of bed until the physio comes to see you and it'll be at least three days, probably longer after the surgery you've had, before they work with you on transferring to a chair.' The nurse, who looked young enough to be Connie's grand-daughter, smiled, but it did nothing to quell the panic rising in her throat.

'You don't understand; I need to go and speak to someone. To ask her to give back something I should never have given her. I thought I was going to die, you see, otherwise I'd never have done it. Please.' Her head felt fuzzy, like someone had stuffed it full of cotton wool, but it wasn't as if she was talking complete gobblede-gook, so why the nurse couldn't seem to understand the urgency of the situation was beyond her.

'It's okay, Connie, you're safe now.' The young nurse had adopted what she obviously thought was a reassuring tone, but she'd also pressed the buzzer by Connie's bed to summon more help. 'You're perfectly stable and I can promise you you're not going to die. There's plenty of time to sort out whatever it is you're worrying about, but if you keep trying to get up you could really hurt yourself.'

'A lot more people could get hurt if I don't. Richard can't see that letter; I've got to get it back.' Connie couldn't seem to make her understand. The plan, when she'd come down to Port Kara, if you could call it a plan, had been to try and find Richard. To stand with him, face to face, and work out whether handing over the letter was a good idea, or the most stupid idea anyone had had since Anne Boleyn had decided that flirting with Henry VIII would be her path to happiness. Now the consequences of Richard reading the letter seemed almost as disastrous. Connie had only written it down in the first place because she'd known he wouldn't listen to everything she needed to say once he found out the truth, and a letter could be read again at a later date. But if she'd been certain she wanted him to know the contents of the letter, she could have just posted it. The same way that if she'd been sure she wanted her niece to know the truth, she could have sent Darcy a letter, or even an email, telling her everything, instead of sealing the envelope with her name on it and hiding it inside the treasure chest that had fascinated her niece since she was a child. But now not only was Richard's letter out there, in the hands of a doctor who might already be planning to forward it on to him, but she'd also told her to contact Darcy and explain to her niece exactly where the secrets she'd buried for so long were hidden. Which meant it was going to take a lot more than a young nurse to stop Connie getting out of bed now.

'You've got to try and stay calm.' The nurse let go of a long sigh as her colleague came to the other side of the bed. 'Thanks for your help, Helen. Connie's very agitated and I've told her that trying to get out of bed too soon is dangerous and could cause her a serious injury.'

'Chloe's right.' Helen was probably a good twenty years older than the other nurse. She had the dark blue uniform of a sister and a firm hand against Connie's shoulder. She looked like she'd been around the block and back again, and she'd probably seen it all before. 'Now why on earth would you be wanting to get out of bed when you know it could do you a lot of harm?'

'I gave the doctor a letter, to pass on if anything happened to me, and I need to get it back.' Connie was getting frantic now. No one was listening.

'But nothing has happened to you, so there'd be no need for the letter to be passed on.' Helen made it all sound so simple, but Connie knew that people didn't always follow even the simplest of instructions. She'd seen it time and time again, with some of her students at the university.

'What if she misunderstood and thought I wanted her to pass the letter on regardless? I need to tell her to give it back to me, or at the very least get rid of it.' Connie was finding it difficult to breathe. Maybe that was the nurse's plan, to keep forcing her to explain the problem over and over again until she ran out of the energy to fight any more. 'Let me get out of this bed. Now!'

'I can't do that and you need to calm down before you start upsetting the other patients.' Helen had a hand against Connie's shoulder again, pushing her firmly but gently back down onto the bed. 'But if you tell me who you gave the letter to, I'll see what I can do to help.'

'She said her name was Danni; she came out to the crash and they told me when I got here that she saved my life.' Connie was almost beginning to wish she hadn't, because once this secret got out, it could never be buried again.

'That's Danni Carter, one of the doctors from A&E. She came up to see you when you were down having your second op.'

'Oh, thank God.' Connie finally stopped pushing against Helen's hand and relaxed back against the pillows. 'Did she leave the letter?'

'No, but she said she'd come back when she was next on shift and I can try and get a message to her if you like? Whatever is in this letter must be pretty important if you're willing to risk getting hurt to try and retrieve it.' If Helen was hoping to find out the details, she was going to be disappointed. There were already too many people who knew more than Connie wanted them to.

'Can you tell her I need to see her as soon as possible and that whatever she does, not to give the letter to anyone but me?'

Chloe exchanged a look with Helen, making it clear her interest was piqued too. But this was Connie's life, not some sort of soap opera.

'And have you got some paper I could use, please? If I'm stuck in this bed, there are some other letters I could spend the time writing.'

'They'll be bringing round the hospital trolley in about twenty minutes; they usually have cards and notepaper on there.' Helen suddenly sounded a bit sniffy, as if Connie's reluctance to let her and Chloe in on the details of the letter had somehow offended her. 'And if you promise not to try and get up again, I'll get a message to Dr Carter.'

'I promise and thank you.' Connie breathed out, finally allowing her body to relax just a little bit, all the while keeping her eyes trained on the entrance to the ward. As soon as that hospital trolley arrived, she was going to buy every scrap of writing paper they had.

* * *

Connie was like a cat on hot bricks. Every time one of the nurses came along, she expected it to be Helen with the news that she'd been in touch with Danni, or even better that she was holding the letter in her hand. But so far there'd been no sign of her.

Half an hour after she'd last seen Helen, Connie heard laughter drifting from some of the bays further down the ward and, five minutes after that, a woman came into Connie's bay pushing a trolley laden with newspapers, magazines and the sort of treats that no doctor could possibly recommend.

'Hello, my love, it looks like you've been through the mill.' The woman pushing the trolley smiled and Connie had the feeling they'd met somewhere before, but in the fuzziness of her brain she couldn't recall where. Or maybe she just had one of those faces. After all, Connie hadn't been to Cornwall, let along Port Kara, in decades.

'I was in the bus crash.' Connie blinked a few times, determined not to cry. But every time she'd closed her eyes since the accident, it was like she was back inside the bus. The terrible sounds of screams as it careered out of control. She couldn't claim her whole life had flashed in front of her, but she'd been certain she was going to die and the only thing that had flashed in front of her was the faces of the people she owed an explanation to. The thought that she could so easily have missed the opportunity scuppered any chance she might have had of holding back the tears.

'Don't upset yourself. I know you've been through a horrible experience, but you're safe now and it's going to be okay.' The woman abandoned her trolley and moved closer to the bed. 'What's your name, my love? I'm Gwen.'

'Connie.' She blinked again. Crying in front of anyone, let alone a stranger, wasn't the sort of thing she did. Connie prided herself on being professional and resilient, stoic even. She'd had to be. There'd never been anyone around for her to lean on, especially since her sister had died.

'Well, Connie, the thing you've got to do now is take care of yourself to make sure you get better as soon as possible. Treat yourself to all the little things you don't normally do, or have time for. You look to me like someone who keeps yourself very busy. What do you do for work?'

The question took Connie by surprise. More often than not

lately, people would just assume she was retired. 'I'm a university lecturer.'

'Now that does sound demanding, and I bet it's been a while since you've had the chance to read just for pleasure? But the one upside of being in hospital is that now you have.' Gwen turned back towards her trolley, pulling it closer to the bed. 'There's plenty of reading material on here, but I'm happy to go to the library in the village if there's something else you'd like? They've got audio-books too and I've got a portable CD player and headphones you're welcome to borrow. I've really got back into reading since I retired from midwifery and I'm working my way through the classics.'

'That's on my bucket list for when I retire too.' Maybe Gwen had a point about making the most of the time while she was stuck in hospital, and losing herself in a book might even take her mind off the missing letter for a little while. Although she very much doubted she'd be able to concentrate on anything until that piece of paper was safely back in her hands. 'What would you recommend?'

'I've just finished *Lady Chatterley's Lover* and last night I started *Emmanuelle*, but then I like my books like I like my life. A little bit racy.' Gwen grinned, but it was clear she wasn't joking, and for the first time Connie smiled too. She still wasn't sure whether she really did know Gwen from somewhere, but she knew already liked her. It was hard to place her age, but the other woman was still attractive, with shoulder-length blonde hair and a twinkle in the blue eyes that were trained on Connie. She clearly wasn't conforming to the stereotype of a woman over sixty and Connie felt certain Gwen would know exactly who Led Zeppelin were too.

'I've read *Lady Chatterley's Lover* before.' There was a phase – after Richard – when Connie had read every book she could find about star-crossed lovers, searching for a happy ending, to give her some hope that things could work out. *Lady Chatterley's Lover* had held a particular appeal, given that the heroine was also called Connie. But that was the problem with forbidden love – it never ended happily, and real life had certainly mirrored fiction in that respect.

'I reckon Mellors is worth a revisit; your namesake certainly thought so.' Gwen smiled again. 'But I'm happy to pick up any kind of book you'd like. Or I've got magazines here, everything from the *Angling Times* to *My Weekly*. Just take your pick.'

'What I really need is some writing paper and a pen.'

'That doesn't sound like relaxing to me.' Gwen raised her eyebrows. 'But if that's what you want, I've got some notelets on the trolley, but we've got some proper writing paper down in the shop. I can nip back down there and get you some?'

'Thank you. I don't think notelets are suitable for the sort of letter I want to send.' Connie wasn't even sure what she was going to say in the new letter to Richard, but she'd always found writing cathartic and it certainly felt more productive than sitting around and waiting.

'Do you want to talk about it?' Gwen looked at her and to Connie's surprise she realised she did. When the nurses had questioned her about the letter, the last thing she'd wanted to do was share any information, but there was something different about Gwen, and it was driving her mad wondering whether Richard already had the letter. She needed someone to talk to and for some reason Gwen seemed like the right person. She was around the same age as Connie and wouldn't fall over in surprise at the idea of someone her age having had a past. Sometimes young people seemed to think they'd invented love. And sex.

'I need to write to an old friend. I've already written him one letter, but I don't think I put what needed to be said in the right way. When I had the accident, I gave the letter to one of the doctors to give to Richard, and now I don't even know where it is. I need to write another one, explaining things more clearly. But I don't know where to start.' If Gwen was still following all of this, she was doing well, because it felt really mixed up, even in Connie's own head.

'What do you want to tell him? I always think being honest and upfront is the best policy, although sometimes I do get told off for it.' Gwen pulled a chair up to the side of the bed. 'Maybe talking it through will help you work out the best way to explain things to Richard. I'm happy to be a sounding board if you think that might be useful?'

'I can't hold you up.' A frisson of nerves was already gripping Connie's insides, but Gwen was right. She needed to say it out loud to make sense of it herself, before she had a hope of explaining it all to Richard.

'That's the great thing about being a volunteer; I don't have to answer to anyone. Just tell me as much or as little as you want, and I promise I won't judge you for any of it. After over forty-five years as a midwife, I think I've heard everything.'

Connie sighed and closed her eyes as she began to speak. 'Richard was thirty-one and I'd just turned thirty. We weren't stupid kids and we should have known better.' Logic had gone out of the window the first time Richard had looked at her, and when he'd touched her, she'd been lost to any reason. Otherwise she'd never have let herself fall as hard as she had, knowing all the time that it couldn't lead anywhere. 'I was down in Port Kara for the summer. Working at the university meant summers could seem endless, and back then I had ambitions of writing a classic novel of my own. I'd always loved history, because it felt more like listening to stories than having to work, like I did for all the other subjects. I had an idea for a story about evacuees sent to Cornwall in World War Two. So I rented a house three roads from the beach and I could almost feel it pulsing in the air, this urge to get words on the page. It was like the town itself was telling me a story. I couldn't type fast enough and that first week alone I'd written more than fifty pages. When I wasn't writing, I was walking. Hours spent on the beach, listening to the breeze as it whispered the next part of the story. You probably think I sound crazy.'

'No, I don't!' Gwen's response was emphatic. 'It sounds like the ability to harness magic, and not the sort me and my Barry do.'

Connie furrowed her brow, wondering what she might be about to hear, but then Gwen shrugged. 'Barry the Magic Man and the Great Gwendini have got nothing on you!'

As Connie laughed, some of the tension immediately lifted. If Gwen's intention was to put her at her ease, it was working. She'd been accused more than once of taking herself too seriously, so Gwen was probably the perfect person to share her story with. 'Oh, I don't know, I think the Great Gwendini might have more magical powers than you think, because the only other person I've told everything to before is my sister.'

'In that case I'm honoured, but you don't have to tell me anything else if you don't want to.'

'No, I do.' Connie breathed out. 'It was on one of those walks when I met Richard. I didn't think those bolt-of-lightning feelings that only exist in romance novels were real. But then I saw him, and it just hit me. I could tell straight away he felt it too. For a few minutes I actually lost the ability to speak.'

Gwen was leaning forward now, her attention focused, but she wasn't saying anything and Connie was grateful. Now that she'd started, she just wanted to get it out. 'I dropped my sunglasses on the sand and we both bent down to pick them up. His hand touched mine and it was like every cliché in every love story I read as a teenager. It was pure electric. I wasn't some innocent kid, there'd been others before Richard, but within twenty minutes we were back at the house I was renting. I didn't ask then if he was free to be with me, because I knew it wouldn't matter what his answer was. Maybe everything that happened after the summer was over was my punishment for rushing in the way only fools ever do.'

'He had someone else?' Gwen was looking at her, but she'd kept her promise. There wasn't a hint of judgement in either her face or her voice.

'He was engaged, but he didn't love her.' Connie shook her head. 'Oh, I know you're probably thinking that's the oldest line in the book, but she didn't love him either. They both came from farming families and their farms were having trouble staying afloat. It was more of a business merger than a relationship, but Richard and Fiona felt a huge sense of responsibility. I knew he'd never choose me over his duty. Instead, I told myself the summer would be enough. I wanted to be with Richard every second he had spare and, as I got to know him, I realised our connection was a million miles away from being just physical. That's when things got tough. If it had been just that, walking away at the end of the summer would have been so much easier. But as it was it broke my heart.'

Gwen put a hand on her chest, almost as if she could feel the heartbreak Connie had experienced back then. 'I can't believe he didn't ask you to stay.'

'He did.' The memory of it could still take Connie's breath away. 'But I knew he'd regret it if he lost the farm and everything his family had worked generations for. So I said it was over and that it was only ever a summer fling for me, but it was a lie. I loved him, I never stopped and no one else has even come close.'

'And that's what you want to tell him?'

'I need to. I don't know if he and Fiona are gloriously happy with six kids and twenty-eight grandchildren, but it's like it's burning inside me. I've kept it hidden for all these years, but I need him to know.'

'Just tell him that and, if you haven't already done so, for God's sake finish that book you were writing! It would be straight on my list of must-read novels.' Gwen smiled again; she made it all sound so easy.

'But what if he and Fiona are still together?'

'Then tell him you need him to know you always loved him, and that the summer meant a lot you. After that you wish him and Fiona well and walk away again. You've done it once and you can do it again.' Gwen almost had her believing she could. 'At least that way the burning urge to tell him the truth might finally ease off, and you can get on with the rest of your life. And if he's not with Fiona any more, well, who knows where it could lead? If you tell me his second name, I can probably find out in five minutes whether he's still married.'

'I've sat at my computer a thousand times wanting to do that. To type his name into the search engine and find out if Fiona is still a part of his life, but it's not as simple as that and telling him I love him is only part of what he needs to know. If he discovers what else I haven't told him, there's a very good chance that any happy memories he has of that summer will be gone forever, and he'll hate me as much as I still love him.'

'What secret could possibly be that bad?' Gwen leant forward again, and the silence seemed to go on for an eternity before Connie finally took a deep breath.

'There was a baby. Richard's baby. I gave his child away without even letting him know he was a father.'

7

Danni had two hours of her shift left. As soon as she was finished, she was planning on going up to see Connie. Helen, one of the nurses, had sent her a message saying that Connie had asked to see her and that she was worrying about the letter she'd given her.

'*I've got no idea what it's all about, but hopefully you have.*' Helen had left the voicemail message, sounding every bit as confused as her words suggested. '*She seemed agitated, and she definitely didn't want to talk about it, but you can fill me in later if you like!*'

St Piran's was a small hospital, and everyone more or less knew everyone else. Danni had got to know Helen a bit better than most of the other nurses outside of A&E, because she was one of Aidan's best friends and they'd both been to a BBQ at his place. But there was still zero chance of her sharing any of the details that Connie had given her. As tempting as it had been, once she'd looked Richard up on Google, Danni had resisted the urge to open the letter. She knew what it was like to have a secret and what Connie was concealing was none of her business. She'd promised to deliver one letter and one message, if the need had arisen, that was all, but thankfully Connie could now do that herself.

'That's a new one for me, someone calling an ambulance for period pains.' Esther's voice brought Danni back to the present, as a young patient and her friend, who'd been brought into A&E by the paramedics an hour and a half before, disappeared back out through the double doors. 'I've seen patients with burst cysts and endometriosis before, when the pain relief we offered could barely touch the pain. But as soon as Mia was given some paracetamol, she was fine.'

'I thought the chap in bay six, who I've just sent home after removing his splinter, was taking the proverbial, but at least he didn't call an ambulance.' Aidan rolled his eyes as he walked towards them.

'It wasn't Mia's fault; she's only eleven and the poor kid had no idea what to do.' Esther shook her head again. 'If someone had told her that paracetamol and a hot water bottle might be enough to ease the pain a bit, they'd never have called an ambulance.'

'You're right and what worries me most is that her mother seemed to think it was all a big joke.' Danni was with Esther on this. The two young girls, who'd evidently been left home alone overnight, weren't to blame for wasting the paramedics' time. From what they'd told Danni, Mia hadn't been having periods for long and the pain that had accompanied the start of her latest period had terrified her. When her mother hadn't answered her frantic calls, her best friend, Bella, had called an ambulance.

When the paramedics had also been unable to reach Mia's mother, they'd brought her in. Mia's mum had eventually responded five hours after her daughter's first panicked phone call and when she'd arrived in A&E to pick the girls up, she'd found it hilarious, but she might not be laughing soon. Esther and Danni had agreed that the incident needed to be reported to social services. There might not be a set age for children to stay home alone, but not staying in contact definitely pushed it into the realms of danger, as far as Danni and Esther were concerned.

'My mum wouldn't even let me go to the corner shop for a pint of milk on my own until I left for university!' Esther laughed, but Danni knew her family well enough to know it was probably true as they were incredibly protective of Esther. After Danni's father had died, nobody had ever really cared that way about her. Except Esther, who had stepped into the role of family when she'd realised it was a vacancy that needed filling in Danni's life. And Danni wasn't sure what she'd have done without her.

'Can you imagine doing that? Just going away and leaving your kids for the night? I can't even leave Babs and Ange for a night without making sure someone is going to check on them.' Aidan pursed his lips. 'Jase says I've made a rod for our backs with the way they're treated, but they are dames after all.'

'Okay, you've got me. I'm thoroughly confused now.' Esther looked from Aidan to Danni and back again. 'I thought you were talking about your kids for a moment.'

'Babs and Ange as kids' names – how old do you think I am?' Aidan laughed and Esther tried to dig herself out of the hole she'd just climbed into.

'No, no, it's not that. All those old-school names are coming back, aren't they? My friend is expecting twin girls and she's going to call them Hazel and Irene.'

'Babs and Ange are cats.' Danni knew what Aidan was going to say next before he opened his mouth.

'Not just any sort of cats – they're Scottish Folds. They're the Aston Martins of the feline world.' Aidan put his hands on his hips, as if daring anyone to challenge him.

'Okay, but why Babs and Ange? Wouldn't Scottish names have made more sense?' Esther screwed up her face.

'We named them after our favourite actresses. Barbara Windsor for Jase, and Angela Lansbury for me. God rest their souls.' Aidan made the sign of the cross as he spoke. 'What more fitting tribute could you have to two powerful women, who were both way ahead of their time, than naming the two most beautiful cats in the world after them?'

'Well, when you put it like that, it makes perfect sense.' Esther laughed. 'It reminds me of when we got those goldfish and named them Idris, Styles, Efron, Jackman and Ryan.'

'Good choices.' Aidan grinned. 'But the question remains, which Ryan? Reynolds or Gosling?'

'That was the joy of choosing Ryan – he could be either and we'd happily have taken both.' Danni shrugged.

'Me too.' Aidan winked. 'But having pets together means there was a serious commitment between you two. I knew you lived together, but I had no idea you were that settled. Who got custody of the fish when you split?'

'Essie didn't want to leave me all alone in the world. So I got the goldfish and she got Lucas.' Danni hadn't meant it to come out the way it did, but Aidan clearly wasn't going to let it pass.

'Ooh, have I touched a nerve? What was it? You committed to getting pets together and then Esther ups and leaves you for some-body new, leaving you holding the goldfish bowl.' He was laughing and, thankfully, so was Esther. If she'd picked up on the hurt behind Danni's comment, she wasn't showing it.

'In my defence, it wasn't a conscious decision to commit to pets, was it, Dan? We got left the goldfish in a will.'

'Okay, now I feel as if naming my cats after a couple of theatrical dames is very basic. You're going to have to tell me the rest.'

'We had this patient who used to come into A&E on a regular

basis, Christine.' Danni turned towards Aidan. 'She had COPD and she couldn't get out and about as much as she wanted, so she filled her house with pets. When she died, she left a note in her will setting out exactly who she wanted the animals left to. Me and Essie got the fish, her favourite paramedics were given joint custody of the bearded dragon, but it was her carers who hit the jackpot.'

'Did she leave them her house?' Aidan looked really animated, but Danni was going to have to disappoint him. There was no financial payoff for Christine's hard-working carers.

'Not quite – Christine lived in a flat owned by the housing association. Her carers got a tank of stick insects, two tarantulas and a royal python called Nigel.' Danni laughed again. 'It was testament to how much we all thought of Christine that everyone accepted the legacies left in her will.'

'Are all the goldfish still alive?' Aidan was really invested now.

'Efron died of a broken heart just after Esther moved out, but thankfully the rest of the gang got over the heartbreak.' Danni grinned. She'd got away with revealing a chink in her armour before and no one seemed to have noticed that she really had been devastated when Esther had moved in with Lucas, and only partly because she was losing her best friend as a flatmate. She needed to make sure they didn't see beyond the jokes. 'But when I moved down here, they were able to leave the confines of the bowl and start a new life in the garden pond.'

'And do you still keep in touch with the stick insects?' Aidan laughed as Danni shook her head.

'They never call, they never write. But what can you do?'

'We could always—' Esther was cut off midway through her sentence as the red phone at the side of them started to ring. It was a trauma call that would let them know the details of the latest emergency on the way into them. Life in A&E couldn't ever be predicted and there was never too much time to dwell on anything else, which was just one of the reasons why Danni loved it.

* * *

Esther had taken the call and briefed the others on what to expect. It was a young boy, on his way in with a suspected open fracture of the tibia and fibula bones.

'Oh God, if the bones are protruding, I think I'll pass on that one.' Aidan grimaced. 'I was actually sick the first time I saw that in real life. Come back, splinter man, all is forgiven.'

'There's no protrusion through the skin, but the shape of the lower leg is highly suspicious and it's a football injury, so there's a good chance the paramedics are right.' Esther wrinkled her nose. 'That's why watching Netflix is the safest hobby.'

'Until you realise that you've eaten your body weight in pizza, while you've been binge-watching, and you drop down dead from a massive heart attack.' Aidan wasn't looking at Danni as he spoke, but Esther was and she'd obviously seen her reaction. People made throwaway comments about having heart attacks all the time. They didn't mean anything by it, but the image that Aidan had unconsciously conjured up had her father's face at the centre of it. Aidan might have been willing to talk about his struggle with open fractures, but Danni didn't want anyone to think the ghosts of her past might affect the way she worked. Except Esther already knew that they did.

'You carry on with the walk-ins, Aidan. I'm sure Danni and I can cope with the trauma case.'

'I've got my tweezers at the ready!' Aidan was as good as his word, disappearing to check on other patients and making sure he'd be well out of the way before the ambulance arrived.

'Are you okay? I know he was only joking but...' Esther put a hand on Danni's arm once Aidan was gone.

'I'm fine. I wouldn't be in this job if that sort of thing still bothered me.' Danni screwed up her face, aware that her best friend probably knew it did still bother her, but that she'd found a way to push these things down. Sometimes she worried that all the things she'd pushed down might suddenly come to the surface one day, but for now they had a trauma call to deal with and ten minutes later they were in the thick of it.

'This is Ollie, he's eight years old and he was playing football at his primary school when he stopped to block a ball. His foot got stuck in a divot, but the rest of his body kept moving.' The paramedic opened his mouth to say something else, when a muffled voice interrupted.

'Then my bone went crack.' The little boy widened his eyes as he lay on his back, the mask over his nose and mouth administering painkilling gas.

'That must have been scary.' Esther took hold of Ollie's hand and he nodded his head.

'There's an obvious change to the shape of the lower left leg, indicating an open fracture.' The paramedic turned his attention back to Danni. 'Although there's no penetration of the skin, there is some evidence of a small wound. We've stabilised the break and administered antibiotics, as well as pain relief. This is Miss Phipps, Ollie's teacher, and Mum and Dad are on their way in from work.'

'Thank you for everything you've done.' Danni hadn't got to know all the paramedics who served the hospital yet, but she'd been impressed by what she'd seen so far and today was no exception. She knew only too well the pressure of being first on the scene, but the A&E team could take over now.

'I'll never forget that sound.' Miss Phipps, who barely looked old enough to be out of school herself, went pale as she relived

Ollie's accident. 'And the shape of his leg, it was like that scene from *Harry Potter*.'

'Why don't you come through to the bay with Ollie and take a seat.' Danni gently guided the younger woman by the arm. Miss Phipps was doing herself no favours by recounting the details and, if she didn't take a seat soon, there was a good chance she might faint. Then they'd be left with two casualties on their hands.

'How are you doing, Ollie?' Esther had always been brilliant with the children who came into A&E. At their old hospital, if any of the doctors ever had a young patient who kicked and fought against being examined, refused medication or other treatment, all they had to do was ask Esther to help out and they'd be able to do what they needed.

'Is my mum coming?' Ollie's words were still muffled by the mask, but thankfully the pain relief was doing its job.

'She's on her way, sweetheart, and we'll be able to tell her how amazing you've been.' Esther exchanged a look with Danni, both of them knowing that the next hour or so might get even tougher for Ollie. They'd need to examine him and send him down for an X-ray to check the position of the break. He might also need a scan to assess any damage to the soft tissues around the break and then there'd be a discussion about whether he was going to need surgery. If it was an open fracture, then the break would be stabilised and Ollie would be booked in for surgery the next day. But if the trauma and orthopaedic team had additional concerns, he might even face emergency surgery as soon as an operating theatre was available.

'We're just going to have a quick look at you and by the time we've done that, your mum and dad should be here.' Danni gave Ollie a reassuring smile and followed on behind as he was wheeled into one of the bays. Gary, one of the other nurses, completed the handover with the paramedics and Danni started the examination. It wouldn't have taken seven years of medical school, or the specialist training she'd completed afterwards, to tell her that this was definitely an open fracture. The angle of the resulting deformity in the shin also left her in no doubt that both the fibula and tibia were involved. She just hoped when Ollie had his scan, it would be one break across the bones rather than several.

'One of my friends is going to come down and take a look at your leg too, Ollie. He's another type of doctor, who specialises in helping people when they've hurt their legs.' Danni smiled again, making it sound as easy as sticking a plaster over a cut. There was no doubt in her mind that Ollie was going to need surgery. Given there was a small puncture wound where part of the bone must have pierced the skin, even though the bone was no longer visible, the surgeons would at the very least want to wash out the wound to prevent infection. Looking at the break, it was very likely to need realigning and probably pinning too, but Ollie didn't need to know any of that yet. Although judging by Miss Phipps' face, he'd probably have dealt with the news better than she would. 'Gary, please could you do me a favour and ask if one of the surgeons can come down when we've got the results of Ollie's scan?'

'He needs an operation?' Miss Phipps was reacting in exactly the way Danni had feared she would. 'Oh my God, oh my God! I knew I shouldn't have said I'd cover the PE lesson. We have a specialist coach come in for football, but Duncan's got food poisoning and the Head said I'd be fine. But I don't even know the rules! I suggested we spend the time making papier-mâché heads for the puppets we're using at Harvest Festival, but she said the kids needed fresh air and now Ollie's going to have to be sliced open and—'

'Miss Phipps!' Danni and Esther spoke sharply and in unison, silencing the young teacher, who stared back at them, her mouth still moving, but no words coming out. She was obviously distraught, but this was about Ollie and keeping him as calm as he had been since he'd arrived.

'Why don't I take you to go and get a cup of tea; you look like you could use one.' Esther took hold of her elbow. 'Ollie will be fine with us for a bit; he's going down for his scan now anyway.'

'Okay.' The young woman nodded, looking relieved at the opportunity to leave and not have to catch sight of Ollie's injury again.

'Thank you.' Danni mouthed the words to Esther as she took Miss Phipps away. If anyone could make Ollie's teacher feel better, it would be Esther. Danni had witnessed it countless times in the years they'd worked together. Esther just had this way of making people open up and feel it was okay to talk about whatever was worrying them. One girl had been very unwell when she'd come into A&E and her symptoms had suggested an overdose. She'd been adamant she hadn't taken anything, until Esther had spoken to her on her own for a few minutes. After that, it had all come tumbling out. The breakdown in the relationship with her mother, an aggressive stepfather who belittled them both, and years of pent-up hurt that had culminated in her swallowing every pill she could get her hands on. If Esther hadn't got the full story when she did, that girl might not have survived. So there were no better hands for Miss Phipps to be in.

'Right, let's get you along to your X-ray then, young man.' Danni wanted to go down with him and see the results for herself. Half an hour later they were back in A&E and there was no doubt about either the open nature of the fracture, or that Ollie would need surgery to correct the injury. By the time they got back, Ollie's parents had arrived.

'Hi, I'm Danni, one of the doctors taking care of Ollie. He's been an absolute star.' She had been about to explain to his parents what the X-ray had shown, but Ollie's mum was too fast for her.

'Oh, sweetheart.' His mother leant over him. Ollie had been given some stronger pain relief since arriving at the hospital, so he was no longer wearing the face mask. 'This is why I didn't want you playing rough sports. There's too much risk of you getting hurt.'

'I'm fine, Mum.' Danni had been telling the truth when she'd told Ollie's parents how brilliant he'd been, but for the first time he was looking upset. 'I love playing football; please don't make me stop.'

'It's all right, champ, we won't stop you playing.' Ollie's father looked at the little boy's mother. 'We can't wrap him in cotton wool forever, Jen. I've been telling you that for eight years, and these things happen.'

'Not to my son. He's all we've got.'

'Which means he deserves the best life possible. I'd broken my right arm twice by the time I was his age. I fell out of the same tree both times, nicking plums from a house at the end of our road with my brother.' Ollie's dad shot Danni a rueful grin. 'And those summers are still some of the best memories of my life.'

Ollie's father looked directly at the little boy. 'Just don't tell your nanny Pat that, son, or she'll have mine and your uncle Carl's guts for garters, even all these years later.'

'I won't, Dad. I promise.' The little boy looked very solemn for a moment and then he grinned. 'But can I tell her how loud the crack was when I broke my leg? Miss Phipps nearly fainted!'

'I don't think your mum is quite ready to hear that story yet, Ollie.' Danni had a horrible feeling that Miss Phipps wasn't the only one who'd be in danger of passing out if he carried on, and she turned towards his mother. 'The X-rays show there's an open fracture of both the tibia and fibula bones in his left leg, but each bone is only broken in one place. I know it sounds very scary, but the surgical team are on the way down to discuss the best way to get Ollie on the road to recovery as soon as possible.'

'Where's his teacher? She should have made sure this didn't happen.' Danni didn't fancy Miss Phipps' chances much if Ollie's mother got hold of her. 'Go and find her, Dean; I want to hear from her how on earth this happened.'

'It was an accident, Jen. Come on, blaming anyone isn't going to help.' Dean moved to comfort his wife, but she wasn't ready to listen.

'This is our boy lying here, our only child and all because the people we trusted to take care of him couldn't do their job properly.'

'These sorts of accidents happen all the time. Don't they, Doctor?' Dean turned towards Danni, who nodded slowly. Whatever the school might or might not have done wrong, laying blame at anyone's door right now wouldn't change anything and it was clearly upsetting Ollie.

'I've seen countless injuries of this type during my career and as scary as they might seem, the human body is amazing and Ollie will be running around again before you know it.'

'But he needs an operation. He's only eight years old for Christ's sake and anything can happen with an anaesthetic.' Jen was clearly working herself up into a frenzy and Danni could really have used Esther's calming influence.

'The risks are tiny for someone of Ollie's age who is otherwise healthy.' Danni could tell that her words were doing nothing to comfort Jen, but then Lucas pulled back the curtain and came into Ollie's bay.

'I can hear you lot from down the corridor! Can anyone come to your party, Ollie, or is it invitation only?' Lucas winked at the little boy and some of the tension immediately left Ollie's face. 'I'd heard we had a football star in the hospital, but I had no idea you'd brought all your fans with you.'

'These are Ollie's parents, Mr and Mrs Hudson.' As Danni said their names, Ollie's mother thrust a hand out towards Lucas.

'Call me Jen, please, and my husband is Dean. Are you the surgeon?'

'If Ollie lets me have the job. How does that sound to you, buddy? We can put everything back where it's supposed to be and then we'll put a special type of hard bandage over it to protect it while it heals, called a cast. The best bit is you get to choose the colour of your cast; we've even got some glow in the dark options.'

'Cool!' Ollie's face had completely transformed since Lucas had arrived.

'Can you still get them signed? My brother did a whole cartoon strip on one of my casts when I was a kid.' Dean laughed. 'My mum said if he'd have put half as much effort into his homework, she'd have been a happy woman.'

'They're not quite the same as they used to be, but the thicker marker pens still work.' Lucas looked from Dean to Ollie. 'So, what do you think? Shall we go and get this leg of yours sorted out?'

'Yeah, and I can't wait to see my leg when it gets dark.' Ollie turned towards his dad. 'Can you send Miss Phipps a picture later, Dad, to cheer her up? Then she can show the rest of the class.'

'What do you reckon, Jen?' Dean turned towards his wife, who smiled for the first time.

'I think we can do that.'

Things swung into motion quite quickly after that. Lucas examined Ollie and reviewed the results of his X-rays, while consent forms were organised for his parents to sign. Esther arrived back, after waiting with Miss Phipps until her partner came to pick her up. She'd apparently been too scared to come back to A&E after she'd seen Ollie's parents heading in, which had probably been the right decision given how Ollie's mum had reacted. At least until Lucas had arrived.

'You were amazing with Ollie and just your presence seemed to calm his mum down.' Danni walked along the corridor with Lucas as he left the department to head up to theatre to prepare for Ollie's operation.

'I could only do that because I already knew what to say to them and what treatment Ollie was going to need.' He turned to face her, and she felt the impact of Lucas's presence every bit as much as Ollie's mother had. 'I knew that your examination of him and the analysis of the X-rays would be accurate. This has always been my favourite team, Dan. You and me.'

For a moment she couldn't speak and the only thing she could think of was this man standing right in front of her, but she forced herself to blink three times so that she could conjure up another image, and the words it provoked came tumbling out of her mouth. 'You should have seen Esther with Ollie's teacher. The poor woman was beside herself, but Esther just did that thing she always seems to do and made her feel better. I don't know how she does that. She was brilliant with Ollie too. You two will make such fantastic parents one day. You're so lucky to have her.'

'I know, I just wish—'

It was Lucas's turn to get cut off as Esther came through the double doors just ahead of them, her smile making Danni's scalp prickle with guilt. Why couldn't she love someone else? *Anyone else.* It didn't matter who it was, as long as it wasn't Lucas. She was the worst person in the world for feeling the way she did.

'I know that look. What are you two up to?' Esther was still smiling, but nausea swirled in Danni's stomach all the same. 'I hope you aren't cooking something up for my birthday again. That zip wire over Penrhyn Quarry was enough excitement to last me for the rest of my life. If you're planning anything, nice and simple works for me.'

'It works for me too.' Danni didn't look at Lucas again, but she hoped he got the message anyway.

* * *

'I'm sorry about the way Jen was when we first got here. She's just gone to call her parents to let them know what's going on, but she feels really bad about it.' Dean looked at Danni as she came back to the cubicle, just before Ollie was due to be taken up to theatre. 'I know all children are precious, but we thought for years we'd never get to have a child of our own. He's the result of six rounds of IVF and it's been all I can do to get Jen to let him do the usual stuff an eight-year-old boy wants to do. But everyone here has been great and we're really grateful.'

'There's no need to apologise. I can't imagine how terrifying parenthood must be, but you've got an amazing little boy.'

'We're very lucky, aren't we, Jen?' Dean looked up as his wife came back into Ollie's bay.

'The luckiest.' Ollie's mum took hold of his hand as she spoke, and Danni moved towards the head of the bed.

'Right then, young man, I'm going to leave you with your mum and dad now, so you can have them to yourself for a bit before you go up and get that amazing cast Lucas promised you. I wish all my patients were as good as you.'

'If I don't play for Man City when I grow up, I might be a doctor. Or maybe an ambulance driver, 'cos they get to drive really fast and have lights and sirens and all of that stuff.'

Danni couldn't help laughing and Ollie's parents did too. He really was a great kid. 'I bet you'll be brilliant at whatever you do.'

'Thank you.' Jen reached out and touched her arm as Danni

left, and she nodded. She hadn't done anything really. It had been the paramedics who'd stabilised Ollie's injury and got him to the hospital, and now Lucas would get him on the road to recovery. But it was a group effort, and it was why she loved working as part of a hospital team. She hated the thought of having to give that up, but she would if it came down to a choice between that and ever crossing the line in her relationship with Lucas. She was just praying she'd never have to choose.

8
_____

Connie was certain her blood pressure reading would have gone back down to acceptable levels by now, if she wasn't still waiting for Danni to return her letter. How the hell was she supposed to 'relax and concentrate on getting well', as the nurses kept telling her, if she had no idea where the letter was? For all Connie knew, the doctor might be one of those people who thought she knew what was best for others and who'd decided that posting the letter was the only possible course of action. She couldn't bear the thought of going into surgery for a third time and not knowing where the letter was.

Her memories of the day of the accident weren't as clear as she'd have liked them to be and every time someone had come into the ward who looked even vaguely like the young doctor who'd treated her, Connie's hopes would surge, only for disappointment to wash over her when she realised that it wasn't Danni. So it took a while for her to realise the moment had finally come.

'Hi, Connie, how are you doing?' The woman standing at the side of her bed had long, wavy, dark hair and eyes the colour of amber. It was the eyes that Connie would have recognised, even if four years had passed, instead of four days. They were the eyes she'd looked into when she'd been terrified that her life might be slipping away, without Richard ever knowing the truth.

'Have you got the letter?' There was so much she needed to say to Danni, so much she wanted to thank her for, but she couldn't think of anything until she knew where the letter was.

'It's right here.' Danni passed it to her, and Connie could tell the seal hadn't been broken and the respect she had for the young doctor rose even higher.

'Thank you.' She sighed, but there was still one more question she needed to ask. 'You didn't contact Darcy, did you?'

'You asked me not to, unless something happened to you. And you're still here, just like I said you would be, so I haven't been in touch with anyone. But I think it would be good to let your family know what's going on. They must be so worried.'

'One of the nurses gave my phone back after my operation, but I didn't want to contact Darcy in case you'd already spoken to her. She won't be worried; she knows I sometimes go out of contact for a few days when I'm on a research trip and that's what she thinks I'm doing here. But I'll phone her now I know you haven't called her. I don't want her to see any reports of the accident online and panic that I'm seriously hurt. I'm just terrified that when she finds out the truth about me, she might never want to speak to me again.'

'Whatever it is, it can't be that bad.' Most people would have asked outright what the secret was, but not Danni. 'And hasn't everyone got something they'd rather not everyone knew about?'

Connie narrowed her eyes. It wasn't just what Danni had said that made her wonder if the young woman was also keeping a secret, it was the expression on her face. 'Do you ever worry that people wouldn't feel the same way about you, if your secret came out?'

'None of my secrets are that exciting.' Danni attempted a shrug, but Connie was more certain now than ever that there was something significant the young woman was hiding.

'How about if I tell you mine, you tell me yours? I think I owe you an explanation, as you were good enough not to go snooping for yourself.'

'Ah, well, that's not strictly true.' Two spots of colour had appeared on Danni's cheeks and Connie couldn't keep the sharp edge out of her voice.

'You opened my letter?' She hadn't spent her entire working life as a university lecturer without developing the ability to hold a person's gaze when she was asking a question, until they felt they had no choice but to answer.

'Oh no, nothing like that.' The spots of colour had flooded Danni's whole face now. 'But I did google Richard. I wanted to check that he was still at Trengothern Hall, and I was intrigued to see what someone who'd been so important to you looked like. I'd never have betrayed your trust and opened your letter, though, because the truth is I have got one secret that I'm terrified I might not always be able to contain.'

'I bet it's not as bad as mine.' Connie was going to share her secret with the young woman standing next to her bed, whether Danni returned the favour or not. Speaking about it to Gwen had helped get things clear in her head and to make the decision to tell Richard before she breathed a word to Darcy, or anyone else it might affect. That was the thing with secrets: they lost their power once they were out in the open. They could still cause damage, there was no doubt about that, but she was certain now that keeping the secret in the first place had caused the most harm of all. Connie took a deep breath and ten minutes later she'd told Danni everything, the same story she'd shared with Gwen, each telling proving slightly easier to get through.

'Giving up the baby must have been an incredibly difficult decision to make all by yourself. But you were trying to protect Richard and make sure he didn't lose the farm, or end up resenting you for it.' Danni was making the same excuses for Connie that she'd made for herself for the last thirty-eight years, but it was no good. Nothing could justify what she'd done, even though there wasn't a trace of judgement in the younger woman's voice.

'Most people wouldn't be so understanding, and I wouldn't blame them if they weren't.' Connie looked down at her hands, knotted together in front of her. When she looked up again, Danni had turned away and was glancing over her shoulder as if to make sure no one was around to overhear them.

'I wish my secret was even half as selfless, but it's not. My biggest fear is that one of the most important people in my life will find out and hate me because of it. My only hope is that one day the thing I'm keeping from her won't be true any more, and then I won't need to keep it secret.'

'Does anybody know about it?'

'I think one person does.'

'Would it help if you told me?' Connie deliberately kept her expression neutral. She didn't want to pressurise Danni, but finally being able to tell the truth about Richard and the baby had helped make the whole thing feel a little less overwhelming. 'You don't have to, but it might ease your burden and I promise it won't go any further.'

'I'm in love with my best friend's fiancé and I've spent the last seven years praying that she'll fall out of love with him, find someone who makes her even happier, and leave the way clear for him to realise he should have been with me all along. Even saying it out loud makes me cringe. I sound like a pathetic, love-sick schoolgirl, not a woman in her thirties who ought to know better.'

'You sound like someone tortured by feelings you wish you

didn't have, and we can't help who we fall in love with. Trust me, I know as well as anyone that life would be a whole lot bloody easier if we did.' Connie had convinced herself that she recognised a kindred spirit in Danni and now she knew for sure. On the surface, the younger woman's secret might not seem nearly as devastating, but Connie remembered only too well the unbearable ache of longing for something she couldn't have. Thoughts of Richard had filled her every waking moment in the early days, and Danni was having to contend with feelings of guilt towards her best friend too. That was no easy burden to bear. 'Have you ever done anything about the way you feel?'

'Run away from London to bury myself in a new life in Cornwall, where I wouldn't be faced with seeing him every day. We worked together and I thought getting away would help me finally get over him.'

'I'm sensing a "but"?'

'They followed me.' Danni sounded exhausted. 'And now I'm back to seeing both of them on a daily basis. Every time she looks at me, or asks for my opinion about their wedding plans, I feel like the worst friend – no, scratch that, the worst person – in the world.'

'If you weren't a good person, you'd have already acted on your feelings, because hers wouldn't have mattered to you as much as your own. But by keeping this a secret, you've put her feelings first every single day for the last seven years. Only a very good person would do that.'

'It doesn't feel that way, and I hate myself for loving Lucas.'

'And is he the one person you've told your secret to?' Connie could see why Danni would feel bad about telling Lucas, because even if he didn't reciprocate her feelings, keeping his fiancée in the dark about them, when he knew, was a betrayal in itself. But Danni was already shaking her head.

'I didn't tell him. I've never told anyone except you, but I think he knows anyway. There've been times when we've come so close...' Danni frowned, hesitating for a moment. 'One night we almost went too far, another step in his direction and I'd have risked more than a decade of friendship with a woman whose whole family have taken me in as one of their own. I knew then that I had to leave, because I wasn't going to be strong enough to keep doing the right thing when we were working so closely together. Esther is the kindest, most beautiful soul and the thought of hurting her is the only thing stopping me from acting on how I feel about Lucas. Except now they're here, and he's back working in the same hospital. So, what do I do? Run away again? Find somewhere to go where they'll never follow me?'

'You could just tell her.' Connie was fully aware she was making it sound far easier than it was, and Danni recoiled as if she'd been slapped. 'Hear me out. The power of your secret, and the danger of it, lies in the fact that Esther doesn't know. It's torture for you, I can see that, but I'd bet my last pound that it's exciting for Lucas. If Esther knew, it would take the pressure off you taking all the action to stop anything happening. And it would kill the excitement for Lucas stone dead.'

'And probably my friendship with Esther with it.' Danni looked close to tears.

'Either way I don't think it can survive. If you don't tell her, you've got two choices. The first is to keep running, and what kind of friendship can the two of you possibly have then? Your other choice is to act on the way you feel and that can only ever end in disaster, with your friendship blown apart forever and you as the villain of Esther's life story. But if you tell her, she's likely to choose to distance herself and Lucas from you, so that nothing ever happens. Yes, you'll lose the friendship you once had, but you won't be the one person in her whole life she wishes she'd never met and, who knows, maybe one day she'll find her way back to you.'

'You think someone else will come between Lucas and Esther?'

'From what you've said he seems willing to push the boundaries. How long will it really be before he pushes one of those boundaries so far that it breaks?' Connie shrugged. 'I can almost guarantee it. But don't you dare put your life on hold waiting for that to happen. Would you really still want Lucas if he did that to Esther?'

'No.' Danni's eyes met Connie's and they revealed the truth before she could admit it herself. 'I don't want to want that, but it's like I don't have a choice.'

'And that's exactly why Esther needs to know. It's the only thing you can control. I should have been honest a long time ago about how I felt, but I spent four decades fighting it and it still hasn't gone away. Don't waste half a lifetime like I did. Seven years is already far too long.'

'If you think I should do that, why didn't you change your mind and tell Richard how you felt?'

'Because I made a deal with myself that Richard could be mine for the summer, but then he had to commit to Fiona. The summer we had was glorious in every sense of the word, and I knew if I admitted to Richard that I loved him, he'd want to call off the wedding. Even when I discovered I was pregnant, I couldn't go back on the promise I'd made myself. Later on, when I wished with every bone in my body that I could, it was already too late.'

'That sounds like something out of a Jane Austen novel.'

'It felt like it too, at times, but no matter how distraught I was, I kept telling myself what he didn't know couldn't hurt him. For Richard it would always be just a summer fling and he'd probably got over me by the time autumn came.'

'Do you really think he did?' The emotion on Danni's face was naked. It was obvious she didn't just *want* to hear how things had panned out for Richard, she *needed* to know. If he'd got over his feelings, then maybe she could too. But sadly, Connie was in no position to offer any such reassurance.

'I've got no idea; all I know is that I never did.' She sighed; it had been exhausting to hold on to all of this for almost four decades and now she was stuck here, in this bed, unable to finally tell him the truth about all of it. 'It was different back then. There was no social media, thank God, or I'm not sure if I'd have been able to stop myself from searching for him. Imagine the torture of looking at photographs of the person you love marrying someone else.'

Even as the words came out of Connie's mouth, she wanted to grab them and stuff them back down her throat. Danni was going through that sort of torture, on a daily basis. 'I'm sorry.'

'It's okay and I can see how that would have made it easier to resist contacting him.' Danni's eyes were glassy. The poor girl had tried to escape the way Connie had, but even moving to Cornwall hadn't been enough. 'I can't believe you weren't ever tempted to get in touch with him, even when the internet came along.'

'Oh, I wanted to, about a hundred times a day.' Connie sighed. 'But I told myself I'd made a choice all those years ago and that I had no right to come crashing into the life he'd made for himself. For all I know, he could have spent the last thirty-eight years being blissfully married to the love of his life. And, selfishly, I didn't want to know that. Ignorance is bliss and I can tell myself that I was the only one he ever really wanted, just like he was the only one for me. I still don't want to see pictures on Facebook of him and Fiona side by side, though.'

'There aren't any.' It was Danni's turn to clamp a hand over her mouth. She was clearly prone to blushing, as a flood of bright red swept right up to the roots of her hair. 'Oh God, I'm sorry, but when

I googled his name, I wanted to know if he was still at Trengothern Hall, just in case I needed to deliver the letter, but then I found him on Facebook. There's no sign of Fiona, or any other partner come to that.'

'He's on his own?' It was almost as if Connie had been holding her breath for the best part of four decades as Danni nodded. When she finally breathed out, she wasn't sure how to feel. If he was on his own, either Fiona was no longer a part of his life, or she never had been. There was a chance Connie had wasted the last thirty-eight years and given up on her chance to be a mother for something that had never even happened. For a moment it was like she'd forgotten how to breathe altogether, but then she took a long, shuddering breath.

'Are you okay?' Danni took hold of Connie's hand and she managed to nod. 'I don't understand why he didn't try to find you either.'

'He started writing from the day I left. When I got the first letter, I didn't reply and, when he wrote the second one, he told me he'd try twenty times, one for every week between me leaving and him marrying Fiona, and then he'd stop. Every single time I got a letter, I wanted to send one straight back telling him how much I missed him, or drive back down here and tell him I felt the same way about him, but I didn't. This time, he was true to his word, and the twentieth letter was his last.'

'But you think now's the right time?'

'I've got no choice. There's a reason I need to see him. I need to tell him about the child I gave up for adoption. I wrote him a letter in case I got down here and couldn't find a way of persuading him to meet me, but the plan was always to tell him face to face if I could. The letter was just a back-up; some things warrant more than words on a page. But however he hears it, he's going to hate me and I deserve it.'

'He's not going to hate you. He might be angry at first, but if you tell him what you've told me, he'll understand you did it because you loved him.'

'If I was in Richard's shoes, I don't think I'd be able to forgive what I did. I made my choices, but in doing so I robbed Richard of the chance to make his. Now I've got to tell him that the baby he didn't even know existed is grown up and searching for answers that will lead straight to Richard's door. I've got to speak to him and tell him myself, before someone else does.' Connie let go of another long breath and looked at Danni. 'I've done some awful things in the name of love, and I know to my cost that secrets always catch up with you in the end. Which means the best advice I can give you is not to keep any.'

She watched as a series of emotions crossed the younger woman's face. It was too late for Connie to get her happy ever after, when she'd stolen so much from the man she loved. But maybe Danni might still stand a chance of getting hers. And, for some reason, the idea made her feel just the tiniest bit better.

9
———————

'Are all the A&E staff having a break at the same time, or what?' Chloe, one of the nurses from Tewyn Ward, grinned as Danni walked into the hospital shop. St Piran's was small enough for most of the staff to know each other, even if she and Chloe hadn't joined at the same time and gone through some of their general induction training together. Aidan and Amy, who were both nurses in the A&E department, were already in the shop buying what looked like enough chocolate to feed a small army.

'I don't know about these two, but I'm finished for the day.' Danni returned Chloe's smile, but she was still reeling from what Connie had told her. The poor woman had longed to be with Richard all these years and had clearly been heartbroken about giving up their child for adoption, yet somehow she'd kept that to herself in a misguided attempt to protect him. If that wasn't love, she didn't know what was. But Connie seemed to have painted herself as the villain of the piece and she was clearly scared that Richard would do the same thing when he finally found out the truth. Danni had it easy in comparison. Nothing had been done that couldn't be undone. She just needed to find a way to fast-forward getting over Lucas. But for now, she was craving a sugar hit. It had been a long day and she needed a boost of energy for the journey home. Sometimes taking the healthy option and having a piece of fruit just couldn't cut it. That was where the hospital shop came into its own and she'd rugby tackle Aidan to get to the last Star Bar if she had to.

'We've both got two hours to go.' Amy made it sound like three weeks instead of two hours; the weariness in her voice would have given away how tired she was feeling, even if her face hadn't. 'But we're planning on going out after that, hence all the chocolate. Aidan has promised to be my wingman; even Gary's coming along. I'm not sitting around waiting to see if Zach decides he's moving back in for a third time. He's had his last wobble about committing, as far as I'm concerned.'

'The best way of getting over one man is to get under another.' Gwen, who was standing behind the counter, dropped a perfect wink. 'Although I've always preferred getting on top myself.'

'Yes, Gwen!' Aidan reached out to give her a high five, dropping some of the bars of chocolate he'd picked up onto the counter in the process.

'You should come with us, Chloe. And you, Danni.' Amy looked towards them. 'I think a few of the others might be coming, and Gary's threatening to show us his best moves. That's got to be worth coming along for on its own.'

'Thanks, but I think I might need an early night.' Danni's excuse felt as feeble as it sounded and she'd been about to add something to make it sound less pathetic, when someone touched her arm.

'Anyone would think you're stalking me. First you're up on the ward with one of my patients and then you show up when I'm on a break. Not that I'm complaining.' Lucas's smile mirrored the warmth in his voice.

'I can't be stalking you, seeing as I was here first.' Danni knew she sounded defensive despite the failed attempt to keep her tone light.

'Well, as long as we're both here, do you want to grab a coffee?' The Costa Coffee machine in the shop beat anything the hospital restaurant had to offer, regardless of the grand-sounding name the restaurant had been given. King Arthur's Table made it sound as if there were banquets to be had, but the fact that so many staff raided the hospital shop at break time instead said a lot. There were three bistro-style tables outside the shop, too, which was at the entrance to the hospital, perfectly positioned to watch the world go by, making it feel almost like a pavement café. But even if Lucas had been offering to take her for a coffee on the banks of the Seine, her answer would have been the same.

'I'm going home. Sorry but it's been a long day.'

'Surely you've got ten minutes spare for me? Something happened in theatre and I need to offload. You've always been the best person I know for that.' Lucas's eyes searched her face. She'd lost count of the number of times he'd recounted stories about his working day to her, and she'd always told him what he needed to hear – that any negative issues weren't his fault. He'd tell her whenever he'd overcome a tricky situation in the operating theatre, too, and she'd be just as generous with her praise as she was with her reassurance. Lucas knew he was a brilliant surgeon, but he seemed to need to hear it from her to believe it. It was something else she put down to him losing his mum and dad. He had no parents whose pride he could bask in and, somewhere along the line, she'd become the person who filled that gap for him.

'I can't.' Danni shrugged, making a spur-of-the-moment decision. Things between them couldn't fall back into the same pattern they had in London. She needed to put some new restrictions in place, because it didn't look like Lucas would. 'I've got to go home and take Brenda out, before I get ready to go out on the town with this lot.'

'You should come, Doc.' Amy gave Lucas a look that said he'd be more than welcome. 'It's going to be a wild night.'

'As tempting as that sounds, I'm on call until ten tonight and I don't think I'll be fit for anything but my bed after that.'

'If only you were single, I'd have skipped the night out and kept the bed warm for you.' Amy clearly wasn't joking when she'd said she was determined not to wait around for Zach. It wasn't the first time Danni had seen women, and men, react this way to Lucas, but it made her wonder how Esther dealt with it, especially as he just seemed to find it funny.

'My loss will be someone else's gain, I'm sure. Just make sure you look after this one.' Lucas gestured towards Danni. 'She means a lot to me.'

Danni looked at the floor. She was starting to think that Connie might have been right when she'd said it was Lucas pushing the boundaries between them. And he didn't seem to care if that was obvious to other people too. Amy or one of the others could easily repeat what he'd said about Danni to Esther. Would his words just sound like friendly concern to her? Because it didn't feel that way to Danni. There was a proprietorial tone to Lucas's voice, and he'd adopted it before, when one of the registrars at their old hospital had made it obvious he was interested in Danni.

She hadn't wanted to date Ben, but she'd liked him as a friend, and they'd been to see a couple of films together. Lucas had acted like a jealous boyfriend, and she hated the fact that part of her had liked it, at least at first. But then it had started to become awkward when Lucas had taken to joining them every time he saw them together, commencing a game of one-upmanship Ben didn't even seem interested in playing. Lucas had made it clear he considered his role and skills far superior to Ben's. He'd doubled down on telling Danni – whenever Ben was in earshot – about the latest life-saving surgery he'd been involved with. She'd been flattered that he seemed desperate for her opinion of him to exceed her opinion of Ben. But what Connie had said had touched a nerve, and she was starting to wonder how much of that had been about her, and how much of it had been about Lucas 'winning' the competition for her attention. She didn't belong to him, and he certainly didn't belong to her. She had to start making that clear.

'We can't make any promises, I'm afraid.' Aidan was stuffing bars of chocolate into his pockets as he spoke. 'I first met my husband at the bar we're going to, and we were on a plane to Ibiza less than twenty-four hours later.'

'We'd better say goodbye now then, just in case you're jetting off somewhere by this time tomorrow.' Lucas turned to face Danni and, before she knew it, he'd closed the gap between them. Kissing her just far enough away from her mouth to pass it off as just being a friendly peck to anyone watching, but close enough for every nerve ending in her body to go on high alert. The worst part was she had a horrible feeling he knew exactly what it was doing to her. She'd never suspected that he might enjoy the danger of the tension between them, until Connie had mentioned it, but now she couldn't get that idea out of her head. When Danni had first started to think Lucas might have strong feelings for her, she'd assumed that – like her – it was his love for Esther that stopped him acting on them. The thought that it might all just be a game to him made her stomach turn. It couldn't be true.

Danni barely said another word in the midst of the flurry of activity that followed, with Lucas getting the coffee he'd come for and the others paying for the snacks they'd chosen. It was only when it was just her and Gwen left in the shop again that she finally felt less on edge.

'So, are you really going to go on that night out with Aidan and the others?' Gwen narrowed her eyes as she took the Star Bar from Danni's outstretched hand to scan the barcode.

'I think I'll just go home and snuggle up with Brenda.' The truth was, Danni had never really had any intention of going. She'd just wanted to say something to stop Lucas asking her to hang out with him and it had worked. But the thought of going out to a bar, with Amy determined to find someone to help her get over her boyfriend and Aidan and the others cheering her on, did not appeal to Danni one little bit. Especially as someone was bound to suggest that she should be following Amy's lead and looking to 'have a bit of fun'. As sad as it might seem, these days her idea of fun really did involve curling up with Brenda on the sofa, and getting lost in a good book. Staying home and letting life pass her by was a habit she'd got into over the years, long before she could use the dog as an excuse. There'd been no danger of her dating Ben, even before Lucas had wedged himself between them, because she was waiting for a fantasy that was never going to happen. Lucas wasn't going to suddenly turn up at her door and tell her that Esther didn't want him any more, and that he was glad because it had been Danni he'd loved all along. She'd wasted so much time wishing for that, but suddenly she wasn't even sure if she wanted it. Either way, Connie's words were ringing in her ears; she'd spent forty years longing for someone who could never be hers. And the thought of that turning out to be the story of Danni's life too made her shiver. So, even before Gwen fixed her with a look that clearly said she meant business, Danni was starting to wonder if she should take Amy and Aidan up on their offer after all.

'You should go.' Gwen's words sounded more like an order than a suggestion. 'Don't waste your time loving someone who'll only ever really love themselves.'

'I'm not in love with anyone.' This was exactly what she'd been afraid of when Lucas had told the others to take care of her. And

Danni shook her head vigorously enough to make it ache, but she could tell from the expression on Gwen's face that she wasn't convinced.

'Whether you are, or whether you just think you are doesn't matter, because it's holding you back from the life you could be living. Either way, you should go on the night out, my love, and keeping going to new places and trying new things until you don't have to force yourself to do it any more. It's the only way.' Gwen handed her the chocolate bar. 'And this is on me; you get one free chocolate bar with all my best advice.'

The weird thing was that Gwen's advice had almost echoed what Joe had said, except he'd been talking about getting settled in her new life in Cornwall. But suddenly it was obvious just how linked those two things were. Moving on from Lucas and finally being able to call Cornwall home – and really meaning it – weren't two separate things, and she had to do whatever she could to make both of them happen. 'Thank you for the advice and the offer of free chocolate, but I need to pay for it.'

'It's my treat, God knows you deserve it with the hours you put in, and we'll say no more about it. Just promise me you'll think about what I've said.'

'I will and thanks again.' Putting the chocolate bar into her pocket, Danni looked at her watch. There was plenty of time to walk Brenda, have a cuddle on the sofa and still get changed in time to meet the others after work. There was no excuse not to. After all, no harm could possibly come from taking Gwen's advice.

10

Bar None was more of a club than a bar, and it had evidently become much harder to get into since Aidan had met his husband, Jase, there. Over the past ten years, Port Kara had become something of a celebrity hotspot, with the stretch of sand at the end of the main beach belonging exclusively to the properties in that part of the bay, just beyond the original lifeboat station. The Dunes, as the area was known, had come to rival Sandbanks in Dorset, because of the rich and famous who owned properties there. Not that Danni ever expected to see any of them arrive in A&E at St Piran's. No doubt a helicopter would whisk them off to the nearest private hospital, should a medical emergency ever arise.

Luckily, despite the town going up in the world, almost everyone seemed to know who Aidan was and he could access places that the rest of them would almost certainly have been turned away from.

'Thanks, Shane.' Aidan gave the burly bouncer on the door a peck on the cheek as he waved the group in.

'Is there anyone you don't know?' Danni smiled as Aidan turned back towards her, once they were inside.

'I'm Shane's coming-out story. Before he met me, he was so used to hiding in the closet, he could see better in the dark.' Aidan grinned. 'Thank God for me!'

'That's what we all say.' Amy linked an arm through Danni's. 'Come on, we've just got to trust in Aidan and follow his lead to guarantee that a good time is had by all.'

'I can't stay too long; I need to get back for the dog.' Danni had no idea if Amy or any of the others even heard her as she was dragged onto the dance floor. The drinks kept coming thick and fast, and there was no sign of Aidan having paid for any of them. There was probably a story behind that, too, but there'd have been no chance of Danni hearing it, even if Aidan had been in the mood to explain.

This sort of thing had never really been Danni's scene. Even at university, she'd been too self-conscious to let herself just relax and dance. She'd always felt at five feet ten like she stood out too much, when all she'd longed to do was to blend in. The drinks helped a bit, but watching Gary was probably the thing that made her most willing to dance, not caring so much what anyone else might think, because he clearly didn't give a damn. Gary was a fifty-something grandfather of one, who looked perfectly at home standing in the centre of the dance floor in a lively bar, twirling his arms around like two out-of-control windmills and doing what looked like a very slow-motion version of the Riverdance with his feet. It was hilarious, but the fact Gary was obviously loving it meant it was the most fun Danni had had in ages.

Amy turned out to be a fast worker too, and her plan to move on from Zach didn't take long. She'd persuaded a guy at the bar to start buying her drinks about half an hour after they'd arrived and when Danni glanced over at them twenty minutes later, they were kissing in a way that suggested they were now oblivious of everyone else. Despite Amy achieving her aim to meet someone new, Danni had been relieved to discover that Bar None wasn't the sort of place where everyone seemed to be there with that intention. Despite telling herself that meeting someone else might well be the best way of finally getting over her feelings for Lucas, trying to get to know someone in a bar, where the only possible way of having a conversation was to speak at an unnatural volume, wasn't for her. Dancing was good for the soul, though, and Aidan seemed determined not to let her off the dance floor until he was good and ready. It took three attempts before he finally agreed to let her have a break for a drink and even then he put a time limit on it. Probably aware that there was a good chance she'd forget how much fun she'd been having and make a bolt for the door, otherwise.

'Come on, we can't let these youngsters show us up, especially not when Gary hasn't sat down since we got here.' Aidan grabbed hold of her wrist when she tried to order another drink from the bar, in the hope he might get sidetracked and let her rest until her feet stopped aching quite so much.

'I should probably be offended that you're calling Chloe and the others "youngsters" and not including me in that, but I'm too tired to care that you're implying I'm old.' Danni shrugged. She really was exhausted, and if anyone had said earlier in the day that she'd spend two hours dancing non-stop that night, she'd have told them they were mad. She'd have to break it to Aidan that she was leaving at eleven thirty, no matter how much he might try to protest. It would be easier to get a cab if she left then. Her cottage was only about a mile and a half from the bar, but she had far too much imagination to walk home alone. She tried not to think about the fact that there'd be no one at home to even miss her if she didn't show up.

'Listen, Dan, I'm not saying you don't look great and if I was that way inclined I'd be showing you all my moves, to try and make sure you came home with me tonight.' Aidan pursed his lips and gave her a look that dared her to even try and resist. 'But as unacceptable as it is to me, I'm forty-three on my next birthday and you're almost closer to forty than thirty, so we've got to face facts.'

'Not until I pass the thirty-five mark I'm not, but I'm starting to wish I was your type. At least that way I could witness your best moves, instead of having you confront me with home truths I don't need to hear.' Danni laughed, but the fact the years were creeping by wasn't lost on her. In many ways thirty-four was still young, but having a family of her own was a journey she'd expected to have started on by now. Ever since her father had died, and her mother had begun a new life with Paul, Danni had felt rootless. She longed to have that sense of belonging again, and build the sort of family that Esther's parents and grandparents had. As it stood, it was just her and Brenda, and if she didn't find a way to move past her feelings for Lucas once and for all that wasn't likely to change.

'I thought there was someone else whose type you wanted to be.' It was almost as if Aidan could read her mind, but she furrowed her brow as if she had no idea who he was talking about.

'Like who?'

'Like a certain surgeon who's followed you to Cornwall. But he's not good enough for you, Danni; he's already in love with someone else.' Aidan pulled a face.

'Yes, his fiancée, who also happens to be my best friend. So even if I was interested in him, which I'm not, I wouldn't—'

'I wasn't talking about Esther.' Aidan cut her off. 'The only person Lucas is really in love with is himself. I realised it the first time I ever met him.'

'What do you mean?' Danni had picked up on the fact that Aidan wasn't Lucas's biggest fan, whenever he'd been down in A&E. But they were both big personalities, and that wasn't always a good mix.

'I heard him telling the daughter of the bus driver who died that *he'd* done everything he could to save her father's life.'

'Are you sure he didn't say *the team* did everything they could? That's what I told Dave's wife.'

'I know what he said.' Aidan folded his arms across his chest. 'And I heard him call one of the kids he came to assess a little brat. It was under his breath, but I definitely heard it.'

'He wouldn't do that. He loves kids and he's brilliant with them. Everyone says so.' The skin on Danni's scalp was prickling. She might be starting to question whether Lucas enjoyed taking risks by pushing the boundaries of their relationship, but she refused to accept that he wasn't who she thought he was in every other way. She'd spent seven years loving him but, if what Aidan was saying was true, then she'd never really known him at all, and she didn't believe that. She couldn't.

'Of course they do and that's the whole point. It's an act he puts on, but he's not fooling me.'

'I've worked with him for a really long time and I'd definitely have seen something.' Danni's determination to defend him was making her eyes sting.

'There are none so blind as those who will not see.' Aidan raised his eyebrows, and she'd been about to ask him what the hell he meant by that when a familiar voice cut through the noise around them.

'Danni! I didn't know if you'd still be here.' Esther was making her way through the crowd of people to get to the bar. She didn't have to push; the crowd seemed to part to make way for her, and in that moment it was obvious why Esther had never seemed insecure about the way people looked at Lucas, because they looked at her like that too. She had the sort of incredible bone structure that suited her pixie-style haircut perfectly. It would have made Danni want to chop off all of her own hair, if she hadn't come to the conclusion a long time ago that she had a funny-shaped head. When she'd mentioned it to her hairdresser, he'd just laughed and said she was talking rubbish, but either way she couldn't possibly pull off a haircut like that. The ability Esther had to turn heads probably explained why it had been so easy for her to get into the bar, too.

'Aidan won't let me leave and I had to beg to be allowed off the dance floor for a ten-minute break.' Danni grinned, her body flooding with relief when she realised this was her opportunity to cut off the difficult conversation she'd been having with Aidan, especially once she was certain Lucas wasn't with Esther. 'I didn't know you were coming.'

'Neither did I.' Esther wrinkled her nose. 'But Lucas got called in to cover emergency surgery on a guy who's had a motorbike accident. So it was a toss-up between coming here, to see whether Bar None really is the celebrity hangout it's meant to be, or heading home and eating dinner alone... again.'

There was something in Esther's expression that would have made Danni question her further if they'd been alone. She looked sad. It had only lasted for a split second before Esther had shaken it off, but Danni had seen it. As soon as she got the chance to speak to her, without Aidan listening in, she was going to do it. She couldn't bear the thought of Esther being unhappy, and the prospect of that having anything to do with her and Lucas made her chest feel tight.

'And you decided you didn't want Danni's average Friday night to become yours too!' Aidan laughed, dropping a wink in Danni's direction. He really was handing out his version of home truths like sweeties, but Esther was shaking her head.

'Any excuse to spend time with my best friend works for me, and someone let slip that Gary's dance moves became legendary after the Christmas party last year.' Esther reached out and squeezed Danni's hand as she spoke. She'd been protective ever since she'd learnt more about Danni's past, and every time anyone made a joke about Danni's private life, she always shot them down.

There'd been a paramedic called Craig when they'd worked in London, who seemed determined to paint Danni as some sort of Miss Havisham figure, ever since she'd turned him down at the Christmas party. He'd made little comments or digs whenever she saw him, and then there was the evening when one of the nurses had told anyone who'd listen that she'd got engaged on the holiday she'd just come back from. Craig had passed on his congratulations and then made a joke that the only chance Danni had of getting engaged would be if she proposed to her cat. She'd just rolled her eyes and chosen to ignore it, but it had been like someone had lit a firework underneath Esther. She'd charged towards Craig and, if Danni hadn't managed to stop her, she wouldn't have fancied his chances, despite the fact he was at least a foot taller than Esther.

When they'd spoken about it afterwards over a bottle of wine, and Danni had asked her why the comments had bothered her so much, Esther had said she couldn't stand the thought of someone like Craig thinking he was better than Danni, just because she'd chosen to be on her own. Then she'd said something that Danni had never forgotten.

'What that moron doesn't seem to realise is that you could be with anyone you wanted. But you've chosen to be on your own, because you'd rather do that than be with the wrong person. One day you'll meet someone who's made exactly the same choices as you have, and stayed single until they met the right person. And you'd never take someone else's right person away from them, even if you knew you could.'

For a moment Danni hadn't known what to say, and her eyes had met Esther's for less than a second, before her friend had laughed and topped up their glasses. 'Sod that idiot anyway, any woman in their right mind would rather propose to her cat than end up with him.'

It couldn't have meant anything, because if Esther had even an inkling of Danni's feelings for Lucas, there was no way their friendship would have survived it. As for being on her own, most of the time it didn't bother her. And Esther was right that she'd much rather be on her own than with the wrong person. But it would have been a lie to say she didn't want to find someone to have a family with, and maybe it was time to be a bit more proactive, especially after what Connie and Gwen had said.

'Gary's moves more than live up to the hype.' Danni couldn't help laughing as she looked over to where he was dancing with Chloe and some of the other nurses. He looked a bit like someone making their way across the beach when the sand was too hot to stand on, hopping from one foot to the other. 'But I was just thinking about making a move. Maybe I can pass the baton on to you and Aidan will finally let me leave.'

'No way! If you're heading home, I'm coming with you.' Esther widened her eyes. 'We haven't had a girls' night in for ages.'

'It's eleven already.' Danni didn't miss the look that crossed Aidan's face and even she had to admit that it sounded like an excuse, especially as she wasn't working the next day.

'Ooh eleven o'clock, you party animal. Amy's not going to be happy if you head off. Her goal for tonight was to get you and her a date for the fundraising ball. It might not be until December, but she seems to think the closer it gets, the harder it'll be.' Aidan gestured over to where Amy was still kissing Zach's replacement. 'It looks like she's cracked it, but you're going to have to go with Gary at this rate.'

'I could do far worse.' Danni took a deep breath; if she committed to it now, in front of Esther and Aidan, then she wouldn't be able to back out. She looked towards her best friend. 'Okay, you can come back with me for a late girls' night in, if you promise to help me with something.'

'Anything.' Esther was already nodding. 'What is it?'

'I'm going to set up an online dating profile.' It had been another spur-of-the-moment decision, but she'd been telling herself all night that she needed to do something drastic to change things between her and Lucas. This was something that would send a clear message to Aidan, Gwen, Connie and, most of all, Lucas, that her life in Cornwall wasn't going to turn into a carbon copy of the one she'd had in London. 'Amy's right, I need a date for the fundraiser, but I don't think meeting someone in a bar is going to work for me.'

'Are you really going to do it? I can't believe it.' Esther looked like a kid on Christmas morning as she turned towards Aidan. 'I've been suggesting she should do this for years.'

'So why now?' Aidan narrowed his eyes and Danni let out another long breath.

'It just feels like the right time. After all, as you just so kindly reminded me, before long I'm going to be closer to forty than thirty!'

'In that case, I'm coming with you, because this has got to be done right. And before I met Jase, I was an online dating sensei.'

'Right, we're getting out of here now, before you change your mind.' Esther linked one arm through Danni's and Aidan moved to her other side, all but frogmarching her out of the bar. It was too late to pull out now, and the truth was she didn't want to. She'd tried everything else she could think of to move on from Lucas, and there was nothing left to lose. But if she didn't do it, there was every chance she could end up just like Connie, letting the decades pass her by. Suddenly the prospect of launching herself into the world of online dating didn't seem so scary after all.

* * *

'I wish we could just see a few of the profiles, so we know whether it's even worth bothering to go to all the hassle of signing up.' Danni could tell from the expression on Aidan's face what his response was going to be, before he even opened his mouth.

'The whole point is that you have to sign up first before you can start checking out other people's profiles on this site. That way, if you like what you see, you can let them know straight away.'

'I don't know what to write.' Danni sighed, trying a different tack to get out of something she was already wishing she'd never started. 'It's hard to come up with hobbies that sound even remotely interesting, when all I seem to do is work and fall asleep in front of box sets.'

'Hmm.' Aidan looked at her, with his head slightly to one side. 'How to spin this... I know, what about: *I have a real passion for my work in medicine, but I love to unwind in front of the latest must-see TV at the end of the day. If I show you my recommendations, will you show me yours?* That could work.'

'Still makes her sound like a workaholic with no energy for anything but TV.' Esther shook her head. They were talking about her like she wasn't even there.

'But I am a workaholic with no energy for anything else except TV.' Danni shrugged. 'There's no point in me pretending otherwise, because they'll only end up disappointed when they find out the truth.'

'Maybe if there was someone special in your life, you'd stop being such a workaholic and find the time to try some new things.' Esther peered over her shoulder at the laptop. 'You like travelling, and you're always saying you'd love to do more of that. You like walking, and animals, and you're good at DIY. Although I definitely don't think we should put cooking down as one of your skills.'

Esther wrinkled her nose at that last comment and Danni laughed. 'In my defence, I didn't know I was having guests tonight and you can only work with the ingredients you've got.'

'Is frozen pizza an ingredient?' Aidan scrolled further down. 'Okay, let's come back to hobbies and interests, and do some of the other questions instead. Here's one: *How would your friends describe you?*'

'Ooh, that's a good one.' Esther almost jostled Danni out of the way altogether with her eagerness to look at the screen. 'What would you say, Aidan?'

'That she's got low self-esteem.' He made it sound so matter of fact, as if he was saying she had brown hair, or hazel eyes. But no one could take low self-esteem as a compliment, especially not someone who had it.

'Well, thanks.' Danni bit her lip. Aidan really had been knocking back the truth serum. It wasn't the first time someone had said it to her. Joe drove her mad sometimes, psychoanalysing every conversation they had. One bit of unwelcome advice had really stuck in her mind. She'd told him about a friend from the hospital in London who kept asking to borrow money. She'd wanted to say no, but couldn't seem to find the words.

'Just tell them no, it's a simple as that.'

'Not for me it isn't.'

'That's our so-called mother's fault. She's why you've got such low self-esteem and why you feel the need to be such a people-pleaser. But you don't have to do those things to make people like you, Dan. The people who really like you do it because they can see how great you are, not because you bend over backwards to make their lives easier. Those people don't like *you*, they just like what you do for them, or how you make them feel.'

Aidan cleared his throat, jolting her back to the present. 'I was about to say she's got low self-esteem, but she shouldn't have, 'cos she's brilliant.' He started typing in the box next to the question and Danni didn't even try to stop him, because she'd already decided to delete the profile after they'd gone. 'What about you, Esther? I've only known Danni less than a year, but you two have known each other forever.'

'I was going to say the same, and that it makes me sad she doesn't realise how great she is, because she's better than me, she's better than everyone, and I feel lucky to have her in my life.'

A lump of what felt like concrete seemed to have wedged itself in Danni's throat. She didn't deserve Esther's opinion of her; she didn't even deserve her friendship. But she needed it more than anything else in her life, and she was determined to hold on to it, whatever it took.

'Hmm, I think that might be the gin talking and we don't want to lay it on too thick.' Aidan grinned, saving her from having to respond. 'We could say hardworking, and she never asks anyone on the team to do a job she wouldn't be prepared to do herself, but we don't want it to sound like a reference either.'

'God, am I really that boring?'

'No! You're funny and kind, and—' Whatever it was that Esther had been about to add, Aidan cut her off.

'And you know more about seventies and eighties music than anyone I've ever met.'

'My dad was a massive fan; he played that music every day when I was little. There was no way to escape it.' Danni still found it hard to listen to certain songs that came on the radio. They had the power to make her feel as if her dad was sitting right there next to her, and it was like a punch in the stomach every time she turned around and realised, all over again, that he was never coming back.

'There are so many things I could say, but what's important is —' For the second time in less than a minute, Esther got cut off, and Danni caught her breath when she suddenly realised that Lucas was standing in the room.

'Sorry, I did knock, but no one answered, so I thought I'd better just come in.' If Danni had been harbouring any hope that the next time she saw him, all the feelings would have miraculously disappeared, those hopes were dashed as soon as she looked up. It wasn't something she'd ever felt with anyone else, and she wasn't sure she could have put her feelings into words if she'd tried. She had to at least try to act normal. It wasn't even a surprise arrival; she'd known he was going to come over and pick Esther up after he finished work.

'Sorry, I've got a rowdy crowd in tonight.' Danni painted on a smile. 'Can I get you something to drink?'

'I'm fine, but the pizza looks good.'

'It isn't, as these two will tell you, but you're welcome to eat as much of it as you can stand.'

'Thanks, I'm starving.' Lucas grabbed a couple of slices of the long-cold pizza. 'Should I ask why on earth the three of you have ended the night huddled around a laptop, instead of at Bar None, or am I better off not knowing?'

'Probably better off not knowing.' Aidan shrugged. 'But I'm going to tell you anyway. We're trying to get little-miss-single-and-oh-so-ready-to-mingle a date, by setting her profile up online.'

'You're online dating?' Lucas made it sound akin to Danni deciding to drink her own urine.

'I might, I just thought—'

'No "might" about it – you are.' It was Esther's turn to cut someone off for a change, and she clearly wasn't going to accept a debate. 'We were just trying to fill in the section about how Danni's friends would describe her. What would you say about her, Lucas?'

'That she always puts other people's feelings before her own.' Lucas caught her eye for a split second and she was certain that everyone in the room must be able to hear her heart beating, because of how hard it was thundering in her chest. She had no idea what Lucas was playing at, but whatever it was, it was crossing the line she'd been so determined to draw between them. The idea of doing it had been so easy in theory, but now that he was standing in front of her, all her resolve seemed to evaporate. She didn't even dare to look in Esther's direction, but what her friend said next took her completely by surprise.

'That's exactly what I was saying, or at least trying to say. I don't think I'm quite as coherent as I thought I was, after three of these.' Esther raised her gin and tonic. With Aidan taking over the role of barman the moment they'd got in, and pouring very generous measures, it was surprising they'd managed to fill in any of the profile at all. At least the alcohol seemed to have softened his attitude towards Lucas, although that might also have been because he was relying on him for a lift home.

'So, it's agreed then?' Aidan raised his eyebrows. 'We're going to put "funny, kind, hardworking and selfless" as the words we'd all use to describe her, and then maybe "seventies and eighties music nerd", just to avoid making it sound like Danni has written all those things about herself. No one can be completely perfect. It's no fun if someone's too much of a goodie-goodie anyway, is it, Lucas?'

'No fun at all.' Lucas caught Danni's eye again, and she might as well have been standing in the middle of the room naked given how exposed she felt. Thank God the other two were too drunk to notice. 'But as entertaining as all of this is, if you want a lift with us, Aidan, I'm going to have to take you and Esther home in a bit. I'm on call early again tomorrow.'

'I think Danni can finish the rest without us, but if you don't show us a completed profile by the next time you're on shift, we're making our own one for you and there won't be a thing you can do about it. Isn't that right, Esther?'

'Absolutely, but right now I need you to help me find my shoes and jacket, because I've got absolutely no idea where they are.'

'Me neither.' Aidan and Esther headed out of the living room and down the hallway in an attempt to find their missing footwear. They'd barely even left the room, when Lucas reached out and took hold of one of Danni's hands.

'Don't start dating some guy you meet online, Dan. It isn't you.' He was staring at her so intently, she could feel goosepimples coming up all over her skin, but she forced herself to hold his gaze.

'So, what should I do then? Spend my life with just my dog, watching my friends building their lives together for another four or five decades, and then die alone?'

'It doesn't have to be like that. We could—'

'No! We couldn't.' Snatching her hand away, despite every fibre of her being screaming at her not to, she pushed him towards the door. 'Go and help Esther find her stuff, and start counting your blessings about how bloody lucky you are to have found her.'

Danni pushed him again as they got out into the hallway, almost sending him cannoning into Aidan, who was bending down to put on his shoes.

'Trainers found and unharmed apart from a liberal coating of slobber. Thank God.' Aidan stood up to look at Danni. 'Make sure you finish that profile and activate it, you hear, or there'll be consequences you'll come to regret.'

'Oh, I know there will, and I promise it will be up and running by the time I'm next in work.'

As Danni saw them out, her goodbye to Lucas was much less effusive. Despite the amount of time she'd spent with him and Esther over the years, she'd always kept up her guard and made sure she was never too affectionate with him, which made the times he'd almost crossed the line even more inexcusable. But he seemed to take that risk more and more often. Danni's treacherous body might not have caught up with her brain yet, because it was still responding to his physical proximity the way it always had, but something inside her was starting to shift.

11

Danni was as good as her word and her dating profile was live by the time she started her next shift. She still wasn't convinced that it was the way to go and it was so hard to imagine meeting anyone. But she knew for certain she wasn't imagining it any more. Lucas was aware of how she felt and he felt something too. It was time to throw everything at her plan to get over him. Moving to Cornwall hadn't been enough. She'd also started looking for jobs overseas too and she was already partway through an application for a post in Sydney. Esther wouldn't uproot the new life she and her family had just started in Cornwall, so there was no danger of her following Danni to the other side of the world. She'd be hurting her best friend by leaving, but not half as much as she'd be if Danni's relationship with Lucas crossed the line even once.

The best-case scenario was that Danni would meet someone, fall head over heels in love and be over Lucas before she knew it. And at least if Danni ended up in Sydney, she'd be closer to her brother, Joe. She missed him more than she would allow herself to admit, and the far too infrequent trips to see one another only seemed to make that worse.

'Any updates on matches?' Aidan asked her the question at least once an hour when they were on shift together. But even if there had been someone who looked like a possibility, the last thing she would be doing was giving Aidan the opportunity to pass judgement on her preferences.

'She'll tell me before she tells you.' Esther suddenly appeared from one of the cubicles, holding a stack of disposable kidney dishes. 'If she doesn't, I'll be finding myself a new bridesmaid.'

'I will tell you first, I promise. But, as I keep saying, there's nothing to tell anyone yet.' Danni gestured towards the dishes. 'Dare I ask why you need so many of those?'

'Someone's put about forty of them in bay six. It's no wonder the rest of the cubicles are empty.' Esther shook her head. 'I think the play specialist was using them to make hats when Gary and Dr Daniels were trying to get the piece of Lego out of that little boy's nose.'

'Kidney bowl hats can make a great distraction; you just need to ensure they're empty first. I made that mistake once and discovered there are way worse things than having egg on your face!' Aidan laughed, and Danni didn't doubt for a moment that he could've distracted a child from an uncomfortable procedure if the need arose. But the department was sometimes lucky enough to be able to call on a play specialist, who was based in the children's ward, and whose job it was to use play to help minimise children's anxieties when they were going through treatment.

'Remind me never to ask you to help me plan a children's party.' Esther rolled her eyes before Aidan spun around to face her.

'Ooh, have you got something to tell us?' Just asking twisted something in Danni's gut, but one day, even if it wasn't now, she knew Esther would be saying yes to that question.

'No, because I'm planning on being able to drink on my honeymoon. What's the point of staying in a hotel with a swim-up bar if you're stuck on orange juice?'

'You've booked the honeymoon, then?' It was a weird situation. Danni desperately wanted to hear the details, but at the same time she didn't want to picture Esther and Lucas walking hand in hand along golden sand. It was like asking to be tortured. As it was, Gary made sure that Esther's response was going to have to wait.

'Stand by your beds – we've got two emergencies on the way in. A suspected appendicitis and a second patient, who has fallen from a ladder and has what they think is a badly broken shoulder.'

'We'd better call the surgical teams to let them know. They might need to cancel elective surgery to keep a theatre free if it is appendicitis. And the orthopaedic surgeon will want to assess whether the second patient's proximal humerus needs repairing.' Danni turned towards Aidan, who pretended to swoon.

'If you try out that sort of chat on your profile matches, they'll be eating out of your hand.' Aidan laughed again, before disappearing to make the calls. Danni didn't even want to think as far ahead as having to make conversation with anyone who might match her online. She'd been surrounded by medical professionals in her personal and professional life for so long, it was almost impossible to imagine a 'normal' conversation. She'd worry about that when she had to. For now, there was work to be done, and she'd take a ruptured appendix over a date with a stranger any day.

Danni had her suspicions almost as soon as she saw the patient being wheeled into A&E. The woman's face was contorted with agony one moment and then seconds later the horrendous pain she was in seemed to pass.

'Did you ask her if she could be pregnant?' Danni lowered her voice as she followed the paramedics out of the cubicle after they'd completed the handover. The patient, Roxy, was accompanied by her partner, who was watching her like a hawk. If Roxy was pregnant, but hadn't told her partner, there might be a good reason for it.

'She insists not.' The paramedic shook her head. 'Her partner's had a vasectomy.'

'Okay, thanks.' Despite her colleague's response, Danni couldn't shake the niggling doubt that this wasn't going to turn out to be the sort of emergency the A&E department could deal with. Appendicitis pain could come and go in the early stages, but by the time it got as severe as it seemed to be for Roxy, it was usually constant and located in the lower right-hand side of the abdomen. Something wasn't right.

'Essie. Have you got a sec?' Danni called out to Esther as she saw her emerge from another cubicle, hurrying towards her as she did.

'Of course, what's up?'

'I've got the patient with the expected appendicitis in my bay, but I think there might be something else going on.' Danni kept her voice at the same reduced level she'd used to question the paramedics. 'There's a chance she could be in labour, but I don't think she'll give me an honest answer in front of her partner, because she told the paramedics he's had a vasectomy.'

'Oh God. Does she look pregnant?'

'No, but that doesn't necessarily mean she isn't. She might not be full term or, even worse, it could be an ectopic pregnancy. I need to find out if there's any chance it could be that as soon as I can.' Danni shivered, despite how warm it was in the department. When she'd been on rotation during her training, a woman had come into A&E with a ruptured ectopic pregnancy. It had been touch and go whether she'd survive. In the end, she'd lost her second fallopian tube, after losing the first to a previous ectopic pregnancy just a year before. For the patient, it had seemed to be a fate only slightly preferable to death. She'd still been screaming at them not to let her lose her chance of having a baby when she'd been taken up for surgery, and Danni would never forget the look on her face. If Roxy was going through something similar, the sooner Danni took action the better.

'What do you need me to do?'

'If you can just take her partner off for a few minutes. Tell him there's some paperwork the two of you need to complete or something, so she can be admitted. Anything, just so I've got the chance to talk to her alone.'

Danni had to hand it to Esther. The way she'd spoken to Roxy's partner, Duncan, about him needing to go with her to register as next of kin, almost had Danni convinced. Within a minute of her following Danni down to Roxy's cubicle, Esther and Duncan had disappeared to complete the fictional paperwork.

'I know the paramedics have already asked you this, but I need to check again. Is there any chance you could be pregnant, Roxy?'

Before the other woman even spoke, Danni could tell from her expression that she'd been right. And when Roxy's face crumpled as she started to cry, all Danni could do was put an arm around her shoulders.

'It's all right. We can sort all of this out. The most important thing to do is to get you the right sort of care.' Danni kept her tone even. 'Have you got any idea how far along you might be?'

'I kept telling myself it couldn't be true. Even when I felt the baby moving, I convinced myself it must be IBS or something.' Danni had to concentrate hard to make out what Roxy was saying because she was crying so much. 'Duncan had his vasectomy eight years ago, after his ex went on and on about him doing it. But within six months she'd left him for her boss. Duncan's lovely, but he's paranoid about me cheating too, and he's never going to believe this baby is his.'

'It's okay, Roxy, these things have a way of working themselves out. But none of that matters for now; we just need to keep you and the baby safe.'

'But it is his baby, it really is!' Roxy was verging on hysterical now and, if Duncan was anywhere nearby, he was going to find out the news in the worst possible way. 'If I can't even convince you, how am I supposed to convince him?'

'I believe you.' Whether Duncan would believe it – without having to go through the sort of DNA tests that would damage any relationship – she didn't know. But she was certain Roxy was telling the truth. Pausing as another pain racked the other woman's body, Danni held on to her hand, hoping she was at least offering some comfort until the contraction subsided. 'I know this is really hard, but you're either going to have to tell Duncan what's going on, or ask him to leave, because I need to let the team from the maternity unit know what's happening.'

'I can't. He'll walk out and I can't do this. Not on my own.' Roxy's eyes were bloodshot from all the crying and she was already exhausted. 'I didn't think I'd ever get to have a baby of my own. Dunc's got Milly, his ten-year-old, but his ex didn't want any more kids. He said he always wanted another one, but we decided against a reversal because he was worried about things between us going the same way, and not getting to be with his child every day. He's missed out on so much with Milly and he didn't want to risk it again.'

'He's going to be shocked at first, but I'm sure he'll realise you're telling the truth and there are ways to prove it if it comes to that.' Danni resisted the urge to add that if Duncan knew Roxy well enough, he'd know she was telling the truth, because she knew from personal experience that it might not be the case. After all, no one knew Danni better than Esther did and she'd been lying to her friend by omission from the moment Lucas had walked into their lives.

'Can you be here when I tell him?' Roxy's eyes were pleading with Danni, but she didn't even hesitate before she nodded. It might be an awkward conversation, but if there was any chance of Duncan reacting violently, then proving that he was the father of her unborn baby might be the least of Roxy's worries.

* * *

Danni had promised Roxy she'd be as quick as possible when she'd gone to make the call to the maternity unit to let them know her patient would need to go up to labour and delivery as soon as possible. True to her word, she was back with Roxy in less than five minutes, arriving in her cubicle just ahead of Esther and Duncan.

'Have they given you anything for the pain, darling?' Duncan was immediately at his partner's side, his face a picture of concern. He didn't look like the sort of man who'd immediately assume the worst of the person he so clearly loved. But the past could damage you in a way that was hard to ever fully undo. His ex had cheated on him, which made the prospect of someone else doing that seem far more likely, no matter how hard Duncan might have tried to fully trust Roxy.

'They'll give me some pain relief when I get up to the mat… the ward.' Roxy bit her lip and Danni moved to the other side of the bed. She could see Esther out of the corner of her eye, and she silently willed her to stay with them too. Esther might be tiny but, if Duncan did kick off, she'd know the right thing to say to somehow make it better, or at the very least not to make the situation even worse. Roxy turned towards Danni, the pleading look back in her eyes and, when Danni raised her eyebrows, Roxy gave an almost imperceptible nod of her head. She needed help to get the words out, otherwise the midwives could be down in A&E before she'd even broken the news to Duncan.

'They're going to be moving Roxy to another department soon.' Danni glanced at her patient, who gave a more certain nod this time. 'She needs to go to the maternity unit. She's in labour and based on the frequency of the contractions, the baby's arrival could be pretty imminent.'

'Pregnant? She can't be.' Duncan's face was a mask and, other than the widening of his eyes, his reaction was impossible to read as he turned to face Roxy. 'You're not, are you? You can't be!'

His voice had risen on every word, and Roxy nodded. 'I am and it's yours. I promise, something must have happened to stop the vasectomy from working and I—'

'How long have you known?' Duncan's tone was just as difficult to interpret as his expression. Danni couldn't imagine how hard this was for Roxy, because even she was holding her breath.

'Six months.' They were two such tiny words, but the timespan they encompassed suddenly seemed like forever. Just imaging Roxy keeping something like that to herself for six months, out of fear about how Duncan might react, made tears spring up in Danni's eyes. The fact she'd been keeping a secret of her own for over seven years suddenly seemed like nothing in comparison. This was a whole new life, and nothing in the world could stop this secret from finally being uncovered. There was a force bigger than any of them about to bring it kicking and screaming into the world.

'I can't believe you went through all of that on your own. Jesus, why didn't you tell me?' There was no hiding what Duncan was feeling any more. He was crying as he folded Roxy into his arms.

'I didn't know if you'd believe me about the baby being yours.' Her voice was muffled by his embrace, but there was no mistaking the next sound, or its cause, as another contraction took over and Roxy let out a low moan.

'Sounds like we're in the right place!' Bobby, one of the midwives, who Danni had met during her orientation training, grinned as he came into the cubicle, followed by a second member of the maternity team. They hadn't even had the chance to introduce themselves, when Lucas suddenly arrived too.

'I'd recognise the sound of the pain caused by a broken shoulder anywhere.' Looking up as he said the words, he met Danni's eye and she shook her head.

'Wrong cubicle and you've clearly been on the surgical team for too long!' Esther caught hold of her fiancé's arm and laughed. 'Everyone knows nothing trumps childbirth, but I'll show you where your patient is. Good luck, Roxy.'

'Maybe we should have asked him to stay on anyway.' Bobby grinned again as Esther and Lucas disappeared. 'Because when my wife was in labour for the second time, she very nearly pulled my arm out of the socket.'

'Fair's fair.' The other midwife nudged him in the side and smiled at Roxy. 'I'm Jess, and this is Bobby. We'll take you along to the maternity unit and get you checked over properly, but I hear the contractions are coming quite regularly.'

'It certainly feels like it.' Roxy's voice was quiet, as if she still couldn't believe it was okay to admit what was going on.

'Roughly every five minutes since she got here.' Danni laid a hand gently on Roxy's shoulder, choosing her words carefully. 'It's all been a bit of shock, though, so Roxy hasn't had the usual ante-natal checks.'

'We get a lot more of that than you might imagine.' Jess smiled in a way that was bound to help convince Roxy it would all be okay, because it certainly had that effect on Danni.

'You're going to be the best mum, and I'm going to get to be a dad again.' Duncan's eyes were still wide with wonder, but there didn't seem to be any question in his mind that he was the father. 'I can't believe I'm getting the chance to do this with the love of my life.'

'That's always a good place to start.' Bobby laughed, but he looked like a man who knew a thing or two about the toll that sleepless nights could have on any relationship, no matter how strong. Yet watching Roxy and Duncan leave for the midwifery unit, Danni somehow knew they were going to make it. There might be some tough conversations to come about why Roxy had kept the pregnancy a secret for so long, but the way Duncan looked at her, it was obvious he didn't just believe her, she was the centre of his world too. Only one person had ever looked at Danni like that, but the trouble was, he looked at her best friend like that too.

12

———

Danni's shift had finished, but before she headed up to see Connie, she needed a coffee from the hospital shop. It hadn't been a particularly busy shift, at least not by A&E standards, but she felt drained all the same. Sometimes her mind just seemed more determined to overthink things than others. She'd spent a lot of the shift thinking about Duncan and Roxy, and wondering how they'd got on, which made her wonder if she'd ever have that – not just a partner, but a family of her own. Almost eight years had gone by with her waiting on the sidelines of life, in the hope that Esther might decide she didn't want Lucas after all. But the truth was, that was never going to happen. And, even if it did, Danni getting involved with him afterwards would mean they couldn't salvage their friendship.

No one wanted their best friend having a relationship with their ex-fiancé. There were too many messy feelings involved. Not that Esther had ever shown any sign of wanting to end things. Lucas was the only person who'd ever given an indication that things might not be as perfect as they seemed. It had only been a handful of times, and it was almost a cliché – a version of the whole *my partner doesn't understand me* sort of line. But each time he'd looked into Danni's eyes and told her that no one would ever get him the way she did. When she'd next see Lucas and Esther together, still looking every inch the perfect couple, her confused little heart would soar and sink all at the same time. Esther for her part had never expressed any doubts and, if things ended when she didn't want them to, the messy feelings left behind would be like a hand grenade having gone off.

Now she was back to standing on the sidelines of her own life. But she really did want a family of her own. She wanted someone holding her hand, marvelling at the fact that the two of them were going to have the adventure of parenthood together. She just had to hope that the online dating would at least help with the possibility of finding someone to do that with – someone who wasn't Lucas.

Danni was just mulling over whether a family-size bag of Maltesers might be in order, when a voice behind her made her jump.

'Are you going to eat all of those by yourself?' There was a teasing tone to Lucas's voice, but for some reason she felt the need to explain why she was holding two bags of chocolate in her hand.

'They've got a two for one offer on Maltesers, but one's for a patient.' She hated the way her body reacted to his proximity, like it was crying out for his touch. Her eyes swept over him, searching for something that might change the way she felt, but knowing deep down it wouldn't matter if he had spinach in his teeth, toilet paper stuck to his shoe, or even if his hair suddenly fell out overnight. The physical attraction had been instant, but what she felt for him now had built up over so many shared moments together. She wouldn't have got through some of the early training without him and he'd joked all the time about her being his work wife, until it had almost felt like she really was his other half. Except he went home to Esther every night, leaving Danni with a gap in her life whenever he wasn't around. So as physically attractive as Lucas was, it wouldn't matter if that changed.

'I've told myself that story before, or that I'm buying one bag for a colleague, but I always end up eating both.' Lucas laughed and placed a hand on her shoulder, his fingers stretching towards her collarbone, making her body jolt as they made contact with her skin. 'Tough day?'

'Quite quiet, but you know what those days are like. There's too much time to think.' They exchanged a look and she felt it again: that connection with him she didn't have with anyone else in the world. He understood her so well, because he'd been through it too. He'd lost *both* parents to cancer in quick succession. His mother when he was fourteen, and his father just a year after he and Esther had started dating. Danni had gone to the funeral and, when Lucas had got up to speak, he'd credited Esther and Danni for getting him through the darkest days of his life. It was the first time he'd told Danni that he loved her, by announcing publicly how much he loved the two women sitting in the fourth pew from the front, and how grateful he was that they'd come into his life. He hadn't separated them out, or explained to anyone who might not already know that one of them was his girlfriend and the other one was... what? A colleague? A friend? A work wife, who'd never be the real thing? She'd wrapped the words around her all the same: '*I love you so much.*' And she'd played them on repeat in her mind countless times, in countless imaginary scenarios. He'd said it since, in the way that friends did. Sometimes at work, sometimes in front of Esther, but it had never been quite as powerful as the way he'd said it at his father's funeral.

'You know you can always talk to me, don't you?' Lucas's fingertips were still brushing against her skin; if he trailed them even an inch lower she wasn't sure she'd be able to stop herself from reacting in the way her body was already begging her to do.

Instead, she jerked away, pretending to reach up for a box of chocolates on the top shelf.

'Thank you.'

'Something's up; I know you. And, whatever it is, eating your body weight in chocolate isn't the answer.' Lucas looked at her. 'You know you can tell me anything, don't you? If I hadn't had you to talk to sometimes about Mum and Dad, I think I might have had to give up medicine altogether. Do you remember that patient who looked so like my mum that I almost convinced myself she'd faked her own death?'

Lucas was laughing, but Danni knew it had taken him a long time to be able to see the funny side of that situation. It had been over twelve years since his mother's death at that point, but his grief had still seemed so raw. Getting him through that and talking to him into the early hours of the morning, when she should have been studying, was just one more thing that had bonded them together. So she knew she really could tell him anything. Except one thing.

'The couple you barged in on, in the cubicle, they were having a baby. It was all a bit of a surprise, but it got me thinking that it's what I want. A family of my own. I know it won't change the fact that Dad died, and Mum skipped out on family life, but I still want a second chance to have one. Sometimes I think I've wasted all this time, when I should have been focusing on that.'

'Building your career isn't wasting time.' He held her gaze for what felt like an agonisingly long moment. 'And neither is building a friendship like ours. I need you, Danni; I always have and I always will.'

'I keep wondering what happened to them. I was thinking of taking some different chocolates to the maternity unit, to see how they're getting on.' Danni had to change the subject, because they were right back on the dangerous ground they'd been on before she'd left London. Maybe Joe was right, maybe they really were co-dependent. Lucas needed her to fill a gap in his life, and she desperately wanted to be wanted, the way her mother had never wanted her and Joe.

'Rumour has it he'd had a vasectomy, so no wonder it was a shock.' Lucas raised his eyebrows. No one but Danni had been in the cubicle when Roxy had spoken about that, but she'd been very upset and quite loud, so almost anyone walking through the department could have overheard and passed the gossip on. But she hated the thought that Roxy's fear was being turned into entertainment for other people. The fact Lucas had clearly been involved in spreading that rumour made her feel nauseous, because it meant Aidan might not have been so wrong about him after all.

'It was, but he never doubted her. It was obvious she was telling the truth.' Danni felt almost defensive of Roxy, her scalp prickling at the idea that she was the current topic of hospital gossip.

'I don't think I could ever trust anyone that much.'

'Not even Esther?' Danni waited for his answer, and he fixed his eyes on hers again as he spoke.

'Not even myself.'

Catching her breath, Danni forced herself to turn away. Her head was aching from the effort of trying to work out what was going on. She'd been so sure she knew the real Lucas, and that she might be the only person who really did, but now she was starting to doubt her ability to tell what was real and what was a game. Despite all that, there were still moments when it was like the rest of the world had disappeared when they were together. But whatever was really going on, she wanted it to stop. 'I'd better get a card to go with the chocolates, I suppose. You can't congratulate people on becoming new parents without giving them a card.'

'I don't suppose you can.' Lucas didn't move to touch her again, but he stepped closer as he lowered his voice. 'You know where I am if you need to talk. Anytime, about anything.'

Keeping her eyes firmly fixed on the cards until Lucas had paid for his coffee and left, Danni finally let go of a long breath. Selecting a gender-neutral congratulations card, she took the armful of chocolate she was now carrying over to the counter, where Gwen was waiting.

'I'm off to see Connie.' She smiled at the older woman, who returned the gesture.

'She'll be glad to see you, and it'll be good for you to talk to someone too. Someone who might be able to give you a bit of useful advice.'

'About what?'

'About how to avoid getting your heart broken, and how to avoid breaking someone else's heart, especially if that someone else is a person you love.' The look Gwen gave her was so knowing, there was no doubt who she was talking about, even before she spoke again. 'Be careful of him, Danni; he's not worth losing your best friend over.'

The insight that this woman, who barely knew her, had into Danni's life knocked the air out of her lungs for a moment, but the brutal truth had the power to do that. She couldn't risk losing Esther; it was what had given her the strength to push Lucas away every time he'd given her the opportunity to take things between them to another level. But if the situation was obvious to Gwen, there was every chance Esther might see it too, and be the one to walk away from their friendship. Danni couldn't let that happen, whatever she had to sacrifice to prevent it.

'I'll give Connie your love.' Trying desperately to adopt a neutral expression, she touched her debit card against the scanner to pay, and scooped the chocolates up with the haste of a contestant on *Supermarket Sweep*. She had to get out of there as soon as she could and, if things didn't change soon, she had a horrible feeling she was going to have to leave St Piran's even sooner than she'd feared.

* * *

'Maltesers? Did Gwen tell you they're my favourite?' Connie's stomach was already rumbling at the sight of the bag of chocolate that Danni had just placed on her bedside cabinet. The hospital meals weren't quite as bad as their reputation, but the consistency of most of the dinners reminded her of baby food. Last night's had been shepherd's pie slopped onto the plate, with the morsels of meat impossible to find amongst the mash and gravy, even if it did taste okay as long as you closed your eyes. She remembered feeding Darcy stuff that looked similar, sometimes out of a jar, and sometimes homemade by Connie's sister, Janice. Darcy had been an expert at projecting rejected mashed potato across the width of the room when the mood took her, but Connie had always enjoyed feeding her nonetheless. It was a privilege she never thought she'd get when she'd made the decision to give her baby up.

At the time it had felt less like a decision and more of a necessity. Connie and Janice had grown up without a father around, and with a mother who was forced to work two jobs just to keep a roof over their heads. She'd worked so hard that her daughters had more or less had to bring themselves up, and she had drummed into them that education was their way out of the same poverty trap she'd been caught in. She'd been so proud of Connie's qualifications and her becoming a lecturer. One comfort from her mother's death was that she'd never known about the pregnancy. Connie had breastfed her newborn baby, despite the toe-curling pain, and the even more excruciating fear that it would make the bond between them even stronger than it had been when she'd first looked down at her baby's face. In that first moment, she'd known she had to make sure the baby had the chance of a childhood different to her own. Janice and her husband, Peter, had thought so too, and it had all been agreed before Connie had even had the chance to consider changing her mind.

'No, Gwen didn't mention it.' Danni smiled. 'It was just a lucky guess, but surely everyone loves Maltesers?'

'My niece, Darcy, does. Always has, but she tells me she's craving them even more now she's pregnant. I couldn't get enough chocolate when I was pregnant either, so she takes after me for that.'

'It sounds like the two of you have got a lovely relationship.' Danni sat down next to the bed and Connie couldn't help noticing how tired the younger woman looked, as if she had the weight of the world on her shoulders.

'We've always been close, but even more so since her parents died. My brother-in-law, Peter, was fifteen years older than my sister and I always used to tease her that she chose him because our dad was never around, but I knew it wasn't true. They were one of those couples who were made for each other.' Connie sighed. 'With the age gap, none of us ever expected her to go first. She got sepsis and it was all so quick. Peter was like a shadow of himself, and I think he only hung on for another eighteen months for Darcy's sake. He wanted to go the moment Janice was no longer here.'

'That must have been really hard for your niece. I've got a friend who'd lost both his parents by the time he was in his twenties, and it can have a huge impact losing your support network that young.'

'It can; Darcy was in her early thirties by the time Peter died, but she never made it about her. She was just sad they were gone and then, later, that they'd never get to meet the baby she's expecting. I still find that painful too, but I'll just have to be a grandparent for all three of us.'

'Darcy's lucky to have you.' An unreadable expression crossed Danni's face and Connie found herself wondering, not for the first time, why such a busy young woman would want to take the time out to keep visiting her. She was grateful for it, but there must have been better things Danni could have been doing with her time.

'I'm the one who's lucky to have her in my life. I didn't think I'd ever get to be involved in raising a child, even from the sidelines.' Connie would never stop being grateful to Janice and Peter for their support, and even after all this time, she was certain she'd made the right decision. But with Darcy about to have a baby of her own, it suddenly felt as if the secrets from almost forty years ago were desperately trying to bubble to the surface. It was time to tell the truth, but, being stuck in this hospital bed, she couldn't do it alone. 'I need your help with something.'

'Of course.' Danni was immediately up on her feet. 'Do you want me to help you move into a more comfortable position?'

'No, it's not that. I need you to take the new letter I've written to Richard.' Connie had thought long and hard about all the options there were for getting in touch with Richard and, if she couldn't see him face to face, she was certain now that this was the best way. 'I know I could email or message him online, but he needs to see my handwriting to know it's true. I might be flattering myself to think he'll remember what my writing looks like almost four decades later, but I'd never have forgotten his from the notes we wrote each other when we were together, even if he hadn't sent me all those letters afterwards. There's a photograph in the envelope too and I need him to see that when he reads the letter. Downloading it from an email just won't be the same. Please, I know it's asking a lot, but I can't do much stuck here and they keep delaying my discharge to rehab, because they're not happy with my scans. I could ask Gwen. She's lovely and I know she'd do it, but—'

'But she'll get too involved?' Danni had read Connie's mind, and she tilted her head. 'Of course I'll do it, but you've got to be really sure because once this secret is out, there'll be no way of hiding it again. Not for you, not for Richard and not for Darcy.'

'I know, and I owe it to Darcy to tell her the truth myself, but I want Richard to know first. He's the one the secret has been kept from for the longest.'

'I hope it works out for you; it mut be a really hard to...' Connie didn't hear the rest of what Danni was saying, because the whole world had stopped. Or at least it would have done, if a man hadn't been walking towards her bed.

'Oh my God.' She recognised the only man she'd ever been in love with instantly; he'd hardly changed a bit, but it couldn't be him, almost forty years had passed. She said his name out loud all the same. 'Richard?'

'It might have been that once, but my name's Charlie now.' The man towering above her bed suddenly smiled, the dimple in his right cheek exactly like her own. 'Hello, Mum.'

13

'I should go.' Danni's face was the perfect mirror for the shock that had taken Connie's breath away. She'd known this moment was coming as soon as she'd got the email from Darcy, three weeks before.

Hey, Auntie Cee! Your little great nephew is kicking the hell out of my womb and I've not been sleeping very well. I was online at 4 a.m. this morning when an email came through from that DNA ancestry website I joined. It says I've got a first cousin match! Looks like that disappearing dad you and Mum had must have had some other children. All those years of me begging you to have a baby when I was younger, so I'd at least get a cousin if I couldn't have a sibling, and it looks like I've had one out there all along!!! He wants to get in touch and I'm going to do it as soon as bubs is here. I don't want to arrange a meet-up with my new cousin while there's a very real danger of me wetting myself if he makes me laugh 😊. Hope that's okay with you? How exciting, you've got a nephew! Xx

Even without all the exclamations and emojis, Darcy's excitement had been palpable. Connie had needed to act straight away and get to Cornwall, to try and track Richard down before their son somehow managed that too. For all she knew, Richard might have been registered on the same DNA website, but even if he wasn't, there'd been less than two months until Darcy's baby was due to find Richard and tell him, before her niece. Richard had a right to know first.

It would have been impossible to put Darcy off from contacting her cousin for any longer than that, and she wouldn't have wanted to. Her niece had already lost both parents and theirs was such a tiny family – she needed every member of it she could find. Otherwise, when Connie was gone, there'd be no one left on her mother's side. Finding the baby she'd named Saul had been something she'd only dared dream of, but had longed for all the same. When she'd let him go, Connie had made a promise to herself that she'd wait until he came looking for her – if he ever did – rather than trying to find him first. She'd chosen the name Saul because it meant 'borrowed', and that was all he'd ever been to her, a precious gift, borrowed for the time that had ticked by far too quickly until he'd been taken away. Yet now he was standing in front of her, in the flesh, all grown up and well over six feet tall. He bore no resemblance to the tiny newborn she'd held in her arms, yet she knew for certain it was him.

'Don't go, please.' Connie reached out a hand towards Danni. She had no idea how this man, her son, who called himself Charlie, was going to react to finally meeting her, but she needed a friend.

'You don't need to leave on my account.' Charlie smiled again and for the first time she noticed that, as much as he looked like Richard had all those years ago, his eyes were exactly like her sister, Janice's. They were the same almost sky-blue colour, and even the same shape. And suddenly it felt like Janice was in the room too, willing this to work out the way she would have wanted it to.

'At least take my chair.' Danni moved to stand up, but Charlie shook his head.

'There's another one over there. I'll go and grab it, if you don't mind?' He looked at Connie and it was all she could do to nod. Part of her wanted to reach out and grab him, to make sure he was real, to hold on and never let go. But this had to be at his pace, and she needed to protect herself too. He might just be curious and want one meeting and nothing else, even if she was already praying that wouldn't be the case.

'Have you spoken to Darcy?' Connie was still struggling to breathe and speak at the same time, but she had to know how much her niece had been told.

'Not in person, no. She replied to my message about our DNA match, saying she wanted to meet up after she's had the baby. But she told me who she was and who you were, explaining that I must be related to your father, who walked out when you were a baby.' If Charlie saw the irony in that, there was no trace of bitterness in his voice. 'But all the time I was growing up, when I'd blow the candles out on my birthday cake, Mum would tell me to make a wish for Connie too, because you'd made her biggest wish come true when you'd allowed her to adopt me. So I always knew my birth mother's name was Connie. As soon as I read your name in Darcy's email, I realised it was you. But it was obvious Darcy had no idea, and I wasn't about to be the one to tell her. Instead, I dug around a bit on Facebook and found you via Darcy's profile. Having a surname as unusual as Berrycloth made it easier to search for information. I kept going online every few days, wondering if I should drop you a message, but then your name came up in an online article about the bus crash, and I didn't want to wait any more. I'm sorry to turn up like this; I just didn't want to be one of those people you read about, who finally decide to track down their birth parents only to find out they're too late.'

'I'm not going anywhere. I couldn't even if I wanted to.' Connie smiled for the first time and if she hadn't had such a terrible singing voice, she might even have broken into song. There was so much joy bursting inside her, now that her son was within touching distance after so long. Not even the fear of what would happen when he found his father didn't know he existed could dampen her happiness in that moment. Something primeval inside her had loved Charlie for all these years, throughout their absence in one another's lives, but even though she'd only just met him, she already liked him too. This earnest man, who was clearly more worried about everyone else's feelings than his own, reminded her so much of everything she'd loved about his father. And she needed him to know just how much it meant to her to see him again. 'I'm glad you're here. You might not believe it, but I've dreamt of this moment from the day I had to say goodbye to you.'

'I've got to admit you weren't what I was expecting.' There was still a complete absence of bitterness in Charlie's voice, but curiosity was written all over his face. 'I thought maybe you'd been really young when you had me and that's why you chose adoption, but your profile at the university said you've been teaching for over forty years, since before I was even born.'

'It wasn't an easy decision, but your father…' Connie trailed off. She couldn't lay any of the blame at Richard's door when he hadn't even known about Charlie's existence. It had all seemed so black and white back then. Having the baby adopted was the best thing for everyone, except Connie, and her pain was the price she'd had to pay for keeping the whole thing secret. But she couldn't tell Charlie the whole story, not until Richard at least knew there was a story to tell.

'I promise I will tell you everything, but I just need a little bit more time.' Connie glanced at Danni, who gave the tiniest nod of her head. 'I need to speak to Darcy and to your biological father, and then I'll answer whatever questions you have. Talking to him first is the only reason I didn't contact you as soon as Darcy told me there was a DNA match online. Just give me a few more days, please.'

'I've waited thirty-seven years, so a few more days can't hurt.' He smiled again and something in Connie's chest twisted. The urge to take her son in her arms was almost as overpowering as the urge to hold on to him tightly, and never let go, had been on the day she'd handed him over.

'As a doctor, I can promise you she won't be running off anywhere, anytime soon.' Danni squeezed Connie's hand. 'But thankfully she's going to recover from all of her injuries with time.'

'I'm more grateful for that than you'll ever know.' Either Charlie was the most fantastic actor in the world, or the most forgiving person. But then perhaps there was nothing to forgive. Connie hoped with all her heart that was true, but she had to know.

'Were you happy growing up? Was it the right decision?'

Even before Charlie answered, his eyes lit up, and Connie felt a wave of relief wash over her entire body. 'I had the best childhood you could hope for and so much love. Mum's an artist and Dad's a music teacher. The house was always full of creative people and so I guess it's no surprise I ended up being a writer. Mum taught me a lot too, so when I wrote my first children's book, I was able to illustrate it myself. I'm sure that helped get me a publishing deal and now I get to make stuff up for a living. It means I can base myself anywhere, so Maggie and I have rented a cottage in Port Kara for the next six weeks. I thought it would give you and me an opportunity to get to know one another properly, and I can be around to help out while you recover. But, if things don't work out between us, that's okay too. I'm not looking to fill a gap in my life, because there's never been one. It just struck me that I write stories for a living, but I don't know my own. So, what do you think, shall we give getting to know one another a shot?'

'I'd like that and I'm so glad you've had such a lovely child-hood.' Even the tiny sliver of jealousy that had snaked its way into Connie's heart couldn't temper her happiness at knowing that Charlie's adoption had been so positive. She could have asked a thousand more questions and no doubt they would come from both sides, but for now it was just enough that he was here. Stealing another glance at the son she thought she'd lost forever, she crossed one finger over the other beneath the bedsheet that was stretched across her chest. She trusted Danni to do what she'd asked, and deliver the letter. She just had to hope and pray that Richard would be willing to talk once he'd read what she had to say.

14

Brenda had a split personality. When it came to doing anything she didn't want to do, getting into the car for a check-up at the vet's for instance, she acted as if she might well be on her last legs and needed to be carried outside and lifted in. Danni couldn't help thinking that the dead weight of a full-grown basset hound would have been good training for Olympic powerlifters. But as soon as Brenda heard Danni unhook her lead from the coat rack by the front door, she shot out of her basket and skidded to a halt, half on the front doormat and half off it, as her back feet seemed to over-take the ones at the front.

Like most basset hounds, Brenda had a saggy face, which meant slobbering came with the territory and there was now a liberal coating of it up the door. 'Oh Brenda, that's disgusting. It's a good job I love you.'

In all the excitement to get out, she'd knocked into the hallway table, causing the letter to Richard to fall on the floor, right into the path of some more of Brenda's trademark slobber.

'This might be the most important letter Richard ever gets; you do know that, don't you?' Danni laughed as she looked at Brenda, who couldn't have appeared less bothered if she'd tried. Taking a tissue out of the box that had somehow remained on the hallway table, Danni wiped the corner of the envelope. 'Right, good as new. Come on then, let's get going before you can do any more damage.'

Putting the letter into the pocket of her coat, Danni stepped outside the cottage and breathed deeply. When she'd considered leaving London to move back to Cornwall, the fantasy she'd built up in her head could have turned out to be a big disappointment. But, instead, it had managed to exceed expectations and it had taken her right back to the time when she'd been happiest in her life, when her father was still alive and her little family had been intact and impenetrable. But then Lucas and Esther had arrived, and all her dreams of building a life for herself and creating a family like the one she remembered from her childhood had suddenly felt like a distant dream again.

She really didn't want to leave Port Kara or the little cottage that already felt more like home than anywhere had in years. Breathing in again, Danni could taste the salt on her lips, and the sun in the cloudless blue sky above her radiated the sort of gentle, autumnal warmth that made it her favourite season. Most of the holiday-makers and second-home owners would be long gone now too. She could almost picture her father setting up the wickets for a game of cricket on the almost empty beach as she headed across the sand with Brenda. It was still quite early and, despite it being way past the end of the season, the beach would fill up a bit more later. But after witnessing Connie meeting Charlie for the first time the evening before, being in possession of Connie's letter to Richard had felt like even more of a responsibility and she didn't want to delay delivering it for any longer than she had to. There was a lot riding on Richard's reaction to what was in the letter, and Danni knew that Connie wouldn't be able to think about anything other than that until she'd heard from him. It must have been terrifying for her, stuck in the hospital, waiting for news. Danni could feel the nerves bubbling up inside as she set off towards Trengothern Hall.

When she'd searched for Richard online, there'd been a webpage about the self-catering holiday cottages rented out in the grounds of Trengothern Hall, but there'd also been some old pictures of the place on Google Images and the aerial shots had given Danni a good idea of what it looked like now. It had clearly been quite grand in its time and more recent photographs of the hall were still beautiful, with its position high on the cliffs, surrounded by acres of land. But unlike many of the old houses in the area, which were more often than not home to wealthy incomers, Trengothern Hall was clearly staying true to its roots. Danni still didn't know if Richard had married Fiona or not, but the website said the self-catering cottages were set on a two hundred acre working farm, so he'd clearly found a way to hold on to a lot of his family's land.

Taking the coastal path was the quickest way to get to the farm, and Danni relished the opportunity to be so close to the sea, with uninterrupted views all the way out to the headline at Port Agnes, and the Sisters of Agnes Island just beyond it. The coastal path on this side of Port Kara was undulating, sometimes dipping down much closer to where the water broke over the rocks at high tide. And Danni was just reaching that point when a Labrador, with a shiny black coat, came bounding towards her, trying to engage Brenda – who was having none of it – in a game.

'Maggie, come here, girl. Not everyone wants to be your friend.' Danni might only have met him once, the day before, but Charlie had the sort of voice that made it instantly recognisable. It had a rich, deep tone, and when he'd told Connie that he was a writer, Danni had been tempted to ask him if he did the recordings for his own audiobooks. If he didn't, he was missing a trick. It was the sort of voice she could have listened to all day, and it suited him too, which wasn't always the case. He didn't look anything like Connie. He was tall, with curly dark hair and bright blue eyes, which were probably the first thing people noticed about him. When he'd said he was renting a cottage with Maggie, Danni had instantly pictured him having a beautiful partner, but it turned out that Maggie was a Labrador. Although that didn't stop her being every bit as beautiful as Danni had imagined.

'She's okay, don't worry. Hello, sweetheart.' Danni bent down to stroke Maggie's head, which felt like silk beneath her fingers. 'Brenda can just be a bit of an old grump at times.'

'Brenda? That's a brilliant name!' Charlie laughed. 'It's Danni, isn't it? We met at the hospital yesterday.'

'Of course, hello again.' She had no idea why she was pretending to be so nonchalant, or trying to give the impression that she hadn't instantly recognised him and would have done from his voice alone. It wasn't like she sat in on a reunion between a patient and their long-lost child every day, but she just had to go with it now.

'I'm supposed to be working on some illustrations for my next book, but Maggie needed a walk and I need some inspiration.' Charlie smiled again, a dimple appearing in his right cheek as he did and for the first time Danni could see a resemblance with Connie. 'It's certainly the right place to get it. Have you seen the seal pup down on the rocks?'

'On my God, really? Whereabouts?' Spotting seals had been an obsession for Danni for as long as she could remember. It was just one more memory she had of her father, who had taken Danni and her brother searching for wildlife whenever he had time off from work, but especially when they had the chance to get to the Atlantic coast. More often than not, her mother would stay behind to indulge in whatever her latest passion was. Her father had always been supportive, and given her mother so much time without the

children when they were on holiday, that Danni had never noticed
how hard her mum found it to cope with her own offspring. At least
until her father had died, and then it had been brutally obvious.
They were still happy memories, though, and Danni had spotted
seals with her father many times, but rarely a seal pup.

'Just down there, see?' Charlie moved closer to her, pointing to
a crop of rocks, jutting out below where the clifftop dropped to its
lowest point.

'It's so beautiful.' The seal wasn't white, as Danni had thought it
would be, but more of a golden colour.

'It must have been born fairly recently; it hasn't even started to
moult yet.' There was an expression of wonder on Charlie's face
that somehow made him even more attractive. Danni had to look at
him again, as the shock of realising she found someone who wasn't
Lucas attractive suddenly hit home. It had been so long since she'd
felt that way, it took her a moment to work out what the sensation
that could only be described as butterflies meant. It was something
she'd wanted to feel for someone else for years, and the realisation
left her with a weird mix of nerves and excitement as Charlie spoke
again. 'It reminds me of Maggie when she was a pup, a bit. The
same huge black eyes, but it was two of Maggie's siblings who had
yellow coats.'

'He looks nice and fat at least.' Danni forced herself to turn her
attention back to the seal pup.

'I think I'm going to have to put him in one of my stories. We're
assuming it's a him, and there's no way of knowing without looking
at its belly, but I'll have to come up with a name.' Charlie turned
towards her. 'What do you think would suit him?'

'Trevor.'

'I can't say it's the first thing that springs to mind when I look at
a cute little seal pup, but why not?' Charlie's eyes sparkled when he

laughed and Danni had a feeling he did a lot of laughing. The sunny disposition he'd displayed when he'd met his biological mother for the first time clearly hadn't been an act.

'It was my father's name.' Somehow saying it to Charlie enabled her to smile too. Her father would have loved this, Danni bumping into someone who was every bit as excited about seeing a seal pup, and who wanted to immortalise the moment in a children's story. It made saying her father's name, without feeling the sting of tears, easier than she could remember it being since he'd died.

'Trevor it is, then.' Charlie snapped a picture on his phone. 'I'll check if there's somewhere we need to report the sighting, in case they're monitoring the health of the seal pups. But other than that, I think it should be our secret. We don't want to risk hundreds of people flocking down here, when it's so close to the lowest point of the pathway. I'd better haul Maggie in the other direction as it is. Otherwise, knowing her, she'll be trying to get down there to investigate further.'

'Sounds like a good plan. It's been nice seeing you again, Charlie.' It really had been lovely, and unexpected in more ways than one, but the letter to Richard still felt as if it was burning a hole in her pocket. 'I'd better get Brenda moving again too, or she'll decide she's finished with walking for the day and I need to get up to Trengothern Hall.'

'Me too!' Charlie held up his hands. 'I promise I'm not some weirdo following you, but that's where the cottage I've rented is.'

'Oh right, of course.' Danni's breath had caught in her throat. Charlie hadn't been there when Connie had asked her to deliver the letter to Richard, so he'd have no way of knowing why she was headed to Trengothern Hall. And he wouldn't be able to piece the puzzle together and work out who his father was before Connie had been given the chance to explain. But it still made her feel uneasy.

'We could walk together.' Charlie hesitated for a moment, searching her face. 'But I won't be insulted if you'd rather not.'

'No, of course, that would be lovely.' She was already wracking her brain about what to tell him if he asked why she needed to go to the farm. She'd just have to say it was about some medical results she wasn't at liberty to share. It was a plausible reason and in a weird kind of way it wasn't really a lie. So she had absolutely no idea why her heart was still thudding as hard as it was.

By the time they reached the track to Trengothern Hall, Danni had discovered that Charlie had never been married, despite living with his girlfriend, Natalie, for eight years, before realising that something wasn't right. Even though Charlie had been the one to break it off, the way he'd described it did nothing to diminish the opinion Danni had formed of him. He'd signed the house over to Natalie, so she wouldn't have to move away from her support network, and had started again from scratch with just Maggie and some furniture his family and friends had wanted to get rid of. That had been five years ago, just before Charlie's first book had been published. Since then, he'd managed to get back on the property ladder and had just sold the house he'd bought, after spending nearly all of the time when he wasn't working doing it up. He told Danni it had been the perfect time to rent a holiday let down in Cornwall while he decided on his next move.

'Do you think there's any chance you'll want to stay around here?' She turned to look at him, surprised at how much she was hoping he'd say yes. But he was already shaking his head.

'It's beautiful, but I doubt it. Mum and Dad are renting a place on the Isle of Wight now, while they look for somewhere to buy. They've always wanted to retire out there and they're close to a beach, which Maggie loves even more than I do. So, I think if they can find the perfect place near to where they are now, we'll look for somewhere close to them.' Charlie breathed out. 'I want to get to know Connie, obviously. But from what I could gather when I looked her up, her life seems to be based around the university in Yorkshire and I'm guessing she'll be heading back that way as soon as she's well enough. And there'll be nothing to keep me down here after that.'

'Of course.' Danni needed to give herself a good shake. It was ridiculous to feel so deflated that someone she'd only just met wasn't planning to hang around. Especially as she had no idea if she'd be staying in Cornwall either. When the thought struck her that she could always look at opportunities on the Isle of Wight, she started to worry that she really was losing it. But it had been more than seven years since she'd felt drawn to anyone other than Lucas, and it was a relief to know she could still feel that way, especially as it meant staying in Port Kara might be a possibility after all. There'd been times just lately when she'd felt as if her feelings for Lucas might finally be starting to fade, and meeting Charlie had helped convince her that it wasn't just wishful thinking.

'We're here.' Charlie paused as they reached the gate and then held up his hand to wave at someone crossing the farmyard. 'Oh and look, there's Richard. You'll be able to talk to him in person.'

'Yes, right, but, um… It's just that the contents of the letter are a bit, er…' She had no idea how to finish the sentence, and was stumbling over her words, but Charlie was smiling again.

'Don't worry, I won't stay and eavesdrop, I promise.'

'Thanks.' Danni went hot, as she always seemed to do when she experienced strong emotions of any kind. Charlie's discretion might have solved one problem, but she still didn't really want to speak to Richard until he'd had the chance to read the letter. If he asked her what was in it, she could hardly lie again and tell him it was medical results – not without the risk of being struck off.

'I'll leave you to it then. Hopefully we'll get the chance to walk the dogs again another time. I really enjoyed this morning, and of course we ought to go back and check on Trevor together. We did name him, after all. So that makes us both jointly responsible for him, doesn't it?'

'I suppose it does.' Her heart was galloping even faster now, but she couldn't tell whether that was down to Charlie, or because Richard was getting closer and closer to the gate.

'My details are on here. Oh God, I probably look like an arrogant idiot who goes around handing out bookmarks to anyone who'll take them. I promise I don't usually do it, unless I'm at a book signing or a talk. But the idea of being an author who hands out business cards makes me cringe even more, so I never got any of those done. Anyway, if all of that hasn't put you off for life, my social media details are on there, so you can message me if you ever fancy going to check on Trevor.'

'I will.' Danni nodded. The more Charlie spoke, the more she liked him. The fact he was self-deprecating and a tiny bit awkward, despite clearly being successful in his career, made him all the more appealing.

'Great, thanks, I'll look forward to that.' For a moment it seemed like he might be about to kiss her on the cheek, but then he clearly thought better of it, and she tried not to feel disappointed as he turned towards the man now standing behind the gate. 'Morning, Richard, I bumped into Danni this morning when she was on her way over here, so we headed back together. I'll leave you two to it now though, I've got to go and make a call. I'll see you both later.'

'Thanks, Charlie.' Richard furrowed his brow, looking at Danni, as Charlie and Maggie headed across the farmyard. The two men shared their height and build. And, knowing what she knew, Danni could see a similarity in their jawlines and the shape of their noses. But Richard was wearing an expression of suspicion that made him look so unlike Charlie, Danni doubted anyone else would be able to see the resemblance between them unless they were looking for it. 'I wasn't expecting anyone. If you're from Cliff and Country Housing, you needn't bother saying anything else, because I'm not interested. I don't know how many times I have to tell you people, it doesn't matter what you offer me, I'm not selling Trengothern Hall so that you can build God knows how many of your so-called executive houses on my family's farm.'

'I'm not from a housing company. I just came to deliver a letter, that's all.'

'Oh, so you're from the council, are you? I suppose you've had a complaint that I'm breaking some ridiculous regulation, have you? I keep telling you it's a smear campaign from the people who want to buy the farm; they're just trying to stir up trouble and force me to sell.' Richard was going red in the face now and the last thing she wanted to do was to upset him, especially when there was no way of knowing how he might react to the contents of the letter.

'I'm not from anywhere, I promise. I'm just dropping a letter off.'

'I suppose you're going to try and tell me you're standing in for Terry the postman, are you?' There were beads of sweat breaking out on Richard's brow. Someone had obviously been giving him a really hard time, trying to persuade him to sell the farm, and she was almost tempted just to blurt out the truth. But that had to come from Connie.

'Just read the letter; it explains it all.' Danni held it out towards him, but Richard crossed his hands over this chest. 'It's from an old friend.'

'I haven't got any old friends and whatever you're selling, or trying to buy, *I am not interested.*' As he raised his voice to shout the last few words, Danni could see the veins bulging in his forehead.

'It's important that you read it. I've come from the hospital, and someone there gave me the letter.'

He was finally holding out a hand towards her, but all the colour seemed to be draining from his face. 'From the hospital?'

She didn't like the way he was panicking and, despite not wanting to tell him who the letter was from, suddenly it felt like she had no choice. 'The letter's from—'

Danni had been so close to saying Connie's name, but the word was ripped out of her mouth as he suddenly crumpled to a heap on the floor.

'Richard!' Her shout was so loud that some of the hens, who'd been hopefully pecking at the dirt in the farmyard, tried to take flight. Leaving Brenda on the other side of the gate, Danni clambered over. There was no way she could force it open without risking injury to Richard.

'Oh my God, is he okay?' Charlie came sprinting across the farmyard, just as Danni stepped down from the gate.

'I don't know. He was getting a bit worked up, then he went a funny colour and just dropped to the ground.' Danni moved to kneel next to Richard as she spoke. There was no sign of any blood loss or obvious injury from him hitting the floor and he was clearly still breathing. 'His pulse rate is very fast, which might be what caused him to pass out. But we need to know why.'

'I'll call an ambulance.' Charlie took his phone out of his pocket. 'He said yesterday that he's been getting bad headaches and that his vision is sometimes a bit blurry. I told him to get it checked out, but I should have made him come with me when I went to the hospital.'

'It's not your fault.' Danni needed him to know that, because if anything happened to Richard, Charlie seemed like the sort of person who would blame himself. When Charlie discovered that Richard was his father, the stakes would be raised a thousand times higher. So he needed to know that none of this was down to him.

'Ambulance, please.' As Charlie spoke to the operator, Danni looked around for something to elevate Richard's legs above the level of his heart. Dragging a bale of straw out of wheelbarrow just to the left of the gate, she silently prayed that everything would be okay. Richard couldn't die without discovering the truth, because if he did it would break Connie's heart, and Danni couldn't bear to think about how much all of that would hurt Charlie too.

15

'You really need to get yourself a life, Dan, if you can't even stay away from A&E on your day off.' Aidan put a hand on Danni's shoulder as he stood behind her, while she reviewed the results of some of Richard's tests.

'Well, if men will insist on dropping at my feet like that, what's a girl supposed to do?' She shrugged, able to joke along with him now that the results of the most serious tests were back and Richard hadn't had a heart attack or a stroke. However, his blood pressure was very high and, given that he wasn't overweight, and didn't smoke or drink, the underlying cause for his hypertension needed more investigation. There was a chance it could be down to undiagnosed kidney disease, diabetes, or even sleep apnoea, and he'd need to stay in for more tests until they could rule out anything serious.

'Are you sure you haven't been clubbing them over the head, just to avoid internet dating?' Aidan raised his eyebrows as Danni swivelled around in her chair to look at him.

'Who's internet dating?' Lucas seemed to have developed a habit of popping up out of nowhere since he'd started at St Piran's.

In his role, he spent quite a bit of time assessing patients in A&E for surgery, but Danni wished he wasn't quite so stealthy. She could have done with him wearing a bell to warn her of his presence, so she could make sure the conversation was steered away from anything she didn't want him to hear.

'Danni is; you were there the night she was setting up her profile. When you came to pick me and Aidan up.' Esther, who'd come out of one of the cubicles just as Lucas had arrived, nudged him in the side and rolled her eyes as she looked at Danni. 'Sometimes I don't think he listens to anything. I don't know why you want a long-term relationship, because once they get comfortable, they also seem to feel able to completely ignore you.'

'I thought the internet dating profile was just a joke.' Lucas was responding to Esther, but looking at Danni, and there was a muscle going in his cheek. The proprietorial tone he adopted whenever she seemed to be getting close to someone else was back too.

'See what I mean about ignoring what I say.' Esther shook her head again, a note of irritation in her voice. 'You haven't got time for any of this now anyway, Lucas. You need to see my patient.'

'That told you!' Aidan wagged his finger, seeming to enjoy Lucas's obvious displeasure at being told what to do, as Esther led the way back into her cubicle. When they were out of earshot, Aidan pulled a face. 'Ooh, do I sense trouble in paradise?'

Danni did her best to look as though she had no idea what Aidan meant. He didn't need a lot of encouragement if there was potential for gossip, but it was obvious there'd been tension between Lucas and Esther. If Danni hadn't loved Esther as much as she did, that might have made her happy. As it was, she was worried about her best friend. Esther usually had the sunniest disposition of anyone she knew. So Aidan was right: there was definitely something going on.

'Those two are usually sickeningly lovey-dovey. Every shift I've been on with Esther since she started, Lucas finds a reason to come down here and she seems to need to show the world that everything between them is hearts and flowers.' Aidan pretended to stick his fingers down his throat. 'He obviously wants to keep an eye on what she's up to, or...'

'Or what?'

'Or there's someone else down here he wants to come and see.'

'Don't be ridiculous. I've told you we're just really good friends. Lucas is like a brother to me.' The heat had risen up Danni's neck despite her protestation, and the outright lie she'd just told. When Aidan had hinted at this before, the night they'd gone to the club, she'd thought it was just the drink talking, and he'd never mentioned it again. She'd been worried about Esther that night too, because she'd seemed sad, but when she'd questioned her friend afterwards, she'd claimed it was just tiredness.

The idea of anyone realising how she'd felt about Lucas for years was mortifying, but not as bad as people starting to gossip about why, whenever he was in the department, he often sought out Danni instead of Esther. Had Esther picked up on it, too? Either way, Aidan was right: things between the two of them didn't seem like they usually were and she'd never forgive herself if that had anything to do with her. Danni had been trying her best to be clear about boundaries with Lucas ever since he'd come back, and she deliberately avoided showing him any type of affection, even the sort that was perfectly normal between close friends. But his hand still lingered on her arm longer than it should do, and their conversations were often more intense than they needed to be. When he'd said he didn't trust anyone completely, not even himself, he'd held her gaze until she'd been forced to look away. She wasn't imagining the way he acted around her, and her attempts to put an end to it hadn't worked. Next time they were alone she was going to have to spell it out and tell him to back off.

'I wasn't talking about you, you idiot! I've come to the conclusion you've got higher standards than that; you'd never let Esther get hurt for a start. Have you seen Dr Sarin, though? Lucas definitely has, and he's not the only one.' Aidan tapped the side of his nose. 'Even I almost fancy her and the idea of being with a woman usually makes my testicles go back up inside my body.'

'Good to know.' Danni laughed, the image Aidan had painted not one she wanted to think about for too long. Laila Sarin was a junior doctor, working in the department as part of her hospital rotation. She was striking, with poker-straight black hair, perfect skin and dark brown eyes that always seemed to be smiling. If Aidan wanted to start a rumour that Lucas was always in the department because of Laila, that was far better than anyone pointing the finger at Danni.

Reaching into her pocket, she pulled out the bookmark that Charlie had given her. He might not be staying long, but maybe a temporary distraction was what she needed.

When Richard had come round from collapsing, he'd refused to get into the ambulance at first. But Danni had insisted and had even gone with him, in case he tried to change his mind en route. When Charlie had offered to take care of Brenda, she'd surprised herself by hugging him. He'd smelt good, like sea air, but with a subtle lemony scent clinging to his skin, and he'd felt reassuring solid, like someone she could lean on if the need arose. Brenda was probably lying stretched out on the sofa in his holiday cottage by now, which meant she'd have to see Charlie again very soon, and the thought made her smile.

'What are you grinning about? You've got that look I only ever get when it's date night with Jase and I know I'm guaranteed to get all his best moves.' Aidan narrowed his eyes. 'You know if there's progress with the internet dating, you owe it to me and Esther to share the update. We were there from the beginning, after all.'

'If there's ever anything to tell, I promise you'll be the first to know.' There was no way Danni was mentioning Charlie to Aidan, and there was nothing to say anyway. Just because the fact that she could be attracted to someone other than Lucas was amazing to her, it didn't mean it was big news for anyone else.

'I'd better be, because I need all the vicarious excitement I can get. One date night a month does not make for an exciting love life, and last week Jase actually suggested we take up knitting. I swear it's only because he fancies Tom Daley, but I am not ready to spend my evenings off listening to the sound of knitting needles clacking together just yet.'

'It's supposed to be very therapeutic.' Danni laughed at the look on Aidan's face. 'I'm going to go in and give Richard the update on some of his results, and let him know he's going to be admitted for further tests. Then I'm going to go home before someone else accuses me of not having a life.'

'Take me as a cautionary tale.' Aidan threw his arms out to the side, like a magician about to announce his big reveal. 'Go and grab all the fun you can, before you settle down and start arguing over where to plant the azaleas.'

'You wouldn't swap what you've got now for all the dating opportunities in the world.' Danni had seen Aidan's face light up whenever he got a call from Jase, or when he came to pick Aidan up from work. He might joke about it, but there was no doubt he was in love.

'I wouldn't, you're right. Knitting and gardening might never be my thing, but I'd rather be doing them with Jase than anything else without him.'

'And you said Lucas and Esther make you feel sick!' Danni grinned, not waiting for Aidan's comeback. She liked the proof that love was out there, and that maybe you didn't need to have loads in common for it to work out. With Lucas it was the similarities between them that had given them a shorthand in their relationship: the loss of their parents, and the resulting disappearance of anything resembling a family life, as well as the passion they shared for careers that had run in parallel. Maybe if you took that away, the strength of the pull she felt towards him would finally vanish completely too. Either way, meeting Charlie had given her hope that things could change.

'How are you feeling?' Danni smiled as she entered Richard's cubicle. Whatever the cause of his elevated blood pressure, and the subsequent fainting episode, it had clearly taken it out of him. He looked exhausted.

'Bloody old, but then I suppose I am.' He managed a half-smile, but Danni couldn't help wondering if the contents of the letter had taken their toll on him too. It was a lot of information to cope with, and he might be struggling to process it all, given everything that had happened. She didn't want to overstep the mark in such a sensitive situation, but she had a duty of care to him and Connie, who'd be desperate to know how Richard had taken the news. 'I'm just grateful you were around to help. If you're going to collapse, doing it in front of a doctor seems like a good idea.'

'It was nothing, but I'm glad I was there too. And you're not old. Sixty's the new forty.'

'Yes, but I'm seventy on my next birthday.' Richard smiled again, looking completely different to the man who'd appeared so bitter and angry when Danni had spoken to him at the farm. Maybe hearing from Connie had changed how he felt about everything. She needed to find a way of asking him about the letter, without making it obvious she knew what it said.

'Did you get a chance to read the letter I brought you?' The muscles around Danni's spine felt as if they'd been pulled tighter. She was far more invested in the outcome than she ought to be, but she cared about Connie, and she couldn't pretend that she didn't want things to work out for Charlie too.

'They put me in this bloody nightie for the scan.' Richard pulled at the material of the hospital gown he was wearing. 'I shoved the letter in the pocket of my jacket when you gave it to me in the ambulance, and I don't know where they've taken my clothes.'

'I'll track them down for you.' Danni bit her lip. Richard had no idea about the contents of the letter and she still couldn't tell him.

'Who was it from? It must be important if they sent you to hand deliver it.' Richard frowned and a deep crease appeared above the bridge of his nose. 'I had some blood tests at the GP's a while back. I thought it must all be okay when I didn't hear, but it's bad news, isn't it? That's why I collapsed.'

'I came in to tell you that your scans are all clear. We're going to run some more tests to rule anything else out, but the chances are the collapse was down to high blood pressure and you can be given some medication to control that. You might need to look at your lifestyle, maybe try to reduce your stress levels, but I don't think it's anything serious, and the letter wasn't about anything medical.' He'd asked her straight out, so she owed him at least a partial explanation. 'Another patient asked me to deliver it to you. An old friend of yours... Connie.'

'Connie? My Connie? Is she here?' Richard was already trying to get out of the bed and Danni put a hand on his shoulder. The last thing she wanted was him rushing up to find Connie, before he'd had the chance to read the letter, especially with his blood pressure as high as it was.

'She's on another ward, but she's okay.' Danni did her best to adopt a soothing tone. 'You'll be able to go and see her once we get your blood pressure under control, but for now you need to rest.'

'I can't believe she's written to me after all these years.' Richard looked as though he'd seen a ghost. And in a way, Danni supposed that he had. 'What's she even doing here? Last I heard she was in Yorkshire. I wrote to her so many times and she never replied.'

'From what I understand she was coming down to try and see you, but then she was involved in an accident and ended up here.' Danni's scalp prickled. That was the problem with a partial explanation: it was so easy to get in too deep. And Richard needed to hear the truth from Connie, not from her. 'I don't know what the letter says, or why she wanted to see you. I'm sure it'll explain why she's here now, and what she wanted to say. I'll make sure I find out where it is, and then you can go up and see Connie on the ward, if that's what you both want.'

'Is she really going to be okay? You promise?' Richard's face was etched with worry.

'I promise.'

'I still can't get over the fact that she's here, after all this time, and that she wants to see me. It's all I've wanted for the best part of forty years.' He shook his head. 'Do you mind me telling you all this? I know you must be busy.'

'Of course I don't mind, but don't feel like you have to explain anything if you don't want to.' Danni had lost count of the number of times a patient had revealed their innermost thoughts or shared their life story with her. Sometimes it was because they'd suddenly become aware of their own mortality, sometimes it was because of the drugs they'd been given, but more often than not it happened when the patient didn't have anyone close to them to talk to. And she had a feeling that might be the case for Richard.

'When I started writing to Connie after she left Cornwall, I promised that I'd stop at twenty letters and I did, but I never stopped loving her. My wife knew it too, I'm sure, so I can hardly blame her for what happened.'

'Your wife?' Danni knew she shouldn't be asking more questions. It was Connie who Richard needed to open up to, but she couldn't seem to help herself.

'Fiona. We were engaged when I met Connie. It was what our parents wanted.' So, he had married Fiona after all. 'When Connie left, I told Fiona time and again that she could do better than me, but she was devoted to her parents. I think she'd have walked over hot coals if they'd asked her to. When Connie ignored all my letters, I felt as if something inside of me had died, but it made it easier to say yes to marrying Fiona.'

'I'm sorry.' Danni didn't know what else to say, but she could see the pain in Richard's eyes. So many wasted years for him, Connie and Fiona, because doing the right thing by others had seemed more important than how they felt.

'I'm sorry too and I'm glad Fiona has found someone she really loves.' Richard sighed. 'She's been married to Terry for ten years now, and I even gave her away at their wedding. Both sets of our parents were gone by then, and I think that's why she felt free to choose what she really wanted. No one deserves what I put Fiona through and I should have had the courage to spare her that.'

'It's not always that easy.' Danni shivered, despite the warmth. She hated the thought that Esther could end up like Fiona, in even the tiniest way, with a part of Lucas always loving someone else. She deserved so much more than that.

'It's as easy or as difficult as you make it.' Richard gave her a level look. 'But honesty is always the best policy in the long run. I just never thought I'd get the chance to see Connie again and to be honest the thought of it is terrifying.'

'Maybe it'll be easier once you've read the letter. Sometimes when there's such a lot to say, it's easier to write it down.'

'What if she doesn't like what she sees? I'm not in my thirties any more.'

'Neither is she, and she won't expect you to look exactly the same as you used to.'

'But she will have built up an idea in her head of what seeing me again will be like. In the same way that I've imagined meeting her again hundreds of times. The reality is going to be different, and I don't want to disappoint her. Do you think some things are better left to the imagination?'

'I don't know, but—'

'Sorry to interrupt, Dr Carter.' Lucas's trick of appearing from nowhere seemed to be becoming a habit. 'But I need to have a quick word with you about a patient I've just seen.'

'Okay.' There was an urgency to his tone, but at least she had an excuse not to answer Richard, before she really did say too much. Turning towards the older man, she smiled. 'After I've had a chat with my colleague, I'll see what I can do about tracking down your personal effects. And one of the other doctors will be along with you for a chat about the rest of the tests. I'll make sure Connie knows you're here too and, when you're ready, you can go and see her on the ward.'

'Thank you, Doctor.' Richard reached out and touched her hand. 'For everything.'

'It was nothing at all.' Breathing out, Danni followed Lucas out of the cubicle and down the corridor towards the consultant's office.

'Who's the patient you need to talk about?' She was almost having to run to keep up with him, but he didn't respond until they'd reached the door of the office.

'It's empty and it might be best to chat in here.'

'Is there a problem?' If a patient had made a complaint about a member of staff, Lucas might want to keep it confidential, but he was acting very strangely.

'I think we both know there's a problem.' As soon as Lucas

stepped inside the office, he manoeuvred her towards a corner of the room that couldn't be seen from the corridor. 'I don't know how much longer I can go on like this, Dan. Wanting to touch you and not being able to. Do you know how much I want you? I picture it every single time I close my eyes. It's killing me.'

'You can't say that; you love Esther.' He was so close she could feel the warmth of his breath on her neck, and she knew only too well the agony he was describing. But she couldn't picture it in the way he did, because the only thing she saw when she closed her eyes was her best friend's face.

'Do I? How can I be sure I love her, if I feel like this about you?' He was pressing his body against hers, and it was so hard not to respond. Despite the doubts she'd had about him recently, it was like muscle memory. She'd spent so long imagining moments like this, then fighting her desperate desire to respond when they happened, it was almost as if her body was acting completely independently of her brain. Something was different deep inside her, though, a feeling of her heart gradually starting to harden against him, as his voice took on a self-pitying tone. 'You're the only one who really knows me. We're kindred spirits, Dan, you know we are. It feels like you're my other half and deep down I think we both know it's always been you and me, all along.'

'Why are you saying this now? You've had more than seven years and you asked Esther to marry you. Maybe if you'd said something early on, before she fell in love with you, we'd have had a chance. But I would never risk losing my friendship with Esther, not for anything.' Anger was bubbling up inside her and the hardening of her heart seemed to be increasing with every passing moment. These games had gone on for long enough, but then Lucas played his trump card.

'Esther has no idea what it's like to walk in our shoes, to lose her family and have to find that elsewhere. We found that in each other, you and me. You can't tell me we didn't. I've told you things I've never said to anyone else, and I know you've done the same with me. We know each other from the inside out, and I still love every part of you. You haven't had that sort of unconditional love since you lost your dad, and I can't believe you want to walk away from it. I love you, Danni, more than anyone else ever will.'

Tears filled her eyes and all the feelings she'd ever had for Lucas threatened to flood back as she looked at him. She felt like that little girl again, being packed off to boarding school because no one wanted her. But Lucas was standing in front of her, telling her that he did, and that he understood what it was like to be where she was. How the hell was she supposed to turn her back on that? All she could do was look at him, but the words just wouldn't seem to come.

'Didn't you hear what your patient just said? It was like he was talking about us.' Lucas took hold of her wrists, pinning her arms above her head. She couldn't fight against it, because she was already using every ounce of strength she had to keep her back pressed against the wall, when all her body wanted to do was arch itself towards his. 'I was standing outside the cubicle, waiting to talk to you and listening to him saying how he'd spent all those years married to the wrong woman and longing to be with someone else. That wasn't fair to any of them, and I don't want to do this to Esther, when it's you I really want. If you're worried about this not living up to the fantasy like he said, I can promise you it will. We're meant to be together, and anything else is just a bump in the road we'll find a way of getting over.'

'We can't.' Tears were choking Danni's throat as she dragged her hands out of his grip and pushed him away. She might be throwing away the chance to be with the person who could turn out to be the love of her life, but she was doing it for her soulmate. 'Esther isn't a bump in the road. She's the best person I know, and she's the best person you'll ever meet too. If you can't love her the way she deserves, then you owe it to her to end it. But don't do it for me, because I've finally realised we can't ever be together. Even if Esther was the one who chose to end it, the two of us ending up together would still hurt her, and that's something I could never live with.'

Yanking open the door of the consultant's office, before Lucas could answer, Danni broke into a run and didn't once look back.

16

'How's Richard?' Charlie met her at the door of the holiday cottage. He was wearing a cream cable-knit jumper and Danni found herself wishing she could ask him for a hug. She already knew he gave good hugs and, after what had happened with Lucas, she really felt as if she could have done with one. She hadn't kissed Lucas; she hadn't even responded when he'd tried to make a move on her. Instead, she'd pushed him away and told him to love Esther the way she deserved or set her free to find someone who could. But it still felt as if Danni had cheated on someone, and that someone was Esther. She'd run all the way out of the hospital, not stopping until she reached the taxi rank outside and asked the first cabbie in the queue to take her to Trengothern Manor.

'He's fine. They've ruled out anything really serious, but they're running some more tests.'

'That's great news. I'm so glad you were there when it happened; you were amazing.'

'I didn't do anything really and it's all in a day's work.' She'd done her best to sound breezy and upbeat, but Charlie could see right through her.

'Hey, what's wrong? And don't say nothing, because it's obvious something is.' He ushered her through the door. 'Let me get you a drink. If you don't want to talk about it, at least tea and chocolate biscuits ought to help.'

'It's just been a rough day, that's all.' Danni sat down on one of the squishy-looking armchairs positioned on either side of the woodburning stove. The autumn days were mostly still mild, but the temperature had started to drop sharply by the evening and there was something unmatchable about the comfort that could be derived from the glow of a real fire. Brenda and Maggie both clearly appreciated it and had obviously taken to one another too. Maggie was lying on her side, her back to the fire, with Brenda's head resting a few inches down from hers. They looked like long-term companions, rather than brand new friends, which made the scene in the cottage even cosier. In fact, the whole place, Charlie included, looked like a photograph from a book about hygge and Danni already knew she wasn't going to want to leave.

'I bet you get a lot of rough days in your job?' Charlie fixed her with his bright blue eyes and she nodded.

'More than our fair share.' Guilt seemed to be dogging Danni, because now she felt bad – not only for lying to Charlie, but for blaming her mood on work. 'It's not just that. I've got this friend and I've found out her partner isn't sure if they should be together. I don't know if I should say something?'

'I wouldn't, mainly because of the fact he's not sure.' Charlie frowned. 'If they stay together, you'll be the one blamed for what-ever rocky patch they might be going through, and there's a chance you could get pushed out of their lives altogether.'

'It sounds like you're speaking from experience.'

'I am in a way.' The cottage was open-plan, and Charlie moved towards the kitchen and flicked the kettle on as he spoke. 'My ex's sister got between us. Telling Natalie that the reason she was disappointed every time a big occasion came around, and I didn't propose, was because I was never going to commit to her. Natalie and Imogen had a huge row, and they stopped speaking. These things have a way of spiralling out of control and I had a horrible feeling their relationship might break down for good if I didn't do something. So I admitted that Imogen was right; I wasn't ready to commit to Natalie like that and I didn't think I ever would be, because something that should have been there was missing. When she asked me what it was, so we could fix it, I couldn't tell her, because I didn't know. I just knew it wasn't there and that it never would be.'

'Wow, that must have been hard.' Every time Charlie spoke, there was something new Danni liked about him. He could have kept stringing Natalie along indefinitely, but he'd chosen to be honest. Lucas could definitely learn a thing or two from Charlie.

'It was, but not as hard as it would have been knowing that I'd ruined Natalie's relationship with her sister. They'd always been close and I knew she'd need to lean on Imogen when we split up. So, although I don't think you should be the one to tell your friend, you could try talking to her partner and suggest he has that conversation with her.'

'I did that today. I told him he needs to commit to her properly or let her go, because she deserves better than someone who isn't sure.'

'I think everyone does.' Charlie might have broken Natalie's heart, but he'd given her the chance to find something more than he could offer her. Hopefully, having gone through that, he'd understand why Connie and Richard had done the things they had. Thinking you were doing the right thing might be well intentioned, but it could cause so many problems. 'Right, now we've sorted that out, can we get on to the really important questions? Tea or coffee?'

'Tea for me, please.' Danni allowed herself to relax back into the chair as she watched Charlie making the drinks. This was exactly what she'd pictured when she'd allowed Aidan and Esther to set up her dating profile: finding someone she could talk to about her day and happily do nothing much at all with. She didn't want to replicate the angst of her relationship with Lucas. She just wanted to love and be loved in return.

* * *

Bringing Brenda to the autumn fundraising fete for the hospital was always a risk. There were too many catering options available, and far too many opportunities for Brenda to attempt a hamburger heist as a result.

'Are you going to be on our team, Danni?' Esther's father, Patrick, raised a questioning eyebrow. 'I hope so.'

'Is that because you think I'm the ideal build to be the anchor of a tug-of-war team?'

'No, it's because I've never met anyone as determined as you. Which is why, sweet girl, I always make sure you're on my team at games night.' Patrick winked and Danni laughed. It was true they were always paired up for the infamous games nights Esther's parents hosted. Danni might be almost as competitive as Patrick, but she'd argue he took the overall crown, given that he'd once ended up dislocating his shoulder trying to win a game of Twister. He'd even insisted on carrying on with the games night after Danni had managed to pop it back into place. His wife, Caroline, had only allowed it on the proviso that the Twister mat went straight into the wheelie bin.

'I'd love to join in, but I can't trust Brenda. She's got the scent of barbecuing meat all around her and, even if I tie her up, she's more than capable of pulling a fence post out when she gets on the trail of something.'

'Could one of your colleagues have her for ten minutes? We need you!' Esther's mum, Caroline, wrapped an arm around Danni's waist. 'Patrick knows he's got to have me and Esther on the team, but having two members who barely pass the minimum height is not going to cut it. We need some leverage.'

'Is that all I am to you, the height factor?' Danni laughed again, knowing the real reason Caroline and Patrick were so determined to include her was because they considered Danni a member of their family. More often than not, her own mother would forget special occasions, like her birthday, but there was always a thoughtful gift from Caroline and Patrick. They'd never met Danni's father, but along with Esther, they always remembered the date of his passing too. They'd send flowers, or chocolates, with a note saying they hoped it would give Danni a lift. And Caroline always texted too, checking that Danni was okay and telling her they were always there if she needed someone to talk to.

It was obvious where Esther got her warmth and empathy from; she'd been surrounded by it her whole life. And Danni loved her best friend's parents almost as much as she loved Esther. All of which meant it had been a relief when she'd discovered Lucas wouldn't be at the fundraiser. She didn't want him there, tainting the relationship she had with Esther and her family. Ever since he'd told her how he felt at the hospital, she'd dreaded the time when she had to face him again. His confession had been too raw, too real and too risky, and it had made her more certain than ever that nothing could happen between them, whatever decision Lucas ultimately made about his relationship with Esther. Danni had expected to feel sad about letting go of the fantasy, but now her overriding emotion was of shame that she'd ever allowed herself to consider it. When he'd played on having been the only one to truly love her since her father's death, she'd almost fallen for it. But the truth was that Esther had done that long before either of them had met Lucas. She didn't know how she could ever have risked that, even if she'd tried to rationalise it by telling herself she only wanted a relationship with Lucas if Esther stopped loving him first.

'We've got Gary and Aidan as well. So our team is a mix of A&E staff and Hamilton family members, with me and Danni qualifying on both counts.' Esther shot her a smile and Danni felt some of the tension drain out of her. In the twenty-four hours since Lucas had pinned her up against the wall, she'd driven herself half-mad with the idea that Esther might somehow know what had happened.

'We're up against the midwives.' Aidan moved closer to the group and lowered his voice, as if he was about to impart some terrible secret. 'I asked Gwen to be on our team, but she chose them and it's a mixture of midwives from St Piran's and some from the unit in Port Agnes.'

'There's eight of them in total, so we'll need to find at least one more person.' Gary began scanning the crowd as he spoke. 'I saw Debbie, one of the healthcare assistants, just now. She's always down the gym, and she could turn out to be our secret weapon.'

'Good call.' Aidan looked at his watch. 'But we've only got ten minutes, so you'd better go and find her.'

'I'm on it.' Gary disappeared into the crowd of people milling around the stalls flanking the 'showground' on all four sides. In truth, it was just a fenced-off square in the middle of the meadow behind the hospital, which had been loaned to the fundraising team by the landowner, and had been freshly mown to host the inaugural Friends of St Piran's fundraiser. Gwen and her team of volunteers who ran the shop had come up with the idea and done most of the organisation for the event and the showground was hosting a series of activities, from a dog show to a dance display, and of course the tug of war competition. But the biggest draw of all would be the stall selling the homemade blackberry ice-cream Gwen was famous for, not to mention the blackberry gin she recommended washing it down with.

'Did you manage to track down Richard's effects?' Danni had texted Aidan, asking him to find Richard's clothes and the missing letter, once she was on her way to Charlie's place in the taxi. She'd needed to get away from Lucas, and the hospital, but she hadn't wanted to break the promise she'd made to Richard. The letter Connie had sent him was too important to be left to chance, and it had been up to her to make sure he got it.

'Would I let you down?' Aidan raised his palms. 'I found them within five minutes of you running out of the place like your arse was on fire and made sure I got all his stuff to him before he was taken to the CDU.'

The clinical decisions unit was a short-stay ward, where Richard could undergo further testing before a decision was made about admitting him. It was a relief to know that by the time Danni went into work the next day, he would have read the letter and had the chance to go and speak to Connie face to face if he wanted to. Danni was just praying it would all work out between them. They'd both sacrificed a lot in the past, but they had the chance of getting to know one another again and, even better, of getting to know their son. 'I knew I could count on you.'

'Always, now it's your turn to make sure we can count on you and get someone to look after Brenda, while we show the midwives who the winners are.'

'What about him?' Patrick pointed to someone behind Danni. 'He looks trustworthy and he's already proved he's a dog lover.'

Turning around to see who Patrick was pointing at, Danni smiled. 'Oh perfect, it's Charlie.'

'Charlie, eh?' Aidan looked in his direction. 'I must concur. He does look pretty damn perfect. And how exactly do we know this Charlie?'

'He's the son of one of my patients.' Danni hoped she sounded more nonchalant than she felt, but Charlie had a weird effect on her. She might only just have met Charlie, but he'd already helped her see the situation with Lucas in a different light and accept that it wasn't her responsibility to sort out the problems between him and Esther. So, even if this turned out to be the last time she ever saw Charlie, she'd always be grateful that they'd met.

'Well, go on then, ask him to look after Brenda.' Aidan put his hand in the small of Danni's back, forcing her to move forward.

'Hi, Charlie,' she called out and waved her hand at the same time, as if there was a chance of him not seeing her, despite the fact he was less than twenty feet away.

'Hi.' He smiled, and crouched down as he got to where she was standing, stroking Brenda's head. 'And hi to you too, beautiful girl.'

'Bet you wish he was saying that to you.' Aidan nudged Danni's side, his stage whisper so unsubtle it made her face go hot.

'I need to ask you a favour.' She hoped pretending she hadn't heard Aidan would make Charlie assume he was talking to someone else.

'If it's within my power, and it's legal' – Charlie smiled as he stood up to face Danni – 'consider it done.'

'Could you look after Brenda for about ten minutes, please? I've been roped into the tug of war contest, and I don't trust her not to go on a raiding mission of the food stalls while I'm gone.'

'Roped in, I see what you did there.' Charlie was still smiling, despite assuming the terrible pun she'd accidentally made had been intentional. 'Maggie and I would love to keep Brenda company, and cheer your team on, of course.'

'Have you got any pom-poms you could shake for us?' Aidan pushed his sunglasses down his nose so he could look over the top of them at Charlie.

'Damn, I left them behind today, at the last minute too.' Charlie shrugged. 'But I'll shout out some motivational advice if you like. "Come on, you can do it. Pull harder than the other team." You know, stuff you could never come up with, without me.'

'I've always liked the idea of a personal trainer, commanding me what to do and when.' Aidan was a shameless flirt, but Charlie was taking it all in good fun. He had the sort of laugh that made Danni want to smile, every time she heard it.

'It looks like we've all got our roles, then; now bring back the trophy or there'll be hell to pay.'

'Yes, sir!' Aidan gave a mock salute and hooked his arm through Danni's, as Charlie had taken Brenda's lead from her. 'Come on, then, let's go and find Gary and Debbie, and get warmed up. We can show those midwives that they might still have Gwen, but we've got the muscle.'

'Do you ever think you might be taking these things too seriously, Aidan?' Esther asked as they all walked towards the other side of the showground.

'Not at all, but someone who should be taking things seriously is Danni, preferably with Charlie if she gets half the chance. Now he is a good enough reason to quit internet dating and never look back.'

'He's only down here visiting his mum while she's in hospital. He'll be leaving soon.' Danni hadn't realised how much that bothered her until she said the words out loud. It was ridiculous; the feelings she'd had for Lucas couldn't really just disappear in an instant. Her brain was just protecting her by using Charlie as a distraction, so she didn't have to process what she'd admitted to Lucas about there being no chance of anything ever happening between them. Or come to terms with the seven years she'd wasted, all the time betraying her best friend's trust. Once Charlie left, she'd have to work through things properly, but that didn't stop her wanting to enjoy his company while she could. Just the thought of them being able to walk the dogs together, and go to check on Trevor, made her smile again.

'So what if he's leaving soon? When I said you needed to get serious with him, I wasn't talking about marriage and babies and all that boring stuff.' Aidan shook his head, as if he was having to explain something ridiculously simple to her for the hundredth time. 'I was thinking more of getting *seriously naked* and having some *serious fun.*'

'Now there's an idea.' When Esther responded, Danni was just glad her parents were out of earshot.

'Please tell me you're not encouraging Aidan's flights of fancy! I barely know Charlie.'

'All I know is that it's about time you had some fun, Dan. It's been far too long. I can hardly remember the last time you even went on a date. What's the harm in practising on someone who'll be gone soon? Even if it's a disaster, you'll never have to see him again.'

'He might not even be interested in going on a date.' Danni looked over her shoulder to where Charlie was now sitting on a bale of straw at the edge of the showground, with both dogs looking up at him devotedly.

'Oh he's interested, believe me.' Aidan's tone brooked no argument. 'And if you don't tell him that you are too, then I will. Because that's bloody obvious as well.'

'I'll think about it.' There was no way Danni was going to

confess to Aidan that he was right. Especially when the idea of spending time with Charlie was more appealing than she could even admit to herself.

* * *

'Do you really think Aidan was right about the midwives cheating?' Charlie asked as he and Danni wandered amongst the stalls, twenty minutes or so after the midwifery team had shown everyone else who was boss. They hadn't just won the first heat of the tug of war contest against Danni's team, they'd also beaten three other teams to take the trophy.

'No, he's just a sore loser and they're clearly made of tough stuff. You have to be if you're delivering babies.' Danni stopped to look at him. 'I worked in obstetrics for a little while, during my hospital rotation. It's hard work and really emotional too.'

'So you've delivered babies?'

'I assisted with a couple, and I've overseen a couple of emergencies. The first was when I was part of a pre-hospital critical care team, and we were called out to an accident. One of the passengers went into labour on scene and the baby was born in a layby, on one of the A-roads leading out of London. The other time was when a teenage girl came into A&E with what we thought at first was a severe water infection, until I examined her and realised the top of baby's head was already visible. We nearly had another emergency delivery in A&E recently, and obstetrics was the only other field I considered going into. But emergency medicine won in the end.'

'Luckily for them.' Charlie held her gaze and she came really close to following Aidan's advice and asking him for a drink, but the moment passed, leaving her feeling like she needed to change the subject.

'Can we go and check out the auction stall? Gwen said there are some great things to bid on.' She didn't speak again until they reached the stall, her eyes immediately drawn to a charcoal drawing of a baby seal. 'Oh my God, it looks like Trevor!'

'It is Trevor.' Charlie smiled. 'When I went in to see Connie, I noticed the poster asking for items to be donated for the auction. I did this when I got back yesterday, while I was waiting for you to collect Brenda, and when I offered it as a prize to the lady on the stall this afternoon, she seemed really pleased. I didn't have time to get it framed, but I said I'd organise it if that's what the winning bidder wants.'

'It's beautiful. I can't believe you did it so quickly.' Danni already knew she was going to bid whatever it took to make sure the picture was hers. After all, it was the baby seal she and Charlie had named after her father.

'I do charcoal drawings of all the ideas I have for my illustrations, before I decide if I'm going to take them any further. It helps me see if they're likely to work with the story, and I couldn't resist drawing Trevor. I've offered some signed books for the auction too. It's not much, but after everything the hospital has done for Connie, I just wanted to help. It's really hard not being able to go in again until she's had the chance to speak to my father and Darcy, but I rang the ward this morning to check how she's doing. They said she's doing really well, despite the complexity of her injury and the organ damage that's prolonging her stay. They also said she's only here at all because of the A&E doctor who went out to the scene of the accident and almost certainly saved her life. I can't believe how close it came to us missing out on getting the chance to meet. I wish I knew who to thank.'

'They won't expect thanks; they were just doing their job.' Danni had no intention of telling him it had been her at the scene, but, when she looked up from the drawing, he was staring at her intently.

'It was you, wasn't it? I'd have known from your response, even if the ward nurse hadn't mentioned your name.'

'I just did the same as any of the emergency team would have done.'

'I'm so glad it was you there with her. And even if you don't expect my thanks, you're getting it.' Charlie touched her hand. It was only momentary, but she found herself wishing he hadn't stopped. 'I can never thank you enough, but if there's ever anything I can do to try, just let me know. I'm up for anything: dog-sitting Brenda, dedicating a book on your behalf, or naming my next baddie after someone you can't stand. I know it hardly compares to saving a life, but as a writer and a dog lover, that's about all I've got to offer.'

'It looks like you've got quite a lot to offer from where I'm standing.' Danni might be dying with embarrassment on the inside, she was so out of practice with all of this, but she was determined to harness her inner Aidan and at least try to flirt a little bit. 'And, if you really want to do something to say thank you, even though there's absolutely no need, you could always take me to dinner. Or just out for a drink. Even a walk with the dogs would do.'

That was it, she'd already blown it. Rambling and lowering the stakes every time she opened her mouth. If she'd gone on much longer, she'd have probably suggested a high-five. She'd forgotten how useless she'd always been at flirting, long before Lucas had put a stop to her even trying.

'There's nothing I'd like more than to take you out for dinner. Or if you want to bring Brenda over for a playdate with Maggie, I could cook dinner for you at my place instead. Oh God, that sounds cheap, I didn't mean it like that, it's just...' It was Charlie's turn to be awkward and stumble over his words, and every time he did, she liked him a little bit more. 'It's just easier to talk than when you're in a restaurant surrounded by other people. And I like talking to you, Danni. I really do.'

'Me too. I like talking to you, I mean, not myself!' They both laughed. Whatever else they did or didn't have it common, the two of them were certainly terrible at flirting. And much to her surprise, that suddenly felt like a really good starting point.

17

Connie jumped whenever she heard footsteps coming down the ward towards her room, ever since Danni had told her that Richard had been admitted to the hospital, and that she'd given him the letter. When Danni had come up to the ward to tell her that Richard had been sent for a scan, and that she'd be staying to review the results, Connie had felt panic and relief all at the same time. She was terrified something might happen to Richard, just at the moment when she'd finally have the chance to tell him how sorry she was for keeping the secret of Charlie's birth from him, but she'd also been relieved that it was Danni who was taking care of him and acting as the go-between, at least for now. Danni had called her again later that day, to say that Richard was doing well, but that he hadn't had a chance to read the letter before Danni had needed to leave. She'd promised Connie that one of her colleagues would make sure Richard got all his effects back when he was moved to the clinical decisions unit, and that he'd be able to read the letter then.

Richard had every justification to be angry with Connie when he finally discovered the truth. What she'd done was unforgiveable in hindsight, despite having felt like it was the right thing to do at the time. But part of the relief was also down to the fact that she didn't have to face that anger just yet. She hated the thought of him being ill, but it might give the news a few days to sink in. Then there might be a tiny chance that something other than anger would feature in Richard's response. Connie could cope with him rejecting her, she deserved it, but she couldn't bear the thought he might reject Charlie too, before he'd had the opportunity to really think about things. The idea of either of them losing out on the chance to know one another for a second time, because of her, caused her more pain than any of the after-effects of the accident.

So the last thing she'd expected, the first time she saw Richard in almost forty years, was for him to be smiling as he walked through the door towards her.

'Rich?' It was a question, rather than a statement, even though she'd have known him anywhere. He looked older, there was no denying that, but not much had really changed. His build was exactly as it had been, no thickening around the midriff for someone who worked as hard at farming as Richard always had. His dark hair was heavily peppered with grey now, but still thick and curly, just like his son's. His skin was tanned from spending so much of his time outside, just as it always had been, and he had a few lines, but not as many as Connie saw when she looked in the mirror. One thing she couldn't help noticing was how few laughter lines he had, which resulted in another stab of regret, because she'd missed out on developing as many of those as she could have too. She just hoped the lack of lines around Richard's eyes were due to good genes, and not an absence of joy in the life he'd lived since she'd last seen him.

'Yes, it's me. Although I know I probably look like Old Father Time these days. But you're exactly the same, Connie. Still the most beautiful woman in any room, and still the only person to ever call me Rich. Can I sit down?'

'Of course you can. And I don't know if being called the most beautiful woman in a hospital ward is everyone's idea of a compliment, but I'll take it.' She smiled as he sat down next to her bed, relief flooding her body that he clearly didn't hate her for the decisions she'd made. Even if all his feelings for her were long gone, she was suddenly desperate to tell him how she'd really felt all this time. And when she started to speak, the words came more easily than she could ever have imagined. 'I called you Rich because I wanted to have a name for you that was never on anyone else's lips. That way, a version of you would always be mine.'

'It always was, even after I married Fiona.' Despite half-expecting it, the news that he'd gone through with marrying Fiona was like someone reaching inside Connie's chest and closing their fist around her heart. She shouldn't have allowed herself so much hope that Danni had been right, and that Richard was still single. It was crazy to think he would be after all these years. Even if it hadn't been Fiona, it would have been someone else. This was going to be a difficult conversation, and she was grateful she'd been moved to a private room at the end of the ward. At least no one else was going to be around to witness her tears when they came, and she knew they would sooner or later, because she was already fighting them.

'How is she?' It was stupid, Connie acting as if Fiona had been a friend of hers. She'd never met her, or even seen her in real life. She'd been away visiting extended family the summer that Connie had spent in Port Kara. And the only time Connie had ever seen her was in the photographs Richard had shown her.

'She's fine. Or at least she was the last time I spoke to Terry.'

'Terry?' Connie had forgotten how to breathe. She'd considered the fact that Richard might have other children, perhaps even a son. But now she was faced with the reality that he had a family with Fiona, the tears she'd known were coming were pricking her eyes. She could have had that with Richard and Charlie, but she hadn't even given it a chance.

'He's Fiona's second husband; they've been married ten years and he was our postman for almost twenty years before that. He only does a couple of rounds a week now, and sometimes I don't see him for weeks on end, if I'm not about when the post is delivered. But we always have a nice chat when I do see him, and he always tells me that Fiona sends her love. I don't know if it's true, but I certainly don't deserve it, because I married her knowing I was never going to be able to love her the way I loved you.'

A thousand emotions seemed to be swirling through Connie's head. He was saying the words she'd longed to hear for four decades, things she hadn't even dared to believe he might still feel – especially once he heard about Charlie. She wanted to reach out and touch him, to make sure that the moment she'd dreamt about for so long was really happening. But if she said or did the wrong thing, he might disappear from her life again as quickly as he'd reappeared. Taking a deep breath, she finally found the courage to speak.

'Oh God, I've been such an idiot. I thought I was doing the right thing by leaving and not replying to any of the letters you sent. It was so hard when I read them not to send you a reply, but I didn't want to jeopardise your future. I knew that one day you'd resent me for losing the farm, but I should have answered. I'm really sorry.'

'I knew you thought you were doing the right thing, but I hoped when you read the letters you'd realise that keeping the farm didn't mean anything if I couldn't have you. I told myself I wouldn't keep trying, if you didn't reply by the time I sent the twentieth one. But then I decided it might be different if I saw you face to face, so I got into my car without telling anyone where I was going, and drove all the way up to Yorkshire to find you. I went to the university and that's when I saw you.'

'You came to the campus?' Connie's scalp prickled. If Richard had been there and had seen her, there was a chance he'd realised she was pregnant. If he had and he'd chosen to get back into his car and drive away again, she wasn't sure how to feel, even if that did make her a hypocrite. She'd hidden it well, until she was six months gone, not wanting her colleagues to ask too many questions. But once spring had arrived, and she'd had to ditch the coats and woolly jumpers, it had been far harder to disguise.

'It was almost five months since I'd last seen you and only a week before I was due to marry Fiona. I got it into my head that if I made some big romantic gesture I might be able to change your mind. I even had a ring. You always said how much you loved spring, especially when the cherry blossom came out. So I decided that when I found you, I was going to take you to the nearest cherry tree I could find, and propose to you right there and then. But then I saw you, and the man who had his arm around your shoulders. I knew straight away he was another lecturer; he just had that intellectual look. It was something I'd never have, and I realised then that you probably hadn't replied because what I'd thought of as a great love affair had just been a way to pass the summer for you.'

'That must have been Tim. I was upset a lot that term, crying all the time at the drop of a hat, which I suppose was to be expected in the circumstances. He was a great friend, always there to comfort me, and the only person I opened up to at the university about what was happening. But there was never anything between us. He was like a brother to me; he still is.'

'Bloody hell. There was really nothing going on with him?' Richard widened his eyes and Connie slowly shook her head.

'He was just a shoulder to cry on and, as for the stuff about you not being intellectual enough for me, that's rubbish and you know it. One of things I loved about you was your intelligence. You knew so many things I didn't. You understood the value of nature and how to treat it, long before everyone else cottoned on to the need to care more about the environment. You were passionate about the things you loved, including me, and I've never had that before or since.'

Maybe Connie should have been taken aback that almost four decades of suppressed feelings and hidden truths were tumbling out like this, but she'd already lain so much bare in the letter, and there was no point trying to hide anything from him now. If he could take the news that he had a son as well as he clearly had, then surely nothing else she said could shock him.

'I wish I'd known how you really felt. I thought all the stuff about not wanting me to lose the farm was just a way of letting me down gently, but when I saw you with Tim...' Richard looked up at the ceiling and shook his head. 'I thought I'd already lost the most important thing in the world, and if I lost the farm too, I'd have nothing. So I married Fiona, and I've felt like the worst person in the world ever since. I only managed to start forgiving myself when I saw how happy she was with Terry.'

'This might be a crazy question, but the older I get, the shorter I realise life is, and I need to ask you this, even if I shouldn't: do you think there's any chance we could still get to have what they've got?' Before Richard had walked back into her life, Connie could never have imagined herself blurting out such a bold question. Not when he was as good as a stranger to her after all this time. If someone else had told her they'd done the same, she'd have called it insanity. You couldn't just pick up where you left off; people could change a lot in forty years. And yet, somehow, she instinctively knew he hadn't. The man she'd fallen in love with almost four decades before was still in there, unchanged in all the ways that really mattered. If he could forgive her for concealing Charlie's arrival, surely there had to be a chance for them, and she needed him to know what she should have said in response to every single one of his letters. 'I came down to Cornwall to tell you that I loved you and that I always have. I know you might find it hard to hear, given that I waited until—'

'Those words would never be hard for me to hear.' He cut her off before she could finish, taking hold of her hands. 'Because they're all I've dreamt of hearing since you left. I don't know if there's any chance of us making it work this time, but I do know I want to try. You're right, people are going to say we're crazy for even considering it, and that we don't know each other any more. But I was always more myself with you than I could be with anyone else, and sometimes I think you're the only person who's ever known me. I'll always regret it if we just walk away again.'

'Me too and I don't care what anyone else thinks, but I'm sure the people closest to us will understand eventually.' This was all happening so fast, it was almost like a dream and even in her wildest hopes, she hadn't imagined it going like this. It was as if it had only been a week since she and Richard had seen one another, instead of half a lifetime ago. They already had a bond that time couldn't break, a son who'd tied them together, even when they were apart. Maybe Charlie was the reason they both seemed so willing to jump back in where they'd left off. But she was still going to have to ask the question she'd been dreading, because it would bring home everything that she and Charlie had missed out on with Richard. 'Did you and Fiona have children?'

'It never happened. I always hoped it would and that, if it did, it might finally bring us closer. If we were a family, I thought maybe I'd grow to love Fiona at last and that she might be happier too. When we tried, and they couldn't find a reason why it wasn't happening, I felt like it was my punishment. I'd married Fiona to save the farm, and I wouldn't even have anyone to pass it on to.' Richard sighed. 'It was no more than I deserved, and in a way I was glad fate made me pay a price for what I'd done. What about you?'

'Not after Charlie. I never married either, I didn't even want to try. I thought that was the punishment I deserved, after giving Charlie up, so I inflicted it on myself.'

'Who's Charlie?'

For a moment, Connie couldn't understand the bewilderment on Richard's face, but then she remembered that when she'd written the letter, she hadn't met their son. So she'd referred to him as Saul.

'Sorry, when I wrote you the letter I didn't know the name his adoptive parents had given him, so I put the only name I'd ever known him by.'

'I still don't understand what you mean. You had a baby you gave up for adoption?' Richard furrowed his brow, shaking his head again. 'I haven't read the letter yet. When they gave me back my things, it was missing. One of the nurses said they've been looking for it everywhere, but that it might have been thrown away by mistake.'

'You haven't read the letter?' Connie felt as if icy fingers were closing around her neck. He didn't know about Charlie, which meant he had no idea what she'd done.

'When did you have the baby – when you were younger? Is that why you didn't want to be with me, in case I didn't understand?' Richard took hold of her hand again. 'It doesn't matter to me, and it wouldn't have changed how I felt. Having a baby when you're not ready for it isn't just hard on the parents, it's hard on the child too and it sounds like you did the right thing by him. I can't believe you were carrying all of that burden when we met and kept it to yourself. I wish I could have helped.'

'I was thirty-one when he was born.' Connie's voice sounded robotic, even to her own ears. It was like she was having an out of body experience and watching herself from above.

'But that was after we met. You'd turned thirty the January before you came to Port Kara. So that must mean—' He looked at her for what felt like forever, his mouth half open as he let go of her hand, and then the penny dropped. 'The baby was mine.'

'Ours.' She had to try and make him understand that she'd done what she did for all three of them. 'Giving him up was the hardest thing I ever had to do, even harder than leaving you here and going back to Yorkshire. But I convinced myself it was for the best. I didn't want you to choose me over the farm, just because I was pregnant. I thought you'd hate me for it in the long run, and that I'd end up on my own with the baby. I didn't want him to have the life that Janice and I had growing up.'

'You didn't even give me the choice.' Richard was already on his feet, his voice scarily calm, despite the muscles in his cheek visibly pulsing. 'You let me go on with my life, not knowing I had a child, because you thought there was a chance I might leave you and the baby over a piece of land? I thought you were the one who knew me best, but it turns out you had no idea who I was.'

The turnaround in Richard's demeanour couldn't have been more complete. Five minutes before he'd been willing to risk everything for the chance of rediscovering what they'd had. But now he was looking at her as if he hated her more than anyone else on earth.

'Richard, just let me explain, please.' If Connie could have got out of bed without assistance, she would have grabbed hold of him, dropped to her knees and begged if she had to, just to get him to listen. But she was trapped in the bed and, for the first time ever, he held all the cards.

'There is nothing, not one thing in the world, you could say that would change what you've done.' Richard's eyes flashed as he leant towards her, every word fired in her direction and intended to wound, hitting their target at point-blank range. 'I never, ever want to see you, or hear from you again. In fact, as far as I'm concerned, you're dead.'

'You don't mean that, you can't.' Connie was pleading with him, the tears she'd always known would come streaming down her face.

'Oh yes I can and, like I said, you don't know me, not really. You never have and it turns out I didn't know you either. The woman I thought I loved all these years never even existed.'

'Richard!' She called his name out, again and again, as he turned on his heel, but despite her plaintive cries, he slammed the door behind him. Richard had been back in her life for less than fifteen minutes and this time she knew he was gone for good.

18

Connie couldn't ever remember crying as hard as she had in the hours after Richard had walked out of her room without a backward glance. When she'd left Port Kara at the end of that summer, she'd cried all the way home, but the tears hadn't felt as if they were coming from her soul the way they did this time. Even when she'd had to hand Charlie over for adoption, which had been like someone removing a limb without the benefit of anaesthetic, her tears had been tempered by the certainty that she was doing the right thing. Now all that certainty had gone and the inability she had to stop herself from sobbing, until her whole body ached, wasn't just for losing Richard a second time. It was for them missing out on having their son in their lives, when she'd clearly been so wrong.

'I got your message to come in and see you.' When Charlie appeared at the end of her bed, Connie had been determined to curtail any more tears, but it was hopeless. The sight of him made things worse. This handsome man, who could have been her son for the last forty years, might as well have been a stranger for all they knew about one another. And when he found out the truth, there was every chance he might react the same way Richard had. It was Connie who'd kept his birth secret, and Richard hadn't even known his son existed because of her. Richard had never rejected Charlie, and their son had every right to lay all the blame at Connie's door, just like his father had.

'I'm sorry, I didn't want to cry, and I don't expect you to feel sorry for me. I just needed to see you and tell you all the things I promised to say before someone else does.'

'Does that mean you've spoken to Darcy and my father?' She nodded and Charlie moved to the chair at the side of the bed, taking hold of her hand as he sat down. 'It's okay, you don't need to tell me anything yet, if you're too upset. I'm just glad I can see you again.'

'It's not you.' The fact that Charlie was so lovely just made her cry all the harder. His adoptive parents had obviously done an amazing job.

'I know me suddenly appearing in everyone's lives must be a bit of a shock. But like I said before, I don't need to fill any gaps, and I'm not looking for some sort of Hollywood ending. I just want to know my story.'

'I know you do, sweetheart, and it's not you they're upset with. Darcy was shocked, but thrilled. She always wanted a cousin and, if I'd let her, I think she'd be halfway here by now. But her baby is due soon and there's plenty of time for you to get to know her, I hope.' As Charlie nodded in response, Connie felt a surge of optimism for the first time. He was clearly keen to get to know his cousin, but he still didn't know that she'd kept her pregnancy from Richard. 'But your father...'

'If he doesn't want to know me, that's okay. I was always aware there was a possibility that one or both of you might not want to rake up the past. I'm just glad you want to get to know me, because I really want to get to know you too.'

The weight in Connie's chest was making it hard to talk. She was terrified that when Charlie discovered what she'd done, he'd take back every word he'd just said. 'I don't know how he feels about getting to know you, because I didn't even get the chance to tell him we'd found each other. He was in too much shock, because until yesterday, he didn't even know you existed.'

'You never told him?' An unreadable expression had crossed Charlie's face but, unlike Richard, he hadn't let go of her hand. 'Was he married?'

'No, but he was engaged.' Connie focused on a piece of fluff on the sheet covering her. She couldn't look at Charlie; she wanted to get it all out and she needed to do it in one go. She didn't take her eyes off the fluff until she'd told him the whole story, exactly the way she had to Gwen and Danni. He needed to know that none of this was Richard's fault. She wasn't sure what she'd expected when she finally looked at him again, but his shock was obvious.

'I know Richard.' All the colour seemed to have drained from Charlie's face as he spoke. 'The cottage I've rented is on Trengothern Hall Farm.'

'Oh my God!' Connie felt as if she'd been winded. She'd made such a mess of things and now Charlie was stuck in the middle. He barely seemed to register that Richard had been unaware of his existence until twenty-four hours ago. But then he looked straight at her.

'Why didn't you tell him you were pregnant?'

'I couldn't risk him choosing us over the farm. My mother had told me and Janice time and again never to rely on a man. She said my father resented having to marry her when she got pregnant with me and that he'd never wanted to be a father. It made me feel as if I'd ruined both their lives and I never wanted you to feel that way, not even for a second. But I know what I did was unforgiveable and I've wished more times than I can count that I hadn't made the decision to let you go, even though as I was sure it was best for everyone else. Especially you.'

'It must have been so hard for you going through all of that on your own and what your mother said to you...' Charlie shook his head. 'That's what's unforgiveable, making a child feel that way. My parents always said that my birth mother had given them the greatest gift when she allowed them to be my parents. I felt special and wanted, every single day, and that's how every child deserves to feel. I can understand why Richard was angry, but I think if I explain all of that to him, maybe he'll see things differently.'

'I love you for wanting to try.' The words came so easily to Connie. She wanted to tell Charlie that she loved him, full stop. She had from the moment she'd held him in her arms. Now, the overwhelming surge of love she'd felt had reappeared, undiminished. But she didn't want to put any pressure on him. He'd said more than once that he wasn't looking to fill any kind of gap in his life, but if he was willing to make space for her, she'd take it on whatever terms she could get. But he had to understand that she and Richard didn't come as a package deal. 'He wouldn't even let me try to explain.'

'It might be different hearing it from my point of view.' Charlie squeezed her hand. 'We've got to at least try.'

'I told him the baby's name was Charlie. Do you think he'll realise it's you?'

'I didn't tell him why I was in Port Kara, and it isn't the most unusual name in the world, but I suppose it's possible.' Charlie furrowed his brow. 'So the sooner I have the chance to speak to him, the better.'

'I can't believe you're being so understanding about this. I don't deserve it.' A fresh crop of tears filled Connie's eyes, but the complete desolation she'd felt before Charlie arrived had shifted into something resembling hope.

'You did what you thought was best for me and that's what a good mother does.' He squeezed her hand again, before leaning forward and kissing her cheek. 'I can't promise it's all going to be okay, but I'll do everything I can to make Richard understand, and I'll come back and see you as soon as I've spoken to him. Even if he wants nothing to do with either of us, I'm really glad I found you.'

'Me too, more than you'll ever know.' Connie closed her eyes as Charlie finally let go of her hand. He was leaving and she didn't want to watch him walk away. He'd promised he was coming back, but there was always the chance that Richard would change Charlie's mind, rather than the other way around. And if that happened, she didn't want her last memory of Charlie to be the one of him walking out of her life, just like his father had.

19

Danni stared at the text message she'd written to Esther for at least five minutes before sending it.

Hope everything is okay. Are we still on for the dress fitting this afternoon? xx

She'd deleted and rewritten it three times already, second guessing whether '*Hope everything is okay*' somehow made it obvious that Danni was expecting things to be anything but. If Lucas had spoken to Esther about any of the concerns he'd shared with Danni, then surely the dress fitting would be off. Even if that didn't mean the wedding was cancelled too, Esther would at least want to pause things until she was certain Lucas could commit to her 100 per cent. Her best friend couldn't settle for anything less than that, not if Danni had anything to do with it. Within a minute, a reply had pinged back.

Of course it is and don't you go pulling out on me now! I'm having enough doubts as it is, and I'll probably go into a complete meltdown if you aren't there xx

A wave of nausea swirled in Danni's stomach, but as sick as she felt about the prospect of Esther discovering that Lucas was having second thoughts, she was relieved her best friend didn't know the truth. He couldn't have mentioned anything about his feelings for Danni. Not even Esther was nice enough to go to a wedding dress fitting with the person who was at least partly responsible for derailing her wedding plans, even if Danni had done it for the right reasons. Witnessing what had happened with Connie had proven that having the best of intentions didn't protect you. Charlie had called her after he'd been to see Connie and had told her how Richard had reacted to the news that he'd been a father for almost four decades. When Charlie had asked Danni whether she'd known Richard was his father, she had to admit that she did.

'It wasn't my place to tell you. But I knew that Connie would, as soon as she'd told him.'

'I'm glad you didn't.' Charlie's tone had been gentle and she'd marvelled again at his complete lack of bitterness. He seemed to have a way of seeing a situation from all sides. 'I needed to hear it from Connie, and to see her face when she explained her reasons, otherwise I might have reacted differently. I think if Richard speaks to her again, and Connie has the chance to really explain, he'll see in her eyes that the only person she wasn't thinking of in all of this was herself.'

'He's a fool if his anger makes him shut you out.' With anyone else, Danni might not have been so frank, but Charlie made it so easy to be honest. He had an open, expressive face, and it would have been easy to work out what he was thinking, even if he didn't just come out and say it. Trying to read between the lines of Esther's text was nowhere near as straightforward.

You're having doubts about the wedding? Shall I call you? Xx

Danni could see the pulsating dots indicating that Esther was responding, and she held her breath, not knowing what to hope for. It would be so much easier to have a meaningful conversation over the phone than by text, but she had no idea what the hell she was going to say. The wait for a reply to come through seemed to take forever.

Ha, ha, funny! Can you imagine Mum if I said I was having second thoughts, I think she might actually kill me after how much she and Dad have shelled out for this wedding 😂 I'm just still not sure about the dress, but you've already cheered me up. I read online that every bride doubts whether she's chosen the right dress, but you're the only person I can trust to be completely honest with me and tell me if I've made a mistake. See you at eleven, and be warned, Mum and Nan want to try and find outfits too. It could be a very loooonnnng day! xx

The nausea was back by the time Danni had finished reading the message. Lucas clearly hadn't told Esther he'd been questioning the decision to get married. But worse than that was Esther's total trust in Danni to be honest with her. She wanted to be worthy of Esther's faith in her, she really did, but she stood to lose so much. Charlie had warned her not to get involved. Of course, he didn't know the details, or that she was the one behind the groom-to-be's doubts. But she didn't want what she had with Charlie to be tainted by the mess she'd managed to make of things with Lucas. He'd be gone by the end of the summer and she needed at least one good memory to take with her if she ended up having to leave Cornwall too.

It was almost ten already. She just had time to take Brenda for a quick walk on the beach, to try to shake off the impending sense of doom that seemed to be building in intensity. Maybe Lucas had tried to say something, but talking things through with Esther had made him realise his doubts were just last-minute nerves. And maybe she and Brenda would spot a flying pig when they were down on the sand.

* * *

'Right, I need you to be completely honest with me when I come out.' Esther's voice drifted from the other side of the bridal shop, where the assistant was helping her into her dress behind a curtained-off area. 'No telling me I look amazing, if I really look like an explosion in a marshmallow factory.'

'We'll be completely honest, I promise.' Danni exchanged a look with Esther's mother, Caroline, and smiled. It wasn't going to be a difficult promise to fulfil, because they'd both been there when Esther had chosen the dress and she'd looked breath-taking.

'Okay, this is it – hit me with it.' Esther emerged from the dressing room and her grandmother immediately started to dab at her eyes with a tissue. How Esther could ever have thought she looked like a marshmallow was beyond Danni. The dress was ankle-length, ivory chiffon, with a solid panel beneath the main part of the dress, and sheer sleeves. A V-neck that wrapped across her body was the perfect shape for someone like Esther, who would have had the figure of a ballerina if it hadn't been for her bust. The dress was classy, with just a hint of sexiness, and there was only one way to describe how Esther looked in it.

'You're so beautiful, especially as you don't even realise it.'

'Are you sure I don't look like a little girl dressing up in my mother's best nightdress?' Esther went up on tiptoes and looked at herself in the mirror. 'Why couldn't I just be a couple of inches taller?'

'Because you're lovely the way you are.' Esther's grandmother, Lilian, held a hand out towards her. 'And you know all the best things come in small packages. Just like me.'

'Well, I do get my lack of height from you.' Esther grinned for the first time.

'And your gorgeous hair colour from your mum.' Lilian looked at her daughter-in-law. 'Although Caroline's comes out of a bottle these days.'

'Nan!' Esther widened her eyes, but Caroline just laughed.

'I wish I had your bust, Essie, but you owe the generosity of that to your father. Patrick's definitely got the boobs for a V-neck.'

'Poor Dad.' Esther shook her head, but she was laughing too, and Danni couldn't help joining in. When she'd first met Esther's family, they'd been warm and welcoming, but she hadn't been sure how to react to the way they teased one another. It was only when Patrick had asked Danni if she was any relation to Ronald McDonald, after she'd tried dying her hair red one summer, that she'd realised they really did think of her as one of the family. Giving each other a ribbing was their language of love and, in addition to the nickname of Haggage that Esther had given her, Danni loved the fact that Patrick's pet name for her was Ronnie. It meant she was an honorary Hamilton.

'He doesn't mind; according to him, they're well-developed pecs.' Caroline shrugged. 'We all think you're beautiful, but the question is, how do you feel?'

Esther looked at herself in the mirror for a long moment, smoothing the dress over her hips. 'Actually, I think I love it.'

'Thank God for that.' Caroline let go of a long breath.

'I've got something for you.' Danni twisted the watch on her wrist, which Esther had bought her for her thirtieth birthday.

Danni hadn't wanted to make a big deal of her birthday as there was no one special in her life who wanted to mark the occasion with her. Her mother didn't even mention it and although her brother, Joe, had sent her a beautiful card and a gorgeous pair of earrings, he was on the other side of the world. So when Esther had suggested that they go to dinner at her parents' house, Danni had just been grateful she had somewhere to go with people who loved her. But when she'd got there, Danni had arranged a surprise party with their friends and colleagues. Caroline and Patrick had laid on a buffet with all her favourite foods, and Lilian had made her a three-tier birthday cake – one for each decade.

There'd been so many gifts, including the beautiful watch Esther had given her, with an inscription on the back.

Time goes by, but you'll always have me

Danni had worn it every day since, and it meant more to her than any other gift she'd ever received. It was priceless, just like the friendship it represented.

She'd searched everywhere to find the perfect gift to match the meaning behind the watch. When she'd seen it, she'd been certain it would go with the wedding dress, but the last thing she wanted was for Esther to feel under any pressure to wear it – especially when she'd clearly been having so many doubts about the dress. 'I don't want you to feel like you have to wear it on your wedding day, but if you like it, it could always be your something new.'

Danni took the box containing a necklace out of her bag and handed it to Esther, watching as her friend read the label.

This infinity knot represents a love that can never end. Marriage is a continuation of that, but whatever life brings you, I want you

to know that this is how I'll always see our friendship. Nugget
and Haggage forever xxxx

'Oh, Dan, I love it.' Esther launched herself at Danni, seeming to forget that she was wearing a wedding dress, and any worries Danni might have had about whether she'd done the right thing disappeared. Even if the worst happened, and Lucas told Esther that his doubts about marrying her were down to Danni, at least she'd had the chance to tell her best friend how she felt about her – how she'd always feel about her, no matter what.

'When you gave me the watch, you made it hard to equal, but I wanted to try.'

'You two!' Caroline put her arms around both of them. 'My girls. I'm so glad we're all back living close together; it wasn't the same with you halfway across the country, Danni.'

'No it wasn't.' Esther looked up at her. 'And you've got to promise me you won't ever pull a stunt like that again, and move away. Otherwise I'm going to ask Aidan to be my maid of honour instead of you.'

'He'd probably organise a better hen night.' Danni wrinkled her nose.

'As long as I'm with the women who mean the most to me, I don't care what we do.' Esther looked at Lilian. 'Although you quite like the idea of a *Magic Mike* night, don't you, Nan?'

'Try everything once, that's my motto!' Lilian laughed. 'After all, you only regret the things you don't do. Remember that, girls!'

Danni forced a smile, looking at three generations of women from the family she'd come to think of as her own. She'd never regret not acting on her feelings for Lucas. But if she lost these women, she had a feeling that, for the rest of her life, she'd regret telling Lucas he needed to be honest. That was the measure of her love for Esther, though, and it was a chance she was just going to have to take.

Charlie opened the door to the holiday cottage and gestured for Danni to go in ahead of him. 'I know this is probably old-fashioned at best, and sexist at worst, but my parents always taught me to hold the door open for a lady. And, seeing as there are three of you, I think you should all go in ahead of me.'

'I'm not offended by it, but I can't vouch for Brenda or Maggie.' Danni laughed as the basset hound let out a low moan, lifting her head into the air, already on the trail of her latest quarry. That was the thing with hounds of any sort: if they got the scent of something, nothing could stop them. And Brenda wasn't the only one who'd noticed what smelt very much like fresh cookies. 'Have you been baking?'

'I promised you biscuits if you came back for a drink after our walk, didn't I? But I didn't think you'd come if I told you I'd made them myself.' Charlie shrugged and his self-effacing charm was definitely part of his appeal.

'I think I'll risk it, but only because I'm a fully qualified medical professional.'

'You can go off people, you know.' Charlie smiled and Danni had an almost overwhelming urge to trace the outline of the dimple that always appeared in his cheek. Somehow she resisted, even though imagining what it would be like to touch him had made her fingers tingle. Apart from a few hugs, mostly to say hello or goodbye, they hadn't had much physical contact. They'd been for a drink and out to dinner, and she'd thought about kissing him at the end of the night on both occasions. Danni had never had the confidence to make the first move, but that didn't stop her thinking about what it would be like to kiss him. Just that morning, on their walk, she'd tripped on an old tree root and Charlie had needed to catch hold of her to stop her from falling. It was hardly romantic, but that didn't stop her body from reacting to his touch.

'Come on in and sit down. What can I get you to drink?' Charlie went into the kitchen area, while Danni took a seat on the sofa, with Maggie and Brenda settling themselves down by her feet.

'Tea would be great, thanks.' On the table in front of Danni was another of Charlie's sketches. It was a of a basset hound, rolling on its back, with its paws in the air, and it was unmistakeably Brenda.

'That picture is amazing; you're so talented.' As she spoke, Maggie made the biggest huffing sound and Charlie laughed.

'You're upsetting Maggie, paying me too much attention and not giving enough to her. She's feeling it lately, especially now she knows Brenda is my new muse. That dog is so funny.'

'Oh sorry, Mags.' Danni leant down and stroked the dog's velvety-soft head. Brenda lazily opened one eye, and then thought better of making the effort to move, closing it again. 'You're a beautiful girl and I know you're still Charlie's favourite.'

'One of them.' He gave Danni a slow smile as he set the plate of biscuits down on the table, making her want to reach and touch him all the more. She really liked having Charlie as a friend, though, and she couldn't risk ruining that, especially while they both needed to be there for Connie. 'Tea's coming right up.'

'Great.' She picked up another sketchbook from the arm of the sofa. 'Are you working on a new book?'

'I'm just playing around with ideas at the moment, but I really think Brenda could have her own series.' When Charlie had gone down to Danni's place, to meet them for their walk, Brenda had come galloping down the hallway with a pair of Danni's pants hanging off her head. Of course they couldn't be the lacy kind, or

even the particularly good kind – they had to be the most volumi-
nous pair she owned.

'I think she's got a bag for life stuck on her head.' Charlie had
raised his eyebrows quizzically, giving Danni the perfect opportunity to play along. Instead, for some reason she'd never understand, she'd told him they were her pants. He'd laughed then, and
because it was Charlie, she'd found herself laughing too. He never
made her feel on edge, or as though she needed to be something
she wasn't. That was something she'd never had before, not even
with Lucas.

'If you write a book about Brenda, just promise me you won't
put in the bit about my knickers.'

'I'm not sure I can make that promise. Kids love stories about
things like that, or any reference to bums and bogeys. It's why I love
writing for them so much.' Charlie grinned again as he brought the
pot of tea over to the table.

'I've ordered some of your books.' It was an admission she
hadn't been planning to make, but she couldn't seem to stop
herself from being honest when she was around Charlie.

'I could have given you some, if you'd asked.' He sat down next
to Danni and her fingers started to tingle again. Stopping herself
from making the first move was becoming more and more tricky.

'Nice girls don't like to ask.'

'You see, that's the problem, because nice guys always think
they should wait until they're asked. So that leaves us with a bit of a
dilemma.' Charlie fixed her with a look that finally allowed her to
reach out to him.

'I don't think it does.' At that point, Danni couldn't have
stopped herself if she'd tried. Leaning forward, she didn't take
her eyes off his until their lips finally met. He didn't move a fraction and there was no attempt by him to duck away. And when
they kissed, it was obvious he'd been waiting for this moment

every bit as long as she had. She'd told herself not to expect it to live up to what she'd been imagining, and that first kisses were always awkward, but it was like they'd been practising for months to get it right, and she desperately didn't want it to end there. When she started to unbutton his shirt, he pulled back to look at her.

'You don't have to, I mean, I...' He shook his head, taking her hands in his. 'I want to, I really, really want to, but I don't want you to feel like it's what I'm expecting. I promise that's not why I was up at six making you biscuits, just to try and lure you here. We don't have to rush into anything.'

'I'm not rushing and I'm not expecting anything. I know you won't be around for much longer, but it's been years since I did anything like this. I really like you, Charlie, and I don't want you to feel pressured either. But if this is what you want, I promise you I want it too.' Danni laughed. 'Just not in front of the dogs.'

'Thank God, because I was about to say the same thing.' Charlie kissed her again and all the things that had held her back from intimacy for so long went out of her head. She just wanted to be with Charlie and, whatever happened between them, she knew she'd never regret finally making the first move. It was time to start living a life of her own again, and she'd always be grateful to him for showing her the way.

* * *

'Where have these wet towels come from?' Danni picked two of them up as she headed towards the lounge area of the cottage. The teapot they'd abandoned almost an hour earlier was still there, but the dogs had clearly made short work of the biscuits when they'd been left to their own devices. Thankfully Brenda had the constitution of an ox and she had a feeling Maggie did too, because Charlie had told her just how many times his beloved Labrador had stolen food she wasn't supposed to eat.

'That'll be Maggie. I left the door to the washing machine open and she likes to take the towels out if she gets the chance. With a bit of training she'd probably make a good helping dog, but as it is she's more of a hindrance.' Charlie rubbed the Labrador's head. 'It's a good job I love her as much as I do.'

'Who wouldn't? Do you think the tea's still drinkable?' Danni picked up the pot to see if the sides were warm. She'd expected to feel awkward or nervous around Charlie, after what they'd just done. With everyone else, she'd always second-guessed what they were thinking after they slept together, wondering if they'd been disappointed, but never even hinting at her own disappointment in how things had gone. Maybe that was why it was different with Charlie, because disappointment was the furthest thing from her mind. Whatever it was that had been broken in Danni by loving Lucas and getting nothing in return, Charlie had done more to help fix it than the mountain of self-help books she'd waded her way through.

'I can make us a fresh pot. How about a sandwich? Are you hungry?'

'Starving.' Her stomach gurgled in agreement and she kissed Charlie again, this time without any expectation. 'Thank you.'

'What for?'

'For making me a sandwich, for all of it, for just being you.'

'Being me is what I do best.' Charlie had summed up everything she liked so much about him in a single sentence. He was always *just him*. 'Give me five minutes and I'll make you the best sandwich you've ever tasted. Well, today at least.'

'Sounds perfect.' Danni curled her legs underneath her on the sofa and Maggie positioned her head on the armrest, staring up with her bright, soulful eyes.

'It's all right, girl.' Danni whispered the words. 'I'm not trying to take your place, I promise. But I really do like him.'

'Did you say something?' Charlie called out.

'No, I was just going to ask if you'd had a chance to speak to Richard.'

'Not yet. He put a note through my door the day after Connie told him everything, saying he was going to stay with a friend in Devon and that I should contact John, in the farm office, if there are any problems with the cottage while he's gone. So I don't know if he's got any idea that I'm the same Charlie that Connie told him about.'

'It must have been a lot for him to take on board, and it's probably for the best that he's taking a few days away. He might be able to see things a bit differently when he's had a chance to process everything.'

'I hope so.' Charlie sighed. 'It's awful seeing Connie so cut up and I know she's hoping he'll get in touch when he's calmed down. Talking of getting in touch, someone is clearly trying to get hold of you.'

Danni's phone had pinged for the fourth time since they'd come back out of the bedroom, but when she lifted it up she pulled a face. 'The last three notifications are all messages from a dating site I was on, asking me if I want to renew my trial membership, because it runs out at the end of the week.'

'And do you?'

'No, of course I don't.' The resoluteness of Danni's response surprised even her.

'I don't want you to feel you've got to say that for my benefit. If I was staying, I'd really be hoping that you wouldn't want to stay on there. Even then, I know it would be wrong for me to ask.' Charlie stared at the floor for a moment, before looking back at Danni. 'But you'll be kicking yourself if you miss the man of your dreams, because of me. I just don't want to know when you've found him. In fact I might have to block you on all social media forever, so I never have to see you with someone else.'

Charlie laughed, but the truth was that Danni felt the same way. She wanted this little bubble they were in to stay that way, even if it was only in her head.

'I don't want to delete the app because of you.' It was only a half-lie, because Charlie was at least partly responsible for her not wanting to renew her membership. Meeting him had proved she needed to follow her instincts, if things were going to change. Looking through profiles online would never enable her to do that, and the types of men who were interested in her didn't help. 'I could show you the sort of matches I get. Then you'll see why I want to quit. I should have known what I was letting myself in for when I saw the name: Soulmate Selections. Honestly, you need to see it for yourself. I'd rather take holy orders than date any of this lot.'

'I wish I didn't have to go.' Charlie gave a look that made her wish he didn't have to go either. 'But as good as Mum and Dad have been about me tracking Connie down, I know it would break their hearts if I stayed down here. Mum had breast cancer last year, and the treatment went well, but I'll never take having them around for granted again.'

'You don't have to explain, Charlie. Like you said, if things were different...' She couldn't quite believe how much she wished they were. But maybe if they had been, none of this would have happened. She'd been able to act on her attraction to Charlie because of the fact he wouldn't be around for long. Otherwise it would have felt like too much of a risk. Knowing it was going to end before it even started felt safer, but that wouldn't stop her missing Charlie when he was gone. 'I just hope you aren't too riddled with guilt when you see what I'm left to pick from.'

'How does the app work?' Charlie sat down next to her.

'Are you going to tell me you're a dating app virgin?'

'Guilty.' Charlie held up his hands, his blue eyes twinkling at the look of shock that must have crossed her face. 'You've seen me in action. I'm awkward enough when I meet a girl I like in the real world, even when there's no prospect of a date. Imagine what I'd be like if I went on a date with someone I'd met online. I'd embarrass myself and make her wish she'd swiped whichever way deleted my profile from her phone forever.'

'You've got no idea how lovely you are.' Danni planted a kiss on his cheek, secretly glad that he wouldn't be signing up to all the apps once he left Port Kara. 'On Soulmate Selections you have to set up a profile and answer a load of questions, including how your friends would describe you. Then you can put a heart on any profiles you like the look of. If you pay a fee, you get matched with anyone whose profile you've selected, as long as they've selected yours too. Men can see the matches, but only women can make the first contact.'

'I feel rejected already.' Charlie grinned as she opened the app and another reminder to pay a hundred pounds to sign up for the next three months popped up on the front page. 'Imagine paying for membership and not getting a single match.'

'Some of them don't deserve a match.' Danni shook her head. 'You can filter by what people are looking for, but I didn't realise at first. Then, when I looked at my matches, the only ones interested in me were the married ones looking for fun.'

'All of them?'

'At least 80 per cent. I'll show you. We'll filter the profiles for the married ones first and I'll like some of them. Then we'll do the same with some people who actually want a relationship. I guarantee you I'll get more matches from the married ones.' Danni applied the filter and started scrolling through. 'Most of these men are lucky to have wives at all. They should be showering them with affection and thanking their lucky stars for what they've found, rather than looking for more on the side.'

'They should be doing that anyway.' Charlie caught her eye for a moment and she had to look away. He'd be leaving soon; this was just a stepping stone into whatever came next. Every time she saw Charlie it got harder to remember that he was only ever supposed to help her move on from Lucas.

Danni laughed. 'You really are too nice for this world.'

'Now there's someone who could probably get as many matches as he wants.' Charlie tried to take the phone from her, but it was like her hand had been welded to it. The face staring back at her was so familiar, she could have described every single detail of it. Danni jumped as Charlie touched her arm. 'Are you okay?'

'I know him.' Swallowing hard, she finally dragged her eyes away from the screen and looked at Charlie. 'You know I told you about my best friend, whose fiancé was having doubts about whether they should get married?'

'Yes.' Charlie's hand was still on her arm.

'Well, this is him, in the photo.'

'Oh God, that's not good. I would ask you if you're sure, but I can tell by the look on your face.' Charlie tried to take the phone again, and this time she relented. 'Maybe if we look at the profile, we'll find something obvious that proves it isn't really him and that someone has just stolen his photo from Instagram and set up a fake profile. Apparently it happens all the time, and they always use photos of guys who look like him. My mum's best friend, Sheila, got duped by someone like that and ended up sending him ten grand of her savings, before she realised that her American pilot boyfriend was really a woman, living in Glasgow. She'd chatted to "him" over video calls and everything, but it's scary how good the technology they use to trick people is.'

'I hope that's what it turns out to be.' Danni closed her eyes for a second, silently praying that Charlie was right. But deep down, she already knew he wasn't. Lucas wasn't having doubts about his engagement to Esther because he was in love with Danni. He just wanted to do what so many before him had done, and give himself an excuse to cheat. And the worst part of it all was that Esther had absolutely no idea who the man she was about to marry really was.

20

Working a shift with the pre-hospital critical care team couldn't have come at a better time for Danni. Her mind was working overtime, thinking about the situation with Lucas and Esther, and whether there was a way to approach it that wouldn't result in losing her best friend. Although the A&E department was almost always busy, there'd be peaks and troughs, which might have given her too much time to dwell on things. But shifts with the pre-hospital team were never quiet. The service had to cover a wide area, filling in the gaps for complex cases when the air ambulance was deployed elsewhere, which meant the chances of having a quiet shift were almost non-existent.

The first job came within twenty minutes of Danni's shift starting. It was a call out to the kissing gate between Dagger's Head and Penwick Point. It was on a track that veered off from the main coastal path, but the views from Penwick Point made it a popular spot for picnics, where couples could take the perfect selfie of a romantic day out.

'Okay, the information we have so far is that the patient's name is Glen, a male aged thirty-three, with a severe bleed and possible break to at least one lower limb.' Jonty, one of the paramedics, gave the briefing as they arrived. There was no vehicular access to the site of the accident, so they were going to have to leave the ambulance at the closest point they could reach, about two hundred metres away from the kissing gate. 'The good news from reports on site is that he's had some initial first aid from an off-duty nurse who works at St Piran's, but the worry is that she'd been unable to stop the bleeding at the time of the last update.'

'Okay, we need to get down there fast.' Danni could feel the adrenaline pumping through her veins. This type of situation always felt like the reason she'd chosen emergency medicine. Even when an incident bore no relation to what had happened to her father, every time she was able to make a difference to the pre-hospital treatment of a patient, it felt like a tribute to him. 'If he's got a broken femur, that could cause catastrophic uncontrolled bleeding and the sooner we can get a traction splint on, the better.'

'Let's go.' Jonty passed some of the equipment out to Danni and Julia, the other paramedic, in what was such a well-rehearsed routine it almost felt choreographed. The team underwent so much training in preparation for incidents like this, they knew exactly what would be needed.

As they moved along the coastal path, to the point where the track led off towards the kissing gate, Danni slipped on the loose surface beneath her feet more than once. There were small stones on the path, almost like patches of gravel, and it was so easy to be wrong-footed if you didn't pay attention to where you were walking.

'I can see them, just up ahead.' Julia called out as the kissing gate came into sight and, just in front of it, there was someone lying on the ground, with a woman kneeling by his side, and a bare-chested man holding his head in his hands crouched on the floor nearby.

'It looks like there might be more than one injury.' Danni picked up the pace, and the woman kneeling next to the patient suddenly looked up.

'Oh thank God.' Danni recognised her immediately. She was one of the nurses working on Connie's ward and her name had stuck in Danni's mind because it was so unusual. And she'd told Connie, on one of the occasions when Danni was there, that it was her first job after completing her training.

'Hi, Thalia. I don't know if you remember me, but I'm Danni, one of the A&E doctors, and this is Jonty and Julia.' She gave the young nurse what she hoped was a reassuring smile. She'd been in this position herself before, having to provide first aid, not long after she'd started her medical training. Despite being the most qualified person on scene, it had still felt hugely daunting, and the responsibility had been overwhelming when there was no one else around to consult with.

Thalia was applying pressure to the wound on the patient's leg, with blood soaking through what looked like it had once been a pale blue T-shirt. She'd elevated the patient's leg too, using two rucksacks. But even before she spoke, it was obvious the steps she'd taken to try and stop the bleeding weren't having any effect.

'I just can't seem to get the bleeding under control. Jimmy gave me his T-shirt, so I could use it when I put pressure on the wound, but it just keeps coming. We managed to get Glen's shorts off, so I could get a proper look at his wound. I can't see any sign of a bone, but he's got a deep gash to his thigh and I think from the pain he's describing that he might have broken his femur. He's got no pain anywhere else, but he's in agony with his leg.' A groan from the patient backed up Thalia's words.

'Thank you, you've done a great job.' Danni gave the young nurse a brief smile before crouching down by the patient. She was relieved to hear that this breathing was regular and even, but she needed to carry out a top-to-toe assessment. 'Hi, Glen, I need to check you over to make sure we don't miss any other injuries that might not be as obvious as your leg. There's no pain in your neck or back, is that right?'

'Uh huh.'

'And you didn't hit your head when you fell?'

'My leg took the full force of the landing.' Glen grimaced in pain, his face completely ashen. There was no time to waste given the extent of his bleeding and they needed to work as a team, while Danni continued her assessment.

'We're going to give you some pain relief, Glen. Is there anything you're allergic to?'

'Morphine makes me really sick. I had it when I dislocated my knee playing football and it was almost worse than the pain.' He grimaced again, emitting a low moan from the effort of talking. 'But this is so much worse.'

'I think we'll try some ketamine in that case.' Danni looked at Jonty and Julia, giving them a small nod; their regular training meant they could all slip seamlessly into action. They'd need to administer the pain relief and check Glen's vital signs, to decide whether the blood loss might be at risk of sending him into shock. They would also give Glen oxygen via a face mask and check his neovascular function, to make sure it was safe to administer the pain relief. All of which would leave Danni free to see if she could stop the bleeding and to complete her assessment of his injuries. He was going to need some antibiotics too, given the risk of infection spreading from the wound on his leg.

'Okay, let's take a look at what we've got here.' Danni lifted up the T-shirt stemming the blood, and there was a large open gash on his thigh. It was clear from the alignment of the upper part of his leg that there was a break of the femur, and Danni turned back towards Thalia. 'Can you reapply the pressure, until I can pack the wound.'

'I didn't want to try that without sterile dressings, in case there was a risk of infection.' Thalia looked like she might burst into tears at any moment. She'd had to make spur-of-the-moment decisions and she was clearly doubting herself.

'You did the right thing.' Danni gestured towards the man sitting further down the track, with his head in his hands. 'What about Jimmy, is he okay?'

'He's just in shock, I think. He saw Glen slip and then keep going until he hit the rocks at the top of the cliff edge.' Thalia shuddered. 'I think it's the idea of what might have happened if he hadn't broken his fall that's really freaking Jimmy out. He managed to pull Glen back up to the path, to stop him falling any further, but he's terrified he might have made the injuries worse.'

'You've both done the best for Glen you possibly could.' Danni briefly rested a hand on Thalia's shoulder, before raising her voice and turning towards the patient. 'Okay, Glen, I'm going to pack your wound now with a sterile dressing so we can stem the bleeding. Then we're going to put a traction splint on to help stabilise the bone, because I think Thalia's right and you've broken your femur. But we can confirm all of that once we get to the hospital. How are you doing?'

'Better now.' Glen's voice was muffled by the mask, but his face was already a better colour as the pain relief started to kick in.

'How are his vitals?' Danni looked towards Jonty and Julia.

'All stable at the moment, including his femoral pulse.' Julia accompanied her summary with a thumbs up and there was an audible sigh of relief from Thalia.

'Great stuff.' Danni gestured towards Jimmy with her head.

'Can you just see how Glen's friend is doing? It's obviously been a nasty shock.'

'No problem.' As Jonty headed off to assess whether Jimmy might need any treatment, Danni got to work packing the wound, before securing it firmly with a bandage. If that didn't work, there were a couple of other things she could try, which would reduce the blood supply to the wound, but there was always a risk those techniques could reduce the blood supply to the rest of Glen's leg too. Thankfully packing the wound seemed to be working.

'It looks like that's stemmed the bleeding.' Danni resisted adding the words *for now*. If it bought them enough time to apply the traction splint, that could help reduce further bleeding too. 'I'm going to apply the splint now.'

Danni moved quickly. Placing the splint under Glen's leg, she adjusted the length, before attaching straps across his thigh and ankle.

'How's your pain, Glen?' Danni addressed the patient, who opened his eyes briefly.

'Yeah, good.' The drugs seemed to be doing their job, so Danni felt confident about applying the traction, which would help realign the broken bone. It was a delicate procedure that always carried the risk of injury to other areas, but things could be far worse for Glen if she didn't do it. Holding her breath, Danni extended the inner shaft of the splint.

'Arrghh!' Despite the pain relief, Glen had clearly felt something. But as soon as the procedure was over, he seemed to relax again.

'That's it, you're doing great.' Danni adjusted the straps as she spoke. 'Julia, can you check the femoral pulse again please.'

Danni checked the pulse in Glen's foot at the same time and breathed out slowly. The bleeding seemed to have stopped and all indications were that the splinting hadn't affected his neurovascular function.

'Is he going to be okay?' Jimmy suddenly appeared at Danni's side. He looked pale and wide-eyed, but relief flooded his face as she nodded.

'I think he's broken his femur and he's got a nasty gash on his leg, but it doesn't look like he's sustained any other injuries. We can't be sure until we get him to the hospital, but we're ready to move now.'

'Bloody idiot!' Jimmy shook his head, but then he smiled, standing next to Glen and taking hold of his hand after he'd been transferred onto the stretcher. 'You scared the life out of me. Only you would think you had to run ahead like that to try and make the proposal a big thing, when you know I'd have said yes if you'd asked me in the middle of washing up.'

'Sorry, I just wanted to make it special.' Glen's voice was still muffled by the face mask, but he looked a lot more comfortable as the group began to make their way along the track, with Jonty and Julia manoeuvring the stretcher. It was a bumpy route back to the ambulance, but they'd decided it would be okay if they took things slow enough.

'Glen was going to propose.' Thalia turned and gave Danni a half-smile, as they edged along the track behind the stretcher, carrying the rest of the equipment. 'I tried to keep him talking while we were waiting and he told me what his plan had been. He wanted to run ahead of Jimmy to get to the kissing gate, so he'd be ready to propose when Jimmy got there.'

'Idiot.' Jimmy repeated his earlier assertion, but there was real affection in the word nonetheless. 'He had it all planned. You know what the tradition at the kissing gate is, don't you?'

'Not really.' Danni had heard the term, but had never really understood why it was called that.

'You have to close the gate to allow the other person to start passing through, but the tradition is that you don't release the gate again until you get a kiss. Glen was planning to say that being allowed through came with the condition of answering a very special question.'

'That's so lovely.' Julia sighed. 'My fiancé said, "It's been three years, I suppose we ought to get married, what do you reckon?" I should have made him work a lot harder!'

'Kara' was the Cornish word for 'love', so over time Port Kara had gained a reputation as a place of romance. Lucas had asked Esther to move in with him when they'd been for a picnic at Penwick Point during a weekend away, long before Danni had decided to move there. It was an area the three of them had holidayed in together, because of Danni's childhood memories. But he was still the last person Danni had expected to see when they reached the point where the track met the main coastal path.

'Someone up at the car park said there'd been an accident.' Lucas sounded breathless as he reached the group. 'Can I help?'

'I think things are under control.' Danni had known Lucas for over seven years, worked side by side with him, and loved him for almost all that time, but now she couldn't even look at him.

'He's got a break to the femur that needed realigning and he's lost a lot of blood from an open wound.' Thalia looked at Lucas, giving the information with the same sort of zeal as a teacher's pet answering a question in class. 'I was wondering if there might be a risk of compartment syndrome, because of how long it took help to get here? I was on my own trying to help him for almost an hour; I just hope I did okay.'

'It looks like you did brilliantly.' When Lucas responded, she lit up like a Christmas tree. Danni recognised that look only too well, because she'd worn it every time Lucas had given her even the slightest praise when they'd worked together.

Lucas kept his gaze fixed on Thalia. 'Are there any symptoms of compartment syndrome?'

'He was very pale and there's obvious swelling to his thigh.' The young nurse was almost glowing now, and the skin on Danni's scalp started to prickle. Something felt off, like Lucas and Thalia were party to a secret, or an inside joke, that no one else was part of. So Danni did what she never did and pulled rank.

'His colour returned to normal once he had some pain relief, he hasn't complained of any numbness and his femoral pulse has been steady throughout.' If she hadn't been carrying so much equipment, she might have folded her arms across her body. 'There are no symptoms whatsoever to suggest compartment syndrome.'

'I think I should follow you back to the hospital, because if he does need surgery, he'll be glad Thalia made that call.' Lucas was in danger of developing a bit of a God complex in the face of Thalia's obvious adoration and there was a familiarity between them that made her almost certain something was going on. The fact he used her name without hesitation meant he knew her and Danni had a horrible feeling it wasn't just through work. But now wasn't the time to ask what Lucas was doing at Penwick Point.

'You can do what you like, but we need to keep moving.' Danni shot a look at Jonty. 'Let's get Glen back to the ambulance and if Lucas wants to come into A&E to assess him when we get to St Piran's, that's up to him. But there's no indication we need to delay transfer any further.'

Danni didn't even stop when Lucas tried to put a hand on her arm. All that mattered for now was getting Glen to the hospital. She'd given Lucas the power for far too long, but it was like her blinkers were finally off, and now she could see all the things that Joe and Aidan had tried to warn her about. It made her want to cringe that she'd been so desperate for his attention, and that she'd believed his feelings for her were real. She'd spent seven years loving a man whose main priority had always been himself, but even worse than that, Esther still did. She didn't speak to Lucas again for the remainder of the walk to the ambulance, but that didn't mean she didn't notice the whispered exchanges between him and Thalia. She was almost certain she heard him apologise for being so late, but she couldn't have sworn to it. She definitely saw their hands brush against each other's more than once, and the thought of what she might be witnessing made her nauseous. Esther was panicking about whether she'd chosen the right dress, when all the time her fiancé wasn't even sure he'd chosen the right person. She wanted to have it out with him, but for now her patient needed her to focus on the job.

'Okay, Jimmy, you can come in the back of the ambulance with me and Julia, while Jonty drives, if you like?' Danni turned to address him as the stretcher was finally loaded into the ambulance.

'Just try stopping me.'

'Are you coming back to the hospital?' Lucas turned to look at Thalia as he spoke, his voice soft and low. Even though they weren't touching, there was unmistakeable intimacy between them, and tears stung Danni's eyes. Esther didn't deserve this.

'I've got my car here.' There was a car park just behind the point where they'd left the ambulance. 'But I'm feeling a bit shaky.'

'I can drive you. Maybe we should get you checked over too, when we get back to St Piran's?' The suggestion might have sounded innocent, but the electricity pulsing between Lucas and Thalia was obvious to Danni, because she'd felt it too.

'I'd like that.' Without a word to the others, Lucas and Thalia headed towards his car and Danni balled her hands into such tight fists that her fingernails dug into her palms. Even if someone had stolen Lucas's identity for the dating site, he clearly had no intention of forsaking all others for Esther's benefit. In fact, Danni was almost certain he'd arranged to meet another woman in the very place where he'd asked Esther to share his home and his life. There was no choice now. If Lucas didn't tell Esther what was going on, then she was going to have to, whatever the cost.

21

Danni had barely slept since Glen's accident. There'd been no evidence of compartment syndrome when he'd undergone further tests at the hospital, and she hadn't seen Lucas or Thalia again. They'd probably gone somewhere else to be together and it would kill Esther if she ever found out. Just weeks ago, the only way she'd been able to cope with his relationship with Esther was to think of the Lucas who was engaged to her best friend as being someone completely different to the Lucas she'd fallen in love with. Now it seemed that neither of those men existed. The fact she was meeting Charlie was the only thing that cheered her up. As soon as she spotted him walking towards her on the beach, with Maggie following on close behind, it was like the sun coming out.

'Morning, gorgeous girl.' He bent down and stroked Brenda's head, making the dog immediately roll onto her back with her legs in the air.

'Do you have that effect on all the females in your life?' Danni grinned.

'Only the four-legged variety.' Charlie slipped an arm around her waist. 'And I can't believe my luck that there's a beautiful woman who actually seems to want to hang out with me.'

'Where is she?' Danni pretended to look over his shoulder and he pulled her even closer to him.

'Why do you do that?'

'What?'

'Try and duck out of every compliment I give you.'

'Maybe I'm not used to them.' Danni forced herself to look at him. 'Or maybe I don't want to get too used to them, because you're not going to be around for long.'

'All the more reason to make the most of the time we've got.' Charlie kissed her and guilt snaked its way up her spine. She shouldn't be feeling like this, or letting herself enjoy the time she had with Charlie, when her best friend was being cheated on and she wasn't doing a damn thing about it.

'Hey, are you okay?' Charlie looked at her as she pulled away, and she nodded.

'Just a lot of work stuff, but I don't want to talk about that.' Slipping her hand into his, she leant against him. 'So where are we off to today?'

'I thought we ought to go and see how Trevor is doing.' The dimple that appeared whenever Charlie smiled was another thing she was going to miss when he was gone. If Danni ever decided to go back to online dating, she was going to have put that down as the feature she found most appealing. 'I've been resisting going back, because I didn't want to risk disturbing him. But if we only go down to the lowest point on the coastal path and no closer, it'll just be a matter of luck if we do see him.'

Danni had an almost overwhelming urge to kiss him again as they started walking towards where the coastal path almost dipped down to the water, and where a series of rocks formed the plateau where they'd spotted Trevor the first time. Charlie's thoughtfulness about the wellbeing of the seal pup was just another item to add to the list of the things she liked about him. She could see how this level of liking someone could easily become something deeper, but they'd known from the outset that this could only go one way. 'How can you be sure it's Trevor, even if we do spot a seal pup?'

'Are you telling me you wouldn't recognise our baby?' Charlie pretended to look appalled and they both started to laugh.

'I mean, I like to think so, but...' Danni shrugged, still laughing as Charlie turned her to face him.

'I'll remember everything about the way you look for the rest of my life.' He wasn't laughing any more; in fact, he'd never looked more serious. 'The way you sometimes try to hide your beautiful face, by looking at me from underneath your fringe. The way your mouth turns up in the corners when you find something funny, but you're trying not to laugh. The way your eyes light up when you talk about something you're passionate about. And don't even get me started on the rest. If I hadn't been there myself, I'd never have believed that someone like you would have chosen to spend time with me.'

She had no idea what to say. There were so many things she wanted to tell him that she liked about him too, and that no one had ever made her feel the way she felt about herself when she was with him. But she couldn't. He was leaving, and maybe that was her punishment for the secret hopes she'd been harbouring about Lucas and Esther for years. All she could do was try and make a joke of it, the way she always did. 'I saw a meme the other day, about finding someone who tells you you're beautiful, even when you look like a potato.'

'I know this is how you deal with compliments, but I'm glad I said it anyway and, one day, I hope you'll finally realise that it's true.' Charlie looked out towards the sea and shouted, 'You're beautiful, Danni Carter, and you're the only one who doesn't see it.'

'You're going to scare Trevor away.' She knitted her fingers through his and squeezed his hand, hoping that would somehow convey all the things she wanted to say.

'No, I'm not. Our Trevor is a brave little pup and I've got a good feeling he's going to be there.'

'I hope so.' It was weird how Danni seemed to be making these little bets with herself just lately: if Trevor was there, everything would somehow work out okay. And if he wasn't...

By the time they reached the lowest point in the path, Danni had built up the significance of Trevor being there so much, she couldn't even bear to look. 'Can you see him?'

'There's an adult seal on the rock, but I can't see a baby.' Charlie's words weren't unexpected, so it was crazy that a hard lump seemed to have formed in her throat.

'How long do seal pups stay with their mothers?'

'Only about three weeks, I think.'

'That seems so soon for him to be all on his own.' Tears sprang into Danni's eyes at the thought of little Trevor facing the world alone. Her emotions were all over the place.

'Oh, wait a minute, that looks like...' Charlie paused for a second. 'Yes, I think that's him, getting out of the water on the far side of the rocks.'

'Really, are you sure?' Danni had forgotten all her earlier doubts about being able to tell whether it really was Trevor and, as soon as she saw him, she knew. 'Look how big he's got!'

'He has and he looks really well.' Charlie's face was the picture of joy and, even without looking in a mirror, Danni knew for certain that hers was too. She hadn't felt this way in a very long time; in fact, she wasn't sure she'd ever felt quite like this.

'Do you think we can stay and watch him for a bit? As long as we don't get any closer?'

'I don't think he'll even notice.' Charlie laughed again as Trevor spread himself out on a rock, making the most of the autumn sunshine while it lasted. 'I brought a blanket and I got some cheese scones from Mehenick's Bakery, when I was down in Port Agnes first thing this morning. I thought I'd put them into the rucksack just in case.'

'You might be the best person I've ever met.' It was as close as Danni was going to get to telling Charlie how she really felt about him and they settled down side by side on the blanket, with Brenda and Maggie stretching out next to them. 'I'm so glad Trevor is okay.'

'Me too.' Charlie turned to look at her. 'I just wish you were. I can tell something's bothering you. I know you said it's about work and I don't want you to feel like I'm pressurising you to talk about it, but sometimes it helps.'

She looked at him for a moment, trying to decide whether sharing her worries would help, but then it all just came tumbling out. 'You know we saw Lucas's picture on the online dating app, and I told you before that he said that he was having doubts about getting married?'

'I remember.'

'What I didn't tell you was that he'd said he was having those doubts because he was in love with someone else. He never said he didn't love Esther, just that he wasn't sure about marrying her if he felt that way about someone else.' Danni sighed. 'I know you said he needs to tell her, but I kept hoping it might not be true. But I was called to an accident at Penwick Point today. One of the nurses from Connie's ward was there looking after the patient until the critical care team arrived. When I asked her later, she said she just happened to be out there walking. But, when we were almost back to the ambulance, Lucas suddenly appeared and, watching the two of them together, it was obvious.'

'She's the one he's in love with?'

'Oh well, yes.' Danni hated the fact she was having to lie to him, in the midst of confiding in him. But she couldn't tell Charlie that Lucas had confessed to being in love with her, otherwise she'd have to tell him everything. And she couldn't bear him knowing she'd spent more than seven years wanting her best friend to end a relationship that meant everything to her. 'I mean, I don't know if he's actually in love with her – maybe. But what I do know, for sure, is that there's something going on between them.'

'You're 100 per cent sure of that?'

'I couldn't be more certain.'

Charlie sighed. 'In that case, I've changed my mind about not interfering. Lucas thinking he might be in love with someone else is one thing, but if he's acting on it... I keep thinking about what it must have been like for Fiona, trying to make a relationship work but knowing she was always Richard's second choice. No one deserves that. At the very least, Lucas needs to tell your friend he's having doubts and admit what's been going on. She might be able to forgive him, if confessing makes him realise she's the one he really wants. But no one should be put in Fiona's position, unless they know what they're getting into.'

'I've got to tell her, haven't I?' It felt as though someone was sitting on Danni's chest just saying the words.

'Maybe give him an ultimatum and one last chance to do it, because I still think it would be better coming from him. Then, if he doesn't, you'll have to, because I don't think you'll ever forgive yourself if you let her go into this marriage with no idea of how Lucas really feels.'

'How about I do that, if you talk to Richard?' It wasn't the same thing at all, but she wouldn't feel so bad about leaning on Charlie for support if he needed her too.

'He's back from Devon, but I still haven't managed to see him in person. I don't want to have to leave him a note, but I thought if I told him I needed to speak to him, he might put two and two together and realise I'm his son. He's not stupid and I know my name's fairly common, but he must realise I'm about the right age and I can't help thinking that's why he's avoiding me.'

'He doesn't know what he's missing.' Danni traced her fingers across Charlie's palm.

'Ever wondered how you've been left to clean up so much mess that's all other people's making?'

'Mmm.' She couldn't tell him that she was slap bang in the middle of the mess that Lucas was making, and that at least part of it was very much her fault. She didn't want Charlie to ever think differently of her, even when he was no longer a part of her life. 'I think you're right about leaving a note for Richard. Maybe you can tell him that you understand he might not want to talk to Connie, but you hope the two of you can meet to talk, even if it's only the once.'

'That would be enough for me. It's all I ever wanted from Connie when I set out to find her, just to know my story. Now, I think she and I can have something more. I'd like to hope Richard and I could too, but I really will be okay if I just him meet him once, as his son and not the tenant of his holiday rental.' Charlie took hold of her hand again. 'I'll write the letter when I get back if you promise to speak to Lucas, because I know it's going to make you really unhappy until you have.'

'I promise.' She looked at Charlie as she spoke, but she wasn't just making the promise to him; it was for Esther too. This could be the catalyst that made Lucas see sense and gave him and Esther the happily ever after she deserved. Either that, or the whole thing could blow up in Danni's face. Whatever happened, Charlie was right: no one deserved to be in Fiona's situation, least of all Esther.

* * *

Danni looked at her phone for what must have been the hundredth time in the last ten minutes. Richard had agreed to a meeting, and Charlie had promised to update Danni as soon as it was over. That had been over two hours ago and there was still no word yet. She just hoped that whatever happened, Charlie really would be okay with it. As much as his childhood had clearly been wonderful, and he had never felt rejected as a result of being adopted, the idea that Richard might not want him in his life hurt Danni's heart. Charlie was such a wonderful person and it really would be Richard's loss if he couldn't see that. But the thought of Charlie feeling any pain made her want to run out of The Cookie Jar café in Port Agnes and all the way to Trengothern Hall.

'I'm so glad you asked to meet.' Danni jolted in response to the sound of Lucas's voice. It wasn't like she hadn't been expecting to see him – after all, she had asked him to come to the café. But it was like she no longer knew him, and she felt as awkward as she might have done meeting a stranger for the first time, knowing she was about to have a difficult conversation with them. Meeting Lucas in Port Kara had felt too risky. They weren't doing anything wrong, but that didn't make her feel any better about getting together behind Esther's back.

'I'm glad you came.' Danni gestured for him to take the seat across the table, but when he reached out for her hand, she snatched it away.

'What's wrong? I thought you finally wanted to talk about us, *properly*.' There was a sort of sleaziness to his tone she'd never noticed before, an assumption that she'd be only too willing to give him whatever it was he wanted. Danni didn't know whether she'd suddenly changed, or he had. Or whether she was only just able to see the person he'd been all along, but she couldn't believe she'd ever have loved someone like that.

'There is no us.' She still couldn't get over the fact that it hurt so little to say those words. It was as if the idea of them being together had always just been a fantasy and that as soon as the prospect of it becoming real had come about, she'd realised she didn't want it at all.

'Come on, Dan, you know that's not true. I've loved you for years and you can't say you don't feel the same way.'

'What about Thalia? Are you in love with her too, or is she just an amusement?'

'What are you talking about?' Lucas sat back in his chair and crossed his arms, looking at her as if she'd suddenly grown two heads.

'I'm not stupid. I know the reason you were both at Penwick Point was because you were meeting up. I saw the way you kept touching hands and how she was looking at you.'

'I was just out for a walk and I can't help the way she looks at me. Lots of them do.' Lucas smiled then and Danni felt bile rise in her throat. He was so arrogant and it was almost impossible to remember what she'd ever seen in him. Maybe the power of the new job had changed him. He was now a big fish in a very small pond, after all, but suddenly she wanted to cry. Where was the person she'd sat next to when they studied late into the night, taking turns to nudge one another awake when their eyes had started to droop? Or the person who'd held her, after they'd witnessed two children getting picked up from the hospital by social services, after their mother had died from a cardiac arrest? Maybe the Lucas she thought she'd known had been an illusion, someone she'd created because that was what she'd wanted him to be. She had no idea, but she missed him, and that was who her tears were for.

Forcing herself to blink back the tears, she glared at him. 'What you could help doing is making a profile on Soulmate Selections.'

She saw the flash in his eyes that told her he'd been rumbled, before he carefully arranged his face into a look of mock outrage.

'People use pictures like mine for their profiles all the time, and half of them on there are claiming to be surgeons or pilots.' His response was so instant, it sounded rehearsed and made him look all the more guilty. Anyone innocent would demand to see the evidence, or at least react in shock. It was like Lucas had an answer for everything.

'I don't believe you.' She held his gaze, and it was as if they'd entered into a staring contest. Eventually he blinked and somehow it seemed to break his resolve.

'Okay, so I might have posted on there to test the waters.' He held up his hands as she started to protest. 'It was only because, when I told you how I felt and you rejected me, I still wasn't sure if I loved Esther enough to marry her. I thought if I could be in love with you, at the same time as I'm in love her, then maybe I wasn't ready. So I posted a profile, just to see what happened, and how that would make me react.'

'I'm sure Esther would feel great about that.'

'Probably no worse than she'd feel knowing that her best friend has wanted our relationship to break down from the moment it began. It was obvious to me from the start, but for some reason she's never been able to see it.' For a moment, there was a twisted expression on his face and the veiled threat was obvious. If Danni told Esther about his dating profile, Lucas would make sure she knew the rest. But then Lucas's face relaxed again. 'The good thing is it worked. I can show you the matches I got, if you like, and you'll be able to see I didn't respond to any of them. The only person who has ever turned my head since I've been with Esther is you. But putting the profile up made me realise what I've got and how much I love her. She's the only one I want to be with.'

'So why did you turn up here, saying you wanted to talk about us?'

'We've always had a connection, Dan, there's no point either of us lying about that.' He looked at her again, the faint hint of a smile playing around his mouth this time. 'And I think that's why I fell in love with you, or maybe I just thought I did because we had all these similar experiences. You knew what it was like for me to lose my parents. I realised that, when I finally told you how I felt, it was the same week as the anniversary of my mum dying. Twenty years I've been without her and, I don't know, maybe I'm scared of loving someone that much again. Marrying Esther and making her my everything, knowing she could be taken away from me at any point, means I'm having to face up to that happening again one day. But all of this has made me realise that the risk is worth it. I'm not going to say I don't love you, Dan, because I do. But I promise you it's not the way I feel about Esther.'

At that moment, Danni wanted to believe what Lucas was saying more than anything else in the world. If all of that was true, things could go back almost to the way they were and the Lucas she'd loved as a friend would never have disappeared. Things would be even better this time, because she wouldn't be *in love* with him any more either. But after all the things he'd said and done, and the way she'd seen him act, it was almost impossible to trust that he meant it. 'What about Thalia?'

'Okay, you're right, she's got feelings for me and maybe I didn't discourage them the way I should have done. But I promise you, on my life, there's absolutely nothing going on between me and Thalia.' He reached for Danni's hand again. 'Don't ruin what me and Esther have got, over someone like Thalia. Because I've got a horrible feeling your friendship with Esther won't survive if you do.'

22

'Sorry it's taken me so long to let you know how I got on, but I thought it was easier to ring than text.' Charlie's voice was warm, and Danni instantly found herself wishing they were face to face, instead of talking on the phone.

'Don't worry about that; I was just concerned about whether everything was okay.'

'I guess that depends on how you define okay.' Charlie let go of a long breath. 'It went pretty much as expected, although to be fair Richard was quite chatty at first and even seemed keen for us to build up a bit of a relationship while I'm here.'

'But?'

'But then I made the mistake of showing some empathy for Connie and telling him that, while I didn't agree with her keeping my birth a secret from him, I could understand why she did it.'

'And I'm guessing that didn't go down well?' She could picture Richard's face as Charlie said that. But that was the thing about Charlie: he seemed to have this ability to see the good in everyone.

'He said I'd never understand, because I'd had a good life despite what Connie did. But he was the one who'd ended up being admitted to hospital and having to tell the staff that there was no one to put down as his next of kin.'

'Oh God, that's sad.' Danni could imagine how that might feel only too well and might one day find herself in that situation. But right now, the person whose feelings she cared most about were Charlie's. 'Are you okay? I know you said you didn't mind as long as you got the chance to speak to him once, but this must be really hard.'

'I'm worried about him, and I don't just want to walk away, when he clearly needs more people in his life than he's got right now.' Charlie sighed again. 'Even if there's a chance he might change his mind and want to see me, he's adamant he never wants to speak to Connie again and I've got no idea how to tell her.'

'I could come with you.' She was probably overstepping boundaries. She wasn't Charlie's girlfriend and having her hanging around while he had a conversation as difficult as that might be the last thing he wanted. But she had to ask, because if he needed her support she'd be there for him every step of the way.

'Actually, I'd really like that. I'm going in tomorrow morning and I thought it was best to just come out with it, like ripping a plaster off.'

'You're probably right and I can meet you there at about ten, before my shift starts?'

'Perfect.' Charlie made it sound as if it was something to look forward to and, despite the awfulness of the situation, Danni really was looking forward to it because he'd be there. 'How did you get on with Lucas?'

'I don't know. He came out with all these far-fetched excuses, but I suppose there's a possibility they're true, if you're willing to ignore the likelihood that he's lying to save his skin.' It was Danni's turn to sigh. 'He promised me everything he's been doing lately was a reaction to panicking about the prospect of one day losing

Esther. He lost both his parents quite young and he said the anniversary of his mum's death was what triggered it all, but he's certain now that Esther is the only person he loves enough to want to marry. I made him promise me he'd tell Esther if anything else happened, or if even the tiniest doubt flared up again between now and the wedding.'

'And do you think he will?'

'I don't know, but I've got to give him the chance to try, because otherwise, if I get this wrong, I could end up being the one who gets pushed out of Esther's life.'

'I think you're doing the right thing. Giving people a second chance, to become the person they should have been all along, is an act of generosity. I just hope, one day, Richard might be able to give that to Connie. But sadly not everyone is as brilliant as you.'

'Brilliant is about the last thing I feel.' There was that stab of guilt again. Charlie really was the most generous and thoughtful man Danni had ever met. But he had no idea who she really was, and she wasn't sure even he would think she deserved a second chance if he knew the truth.

'Well, I know that having you there tomorrow will help Connie feel better about things too. In the circumstances, it feels wrong to say I can't wait to see you, but it's true.'

'Me too, see you tomorrow.'

'See you tomorrow.' As Charlie ended the call, Brenda came over and rested her head on Danni's knee, staring up at her with eyes that understood everything.

'I know I should tell him the truth about Lucas, but there's no point if he's leaving, is there?' Danni looked at the dog, hoping that Brenda would give some indication that her silence was justified, but all she did was let out a long, low howl. It was always a sound that had seemed to encapsulate sadness for Danni and she just hoped it wasn't Brenda's way of predicting what was about to come.

23

When Connie had imagined the man her son might have grown up to be, she hadn't dared dream he'd be as wonderful as Charlie. He was incredibly kind and there wasn't a hint of arrogance about him. Calling her niece to explain why she'd kept Charlie a secret for so long had been relatively easy compared with making that revelation to Richard. Darcy had seemed to understand her reasons and the only thing she'd wanted was to find out everything possible about the cousin she'd always longed for.

Connie had been able to give her the basics and that was all someone of Darcy's generation or younger seemed to need; with Google and social media, she'd been able to fill in all the gaps and find out more than Charlie had revealed of himself so far. And, best of all, it had all turned out to be positive information.

'He's got his own Wikipedia page, Auntie Con!' The look of excitement on Darcy's face when she'd made the video call had matched the tone of her voice. 'He's written eight best-selling children's books and some of them are going to be made into a TV series next year. How amazing is that?'

'It is and I think his parents have supported him a lot; his mother's an artist like Charlie. He plays it down, but I suspect he's had to work really hard to get where he has, even with their help.'

'They sound wonderful.' Darcy had beamed again. 'But luckily for him he's got good genes too. After all, it's easy to trace where he gets his writing talent from.'

'I never finished my novel, and I don't think academic texts compare to fiction. None of this is down to me, anyway.' Connie had been proud of Charlie from the moment he'd been placed in her arms. Her heart was full of love for the little boy who'd been alert and filled with a zest for life, the instant he'd opened his eyes. That pride had only grown as a result of getting to know him, but she couldn't claim any part in his achievements and, as much as she loved Darcy, she hadn't been willing to accept her niece saying otherwise.

'Of course some of it is down to you. You made the decisions that put him on this path.'

Connie had changed the subject after that, knowing that her niece was every bit as stubborn as she was. Later on she'd snuck a look at the Wikipedia page for herself and had discovered that Charlie had donated a hefty percentage of the royalties from his last book to a children's charity. Her son was a good man, who'd had a happy childhood, and the knowledge of that ought to have been enough. Asking for any more was greedy, but she couldn't seem to help herself. She wanted Charlie in her life, and she wanted him and Richard to build a relationship, too. But now one of those things seemed much more likely than the other, even before Charlie turned up for a visit, accompanied by Danni and Gwen. It didn't surprise Connie to see Charlie and Danni together. They seemed to have bonded over caring for Richard on the day he'd been admitted to St Piran's, but she hadn't expected Gwen to be with them.

'This feels like an intervention. Am I in trouble for something?'

She'd struggled to smile much since the conversation with Richard, but somehow it was easy when Charlie was around.

'Of course not. What kind of trouble are you going to get up to while you're recovering from a broken pelvis, and not one but six operations!' Gwen shook her head. 'Not the fun kind, that's for sure.'

'We were just on our way down the corridor when Gwen came out of the shop, heading this way. Shall I borrow an extra chair, so we can all sit down?' Danni looked across at one of the other beds in the bay that Connie had been moved into after her latest operation. The damage her broken pelvis had done to her internal organs had been responsible for three of the six operations, and the other three had been needed to repair the pelvis itself. The final one had gone ahead just the day before, when a scan to investigate the cause of the ongoing pain in her pelvis had revealed that one of the screws seemed to have shifted position, causing the fracture to become unstable again.

'I'll get it.' Charlie took a chair from the bed opposite Connie's, whose occupant had gone off for a physiotherapy session. The four of them exchanged a bit of idle chit-chat about the weather, but Connie only lasted about two minutes before she blurted out the question Charlie must have known she'd been wanting to ask.

'Did you get a chance to speak to your father... Richard, I mean.' Just because Connie thought of him as being Charlie's father, it didn't mean she could expect Charlie to feel the same. Any more than she could expect him to consider her his mother. He'd called her Mum on that first day, but ever since then it had been Connie. She was determined not to let the tinge of sadness she felt every time he said her name affect how grateful she was to have him back in her life.

'I did. It took a while and I don't think he was that keen to talk, even when he finally agreed.' Charlie put his hand over hers. 'I think he's still in shock and it all seems really hard for him.'

'I can't blame him for being shocked. In fact, I can't blame him for any of this; it was all me.'

'Richard clearly feels the need to lash out, but blaming you is just projecting his own guilt. It's something I learnt early on in the counselling course I've been doing.' Gwen looked willing to challenge anyone who might disagree, but Charlie and Danni were already nodding in agreement. 'From all the things you've told me, Connie, he knew what the boundaries were in your relationship, and that the end of the summer would be the end of the two of you. I know he wrote you those letters afterwards, but it was him who'd told you just how much he stood to lose if he didn't marry Fiona. Deep down, I think he knows that by telling you those things he left you with no choice but to keep the baby a secret from him.'

'That's what I think.' Danni was biting her lip and Connie hadn't seen her looking this much on edge since the day of the accident. It was obvious there was something more than friendship building between Danni and Charlie too, and maybe that was what was making her seem so nervous. 'I've got this friend who's had feelings for someone, but it never went anywhere because that person was engaged to someone else. The strange thing is, when there was finally a chance of them being together, my friend realised that nothing could ever happen between them, because of the guilt that would come with it. I think Richard feels so bad about what happened with Fiona that he can't allow himself to build a relationship with you and Charlie.'

'He doesn't want to get to know Charlie?' There was a tigress inside Connie she'd never known existed when she looked at her son, searching for signs that he'd been hurt by his father's rejection. Richard was entitled to hate her, but Charlie was innocent in all of this and, for the first time, she felt something akin to rage bubbling up inside her. Richard was just lucky she wasn't capable of getting out of bed and tracking him down.

'He's not ready yet, but I think he might be eventually.' Charlie was so balanced in how he saw things, and that definitely didn't come from Connie or Richard. 'I just wish I could be as sure that he might change his mind about seeing you.'

'I don't need him to.' Connie forced a smile and, even though her face felt stiff with the effort, she hoped it was convincing. The knowledge that Richard never wanted to see her again might make it feel like someone was trying to rip her heart out, but Richard rejecting Charlie would have broken it forever. If the possibility for the two of them to finally have the relationship they deserved relied on her staying away from Richard altogether, she was willing to do it. 'Is there any chance you might stay on in Port Kara after your rental of the holiday cottage is over, to try and get him to open up to you? I know it should be the other way around, but you've known that you were adopted a lot longer than he has. And maybe when I've gone back to Yorkshire, it'll all be easier.'

'Funny you should mention that, but I've decided to stay around for at least another six weeks.' Charlie smiled and Connie saw the change in Danni's expression; it was as if someone had switched on a bright light. 'I'm not sure if Richard will let me keep renting the cottage, but I'm looking around at other things just in case. And I've only got one condition to agreeing to stay.'

'What's that?' Connie looked at her son, half of her desperately hoping he was going to say what she was expecting him to, and the other half of her terrified that he would.

'That you promise me you won't go back to Yorkshire before I leave Port Kara.' He fixed her with a look of such intensity she found herself nodding.

'I won't.' Even as she thought about all the reasons why she couldn't really agree to Charlie's request, she knew she wouldn't break the promise she'd just made to him. If Richard wanted to punish himself for what had happened, that was his prerogative. But, for now at least, Charlie wanted Connie in his life and she wasn't going to give up that opportunity for a second time. Not without a fight.

* * *

'Connie coped better than I thought she might with the news that Richard is pushing everyone away.' Danni had admired the older woman's resolve from the moment she'd met her. But it was clear that as much as she might once have loved Richard, her feelings for Charlie were on a different level. She'd heard friends who were parents talk about their willingness to die for their children and Connie's reaction to what Richard had said was a version of that. She was willing to come in last place in everyone's list of priorities and be sidelined, or even forgotten, if it meant Charlie had the opportunity to get close to his father.

'She's quite the woman, my mother.' Charlie turned the last two words over in his mouth, like someone grappling with a particularly tricky pronunciation. 'And although I really want to help Richard with the things he's struggling with, and get to know him too, I'm not doing that at the expense of being able to spend time with Connie.'

Charlie paused as the waitress brought over their food, querying whether she could bring them any Parmesan or black pepper.

'Not for me, thanks.' Charlie looked across the table. 'Danni?'

'No, not for me either, thank you.' She just wanted the waitress to disappear and leave them to it. Charlie's announcement that he was staying on for longer had taken her by surprise, and she needed to know if there was anything more to it than getting to know his biological parents. She wanted there to be more to it than that, but like Gwen had said about Connie and Richard, they'd both known where they stood from the start.

'When did you decide—' She hadn't even got to the end of the sentence when Esther suddenly came hurtling towards her. For a moment she went cold, terrified that her friend might be about to launch into a tirade of abuse and tell Danni she knew everything. But then Esther stopped in her tracks and beamed.

'It's okay, Dan, I'm not going to interrupt. I was supposed to be meeting Lucas here for dinner, but he's having to work late, so I'm just picking up a couple of pizzas for later.' Esther looked at Charlie. 'I couldn't not come and say hello, though, and meet the person who's finally tempted Danni to start going on dates again.'

'You're really embarrassing, do you know that?' Danni was like a teenager addressing an overbearing parent, but she couldn't help smiling. Esther had been almost like a surrogate mum when they'd lived together, making sure there was something to eat when Danni had come off a particularly long shift, and checking that she'd got to work safely when there'd been report of an accident on their route to the hospital. So maybe it shouldn't be a surprise that Esther could fulfil the role of embarrassing parent too.

'She's not embarrassing; I like the idea that I might be able to tempt you to do something you don't usually do.' He stuck out his hand. 'I'm Charlie by the way.'

'I'm Esther, Danni's best friend. I've heard a bit about you, but not nearly as much as I should have done by the looks of things.'

'I know a lot about what can be used to kill a person, you know.' Danni was still grinning, despite the blush that seemed to rise up her neck far more often these days. 'And I know how to make it look like an accident.'

'Enough said!' Esther laughed and held up her hands. 'I'll go now. I've got a long evening ahead, writing out place cards for the wedding breakfast, which will keep me from eating these pizzas until Lucas gets home. But just know that I'm going to be ringing you tomorrow.'

'Oh I don't doubt it.'

'And, Charlie.' Esther turned towards him again. 'It's been lovely to meet you. I really hope it won't be the last time.'

'Me too and maybe you can put in a good word for me when you make that call?'

'You can count on it!' Esther gave a little wave, winked at Danni and then disappeared almost as quickly as she'd arrived.

'I'm sorry about that. She just wants me to be happy.' Danni took a sip of the ice-cold water the waitress had brought earlier and hoped it might make her flushed cheeks lose some of their colour.

'I'm not sorry.' Charlie gave her a look that did nothing to help her attempts to appear calm and collected. 'Esther seems really lovely, but I take it her other half is the same Lucas we've been talking about?'

'There's only one Lucas, thank goodness.' As she said the words, it hit her all over again how much she meant them. Lucas wasn't someone she wanted any more, but she didn't want him in Esther's life either. Not unless he could commit to her completely and prove he was worthy of the amazing fiancée he'd had so many doubts about.

'In that case I hope he meant what he said, because no one should get married unless they're certain it's the right thing to do and Esther clearly has no idea.'

'I know.' Danni looked down at the bowl of pasta in front of her, but she'd suddenly lost her appetite. Relying on Lucas to do the right thing was too much of a risk when Esther's happiness was at stake. The trouble was, she still had no idea how to deal with it, without taking an even bigger risk with their friendship.

24

Danni had been speaking to herself almost non-stop since she got up. Well, not speaking to herself exactly, but running through every possible way she could tell an invisible, imaginary version of Esther that Lucas might not be the person she thought he was. The trouble was, none of the imaginary ways of breaking the news had felt right, because it was Lucas who should be telling his fiancée that he'd had a bit of a wobble, but everything was back on track now. At least that's what Danni hoped he'd be telling her. Then at least Esther would have all the information she needed to make a decision. But that depended on Lucas being totally honest, which was why the imaginary conversation with Esther was still going around and around in Danni's head even when she reached St Piran's for her shift.

'Half an hour early.' Danni said the words under her breath as she looked at her watch. It was enough time for her to pop up and see Connie and ask her for some advice. Connie had been through a lot and it was obvious she wished she'd handled some things differently, so maybe it was time to draw upon that experience and hope like hell that they could hit upon the right way of approaching things with Esther as a result. If that didn't work, she might have to enlist Gwen's help, because she was someone who didn't seem to have any trouble just coming out with what needed to be said.

Just inside the double doors of the corridor that led into Tewyn Ward was a small relatives' room, where visitors could wait if patients were having tests or treatment, or where doctors could update family members about a patient's prognosis or treatment plan. There was a glass panel in the top half of the door and, as Danni walked past it, something made her turn and look in. The reaction to what she saw was instant, as if a fist had just been punched into her stomach, making it impossible to catch her breath. She couldn't move either. All she could do was watch as Lucas put two hands on either side of where Thalia was standing, with her back pressed against the wall. They were both smiling, their faces just inches apart, and as Thalia arched her body away from the wall, the gap between them became nothing. She recognised the look of pure longing on the young nurse's face, because she'd seen it in her own reflection every time things with Lucas had almost crossed the line. But Thalia didn't have the loyalty to Esther that had always prevented Danni from acting on her feelings. So there was only one person who could stop this.

'No!' Flinging open the door, she heard the shout before she even realised it was coming from her. Danni was still staring at Lucas and Thalia as they sprang away from one another.

'This is not what it—'

'Don't you dare!' She cut Lucas off before he could turn into even more of a walking cliché than he'd already become. 'Don't even try it, because this is exactly what it looks like.'

'I've got to… I've got to go and see a patient.' Thalia didn't even look at Danni as she mumbled an excuse to leave, and she was clearly terrified by the rage that felt as if it was radiating from every cell in Danni's body. But this wasn't about her; it was about Lucas and what he was doing to Esther. And as far as Danni was concerned, Thalia disappearing could only be a good thing.

'Don't overreact.' Lucas's attempt to reach out to Danni, the moment Thalia had left the room, made her roar.

'Overreact! You're supposed to be getting married. You told me you were certain and that all of this other stuff had proved to you how much you love Esther. So explain to me how grinding your body against Thalia's, and telling her God knows what to get her into bed, helps prove how much you love your fiancée.'

'It wasn't like that.' Lucas looked directly at Danni and she could still remember the first time their eyes had locked, and how she'd felt something she couldn't even describe. But now she knew it was a trick. Lucas had a way of making you feel like you were the only person in the room, the only person in the world, when he wanted to. Except it had just been an act, because he could turn it on and off whenever he chose.

'So, what *was* it like, then?' Every word she said to him tasted bitter in her mouth, but part of her wanted to know just how many more lies he was willing to tell.

'I've just been feeling overwhelmed by the anniversary of losing Mum, and because she and Dad won't be at the wedding. Thalia was just comforting me, that's all.' He sounded so convincing that Danni was beginning to think he believed his own excuses, but she'd heard it all before.

'The anniversary was weeks ago, and your parents have both been dead for a long time; when are you going to stop using that to try and get you out of trouble? You're not a fourteen-year-old coping with life without your mum any more, and it's time you grew the hell up and stopped using your parents' deaths as a way of getting whatever you want from the latest sap willing to fall for it. God, I wish I'd learnt my lesson about you right at the start. I feel sorry for Thalia.'

'No you don't; you're a jealous bitch.' The change in Lucas's expression was like day turning to night and he almost spat the words at her, a look of pure venom in his eyes. 'You've always been jealous of my relationship with Esther, hanging around when we didn't want you there, desperate for attention from both of us, but most of all from me. Now you can't stand it, because Thalia's the one I'm leaning on for support. You knew you could never have me the way you wanted to, because I love Esther, so you got your kicks from trying to be close to me in whatever way you could: telling me about your dad and comparing that to losing my parents. But I've seen through you now.'

'You've seen through me! Are you for real? I should have told Esther a long time ago, but when she finds out about—'

Lucas grabbed hold of her wrist hard, before she could finish speaking, and the heat of his breath on her face made her stomach churn. 'Esther isn't going to find out anything, because there's nothing to tell. She already knows you wish it was you I was marrying. We laugh at you when we're together, you do realise that, don't you? Esther is more sympathetic, of course: "Poor Danni, following you around like a lovesick puppy, I wish she'd find someone who could make her as happy as you make me." But she knows how jealous you are really. And if you go running to her now, trying to tell her that there's something going on between me and Thalia, she'll know you're lying and she'll know why. Because you want the one thing you're never going to get, and you can't stand the thought of her having it instead. It's you who'll be pushed out of Esther's life, not me, and then what will you have? Nothing.'

'I'd rather risk that than know I stood by and let her make the biggest mistake of her life.' Danni's words were full of bravado as she finally wrenched her wrist free from his grasp, and she'd rather have died than let him see the tears that were stinging her eyes. Grabbing the door handle, she bolted from the room, not looking back in case Lucas was behind her. She kept running, down the corridor, out through the double doors. If she looked down, she was convinced she'd be able to see blood seeping through her top, because Lucas's words had been like a blade cutting into her, over and over again.

The things he'd said about her were true, or at least they had been once. When she'd talked to Lucas about losing their parents, she'd really believed they understood each other on a level no one else would. Only now she could see it was part of his plan; he was a master manipulator and it had taken her all this time to see it. Even if it cost her everything, she had to try to help Esther see through the façade as well, before it was too late. With Lucas's final threat that she'd be left with nothing ringing in her ears, she finally stopped running as she reached the entrance to A&E. Taking a deep breath, she went in.

* * *

Danni had wanted to blurt everything out to Esther the moment she'd seen her. But her best friend had been in the middle of treating a young boy with a nasty gash on his forehead, after falling off his bicycle. At the same time, Danni had been dealing with a middle-aged woman who'd presented with the symptoms of a possible stroke, all the time praying that the next patient through the doors wouldn't be someone they'd need to call Lucas down to assess. She needed to speak to Esther first, before Lucas did.

Although, knowing him, he'd still be betting on the fact that Danni wouldn't risk her friendship with Esther by saying anything. Looking back now, she suspected there'd been numerous other women who'd *comforted* Lucas over the years. He'd always claimed the attention she'd witnessed him getting was one-sided, but now she wasn't so sure. In fact, she was almost certain of it.

'We've got another patient on the way in.' Gary's voice behind Danni made her jump. She'd just been able to downgrade the suspected stroke patient when the scan results had shown a TIA, or mini-stroke. Danni had arranged for the woman to be moved to the clinical decisions unit for further observation and tests, before a decision was made by one of the specialist teams about a treatment plan. So she'd been staring into the distance, thinking about the situation with Esther and Lucas, when Gary had alerted her with the news that another patient was about to arrive, and she turned slowly to look at him. 'The patient's a sixty-nine-year-old male who was witnessed having a fall outside a shop on Harbour Street. According to those on scene, there was a brief loss of consciousness, but they're unsure if that's as a result of the fall, or if it's what caused the fall. He's talking and coherent now, with a GCS of fifteen.'

'Thank you.' Danni's response sounded robotic, but she was going to have to rely on going into a kind of professional autopilot until she'd had the chance to speak to Esther.

'He should be here in about two minutes. Oh, hold on, that looks like him now.' Gary was facing the entrance to the department and, when Danni turned around, she realised straight away that she knew the patient.

'Richard?' She might be about to assess his condition, but she didn't need a monitor to tell her that her own heartrate had suddenly shot up. This wasn't just any patient; this was Charlie's dad, and she couldn't bear the thought that the chance for them to get to know one another might be slipping away.

'I've been an idiot.' There was so much sadness in his eyes, it gave Danni goosebumps as she walked by the side of the trolley stretchering Richard into resus.

'Do you want me to call Charlie?' If this moment of vulnerability was the one chance of Richard letting his guard down for long enough to let his son in, she didn't want to miss it.

'I asked the woman who called the ambulance to do it. He said he'd come straight here.' Richard closed his eyes for a moment. 'I'm scared I've left it too late, all because I'm the same pig-headed idiot I've always been.'

'If Charlie's on his way in, it must mean he wants to see you.' Danni wasn't going to tell him she already knew how much Charlie wanted the chance to get to know his biological father; that was a conversation for the two of them to have. But she wanted to be able to give Richard some comfort.

'I know and I don't deserve that, after the way I've treated him. But I'm worried that there won't be any time. I haven't been taking the medication I was prescribed, thinking I could get by myself. But when I felt myself falling and I knew I was going to faint again, I realised just how much of a fool I've been.'

'If it's your blood pressure again, we'll get it sorted. It's not too late for anything and, even though I shouldn't be saying this as your doctor, maybe it's a good thing if it's made you realise what you want.'

'You're some maid, do you know that? It's no wonder Charlie likes you so much.' Richard smiled for the first time and Danni wrinkled her nose as she tried to work out whether *some maid* was a compliment or not.

'It means "what a woman".' Gary grinned. 'It's an old Cornish expression, a bit before your time, but I think you've got yourself another new friend.'

'Thank you.' Danni reached out and touched Richard's arm, wanting to tell him just how much she liked Charlie too. It wasn't the time or the place, but it lifted a tiny bit of the weight that had been pressing down on her since the row with Lucas. If things went the way he'd predicted with Esther, Danni was going to need all the new friends she could get.

* * *

'Well, your blood pressure was sky high, which probably explains why you fainted again, but we seem to have been able to get it all under control now.' Danni fixed Richard with a serious look. 'We're going to need to run a few more tests and admit you overnight for observation. Hopefully it will all just be down to you not taking your medication, but you can't keep taking chances like this.'

'I won't.'

'No, you bloody well won't!' Charlie came into the cubicle where Richard had been moved for further monitoring, with Gary by his side. 'Never mind playing Russian roulette with your blood pressure, you've put mine through the roof.'

'I'm sorry, I really am.' Richard looked and sounded every bit as contrite as a little boy being told off by his dad.

'I'll forgive you if you don't do it again.' Charlie's expression softened as he took Richard's hand and then looked up at Danni. 'He is going to be okay, isn't he?'

'If he follows doctors' orders and your advice, he should be fine.' Danni smiled and Charlie's face flooded with relief. Here was a man who genuinely cared about others and who couldn't have been more different from Lucas if he'd tried. It was almost impossible to believe now that she'd been under his spell for so long, when the goodness in someone like Charlie shone so much brighter. But then maybe that was it: there was no such thing as *someone like Charlie*. Only him.

'Before we move you to the clinical decisions unit for further assessment, I just need to see whether any of your details need updating.' Gary took a step towards Richard. 'Does your mobile number still end in six eight seven?'

'It does.'

'And it says here you've chosen not to list any next of kin, is that right?'

'It isn't that I chose not to, it's just that I didn't have any. At least not until recently.' Richard turned to look at his son and Charlie nodded.

'You do now.'

'Is it okay to put your details? I know it's not been long, but—'

'Of course it is, but only if you promise to come and have dinner with me as soon as you're out of here.'

'Try stopping me.' Richard's smile would have melted the hardest of hearts and the tears filling Danni's eyes were the good ones this time. 'Although a certain brilliant young doctor might tell me I've got to stick to salad leaves and tap water.'

'Everything in moderation, as long as it doesn't interfere with your medication.' Danni pretended to wag a finger at him. 'I'll leave Gary to finish checking your details and I'll go and check if they're ready to move you to CDU.'

'Hold on, Danni.' Charlie caught up with her just along the corridor from Richard's cubicle. 'I wanted to say thank you.'

'What for?'

'For looking after Richard and for giving him and me a chance to finally get to know one another.'

'I didn't do anything. I think collapsing for a second time finally made him realise what he really wanted.'

'Yes, but if it hadn't been for you, I might not have hung around and waited for him to change his mind. I know Connie's original plan was to go back to Yorkshire as soon as she got out of hospital and I could have gone up there to visit. Waiting for Richard would have felt like setting myself up for rejection, if there hadn't been someone else I enjoyed spending time with so much.'

'Brenda will be flattered.' Danni couldn't help trying to brush off the compliment, even if a smile kept tugging at the corners of her mouth every time she looked at Charlie.

'Whilst I do love spending time with Brenda, she comes in just behind spending time with you.' Charlie shrugged. 'It's a close-run thing, but all that slobber of hers means you just about have the edge.'

'So I'm just about preferable to a basset hound with a drooling problem.' Danni tapped her chin. 'I'll take that.'

'I'm glad to hear it, because I'd like to make dinner for you tonight as a thank you. But if you want to bring Brenda, she's more than welcome too. Although, I ought to warn you, this is how love triangles start.' Charlie laughed, but Danni couldn't even pretend to find the words funny. 'Hey, what's wrong?'

'Sorry, just thinking about a patient.' Danni shook her head and tried to shake off the horrible sense of foreboding with it. Lying to Charlie was just one more thing she hated about the situation with Esther and Lucas.

'Oh God, here I am, blabbing on as usual and you have so much more important stuff to deal with. If you can't make it to dinner tonight, don't worry. We can do it another time. If you like, I mean, but we don't have to do that either.' Charlie's affable charm would have been the perfect act if he'd wanted to manipulate someone the way Lucas had, but there wasn't a shred of doubt in Danni's mind that everything about Charlie was genuine. And she liked everything about him too.

'No, I'd love to come, thank you.' Reaching out, she took hold of his hand, watching as the look of concern on his face transformed into a smile that went all the way to his eyes. She wasn't sure she'd ever seen Lucas smile like that. But one thing she knew for certain was that she wanted Esther to have someone who smiled at her that way, whenever they looked at her, and time was running out fast.

25

'Are you sure you don't want to take a rain check on tonight?' Danni didn't think she could have got up and left, even if she wanted to. Brenda was lying across her feet as she sat on the sofa in Charlie's holiday cottage, and Maggie had her head on Danni's knee, staring up at her with those incredible puppy-dog eyes that belied her real age.

'Of course not. When the doctor in CDU said Richard could come home tonight after all, I offered to go and stay with him at the house, but I think we both decided that might be running before we can walk.' Charlie poured some wine into her glass. 'I've told him to call if there's anything worrying him, and I'll pop in and check on him later. Then, in a couple of days' time, he should be feeling much better.'

'And as long as he takes his medication and takes the advice about his lifestyle, he shouldn't have another incident like that.' Danni stroked the top of Maggie's head. 'I think this one really scared him.'

'It did and he said he didn't want to have any regrets.' Charlie let out such a loud sigh that even Brenda opened her eyes and looked up at him, before dropping her head back down on to one of Danni's feet.

'It sounds like you might be pondering some regrets of your own?' One of the most attractive things about Charlie was his ready smile and, even when he wasn't smiling, he always looked like he might be about to. But not this time.

'More a case of what else Richard might live to regret that he hasn't realised yet.' Charlie shook his head. 'He's still saying he wants nothing to do with Connie after what she did.'

'I guess that's his choice, but maybe he'll come round about that too, eventually.' Danni crossed the index and middle fingers on her right hand over one another almost unconsciously. She had to believe that even if people reacted one way in the moment, there was always a chance they'd change their minds. In fact, she was banking on it, otherwise telling Esther about Lucas was an even bigger risk. But this wasn't about her. 'Are you going to tell Connie that he's changed his mind about seeing you?'

'I've got to. The secrets between Connie and Richard are what have caused so many of the problems we're facing now. I don't want to add to that, but I don't want to hurt her, or make her feel like she's being left out either.'

'She'll be sad in some ways, but I think most of all she'll be happy that you're getting this chance. Connie loves you and this is what she wanted for you.'

'That's what love is, I suppose, isn't it? Being happy when things are going right for someone you love, even if you can't have the thing you want for yourself.' Charlie looked thoughtful for a moment, and Danni nodded.

'I know some people think you shouldn't have to sacrifice what you want for other people's happiness, but if you really love someone I don't think you can be happy unless they are.' Danni would never be happy unless Esther was, and marrying Lucas was going to make her friend desperately unhappy in the long run. 'Do you think just coming out with what you need to say is always the best way?'

'Maybe not always, but in this case there's no way to dress it up. Of course I'm still hoping Richard might change his mind about talking to Connie, like he changed his mind with me, and that's something I can emphasise when I speak to her. But I'm not going to lie. The truth always has a way of coming out and I'd rather she heard it from me, the way I want to say it.' Charlie glanced at his watch. 'I'm just going to check on the roast potatoes; can I get you anything else to drink?'

'No, thank you. The wine is great.'

'I'd like to pretend I'm a connoisseur, but it was the wine of the month in the supermarket in Port Tremellien.' Charlie grinned and went back into the kitchen. The wine really was good, but Danni took a huge slug, like she might have done if she was trying to get through a vinegary glass of red, just to be polite. She needed the Dutch courage if she was going to do what she needed to. Taking a deep breath, she typed a message to Esther.

Can we meet? There's something I need to tell you xx

A response pinged back almost immediately.

Everything okay? Do you want to ring me now? We're on our way to the reception venue, to have dinner so we can finalise the menu, but I can meet you straight after. You're worrying me now! Xx

Danni stared at her phone for a few seconds. She didn't want to do this over the phone and she didn't want Esther coming straight from the reception venue to have this conversation; she'd be too caught up in the plans of the wedding to hear what Danni had to

say. She hated the thought of making Esther worry, and there was
always the risk she'd mention those worries to Lucas. So she
needed to word her next message carefully.

Don't worry, I'm fine, but I just need to talk to you about something
when we can get a quiet moment, so not at work! Let me know when
suits you, but no hurry xx

Esther had clearly been watching her phone, ready to reply to
Danni's response, because the next message pinged through
almost instantly again.

Thank goodness for that! Well, now I'm hoping what you've got to tell
me is going to be Charlie related 😊 Can you do lunchtime tomorrow? I
need to get my excitement vicariously because, after nearly eight years,
me and Lucas are like an old married couple already. I've almost
forgotten what those early days are like. Maybe I need to make more
effort with the lingerie for the honeymoon and, as chief bridesmaid, it's
your job to help me pick something out! xx

You know I'd do anything for you and lunchtime tomorrow is perfect.
Shall we meet at 1 p.m. at The Jolly Sailor? xx

See you then and I want ALL the details! xx

It wasn't the first time that Esther had hinted that her relationship with Lucas wasn't as physical as it used to be, which wasn't
that unusual after being together so long. But the fact that Lucas
was clearly getting his kicks elsewhere wouldn't be helping, and
now Esther was starting to question whether she needed to make
more effort. That kind of gradual erosion of her best friend's confidence was something Danni wasn't prepared to wait around to

witness. Esther had always been the light in every room, upbeat and cheerful, and someone everyone wanted around. Danni wasn't going to let Lucas take those things from her, even if she had to be the one to break Esther's heart.

Connie looked forward to her regular visits from Gwen and Danni. They brightened the day and lifted some of the monotony of a long-term stay in hospital. But most of all she loved getting visits from Charlie. Every time she saw him, it was like the empty space that had taken residence in her chest was suddenly filled again. This man – her boy – always came with something to tell her. Whether it was the latest mischief Maggie and Brenda had got themselves into, or an idea he had for the story he was working on, she loved it all. Sharing anything with her son felt like a gift she thought she'd given away for good. But today, she was the one with the news, and she was itching to tell him.

'Oh I'm so glad you've come in – it's been such a great morning!' Connie couldn't keep the smile off her face and she couldn't even wait for Charlie to sit down. 'I've got two amazing pieces of news.'

'You look like you've won the lottery.' Charlie smiled, but she couldn't help noticing a change in his demeanour. He looked tired, but he'd probably been working late on the illustrations for his latest book. He'd told her before that when he was caught up in working on them, the hours could just disappear and sometimes it was only when the sun came up that he realised he'd worked all through the night. Still, she was certain the first piece of news she had to share would perk him up.

'I feel like I have won the lottery! First I get you back in my life and now I'm a great-aunt. Darcy gave birth to a little boy this morning and guess what his name is?' Connie hadn't felt this much like she might burst with excitement since the last Christmas Eve she'd believed in Santa Claus.

'Now do I start with Rumpelstiltskin, or work my way up there from something more traditional like James?' Charlie raised his eyebrows and Connie laughed.

'No, neither of those. It's Augustus Charlie William Clark.' Connie clapped her hands together. 'One of his middle names is in honour of his granddad. But Darcy was so over the moon about finally having a cousin, she wanted the baby to have that link to you from the start.'

'Wow.' Charlie sat down in the chair by the bed with a thud. 'That's really nice of her, especially considering we haven't even met.'

'She wants to put that right. She couldn't come before, but she's keen to bring Auggie, as she calls him, down to visit as soon as possible.' Connie was smiling so much it made her face ache. 'Which brings me to my second bit of news. The doctors are finally certain that I won't need any more surgery, so they're moving me to the rehab centre for a few days' intensive physio and to make sure I can cope. Then I'll finally be discharged from hospital!'

'That's great news, Connie. I'm so pleased for you.' Charlie half-stood and kissed her on the cheek. He was saying and doing all the right things, but he still seemed subdued.

'I know you're planning to stay around to see if Richard changes his mind and, if that's still something you want to do, I'm going to arrange to stay somewhere locally too. At least until I'm fully recovered. I understand you'll have to go back to your own life before long, but if this is the one chance we've got to spend some time together, I'm not going to miss it.'

'Me neither.' Charlie smiled, but there was still something he wasn't saying. 'I've got some news too.'

'Do you need to leave sooner than you planned?' It suddenly

felt as if Connie's heart had jumped up into her throat. Charlie couldn't go; she wasn't ready for him to disappear from her life again. She might never be ready, but she was certain she couldn't face it yet.

'No, I'm still planning to stay on for a while. At least until Mum and Dad make a decision about where they're moving to.' Charlie took a deep breath. 'When you told me about Darcy and the baby, and the news about your treatment, I considered not telling you this. But I don't want there to be any more secrets between us.'

'Neither do I.' She was shaking as she reached out for his hand. Whatever it was he needed to say, she had to listen. The secrets she'd kept had caused so much pain, but somehow fate had given her a second chance with Charlie. So even if it hurt to hear what was coming, she could take it, as long as she didn't lose her son for a second time.

'Richard was admitted to hospital again, because he hadn't been taking his medication.'

'Is he okay?' Her heart still felt like it was lodged in her throat, even when Charlie nodded.

'He is now, but I think it was a wake-up call. He asked the paramedics to let me know he was being taken in and, when I got here, he said he wanted us to try and build a relationship.'

'But that's great news!' Of all the things she'd expected Charlie to say, she couldn't even have dared hope for this, but he was shaking his head.

'It would be, except Richard is still adamant that he doesn't want to see you. I tried to talk him around and explain why you did what you did, but he's just not ready to listen.' Charlie squeezed her hand. 'But look at how quickly he changed his mind about seeing me. We just need to give it more time.'

'It doesn't matter.' As leaden as her heart felt now that it had sunk back down into her chest, she meant what she was saying. 'I lost Richard years ago and I lost you too. I never thought I'd get either of you back, and I can't be greedy and ask for more than I've been given. Having you back in my life is what I've wanted from the moment I watched the social worker walk away with you in her arms. But at least I'd got to hold you and know you, even for a little while. I took all of that from Richard and I'm so glad he's decided to take it back. I'd be lying if I didn't admit I wish he felt differently, but I've missed him for almost forty years and I can cope with missing him for the rest of my life if I have to. But I can't cope with saying a permanent goodbye to you again.'

'You won't have to, I promise.' Charlie's eyes were glassy as he looked at her, and silent tears were already flowing down Connie's cheeks. When she was just a little girl, she'd had to learn in a really hard way that she couldn't have everything she wanted. More than sixty years later she was having to learn that was still the case. And, like the childhood version of herself, she was just going to have to cry it all out until she could accept it.

* * *

Danni stared at the menu, but even the thought of eating made her stomach churn. She'd ordered a large G&T as soon as she'd got to the pub. It was just as well she'd promised herself that she was going to tell Esther everything today – whatever happened – otherwise this drinking for Dutch courage might become a habit.

'Oh good, you're here. I'm starving.' Esther rushed in with her usual whirlwind, planting a kiss on Danni's cheek as she did. 'I think it must be because I ate so much last night at the final tasting session. I'm always much hungrier the day after a big blow-out. I'm sure it stretches my stomach! I'll get us another drink first, though; what are you having?'

'No, I'll get it. You sit down and have a look at the lunch menu. What do you want to drink?'

'A glass of white sounds good, and I'm not on shift again for two more days.' Esther already had her face half-buried in the menu, and Danni's brain was working overtime about whether she should let her friend enjoy her lunch before she broke the news, in case it was the last meal they ever shared together. But the idea of facing their version of the last supper made Danni want to forget all the promises she'd pledged to herself and keep her mouth shut.

Setting her glass down on the table, Danni silently prayed that Esther wouldn't see just how much she was shaking. 'Here you go – I made it a large one.'

'And that is why we'll always be best friends!' If Esther could have chosen something to say that would make Danni doubt her intentions, she couldn't have chosen more perfectly. But it was because Esther was such an incredible friend that Danni had to tell her the truth.

'I value our friendship more than anything else in my life. You've been my family since we first met and you were the first person who was ever really there for me. Moving in with you made the flat feel like the first place I wanted to call home in years, and your family made sure I never had to spend a Christmas or birthday without being surrounded by people who I knew loved me.'

'God, Dan, what's wrong? It's like you're writing me a goodbye note, or a eulogy.' All the colour had drained from Esther's face. 'You're not ill, are you? I kept saying to Lucas that you didn't look or seem like yourself lately. Please tell me you aren't sick, because I don't know what I'd do without you.'

'I'm not sick, unless you count with worry.' This was it, the moment Danni was going to cross a line that couldn't be uncrossed.

Everything she needed to tell Esther felt as if it was bubbling up
inside her and about to overflow.

'Well then, what's wrong? You know you can tell me anything.'

'I know, but I'd do anything not to have to tell you this.' Even
after Danni had taken the deepest breath possible, it still felt as if
she couldn't get enough air into her lungs. 'Lucas isn't being honest
with you.'

'About the stag weekend?' Esther's shoulders visibly relaxed.
'It's okay, he's admitted to me that one of the guys switched the
plans from Barcelona to Amsterdam. It might not be my first
choice of venue, but it's not like I don't trust Lucas.'

'It's not about the stag weekend. And you shouldn't trust Lucas
because he's been seeing someone else behind your back.' For a
moment, everything seemed to freeze, and Esther looked at her for
an impossibly long time, without even blinking. Then she finally
spoke.

'Danni, please don't do this. Please don't make everything
Lucas has been saying about you true.' Her words took the air out
of Danni's lungs again, but she wasn't going to let Lucas's lies stop
her from telling the truth.

'I don't care what he said, but I can already guess. That I'm
lying and delusional, that I'm only saying any of this because I
want him for myself.' Danni was fighting to keep her tone even, not
wanting everyone in the pub to start staring in their direction. 'Do
you know how I guessed that's what he said? Because it's what he
said to me, when I confronted him about his dating profile and
when I saw him pressed up against the same nurse that I know he
was meeting down at Penwick Point. You can ask Charlie, if you
don't believe me.'

'Oh God, that poor man. He's got no idea you're using him in
this little game you've been playing for years, has he?' Esther's
voice was steady, but there was a cold steeliness that Danni had

never witnessed before. 'He's clearly as besotted with you as you are with Lucas.'

'I'm not besotted with Lucas; I can't stand him after what he's done to you.' Danni tried to lean forward across the table, but Esther recoiled, pressing her body as far into the seat opposite as she physically could.

'Oh come on! Do you think I'm blind? I've had to witness the way you are around him ever since we started dating. Trying to create your in-jokes that leave me out, and the way you stare at him when you think I'm not looking. Lucas used to joke about it and the fact he wouldn't have to look far for a rebound fling if I ever left him. But he was embarrassed by it, and all this time I've made excuses for you and tried to pretend to myself that it wasn't true.' Esther choked on her words. 'I used to worry that you'd outgrow our friendship and I was so relieved when you didn't. Now I'll never know if it really mattered to you at all, or if you were just staying friends with me to get close to Lucas.'

'It's because of how much I love you that I never tried to get closer to him than I already was.' Danni's throat was burning. She understood why her friend was angry, but the fact that she was still being manipulated by Lucas made her want to scream. It had taken Danni a long time to work out who the real Lucas was, and she was terrified that Esther might not see it before it was too late.

'Well, thanks very much, you clearly deserve a reward, because according to you the only reason I still have a fiancé is because you didn't snap your fingers and send him running to you instead.' Esther was losing control of her calm now and Danni regretted suggesting they meet somewhere so public. She'd chosen the pub in the hope it would force Esther to listen and that, in turn, it would help her see the truth, rather than just flying off the handle. But Esther was only human and she was reacting in a very human way to something she didn't want to hear.

'That's not what I said.' Danni was almost whispering now, hoping it might make Esther lower her voice too. 'Okay, I'll admit that for a long time I thought I was in love with Lucas, but I always loved you more. And even when there were times when I know my friendship with Lucas could have crossed the line into something more, I'd never have done it, because losing you would be the worst thing that could happen to me. But the other girls don't have any loyalty to you and I've witnessed him blurring those lines with people at work for a long time. It's only now I realise just how far he takes it.'

'There are no other girls, only you and this deluded fantasy you've got that Lucas returns your feelings. He doesn't; he loves me. Only me!' Esther's eyes were wild and Danni was vaguely aware that the people around them had stopped doing anything other than watching them.

'Believe what you want about me. I'd rather that than watch you go into this marriage with a man who came to me and told me he had doubts about marrying you, that he wasn't sure he loved you enough. He even gave that as an excuse for creating an online dating profile. He wanted to risk everything to test how much he loved you.'

'You're lying.' Esther shook her head; the look of desolation on her face was so painful to witness, but Danni was clinging to a shred of hope that it might mean that part of Esther believed her, deep down.

'I wish I was. But you've got to trust me: don't go through with this wedding; you deserve so much more.'

'Stop it! Just stop it!' The anger was back and Esther got to her feet, downing the rest of her wine in one and reaching into her bag before throwing a ten-pound note on the table. 'Nothing you say is going to stop me from marrying Lucas. It wouldn't get you what you want, even if I called the wedding off. He doesn't love you and he never will. I don't want anything from you any more. Stay away from me, and from us. Just get your own life, Danielle. It's about time you did.'

'Esther, don't, please!' Danni called after her, but she didn't turn around. There was nothing else she could have said, even if Esther had been willing to listen. Everything was out in the open now and, just as she'd feared, her friendship with Esther seemed likely to be the only casualty.

All Danni could do was cling to what she'd said to Charlie about love being selfless, but that didn't stop the tears that had been choking in her throat suddenly erupting into noisy sobs. And she couldn't care less how many people were looking at her as she stumbled out of the pub and into a life without Esther in it.

26

Every time Danni's phone pinged, her heart started racing, hoping it would be a message from Esther, saying that she'd thought about everything that had been said and had realised that Danni was telling the truth. But there'd been nothing from her and all Danni's messages to Esther had gone unread. There was one message from Lucas, though.

I warned you how things would turn out if you went around spreading your lies. Now I'm going to make sure everyone at the hospital knows exactly what you're like. Trying to ruin people's lives when you don't get what you want. Nobody wants to work with a stalker.

The words had had the effect on her that Lucas had no doubt banked on. She'd been terrified that she'd need to leave St Piran's to get over her feelings for him and, even now that she hated his guts, he'd still found a way of making sure she had to leave.

'Are you okay? You look miles away.' When Charlie touched her on the shoulder, she jumped. Despite the fact that they'd only known each other a few weeks, he always seemed to be able to tell when something was on her mind. But she couldn't talk to him about this.

'Sorry, I was just thinking about something.' Not even Charlie's offer to go down and see if they could see Trevor had managed to take her mind off things. There was no relief from the constant loop playing in her head, of things she wished she could have said and done differently over the years.

'You look exhausted, and I bet you haven't been eating properly if work has been crazy again. If you don't want to walk for long, we can go back to my place, and I can make you something to eat. You don't even have to talk if you're tired. We can take a leaf out of Brenda and Maggie's book, and just lie about, doing nothing.'

'Thanks, but let's go and see if we can find Trevor first. I could really do with seeing his sweet little face.' Maggie and Brenda were already heading down the slope of the cliff to the lowest point. It was getting cooler and the strength of the breeze would have been reason enough alone for Danni to quicken her pace. But the truth was she was desperate to see the seal pup and find something to make her smile in the middle of the absolute disaster she'd made of her life.

'Whatever you want to do is fine with me.' Charlie walked alongside her in companionable silence, their hands almost touching, and she longed to reach out for that connection to someone she cared about. She'd even called her brother, Joe, leaving a horribly garbled message for him when he hadn't answered. But dragging Charlie into the middle of this felt like it would sully whatever it was they had, even if that would be over soon too. She really liked him, maybe even more than that, and she got the sense that the feeling was mutual, but it probably wouldn't be if he found out what she'd done.

'I think I can see him.' Charlie pointed to the same outcrop of rocks where they'd first spotted the seal pup.

'He's getting so much bigger every time.' Tears were blurring Danni's eyes again at the thought that the seal would soon have lost all of the features that made him so distinctively a pup. Her emotions were dangerously close to the surface, and she wasn't sure how long she'd be able to keep convincing Charlie that she was just overtired from work. It turned out she hadn't even made it as far as getting back to the cottage.

'Okay. Something's wrong and I don't think it's work. You don't have to tell me, but you do have to let me do this.' Charlie wrapped his arms around her and gave her a hug. Other than Esther, he was the only person who seemed capable of understanding when she needed to talk and when she didn't, and somehow reacting with just the right response either way. Burying her face against his chest, she contemplated whether there was any way she might be able to ride this out until he left. All she had to do was bottle up her feelings for a bit longer; she ought to be an expert on that by now after all. But it wasn't that easy with Charlie, because it turned out he'd listened to everything she'd said.

'Is this about Esther? Did you tell her about Lucas?'

'I had to. I couldn't let her go through with the wedding without knowing the truth about him.' She could barely get the words out and she still couldn't look at Charlie, but he was holding her tight and somehow making it possible to believe that things might actually turn out okay.

'For what it's worth, I think you did the right thing. I know I said before that it's safer to stay out of it, but she's your best friend and you'd never have forgiven yourself if he'd ended up ruining her life.'

'But now I'm the one who's ruined it. She won't even read my messages any more.' She finally managed to look up at Charlie as she drew back a little, but he was shaking his head.

'She might feel like shooting the messenger at the moment, but just give it time. She'll realise eventually that this is all down to him.'

'You wouldn't say that if you knew—' She couldn't even finish the sentence.

'Knew what?' Charlie's eyes never left hers and, somehow, the part of her that was desperate for relief decided that a problem shared was a problem halved.

'That I'm the one Lucas said he loved, and that it was because of me he was having doubts about marrying Esther.'

'I still don't see how that's your fault.'

'Because I loved him too. I spent more than seven years fighting it, but apparently still managing to make it blatantly obvious. Esther had to watch her best friend pining after her boyfriend, but she never once said a word. She must have just kept waiting and hoping my feelings would eventually fade. But by the time they did, the damage had already been done.'

'I see.' Charlie released his hold and she missed the feeling of his arms around her the moment he let go. 'Why didn't you tell me it was you who was caught up in all of this, when you were talking about the problems between your friend and her fiancé?'

'It was really hard to talk about.' Danni knew she was making excuses, but Charlie didn't let her get away with it.

'The difficult conversations are the most important ones. I had to sit by Connie's hospital bed yesterday and tell her that the man she's loved for almost forty years wants nothing to do with her.' Charlie clenched his jaw. 'Telling me the truth would have been so much easier than that, so I still don't understand why you didn't do it.'

'Because there was nothing to tell. Nothing happened between me and Lucas, except in my head. And by the time I met you, or at least around the time when I met you...' Danni hesitated, unable to pinpoint now exactly when it was. 'I realised I didn't want anything to ever happen with him. All that wishing and hoping for my feelings for Lucas to go away and they finally had.'

'Are you sure?' Charlie was still watching her, as if he was looking for the slightest nuance in her expression that would suggest otherwise.

'Of course I am – when I met you, when we were together. It just changed everything.'

'I wish that was true.' Charlie stared up at the sky and shook his head, before dropping his gaze to look at her. 'I think I was just a well-timed distraction. Something you were using to divert from the fact that the person you love was about to marry someone else. Feelings like that don't just disappear overnight...'

'I didn't and you're not...' A wave of exhaustion was washing over Danni. She hadn't slept since meeting Esther in the pub and she couldn't even think straight, let alone articulate what it was she was trying to explain to Charlie. Lucas had just been a fantasy, but she was falling for a real person with Charlie, although she could hardly blame him for not believing her. She'd questioned whether her feelings for Charlie were because of her need to find someone who gave her a sense of belonging, and whether she was simply transferring that need from Lucas to Charlie, building up another illusion of the person she wanted him to be. But Charlie was different. He didn't need Danni to massage his ego, and he avoided attention rather than seeking it out. She'd finally found someone who might genuinely be able to give her that sense of belonging, the way Esther and her family had done in a different way, and she'd blown it with all of them.

'Look, I understand, I really do. I wish things were different, but both our lives are so complicated at the moment and maybe it's just as well I'm not going to be here for long, because I already like you way more than is good for me.' Charlie shook his head again. 'If I was staying there'd be a horrible possibility of me ending up as your back-up plan, and no one wants to be someone's Fiona.'

'I like you much more than I should too, but if you were staying it would be nothing like that. You're far too amazing to be anyone's back-up plan.' If she could physically have restrained him from leaving, she might have tried, but she knew she was going to have to let him go.

'I think it's just as well for both our sakes that I won't be around. I hope things work out for you, I really do, but I can't allow myself to care even more about that than I do already. The situation with Richard and Connie is in danger of breaking my heart and I really can't risk letting you finish the job.' Charlie leant forward, kissing her so lightly she almost didn't believe it had happened. 'Good luck, Danni, I'll miss you and, whatever happens, don't ever let yourself become someone's Fiona.'

Before she could even answer, Charlie turned away and called for his dog. 'Come on, Mags, we've got to go.'

For the second time in as many days Danni wanted to call after someone she loved and beg them to come back and listen, without any idea of what she'd say if they did. This time she didn't even try, but the realisation that it was too late for her, and that she already loved Charlie and had lost him too, hit her hard all the same.

Connie's euphoria at being moved to the rehab centre had been dampened by the news that Richard only wanted a relationship with Charlie as long as she stayed out of it. But she was still determined to get through the assessment that would see her considered fit for discharge as soon as possible.

The team at the centre had worked out a programme for her to ensure that by the time she left she'd be able to manage at home on her own. It was a strange concept, the idea of living alone after sharing a busy ward with so many other patients. Even those who weren't within her bay could be overheard at times, and then there was the revolving door of staff who constantly seemed to be coming and going. You could never be lonely, even if you wanted to. And whilst that kind of inflicted communal living was still Connie's idea of hell in many ways, part of her would miss having someone to talk to. The regular visits from Gwen in particular would be something she'd mourn, and she hoped their promise to stay in touch with one another wouldn't turn out to be hollow.

Another person she'd miss would be Danni, but there was a good chance Connie would get to see her again, if her intuition about Charlie's feelings towards Danni were right. The way he looked at her suggested those feelings were more than casual and, if Connie had been Charlie's mum for his whole life, she might have felt able to ask him. But her relationship with her son was still tentative and new, and she was frightened of doing anything that might drive him away, especially after what Richard had said.

Danni and Charlie were still on her mind when Danni walked into the rehab centre. Connie had been in the middle of composing a carefully worded text to Charlie, asking him how things were, aimed at sounding light and breezy. She needed him to know she cared and was thinking about him, without risking becoming over-bearing.

'How lovely to see you.' Connie craned her neck slightly, trying to look past Danni without making it too obvious. 'No Charlie today?'

'No.' It was just a single word, but Danni's eyes were suddenly brimming with tears.

'Oh sweetheart, what's wrong?' Connie was in a high-backed chair by the side of her bed. 'You can sit on my bed, or I'm sure there's another chair we can find somewhere.'

'The bed's fine, although I'm tempted to lie down and pull the covers over my head and not get up for the next few years.'

'Surely things aren't that bad!' Gwen had appeared out of nowhere, making both of them jump – she'd make a good assassin if she ever fancied a change of career.

'Oh trust me, it's every bit as bad as that.' Danni's voice was small, and she didn't even seem to notice when Gwen sat on the bed and put her arm around her. 'I ruined things with Charlie by not telling the truth about what was going on.' Danni swallowed again, as if her words were trying to choke her. 'I told him that my best friend's fiancé was having doubts about getting married because he was in love with someone else. What I didn't say, until it was too late, was that I was that someone else, and that for too many years I'd been praying for him to tell me he felt the same.'

'Lucas Newman.' Gwen screwed up her face as she said his name. 'He's not good enough to clean your boots, or Esther's.'

'Oh please don't say anything to anyone, will you?' Danni gave Gwen a pleading look, but then she sighed. 'I don't suppose it'll matter if you do; I'm going to have to leave St Piran's anyway.'

'Why on earth would you have to do that?' Connie couldn't stand the idea of the hospital losing one of its best doctors over a man who sounded from Gwen's description like a complete waste of space. If it was the same Mr Newman who'd been one of her surgeons, she could see why Gwen had no time for him. He had an ego the size of a house and seemed to revel in the sound of his own voice. But she'd seen him turn on the charm with some of the other staff too, and chameleons like him were often more dangerous than the blatant narcissists.

'Because Lucas is out for revenge, and he'll make sure it's impossible for me to stay on. When I discovered he had an online dating profile and that he was also seeing one of the nurses here, I told him that if he didn't tell Esther, I would.'

'And of course he didn't tell her.' Gwen didn't wait for an answer. 'It might not feel like it now, but you did the right thing.'

'Did I? Charlie questioned why I waited so long. He thinks it's because I've still got feelings for Lucas. It isn't, but I'm starting to wonder if my motives were as pure as I thought they were. I spent forever hoping Esther would be the one to find someone else. I wanted something like this to happen, as long as it didn't hurt her. She thinks I'm to blame, too, and maybe I am. I never gave them the space they probably needed. There was always three people in their relationship, so is it any wonder Lucas decided to make it four?'

'Or five, or six, or seven. I see and hear a lot more than people realise, working in that shop.' Gwen was having none of it. 'Did you ever try anything on with him?'

'No, I'd never do that to Esther.'

'But he tried something with you?' Gwen was like a lawyer cross-examining a witness on the stand and Danni was too exhausted to even try to rebuff her questions.

'More than once.'

'And when you realised you didn't love him any more, why didn't you tell Esther straight away?' Gwen's questioning was relentless.

'Because I couldn't stand the idea of what it might do to her to find that out, and because I couldn't bear the thought of not having her in my life, if she chose to believe him.'

'Bingo!' Gwen threw her arms up in the air. 'Everything you did was because of how much you love Esther. Even when you thought you were in love with Lucas, you put her feelings first. Everything he did was because he keeps his brain in his pants.'

'I want to believe that, but I can't help thinking it would have been better if I hadn't said anything at all.' Danni looked at Connie.

'At least then I wouldn't have lost my friendship with Charlie; it's the best thing that's happened to me in years.'

'He'll get over it. If he can forgive me, he can forgive you for this. But I do understand what you mean about wondering if you should have kept quiet.' Connie's scalp prickled. She'd made so many wrong decisions along the way, she didn't trust her judgement any more. 'When Richard reacted the way he did, I couldn't blame him. I deserved it, but Charlie didn't. I've been wondering ever since if it would have been better for both of them if I'd pretended to Charlie that I didn't know who his dad was, and that he was the result of a one-night stand.'

'I think once he met you he'd have realised that was unlikely.' Gwen cocked her head on one side as she spoke.

'Are you saying I couldn't have a one-night stand?' Connie wasn't sure why, but she felt mildly offended.

'Not that you couldn't, just that you wouldn't. There's nothing wrong with them and I should know' – Gwen dropped a perfect wink – 'but you're the sort who over-analyses everything, not the sort who makes a snap, spur-of-the-moment decision. Which is how you've ended up here, having this conversation.'

'You can't really argue with that, can you?' For the first time, there was a hint of a smile on Danni's face.

'Not really.'

'Good, because no one ever wins an argument with me.' Gwen wagged her finger. 'I was the font of all knowledge when I was a midwife, and it's the same now I'm here. So I'm telling you both that you made the right decisions by telling the truth.'

'Except I should have done it sooner.' Connie couldn't believe she'd managed to live with the secret for so long, but somehow she had. Only now it was out, and like the contents of Pandora's box, it could never go back in again.

'But you heard what Gwen said to me, didn't you?' Danni fixed her with a look, waiting until she nodded. 'You didn't tell Richard because you knew if you did he'd lose the farm. And you didn't want to raise Charlie on your own, because you know how tough that can be. You're the one who had to go through pregnancy, childbirth and making the toughest decision of your life alone. You were just trying to do the right thing.'

'I think I've got an apprentice.' Gwen clapped a hand on her back. 'And I couldn't have put it better myself. You were both just protecting the ones you love, which makes you good people in my book. And good people deserve good things.'

'I don't feel like a good person.' Danni had taken the words right out of Connie's mouth, and an unspoken understanding passed between the two women. They might be able to justify why they'd done the things they had, but that didn't mean they could forgive themselves. All they could do was pray that the people around them would turn out to be far more forgiving.

27
_____

The weather was starting to turn much cooler and the days were now so short that Danni often wouldn't see daylight, either before or after the start of a day shift. The relentless grey that seemed to have settled over Port Kara in the past few days suited her mood, but it didn't make the coastline any less stunning. As Danni walked Brenda on her day off work, the rocks that seemed to rise up from the sea, and gave Dagger's Head its name, had ribbons of fog floating between them, making them look terrifying and breathtakingly beautiful all at the same time. It would have made the perfect location for a tense thriller, or murder mystery, where the victim could disappear forever behind a shroud of fog. The only thing Danni wanted to disappear was the aching void of emptiness that seemed capable of suffocating her from the inside out. It had been almost a week since she'd spoken to Esther, and she hadn't had a response to any of her messages either. It was the longest they'd ever been out of touch, but it was the prospect that this silence might go on for the rest of her life that was killing Danni.

When her brother, Joe, returned her call, it hadn't taken him long to cut to the chase. 'Hey, kiddo, what's up? I got your message and you sounded so downbeat. Mum's not up to her usual tricks again, is she?'

'Not this time.' Danni had felt better just for hearing his voice, and the way he always referred to her as 'kiddo', despite the fact they were now both well into their thirties. It had come to signify the fact he saw himself as her protector, in the face of their father's death and their mother checking out. He'd been the one to drive her to look at universities and the one proudly taking photographs at her graduation. He'd even sent money back from Australia to help support her while she studied and she hadn't realised until much later that he'd had to borrow the money to do it. He came over at least once a year, insisting that she did the same and even sending her the money for the flights until she was earning enough to afford it. Joe must have spent most of his annual leave ensuring he had time with his sister, and she had to stop herself every time from begging him to move back to the UK. That didn't stop her wishing with all her heart that he'd one day decide for himself that home couldn't possibly be more than nine thousand miles away from where she was. She'd thought about following him once her training was finally complete, but the thought of leaving Esther and her family had always stopped her. But now there was nothing preventing her from moving to the other side of the world.

'If it's not Mum, what is it?' The worry in Joe's voice had been obvious, and she should never have called and left that message.

'I'm fine; it was just a bad day a work, that's all. How are things with you?'

'Well, put it this way, I can still tell when you're lying. Come on, Dan, what's up? I know something is, and you know I'm just going to assume the worst if you don't tell me. I'll book a flight over if I have to.' That was something Joe was more than capable of doing and she didn't want that on her conscience too. Things with his girlfriend of two years seemed to be going really well. He was about to complete the sale on his dream house in New South Wales, which had an ocean view and enough room to start a family, but Joe had admitted that securing the property would take every penny of his savings. So the last thing he could afford was an extra trip back to the UK because his kid sister was missing her best friend.

'It's nothing. Esther's not talking to me, that's all.' Her attempt at easy breezy had failed miserably when her voice cracked on the last two words.

'You're joking.' It had clearly sounded as unthinkable to Joe as it was to Danni.

'I wish I was.'

'Lucas, right?' Joe had hit the nail on the head straight away. 'I always knew he'd find a way to come between you two.'

There'd been no point in her lying to her brother, because he'd always been able to see right through her. It wasn't a surprise that Joe had honed in on Lucas being the cause of the breakdown in her friendship either, given how he felt about the man. 'You know I was in love with him, don't you?'

'Love? No you weren't.' Joe's tone had been emphatic. 'Whenever I saw you together I could see what he was doing, and I worked out his game plan a long time ago from the things you told me. He manipulated you to believe you were the only people who understood each other. But you and I know how different what we went through was. We had a mother who didn't want us. He had devoted parents who would never have abandoned him if death hadn't forced them to. That's not something you can compare, but he knew you desperately needed someone to love and be loved by; he just wanted someone to stroke his ego and tell him how great he was. So, yeah, you might have thought you were in love and I suppose that was obvious, but only because you were so guarded around him. I've seen you with your other friends and even some of mine, and you're a hugger. Showing affection is what you do, maybe because we never got any off Mum, after Dad died. But around Lucas, you were always like some sort of staid Victorian maiden, whose reputation and virtue might be sullied by the slightest touch. That's how I knew you liked him, because you were terrified that if he touched you, it might lead to something and you'd never do that to Esther. So I know this isn't because you've done that.'

Joe's complete faith in Danni had made her cry for about the seven hundredth time since the argument with Esther, and when she'd spilt out the whole story to him, he'd listened without interrupting. Afterwards, he'd echoed Gwen, telling her that she'd done the right thing, and that he was certain Esther would come to see that eventually. When he'd admitted it might take years, Danni had broken down again. And, after that, Joe had made the offer she was now seriously considering.

'Why don't you come over here for a bit? You could make it a holiday at first, but they're always looking for doctors and, if you did decide to stay, I'm certain you'd get a visa. I suppose I could put up with having my kid sister around all the time again.' Joe had laughed then, and there'd been such a warmth in the sound that, if Danni had been able to jump on a plane at that moment, she'd almost certainly have done it. After all, she'd already got as far as applying for a job in Sydney. But then she'd looked down at Brenda, sitting by her feet, and even the option of running to Joe had seemed impossible. He'd said the offer to move into his new place was always on the table and she'd thanked him, telling him how much she loved him and how grateful she was that she'd been able to tell him everything. As much of a relief as that had been, it didn't change anything and, even now, a few days later, she had no idea where she went from here.

'You can't go near the edge, girl.' Danni bent down and clipped

Brenda's lead on as they walked into the blanket of fog. The dog was usually very cautious, staying well back from the cliff edge, but Danni couldn't risk anything happening to her. She couldn't bear the thought of losing Brenda too.

'I'm not the only mad fool out in this, then?' The sounds of Charlie's voice, as he emerged out of the fog in front of her, made her scream. 'Oh God, I'm sorry, I didn't mean to scare you.'

He put a steadying hand on her arm, but took it off again almost straight away, making her realise how much she missed the sensation of his touch, even if it had only been an instinctive reaction on Charlie's part. 'It's okay – I'm sorry for screaming in your face like that. It's just the fog. It makes everything look spooky.'

'I love this kind of weather; something about it really helps me to think.' Charlie smiled in that familiar way she'd so quickly come to love. She was really going to miss not seeing that any more.

'I know what you mean.' Danni had wished more than once over the past week that she had the ability to stop herself from thinking altogether, but all that had done was make her brain go into overdrive even more. 'How's Richard?'

'Good, now that he's taking his medication. He asked me to go to his GP appointment with him and she gave him advice on some lifestyle changes he can make that will help too.' Charlie's face clouded for a moment. 'I tried to suggest that letting go of his resentment towards Connie might help with his stress levels, but he still won't even mention her name. He just says he doesn't want to talk about it and the subject is closed for good as far as he's concerned.'

'That's such a shame, but from the outside I can see both points of view. It must be much harder for Richard to do that.'

'I still keep hoping he'll change his mind eventually, but for now I just want to make sure they're both okay.' Charlie was still clearly determined not to take sides.

'You've got to have hope.' A lump lodged itself in Danni's throat, as it seemed to all too frequently these days, as Maggie came over to Brenda and the dogs exchanged an excited greeting. 'She's really going to miss Maggie.'

'She doesn't have to.' As Charlie spoke, something in Danni's chest surged. 'I'm staying on in Port Kara indefinitely. At least until I know Richard and Connie are both fully recovered. The sale on the house my parents were buying on the Isle of Wight has fallen through. Mum's been downloading every episode of *Escape to the Country* she can get her hands on, and they've realised how much more they can get for their money in certain parts of the country, so they're looking at properties all over now. They're viewing some up in Yorkshire this weekend, not far from where Connie lives. So there's no rush for me to find somewhere permanent until I know where they're going to be.'

'It would be amazing if you ended up being close to Connie, but I guess that might be difficult for Richard.' It would be hard for Danni to accept him being at the other end of the country too, not that it really mattered any more. He'd made it clear he didn't want things between them to continue, and she was going to need to leave St Piran's anyway. There was a chance she could stay in Port Kara and commute to work in Truro, if she could get a job at the hospital there, but it would still mean a risk of running into Esther and Lucas. So moving again was starting to feel like the only option.

'Sometimes it takes a while to accept things, but space and time can do wonders in helping people to see things more clearly.' Charlie held her gaze. 'I'm sorry about how I reacted. I don't know, maybe there's some hidden, subconscious part of me that expects to be rejected after the choices Connie made. Or maybe I'm just like every other egotistical male on the planet and I couldn't stand the thought that the person I really, really, really liked might feel that way about someone else.'

'None of this is your fault. I spent so long trying to cover up how I felt, I think I forgot how to tell the truth, even to myself.' Danni had to curl her fingers into a ball to stop herself from touching him. Joe had been spot-on about her doing that sort of thing to protect herself from crossing the line, but it wasn't just the prospect of Charlie rejecting her that scared her. It was the idea that he might not. It would be so easy to fall completely in love with him, but she didn't deserve to have that. Not after the grenade she'd let off in Esther's relationship.

'I know things are far too complicated for both of us to hope for any more than that, but do you think we can at least be friends again?'

She nodded, despite not knowing if that was even going to be possible, when deep down she wanted so much more. 'Definitely. I could use as many friends as I can get right now.'

'Sooner or later Esther is going to realise that you only told her about Lucas to protect her. It's going to be okay.'

'You promise?' She wanted to believe Charlie more than anything, but he clearly didn't want to lie to her after everything he'd said about the importance of honesty.

'I wish I could make you that promise, but she'll be missing you every bit as much as you're missing her, that's one thing I do know for certain.'

'I hope you're right.' Danni made a silent vow that she'd never ask for anything again if the situation with Esther could be fixed. But, when she looked up at Charlie again, she had a horrible feeling she was already telling herself another lie.

* * *

When one of the physiotherapists in the rehabilitation centre had suggested that Connie might want to move into a nursing home to continue her recovery, she'd never felt so old. And she'd reacted with the sort of fiery outburst that her sister, Janice, had always said was the reason she'd never found someone to settle down with. But the truth was she hadn't wanted to *settle*. Connie had never met anyone she'd felt as strongly about as Richard. Now, looking through the treasure box her niece had sent to the hospital at her request, Connie suddenly didn't feel old at all. Almost forty years had rolled back as soon as she'd held one of the envelopes with Richard's writing on the front.

It was the same box she'd told Danni to instruct Darcy to open, if anything had happened to her after the accident. Luckily she'd been able to explain everything to her niece herself instead. But there was someone else who needed to see what was in the box.

'Hello, sweetheart. You look like you've been out in the wind!' Connie smiled as Charlie came into the rehab unit and she fought the urge to reach up and smooth down his hair when he sat by the side of her bed. That was a job for his real mother, although probably not for the last twenty-five years.

'It was wild down on the beach today, but I love it when it's like that, even if I end up looking like I haven't brushed my hair for a month.' Charlie laughed. 'Maggie loved it too and she was chasing around, trying to catch the wind in her mouth.'

'I can't wait to get out and go down to the beach.' Connie sighed. 'That's one thing I'm determined to do before I go back to Yorkshire: walk barefoot on the sand on Port Kara beach one last time.'

'Nothing you do when you get out of here has to be for one last time, unless you want it to be.'

'I don't think the red carpet will be rolled out for me around here.' Connie shook her head, determined not to feel sorry for herself. She'd done what she'd intended to do when she'd made the decision to come back to Port Kara. There were a few loose ends to tie up, and the small matter of being well enough to move back into her cottage, but other than that there'd be no reason to stay. Charlie didn't live in Cornwall and Richard hated her guts. So, whatever her son said, when she stood on the sand, on the same beach where she'd spent so many hours with the only man she'd ever loved, it would be for the last time.

'Richard's just angry, I'm sure he'll—'

'You don't know him like I do.' Connie put a hand on her son's arm. 'But it's okay. As long as I've got you and Darcy, and baby Auggie, that's all that matters.'

She had to believe that was true, but Charlie was giving her a sceptical look. 'Just don't give up on him completely. Not yet.'

'I made my choice all those years ago and I can't expect a second chance, but I do want him to see this.' Connie gestured towards the box. 'And I think looking through everything in there will help you understand things too.'

'What is it?'

'It's the letters from Richard, all twenty of them. And there are also the replies I wrote him; there are twenty of those too.'

'You never sent any of them?' Charlie widened his eyes as Connie shook her head.

'I couldn't, because then he'd have known how desperately I wanted him to choose me. But I knew that would kill him in the end. Or at least I convinced myself it would. Now, I'm not nearly so sure it was the right thing to do.' Connie dabbed her eyes with a tissue. 'There are some old Polaroids in there too, from the camera I had that summer. Ticket stubs from a movie we saw, and even serviettes from the café that used to be on the edge of the beach, where we'd meet as often as we could. I played it so cool then, trying to keep my feelings in check, and I don't think Richard ever knew how sentimental I was deep down.'

'Things could have been so different if the two of you had just been able to be honest with each other.' There was a sadness in Charlie's eyes, but Connie didn't want him to feel that way because of the decisions she'd made.

'And that would hurt a lot more if you hadn't had the loving, happy childhood you did, with two fabulous parents who adore you, and who are clearly every bit as wonderful as their amazing son.' Connie swallowed hard against the emotion threatening to overwhelm her. 'Your mum sent me another care package that arrived this morning. And, somehow, without ever having met me, she keeps managing to fill each parcel with the things I love.'

'She's always had the knack of buying the best presents.' The affection in Charlie's voice was obvious. 'And she wants to put the fact she's never met you right, as soon as possible. She's always said you gave her the greatest gift imaginable and sending the care packages is just her way of starting to say thank you.'

'It's me who's got her to thank, and your dad of course. Because of them, it's so much easier to live with any regrets I might have had and I hope, when Richard sees what's in this box, he might feel the same. There's some paperwork from your adoption and the letter the social worker gave me about the family you were going to, as well as one from your mum. There were no identifying details, but getting those letters helped me so much. I don't expect Richard to forgive me when he reads them, but I hope they help him start to forgive himself.' When Gwen had first suggested that Richard might have reacted the way he did out of guilt, Connie hadn't been convinced. But if there was even the chance that was true, she owed it to him to help alleviate some of that guilt in any way she could.

'I'll give it to him, but I would like to read everything first. If you're sure that's okay? I don't want to invade your privacy.'

'You won't. I'd really love you to see them and know how much Richard and I loved each other, and how much your mum loved you before she even met you. It was what clinched it for me, because she loved you the same way I did: unconditionally.' Connie sniffed, determined not to start crying again, so she made a joke instead. 'And I promise there's nothing in the letters that will make you cringe too much.'

'Well, that's a relief.' Charlie leant towards her, kissing her on the cheek. 'Thank you.'

'What for?'

'For everything you did, and for sharing this with me. I'm just starting to realise how lucky I am to have two mothers who've always loved me so unreservedly. Lots of people don't even get one.'

'No, they don't.' For a moment she was tempted to say more. To ask him if Danni had shared the same story with him as she'd shared with Connie, about her own mother, but that would have been overstepping the mark in an even worse way than smoothing his hair down would have been. If Charlie and Danni were meant to be together, they needed to find a way of making it happen. And Connie knew she was the last person who should be handing out advice, when she'd failed so spectacularly at doing that for herself. Instead, she reached out to her son and allowed the gratitude she had for this moment to wash over her.

28

'I thought Esther was due in today?' Danni took the cup of coffee Aidan was holding out towards her. Part of her had been dreading sharing her first shift with Esther since the argument, but the rest of her hadn't been able to help hoping there'd be some kind of catalyst that would make her best friend realise life was too short for them to carry on like this. Charlie had questioned whether Danni's feelings for Lucas could turn off overnight, after so long. Even though they had, she still hadn't been able to believe Esther would be able to switch off her feelings for Danni just as quickly. She certainly couldn't. Danni had lost other friends along the way, for one reason or another, but Esther was family, or at least she had been.

'She asked to swap shifts with me again. Some kind of wedding prep emergency or something. She seems to be having a lot of those lately.' Aidan pulled a face. 'Which is why I told her she should just have eloped to Antigua and done it on the beach. But she made me an offer I couldn't refuse if I did the swap.'

'Oh really.' Danni tried to keep her tone casual. As far as she could tell, Esther hadn't told anyone what had happened. But it was only a matter of time before people started picking up on the fact that their friendship was apparently over.

'She said I can help her plan her hen do! Can you believe it? I was worried I might be stepping on your toes, but she said you're really busy with other stuff and that you'd understand why she asked me.' Aidan looked mortified when he saw the expression that must have crossed Danni's face. 'Oh God, I have stepped on your toes, haven't I?'

'No, it's fine. I just feel like I've let her down. Talk about being the worst maid of honour ever.'

'Of course you're not. Oh, honey.' Aidan wrapped her in his arms for a moment, then he laughed. 'If anyone needs to worry about being the worst at something, it's Gary. He's trying online dating, but every time he gets a quiet five minutes in this place he practises imaginary golf. He doesn't even seem to realise he's doing it, but if any of his dates see that, his chances will be over before they've even begun.'

Danni looked up just as Gary took another swing of his imaginary golf club, sending his imaginary ball hurtling straight towards the non-existent green. 'Okay, things could be worse.'

'Great shot, Gaz.' The voice congratulating Gary was as familiar as it was unwelcome and, when Lucas came striding down the corridor, it was all Danni could do not to run.

'Thanks, Doc. I've been working on my form.' Gary basked in the compliment and Aidan sniggered, muttering the word *dickheads* under his breath. At least he hadn't been sucked into being one of Lucas's groupies yet.

'I was just popping down to let you know that I'm arranging a curry and drinks the Saturday after next as a sort of work stag do. I'm going to Amsterdam with a few old friends in November, but I wanted to do something with all my new friends from the hospital, to say thanks for making me and Esther so welcome. It's all on me, and it should be a good night.' Lucas was turning on the charm, as only he could, and revelling in playing the bountiful host, while Gary looked beside himself at having been invited.

'Oh wow, thanks, I'd love that.'

'I'll email all the details to you.' Lucas clapped a hand on his back, not seeming to see the irony in the fact he didn't even have the phone number of someone he'd invited to his stag do. Then he turned towards Aidan, pointedly ignoring Danni's existence. 'I would invite you too, mate, but I know you're helping my gorgeous fiancée with the plans for her hen do. We're so lucky to have made so many friends here and it's great knowing just how many people we've got on our side.'

'Yeah, well, I'm team bride all the way. Just like Danni.' Aidan put an arm round her and, if she hadn't have known better, she'd have been certain he was aware of what had happened between her and Esther.

'It's nice she's got such a loyal friend.' Lucas gave him a thumbs up, before catching Danni's eye. It was enough to convey that this was a performance all for her, and that he meant every word of the warning he'd given her. Within seconds he'd headed off down the corridor again, his mission complete.

'I know I shouldn't say it when he's a friend of yours and the love of Esther's life, but I can't help thinking that something about that guy doesn't ring true.'

'You might be right. I just hope she turns out to be the love of his life, but I highly doubt it.' As Danni spoke, Aidan's mouth dropped open. And it was probably only the sound of the red phone ringing with a trauma call that stopped him from launching into an inquisition about what she'd meant. The thing was, she already knew Esther wasn't the love of Lucas's life, because he was. If her best friend was the love of anyone's life, it was Danni's. And now Danni was prepared to step aside and move away for a second time, to give Esther the best possible shot at being happy. If that didn't equate to true love, then she wasn't sure what did.

* * *

When Charlie had asked Danni to come over for dinner at his place, she'd hoped it would give her the opportunity to explain why she'd decided to hand her notice in to the hospital and leave Port Kara. She needed him to know that her reasons for leaving were nothing like they'd been when she'd moved to Cornwall. She didn't need to distance herself from Lucas or her feelings for him. But what she did need was to give Esther the chance to have the life she'd chosen, without a daily reminder of the person who'd tried to talk her out of it. But then Charlie had told her he had his own reasons for asking her around for dinner. He was inviting Richard too, to give him some letters that Connie had been holding on to for almost forty years, and for some reason he seemed to think that Richard might be more open to looking at them if Danni was there too.

'Are you sure this shouldn't be a private moment between you and Richard?' Danni had brought Brenda with her, as instructed, and the basset hound was lying stretched out in front of the cottage's small woodburning stove, with Maggie's head resting on her ribcage.

'It's not like we're going to make him sit here and read the letters in front of us. I just want him to be willing to take the box away with him, and read them in his own time.' Charlie stirred the gravy he was making and looked over at Danni. 'I think if he hears all the things Connie wanted to tell him back then, in her replies to his letters, it might change everything.'

'I hope for Connie's sake you're right.' Brenda started to howl as there was a rap on the door. 'Because it's show time.'

* * *

The dinner Charlie had cooked was delicious and Richard seemed to be in good spirits, telling Danni that he was even thinking about signing up to the yoga class his GP had recommended.

'I'm just not sure that if this old dog gets into a downward position, there'll be any hope of getting me up again.'

'Just be careful. I once had a patient come into A&E who had severe lacerations around a very delicate part of their anatomy as a result of doing yoga in a thong two sizes too small.'

'I'll leave my thong at home for that, then!' Richard laughed and he looked so different from the person Danni had first met, but then Charlie put the box on the table in front of him. 'What's this, the world's biggest box of after-dinner mints?'

'Sadly not.' Charlie was visibly nervous as he sat down next to his father. 'It's from Connie.'

'Whatever it is, I don't want it.' Richard's face had transformed in an instant; all the openness and warmth that had been apparent all evening had disappeared. 'I keep telling you not to mention that woman around me. She's done enough to try and stop us from having a relationship with each other – don't let her do it again.'

'I think if you just look at what's in the box, you'll—'

'No!' Richard's shout cut Charlie off, and he pushed the box away from him, knocking over a glass of water. 'For Christ's sake, how many times do I have to say it?'

'No one is asking you to forgive her.' Charlie furrowed his brow and turned towards Danni, who'd been desperately trying to mop up the water with her napkin, before she looked up at him.

'And you don't even need to tell her you've looked at what's in the box, if you don't want to.' Danni adopted what she hoped was a calming tone. 'I haven't seen what's inside, but from what Charlie has said, I really think this could help you come to terms with everything that's happened. So do it for yourself, even if you don't want to do it for Connie.'

'I can't believe you're on that woman's side too!' Richard was on his feet now. 'No one seems to understand what she's done to me, and she just sits there, painting herself as the victim in all of this.'

'I'm not on anyone's side, Richard, I promise, and if it's upsetting you this much my professional advice is not to take the box, because it's clearly playing havoc with your blood pressure.' Danni sighed. 'But my personal advice would be to take the box away with you, and at least open it to see what's in there. Otherwise you're always going to wonder.'

'If it'll stop the pair of you going on at me, I'll take the bloody box. But she's only got herself to blame if I end up slinging it on the next bonfire I have in the yard.' Richard yanked the box off the table. 'I think it's best if I leave now.'

'You don't have to.' Charlie frowned. 'Stay for a bit; there's no rush.'

'It's all right, I need my bed anyway.' Richard's face relaxed a little as he looked at his son. 'Especially if I'm going to be up early tomorrow to try and squeeze into my thong for that yoga class. I'll see you both later.'

Holding up his hand in a sort of static wave, Richard headed out into the darkness of the night. The silence in the room when he'd left still seemed to be fizzing with the anger he'd so clearly felt.

'Well, that went well.' Charlie tapped a finger against his forehead, which was another of the habits he had when he was feeling awkward, all of which Danni had come to recognise and love.

'Actually, I think it did.' She reached across the table and touched his hand, just for a second. 'You've done what Connie asked and given him the letters. He has all the information he needs; the rest is up to him.'

'I hope he makes the right decision and I really hope Esther does too. You and Connie both deserve a second chance; you were only doing what you thought was for the best.'

Danni forced a smile and slid her hand away from Charlie's. She was almost certain now that he'd give her a second chance if she asked for it, and she desperately wanted one. But she was going to have to walk away from Charlie and her best friend, and she already knew she was going to miss them both for the rest of her life.

29

The last person Connie expected to see when she heard heavy footsteps heading in her direction was Richard. Her spine seemed to go rigid in response and the follicles on her head started to tingle, like a cat whose hackles were rising in readiness to defend itself. She wasn't in the mood for an altercation, not when she'd spent most of the morning bickering with one of the physios who was still trying to railroad her into moving into the nursing home. It wasn't as if having another argument with Richard would get them anywhere. However much he shouted at her, it wouldn't change what had happened. She couldn't make that right and she was exhausted from trying. If going through the contents of the box that Charlie had given him hadn't allowed Richard to at least understand why she'd done what she did, then nothing would.

'If you've come here for another row, you can leave. Never mind how you feel about me, but there are other patients here who are trying to recover from serious illnesses and operations.'

'I'm not here for a row.' Richard wasn't smiling, but he wasn't scowling either and if she'd had to guess what emotion he might be trying to hide, she'd have gone for apprehension.

'What *are* you here for, then?'

'To talk. Can I sit down?' He gestured towards the chair next to the one she was sitting in, which had only been vacated by the pushy physiotherapist ten minutes before.

'It's a free country.' Her scalp was still prickling, and she pressed her lips together in a tight line, ready for when he inevitably started to berate her. That was the thing with her injuries: she couldn't even get up and storm out when she'd had enough of listening to what someone had to say.

'I read the letters you wrote me.' This time, when she looked at Richard, it wasn't apprehension she saw. His eyes had gone misty and there was just the slightest wobble of his chin, as if he was fighting to compose himself. 'I wished I'd known how you really felt about me. I'd have chosen you and Charlie, you know that, don't you?'

'That's the whole reason why I didn't tell you. Can you imagine what would have happened? You'd have had to see your parents' devastation when they were forced to sell off at least part of their farm. You'd probably have had to move up to Yorkshire with me, move into the flat I was living in then, right in the centre of Leeds. It would have been like caging an animal and you'd have ended up pacing up and down, desperate for the freedom of where you grew up, exactly like the lions and tigers do at the zoo.'

'We could have found a way of making it work.' Richard's tone wasn't accusatory like it had been when he'd first found out about Charlie. Now it was pleading, as if they were back there, almost forty years before, and there was still a chance of the two of them raising their son.

'There's no way of knowing that, and one or both of us would have had to sacrifice everything we knew to be together. Maybe we'd have tried and failed, and I'd have ended up raising Charlie on my own. There are millions of amazing single parents out there, but I know I wouldn't have been one of them. I had a great career, but it wouldn't have left room to be a great single parent too, and the thought of living hand to mouth like my mum did was unbearable. I'd never even considered having kids until I met you. But then, for the first time ever, I could picture my children – playing on the same farm where you grew up. Only they never would have done, because the farm wouldn't have been the same, even if you'd managed to hold on to a bit of it. Me leaving and not replying to your letters was never about not loving you. I did all of that *because* I loved you. It was exactly the same with Charlie. The moment I knew I was carrying him, the love I felt for him was overwhelming. And when I saw his face for the first time, I knew I'd never love anyone in the way I loved him. I'd have given my life to protect him and, in a way, that's what I did. I gave up my chance of being his mother – the life that would have been – so he could have the best one possible. And the thing I'm most thankful for, in all my life, is that it turned out to be the right decision. He has the most fantastic parents – just look at the wonderful person he's turned out to be. You must be able to see that.'

'Of course I can, and I read the letter his adoptive mother wrote to you. If I'd had to choose someone else to be his mum, I'd have picked her too. But not over you, because whatever you might think, I know you'd have been a wonderful mum.'

'That's what I'm going to do my best to be from now, in whatever way works alongside the mum Charlie has already got. I don't want to try to take her place, but the way I see it, you can never have too many people who love you.'

'Have you got room for one more?' Richard hesitated for a moment and Connie frowned, trying to work out if he was saying what she thought he was. 'I spoke to Fiona. I drove over to her place, and explained everything to her and her husband, Terry. I told her how guilty I felt and you'll never guess what she said.'

'Probably best I don't try in that case.' Connie managed a half smile and Richard laughed.

'She said there was nothing to feel guilty for. That we both knew what we were getting into, and that she'd never loved me any more than I'd loved her. All she wanted was to get away from a father who thought the best way to keep his children on the straight and narrow was to regularly knock some sense into them.' Richard shook his head. 'She actually thanked me for giving her a home where she felt safe and for allowing her to finally be with the person she loved. She said it was about time I took that same opportunity and, when I told her it was too late, she called me a fool and told me to get myself down here or she'd drive me down here herself.'

'You always did have good taste in women.' Connie's smile had widened, but the look of apprehension was back on Richard's face.

'I know I've been an idiot, but I've got to know if I've completely ruined any chance of you ever feeling the same way about me, as you did when you wrote those letters.'

'I already do. I always have. I've often wished I didn't, never more so than over the last couple of weeks, and I'm far too logical and academic to believe that there's one right person out there for everyone. But, somehow, you've turned out to be the only person I've ever wanted to make that kind of commitment to.'

'Well, I wasn't exactly proposing marriage.' Richard grinned and he suddenly looked exactly like the young man she'd known all those years before.

'Why not? You've already got me pregnant.' She only realised how loud she'd said that last bit when the elderly lady in the bed across from her looked up from her knitting.

'In that case, maybe I'd better do the right thing.'

'Don't worry, I'm going to let you off the hook for that, but if you've got room for me in that farmhouse of yours, I would consider moving in. After all, there's no better way of getting to know someone again than living with them.' Connie lowered her voice and leant forward. 'Although I should warn you that I've got an ulterior motive.'

'Now you're really talking!'

'It's you or a care home.' Connie laughed at the expression on his face. 'They're telling me I can't live on my own again yet, so if you fancy being at my beck and call for the next couple of weeks, we can see how it goes?'

'Will they give me a uniform?' Richard raised his eyebrows. 'Or one of those little upside-down watches nurses used to wear?'

'I don't think so, but would you settle for a kiss?' Connie would know when she kissed him whether moving in and risking giving things a second chance was the right thing to do. Or whether they were just setting themselves up to get hurt all over again.

'I thought you'd never ask.' As Richard closed the space between them and pressed his lips against hers, Connie discovered something she'd never have believed: it turned out that time travel was possible after all, because four decades had disappeared in an instant.

* * *

After the phone call Danni had got from Connie, telling her that she and Richard had reconciled, Danni had felt euphoric. She hadn't even felt the need to sound a note of caution when Connie had told her that she was moving into the farmhouse and that Richard would be helping her through the final stages of her recovery. After all, as Connie had put it, they'd wasted almost forty years already and they didn't want to waste a moment more. It was only afterwards that Danni started to realise Charlie's reasons for staying on in Port Kara had gone. He'd wanted to make sure that both his birth parents were being properly looked after and now he could relinquish any responsibility he might feel, knowing they would be looking after one another.

It meant that Charlie would be leaving Port Kara as soon as his mum and dad had decided where they were moving to. Without Charlie, the last reason Danni had been holding on to for staying would be gone too. She'd already grown fond of some of her colleagues, especially Aidan, but it wasn't enough to make life bearable. Not when Esther was bending over backwards to avoid even working the same shift as her, let alone having contact outside of work.

That's why, at 10 p.m. on a Friday evening, Danni sat down to write. The first thing she wrote was an email to the HR department of the hospital, resigning from her role. And the second was a letter to Esther.

Essie,

I don't know if you'll read this or see it's from me and throw it away before you even look at it. Either way, I need to write it.

I want you to know how much I love you, and how our friendship has meant more to me than anything else for more than ten years. I know you might not want to believe me, but deep down I think you know it's true. I was an idiot for thinking I'd fallen in love with Lucas. I don't know what it was, and I don't want to blame the fact that we both lost parents in difficult circumstances, but that did form a bond between us. There were times when I was treating patients who were at risk of dying in the same way my dad did, and it was only Lucas being there that stopped me unravelling at that moment. But what I forgot was that it was you who stopped me unravelling so many more times, and it was the support of you and your family, as well as Joe, that got me through my training at all.

It's not just that love and support I miss. It's laughing with you, the way only we do, until my stomach hurts and my head aches. Whatever I thought I felt for Lucas, and I know now it was never love, it never even came close to what I feel for you. That's why nothing ever happened, and why it never would have done, even if you and Lucas hadn't been together any more. I wouldn't have traded the chance of a lifetime with him if it meant missing one day of our friendship.

You've got every right to hate me, but I need you to know that I'll never close the door on our friendship. If you ever change your mind, I'll be waiting. If anyone ever hurts you, I'll be there for you and I'll happily track them down and make them pay.

For now, though, I'm giving you the space you need and leaving St Piran's. I owe you the chance of some peace and the opportunity to experience a relationship that's finally lost its third wheel. I pray you never have to come looking for me because you're unhappy, but I hope with everything I've got that one day you'll find it in your heart to forgive me, and that you'll decide to come looking for me because of how happy you are.

Never stop being you, because you're the best person I know.

Danni xx

Putting the letter into a brown envelope, which wouldn't give Lucas any reason to assume it was from her and intercept it, Danni printed off a label to complete the disguise. Writing letters had worked for Connie, but it had taken almost forty years for her to send them to Richard, and Danni didn't even want to think about forty more days without Esther in her life. Jumping into her car, she drove to Esther's house, parking around the corner so that neither she nor Lucas would see her. She even pulled the hood of her jumper low over her face to avoid being seen on the doorbell camera. For just a second before she posted it through the door, she hesitated. There was a chance that the letter might inflame things, but there was nothing to lose when she'd already lost so much. Pushing the envelope through the door, she let it go and turned to walk away. If this was the last chance of saving her friendship with Esther, she was glad she'd taken it, even if it didn't end up changing a thing.

30

Danni had sworn to herself that she wouldn't go back to Esther and Lucas's house, unless she got a response to her letter. But she'd barely lasted twenty-four hours before the urge to drive past their place overwhelmed her. It wasn't like they'd see her, but if anyone had asked her why she was doing it, she couldn't have come up with a logical answer. She just wanted to be able to visualise Esther, inside the house, re-reading the crumpled letter she'd probably screwed up and binned first time around, and slowly realising that her friendship with Danni was worth saving. It might have ranked up there with the same unlikely scenarios that had seen her fantasise, in great detail, about the moment when Justin Timberlake would propose, when she'd been in her early teens. But she had to hope.

Rounding the corner of Esther's road, it suddenly hit Danni how ridiculous she was being. If she could have turned her car around, she would have done. But like the streets in many Cornish seaside villages, the road was narrow, with cars parked on either side in most places. So unless she wanted to attempt what would probably turn out to be a thirty-three-point turn, she was committed to driving past the house.

Please God don't let Lucas be coming out of the door at the precise moment I drive by.

Keeping her eyes firmly fixed on the road in front, she was determined not to even glance in the direction of Esther's front door. And by the time she spotted something large and black hurtling towards her out of the corner of her eye, it was too late to stop in time. As she slammed on the brakes, the object landed on the bonnet of her car with a thud, and a scream filled the air as she skidded to a halt. It took a couple of seconds for Danni to work out that the person screaming wasn't her. When she looked towards where the object had come from, she realised she was almost directly outside Esther's house. At that very moment the front door was flung open, and Esther came hurtling across the path and into the road.

'Oh my God, oh my God, I'm so sorry!' She didn't even seem to take in the fact that it was Danni at first, as she wrenched open the car door. 'I was throwing bags of clothes down to my car and I misjudged that one.'

When Esther finally looked up at Danni, her mouth fell open and all the hostility between them the last time they'd met felt like a distant memory. Esther's concern for Danni was written all over her face, even before she spoke again. 'Are you okay? I could have killed you.'

'I don't think a black bin bag filled with your pants is going to do the job, not even if you've started wearing granny knickers.' Danni grinned and Esther started to laugh.

'What are the odds of me hitting your car with it?' She shook her head. 'What are you even doing down here?'

'I came down because...' Danni sighed. 'I can't even finish that sentence. I came down because I miss you, and I hoped you'd read my letter and I don't know… maybe I hoped there'd be a moment of serendipity, and you'd see me and realise you missed me too. It sounds ridiculous, but given the fact you just hit my car with a black bag you chucked out of your bedroom window, I think the bigger question is why on earth you were doing that?'

'Because going up and down a narrow staircase carrying all my stuff felt like it was only going to end one way, with me at the bottom of the stairs in a pool of blood.' Esther blinked as she looked at Danni, and then widened her eyes. 'Oh, you mean, why am I packing up all my possessions in the first place?'

'Well, yes, that question had crossed my mind.' There was only one logical explanation, but Danni didn't dare hope for it, until Esther actually said the words out loud.

'I'm leaving Lucas and moving in with Mum and Dad for a bit, until I work out what to do.' Esther was resolute and if there was the threat of tears, Danni couldn't see them.

'Not because of the letter?' She bit her lip. She wanted Esther to want more for herself than a man who was hedging his bets, but she didn't want to be the cause of her friend regretting what she'd done. Not when it had already come so close to causing them to lose their friendship for good.

'No, but the letter gave me the strength to do it.' Esther reached out and squeezed her hand. 'I'd had this feeling for a long while that Lucas was almost playing a part in our relationship. Doing all the things he should be doing, but just not *feeling* all the things he should be feeling. And it felt like he was using this, us, as the rehearsal for the real thing when it finally came along. I don't want to be someone's trial run. I want to be the love of someone's life and, when I read your letter, I realised I already was.'

'Why did it take you so long?' It was Danni's eyes filling with tears, and Esther shrugged.

'I don't know, but I could ask you the same question.'

'Maybe he put a spell on us?' Danni raised her eyebrows and Esther smiled.

'He must have done. Either way, the spell was broken by the time I read your letter and I decided that the best thing was for me to go, but I was sobbing while I was packing everything into the bags. Not because I didn't want to leave, but because I felt guilty about ending things and letting everyone down about the wedding.' Esther let out a long breath and pulled her shoulders back, looking nothing like a woman who'd spent the last few hours sobbing. 'But then I found a weekend bag that I was going to use for some of my stuff. Inside it was the bill from a hotel, from February this year, for their Valentine's Special weekend package. And do you remember where I was on Valentine's weekend?'

'You came down here to help me get settled in, because Lucas had to work.'

'Except he clearly didn't, but it turned out I spent Valentine's with my one true love anyway.' Esther's eyes clouded with tears for the first time. 'Is there any chance you can forgive me for what I said? I think I only lashed out because I already knew you were right, but I didn't want to admit it.'

'You're the one who needs to be able to forgive me.'

'There's nothing to forgive.' Esther leant into the confines of the car and gave Danni the best hug she'd ever had in her life. It might have been an awkward space, and the seatbelt might have ended up half-strangling her, but it was a moment she'd been terrified might never come, which meant it was nothing less than perfect.

'Right, now, are you going to park your car over there and help me pack up the rest of my stuff or what?' Esther gestured to a space further down the road.

'I couldn't think of anything I'd rather do.' Smiling as she closed the door, Danni felt the tension ease from her spine for the first time in weeks.

31

'What do you mean there's nothing you can do about it?' Esther put her coffee cup down on the table with a bang. It was an uncharacteristically mild day for late autumn, where the wind had dropped and the sun on Danni's back was strong enough for her to take off her jacket. They were sitting at one of the tables outside the rehab unit, making the most of the weather and the chance to catch up with Connie and Gwen.

'I created a Facebook page setting up the cottage as a holiday let and within an hour I'd taken the first three bookings. And I emailed my resignation into the HR department on Friday night.' Danni shrugged, despite what felt like a lead weight having settled in her stomach when she realised just how brutally she'd gone about severing all ties with Port Kara. 'What can I say – I was going all-in to start again somewhere new.'

'Just explain to HR, and the people who are renting the cottage, that you've changed your mind.' Esther, who had always hated letting anyone down, was adamant. 'You can't go, Haggars; you love it here and everyone loves you.'

'Not everyone.'

'If you're talking about Lucas, stuff him!' Gwen mimed a gesture with the middle finger on her left hand to back up her words. 'He's not worth changing your life for.'

'He told me, even before Esther left him, that he was going to ensure he made things as awkward as possible for me.'

'Well, let him.' Connie, who'd been given the all-clear to leave the unit the next day, was equally emphatic. 'Living your life because of what other people might think, or in an attempt to make other people happy, is a recipe for disaster. I ought to know. Don't let it do the same to you too.'

'Mum and Dad would be more than happy for you to move in with us for a bit.'

'I can't ask them to do that.' It had been a huge relief to know that Esther hadn't told her family about their fallout. She'd said it was because deep down she'd known they'd work things out. But the last thing she wanted to do was impose on them, or anyone else. 'I suppose I could try to find an alternative holiday let for the bookings I've taken. Or maybe even stay in a hotel for those weeks. But it doesn't change the fact that I've handed in my notice.'

'They're not going to want to accept notice from someone with your skills.' It was Connie's turn to shrug. 'Just tell them your plans have changed. They'll be delighted.'

'Not if Lucas has got anything to do with it. He's quite capable of getting HR involved and accusing me of harassment or something.' Danni had always hated the idea of being a victim, but there was no denying that Lucas's status in the hospital outranked hers. 'The fact that I've offered a letter of resignation, and then tried to take it back, would support anything he said about me creating drama at work, or doing stuff just to get attention. It shouldn't be the way it works, but his stock is higher than mine and, if they can only keep one of us, it'll be him.'

'In that case they're idiots.' Gwen looked capable of punching the next person she saw from HR right on the end of their nose. 'Although I might have an idea.'

'You do know your reputation precedes you, don't you, Gwen?' Danni smiled for the first time. 'And I don't want you tying yourself to the railings outside the hospital, in the nude, for my benefit.'

'I've done it before and I'll do it again if I have to.' Gwen laughed. 'But this idea's a bit more sneaky than that, and Craig in the IT department owes me a favour.'

'What have the IT department got to do with it?' Esther furrowed her brow.

'The less you know about it the better.' Tapping the side of her nose, Gwen lowered her voice. 'But Craig and his wife started coming to my belly-dancing classes at the beginning of the year, and his wife said their love life has never been better. So I'm sure I can get him to help out.'

'It's like being in a spy movie. A bad spy movie.' Connie nudged Gwen's arm. 'But as long as it works, and it means St Piran's doesn't lose the best doctor it's got, then I say go for it, whatever it is. And I might just have a little idea of my own.'

'Does it involve belly-dancing IT guys?' Even if nothing Gwen or Connie were trying to do helped, she was so touched that they wanted to try. And the image of Craig from IT performing an Egyptian figure eight was giving her a reason to smile, even in the midst of worrying where she was going to be living, or working, in the very near future.

'Sadly, no belly dancing of any sort, but it might just solve one of your problems.' Connie was already reaching for her phone from her bag. 'You've helped me more than I could ever repay you for, but I want to try. And the fact that having you around means Charlie might be more likely to stay is just an added bonus.'

'You're all so lovely.' Danni took a sip of her coffee so that she didn't have to meet anyone's eye, and they wouldn't be able to see

how much hope was reflected in hers. She didn't want to leave Port
Kara, and she didn't want Charlie to either. But the chances of
stopping both of those things from happening felt almost non-
existent.

* * *

It came as no surprise to Danni that Gwen was the first person to
complete her mission impossible.

'It's all sorted.' She'd come into A&E on the pretence of delivering a coffee order, and had all but dragged Danni into one of the
cubicles. 'Craig's done what he needed to do and you're in the
clear.'

'But I've already had an acknowledgement from HR about my
resignation.' Danni had wanted to scream when she got the email
at the start of her shift, and she'd barely been able to think about
anything else since.

'If you check your emails again, I think you'll find an apology
from them for their error in responding to what was clearly a
computer virus.'

'Okay, you've really lost me now.'

'I told Craig what you'd done in the hope he could get the
email back, but it had already been opened.' Gwen had leant in
closer still. 'So he suggested he replicate the email, but made it
look like it was being sent from every senior doctor and surgeon in
the hospital, with exactly the same wording you used. Then he
went down to HR and told them there'd been a report of a potential virus targeting hospitals, and that he'd put up some new secu-
rity to stop any more getting through, but they might have already
had some. Apparently the head of HR almost wept with relief,
because she thought she was going to have to try and replace all
the senior doctors and that there'd be a big scandal about staff

turnover at St Piran's. All of which meant she was only too happy to accept the story.'

'That's brilliant – scary, but brilliant.' Danni hugged Gwen and had been tempted to lift her off the ground and spin her in a circle. 'I can't thank you enough. Just don't ever go into the business of becoming an evil genius, because you'd be far too good at it.'

'I won't, as long as you promise not to do anything that stupid again. Especially for the sake of someone like Lucas.'

'I promise.' Danni had celebrated the news with the coffee Gwen had delivered, and a slice of the cake Aidan had brought in to mark the fact that the day after would be his birthday.

'Drinks tonight.' Aidan had made it sound like a statement, rather than a question, but she'd been more than happy to accept, despite the fact that she'd worked a nightshift and had promised to meet Charlie for a walk when she finished work. She could grab a couple of hours of sleep after that and still make Aidan's drinks. She didn't want to miss an excuse to celebrate with the colleagues who had quickly become friends, and she definitely didn't want to miss the chance to spend time with Charlie, because that was running out far too fast.

'You look like the sort of photograph that should be on the front cover of book, staring out to sea like that.' Charlie reached her side before she even spotted him. 'The beautiful heroine, awaiting the return of her lover from a long voyage. Something like that.'

'It's probably best you stick to children's fiction.' She laughed as he pretended to look offended. 'I was looking out for Trevor. I just want to know if he's okay, now that he's having to fend for himself. I can't believe seal pups get left by the mothers so early.'

'I've got a feeling Trevor will be fine, but talking of me sticking to children's fiction, I wanted to make sure you never forgot him. Or me. So I've been working on this.' Charlie handed her some papers. 'Don't worry if a sudden gust of wind rips them out of your hands; I scanned the originals to send to my editor for feedback. This is just a print-off. I didn't want us to end up having to dive into the water to try and retrieve them, like we're in a Richard Curtis movie, although I've got to admit I am hoping it might help me wangle one of his happy endings.'

'Oh Charlie, this is beautiful.' Danni traced a finger over one of the sketches, depicting Trevor on the rocks, with the dogs running along the clifftop above him.

'It's about two best friends, Maggie and Brenda, who teach a lonely seal pup all about kindness and the power of friendship. It's a theme that's always popular with the age group I write for, and thankfully my editor is really happy with it.' Charlie reached out and pushed a strand of Danni's hair that had been caught by the wind away from her face. 'But what's even more important to me, is whether you like it.'

'I love it.'

'Then why do you look as if you're about to burst into tears?'

'Because I think I might love you too.' Danni hadn't planned to say anything. It was too soon, too crazy and she'd already messed so much up. But staring at the draft pages in front of her, she didn't have a shred of doubt that Charlie was everything she thought he was. He personified the kindness he'd spoken about, and he was the most open, genuine person she'd ever met. All of that made it impossible not to love him, and as it turned out, just as impossible to keep quiet about it.

'Well, that is good news.' Charlie grinned, the dimple that made her smile every time she spotted it putting in an appearance. 'Because I've persuaded Mum and Dad to move down to Cornwall, on the basis of the sliver of hope I had that you might feel even a tiny bit as much for me as I've felt about you from the first day we met. When I spoke to Connie and Richard about it, I told them people would think I was crazy when I said I'd been in love with you from the start, but they wouldn't have it. I don't know, maybe it's because of what happened to them: nearly losing each other twice because they weren't honest about how they felt. But they told me I'd always regret it if I didn't tell you. But I never thought in a million years you'd say it first.'

'If you tell anyone that, you know I'm going to deny it.' She laughed again and he slid his arm around her waist, pulling her close and crushing the copied pages between them.

'Oh, I'm planning on telling anyone who'll listen. Guys like me aren't lucky enough to get girls like you, so I'll be shouting it from the rooftops.'

'I'm the lucky one.' Danni had made the first move once by telling Charlie she loved him, and she had no intention of holding back any more, or waiting for him to kiss her. Pressing her lips against his, she felt his body respond and the whole world seemed to fade away, until an alert on her phone made Brenda start to howl.

'Whoever that is interrupting the best moment of my entire life, they'd better have a good reason.' Charlie was smiling despite his words, and, at that moment, he looked like someone who would find it impossible not to smile. Which was exactly how Danni felt.

'It's a text from Esther, asking me if I'll go on her honeymoon with her. It was too late to get her money back and apparently the resort prides itself on catering for soulmates, so she can't think of anyone she'd rather go with.'

'I hated seeing you so unhappy.' Charlie gently traced his fingers down the length of her arm. 'I'm so glad the two of you have sorted everything out.'

'Me too and it means I won't need to worry about being homeless for a couple of weeks. After that I'll need to figure something out, until I get the cottage back.'

'Richard has told me to stay on for as long as I like and you're welcome to stay, but I know it probably feels too soon. But Connie had already persuaded him to free up one of the other cottages for you. If you want it, we can be neighbours, as long as that's still not too much pressure. God, why am I so bad at this?' Charlie stumbling over his words in his desperation to get things right just made Danni even more certain than ever about him. Some people wanted the mean and moody type, who played games and kept you on your toes, or pretended to be something they weren't. But she'd been there and done that. Now she knew exactly what she wanted, and it was Charlie.

'If the offer is still open for me to stay with you, then you can definitely count me and Brenda in.'

'Really?' When Charlie put his arms around her again, it felt so right, like coming home with a future that promised to be filled with the people she loved most and she couldn't wait for the next chapter to start.

ACKNOWLEDGMENTS

I'm so excited to introduce you all to the new *Cornish Country Hospital* series, which I hope readers will take to their hearts in the same way they have with the midwives. As I always say, sadly I'm not a medical professional, but I have done my best to ensure that the details are as accurate as possible. If you are one of the UK's wonderful medical professionals, I hope you'll forgive any details which draw on poetic licence to fit the plot. I've been very lucky to be able to call upon the expertise of one of my best friends, Steve Dunn, a paramedic for twenty-five years. I've also been able to draw on the expertise of another friend, Kate Johnson, a hospital consultant, and, as ever, I'll be seeking support and advice in relation to maternity services from my very good friend, Beverley Hills.

You might have noticed that the dedication for this novel is a bit more complex than usual. This reflects the outcome of a competition to name the hospital. While there could only be one winner, the other entrants whose suggestions were used to name hospital wards and departments, were asked if they'd also like to add something to the dedication. All those who said they would have been included.

An extra special thank you goes to Kay Love, who allowed me to name Charlie's dog, Maggie, after her own beloved Labrador. Kay sadly lost Maggie when I was in the early stages of plotting this book, and she helped me bring her beautiful dog to life by sharing some of Maggie's traits, which I hope I've done justice to. Thanks too to the readers on my Facebook page who shared suggestions for character names, Esther and Connie among them. The lead character of Danni was named in honour of my beautiful friend, Danni Starley, who we very sadly lost to cancer two years ago. Danni was a truly inspirational person and her lovely mum, Sally, is a huge supporter of my books, so I couldn't have chosen a better name for the first lead character in this new series.

There are so many people I need to thank for their support. My greatest thanks has to go to the readers who choose my books and continue to make my writing dreams come true. It still amazes and thrills me that I have so many loyal readers, some of whom regularly join me to chat on my Facebook page. You all help me more than you know!

At the end of *A Happy Ever After for the Cornish Midwife*, I wrote a long list of all the wonderful book reviewers who were so fundamental in making that series a success. I am sure I will be compiling a similarly long list during this new series, but for now I just want to thank the book reviewing and book blogging community for all the support they have given me so far.

My thanks as ever go to the team at Boldwood Books for making my dreams come true, especially my amazing editor, Emily Ruston, and my brilliant copy editor and proofreader, Becca Allen and Candida Bradford, without whom this book couldn't have happened. I'm also hugely grateful to Nia, Claire, Jenna, Issy, Marcela, Ben and the rest of the team for their amazing work behind the scenes, and to Amanda for having the vision to set up such a wonderful organisation.

As ever, I can't sign off without thanking my writing tribe, The Write Romantics, and all the other authors I am lucky enough to call friends. And to another of my best friends, Jennie Dunn, for her support with the final read through.

Finally, as it will forever do, my most heartfelt thank you goes to my husband, children and grandchildren. What I do is for you, and always will be.

ABOUT THE AUTHOR

Jo Bartlett is the bestselling author of over nineteen women's fiction titles. She fits her writing in between her two day jobs as an educational consultant and university lecturer and lives with her family and three dogs on the Kent coast. Her first title for Boldwood is The Cornish Midwife – part of a twelve-book deal.

Sign up to Jo Bartlett's mailing list for news, competitions and updates on future books.

Follow Jo on social media here:

facebook.com/JoBartlettAuthor

x.com/J_B_Writer

instagram.com/jo_bartlett123

ALSO BY JO BARTLETT

Cornish Country Hospital Series

Welcome to the Cornish Country Hospital

Standalone

Second Changes at Cherry Tree Cottage

A Cornish Summer's Kiss

Meet Me in Central Park

LOVE NOTES

LOVE IN EVERY CHAPTER

WHERE ALL YOUR ROMANCE
DREAMS COME TRUE!

THE HOME OF BESTSELLING
ROMANCE AND WOMEN'S
FICTION

WARNING:
MAY CONTAIN SPICE

SIGN UP TO OUR
NEWSLETTER

https://bit.ly/Lovenotesnews

Boldwood

Boldwood Books is an award-winning fiction publishing company seeking out the best stories from around the world.

Find out more at www.boldwoodbooks.com

Join our reader community for brilliant books, competitions and offers!

Follow us
@BoldwoodBooks
@TheBoldBookClub

Sign up to our weekly deals newsletter

https://bit.ly/BoldwoodBNewsletter

Printed in Great Britain
by Amazon